SHE CAN KILL

ALSO BY MELINDA LEIGH

MELINDA LEIGH

SHE CAN KILL

Montlake
Romance

Text copyright © 2015 Melinda Leigh
All rights reserved.

Published by Montlake Romance, Seattle

www.apub.com

Amazon, the Amazon logo, and Montlake Romance are trademarks of Amazon.com, Inc., or its affiliates.

ISBN-13: 9781503948693
ISBN-10: 1503948692

Cover design by Jason Blackburn

Printed in the United States of America

For Sunshine
In any world I create, dogs live forever

CHAPTER ONE

Forgive me Father, for I have sinned. It has been eighteen months since my last assassination.

Christopher slowed the car as he approached the turnoff. A visit to his father-in-law's *estancia* triggered equal amounts of guilt—and fear. The ranch was the last place he wished to be. Franco had a job for him. The kind of job he'd been avoiding since his daughter was born eighteen months before, the kind of job that required his expertise with a weapon.

But that's what happened when you married the daughter of an arms dealer.

"Mama," Luciana demanded from her car seat.

Christopher glanced in the rearview mirror. Small white sandals kicked, and her tiny mouth bowed with impatience.

"Yes, my princess," he said. "Mama is here. We'll see her soon."

Eva had driven the seventy kilometers from their Buenos Aires apartment to the *estancia* early that morning to attend a family meeting, while Christopher had made excuses. His economics paper wasn't finished. Luciana needed a nap. The truth was something he couldn't share with his wife or his father-in-law. He couldn't do the job. Whatever sharp edge he'd had in the past had vanished the day his daughter had been born. He'd lost it, plain and simple.

But it was no sacrifice. Love expanded in Christopher's chest. Luciana was perfect. His daughter had made him feel things he didn't know were possible. The moment of her birth had altered him forever. Holding her squalling, brand-new life in his hands had spun his perspective one hundred and eighty degrees. The first time he'd looked into her trusting eyes, he knew his life would never be the same.

He would never be the same.

But as Eva had pointed out in their heated argument that morning, an invitation from Franco Vargas wasn't a request. It was a demand.

So here he was.

He stopped the car at the entrance. Was it instinct or sheer reluctance that made him hesitant to turn down the lane? Two long rows of trees lined the gravel-and-dirt drive leading to the house. Staring down the gauntlet, he lowered the window. The warm breeze sweeping off the pampas lifted the hairs on his neck. Where were the guards? Franco kept surveillance at the ranch as invisible as possible. His father-in-law enjoyed the illusion of being a regular family, but usually, Christopher could spot the sentries. Wary of any deviation from normal, he hovered his foot over the gas pedal. But he had little choice. His attendance was mandatory. The last thing he wanted was for Franco to become suspicious. If he ever guessed that Christopher wanted to take Eva away . . .

That couldn't happen.

He turned between the brick pillars, pausing midway down the long drive to point out a mare and foal in the pasture. From the backseat, Luciana clapped and shouted, "*Caballo*. Horse." With her parents speaking two languages, Luciana seemed to flow between English and Spanish with no effort.

If only the Vargas family really earned their living from polo ponies and wine. But Franco's hobbies were merely a front. The

Vargases' trade in illegal guns went back generations. They were more militant gang than family.

The ranch house was built traditional style: square and low. The barns and polo fields sat to the left of the whitewashed, concrete house. Terra-cotta red tile roofs brightened the landscape. A few outbuildings of similar plain design were sprinkled around the property. Christopher parked in front of the house, amid a cluster of vehicles. The sounds of splashing, music, and the occasional squeal of a child floated on the hot breeze from the back of the house. Near the end of an Argentinean summer, the family would be enjoying the pool. Franco had only two daughters, but there were cousins, uncles, and in-laws involved in the business. For the most part, Eva and the men would gather inside for a business meeting while the other women and children enjoyed the warm afternoon.

Silently, he hoped the business was finished for the day. He'd never admit it to Franco, but since Luciana had been born, Christopher much preferred swimming with his daughter. He felt more comfortable in the backyard with the women, children, and old men.

He liberated the baby from the backseat. Clutching a stuffed brown rabbit in one hand, she kicked her feet.

"You're bringing your bunny with you?"

"*Bebé.*" As usual, she insisted the rabbit was her baby.

Impatient, she called her cousins' names.

"You hear your playmates." Christopher set her on her feet, straightened her yellow, flowered sundress, and took her firmly by the hand. The ranch had its perils. Water, horses, dogs, and sharp tools created lots of opportunities for a curious toddler to be injured.

He bypassed the front door. Franco's head of security and most trusted employee, Nicolas, would be in the hall. Christopher preferred to avoid his scrutiny and silent disdain. Nicolas did not believe a man should be at home while his wife took care of business. His contempt stung. Nicolas had been a mentor to Christopher for years. He'd taught him to handle weapons. He'd taught him to kill.

Heading directly for the backyard, he led his daughter along the side of the house. Luciana's tiny white sandals slapped on the path as they rounded the corner.

An explosion split the peaceful air. The ground rolled, and people screamed. Then the *rat tat tat* of machine-gun fire sounded from the back of the property. Christopher scooped Luciana off the ground. He turned toward the car, but the sounds of engines and tires on gravel stopped him. Pivoting, he ran in the opposite direction. The closest shelter was the barn. More screams, his child's included, pierced his heart.

He raced to save his daughter, but his heart bled for the wife he left behind.

Screaming, gunfire, and the frightened whinnies of horses carried over the lawn. Holding his child, Christopher ran across the grass toward the barn. Just outside the entrance sat a horse van. He glanced into the van's interior as he raced by. A cartridge of bullets lay half-buried under a pile of hay. The intruders had used the arrival of a new horse to launch their attack. No doubt the van's true drivers were dead, their bodies dumped somewhere along the highway. If Christopher had been planning the attack, that's exactly how he would have gained access to the ranch. Horses were his father-in-law's number one weakness.

He entered the cool shade of the barn. A horse neighed. Luciana sobbed. Her cries rose to a terrified pitch.

"Shh, my princess." He needed to quiet her. The commotion covered her screams for the moment, but the second the shooting was over, someone would hear her wails. He turned her face to his chest. Her arms and legs wrapped around his body. Christopher flinched at every spurt of bullets, waiting for one to punch into his own flesh, rendering him incapable of protecting his child. Questions bombarded him.

Who was shooting? Was Eva still alive?

And more importantly, where could he hide? There was nowhere other than the barn. The ranch sat on a flat square of grassland. Few trees dotted its green vastness. The views were spectacular, but the open ground left no way to run without being seen. He had no weapon. Nothing with which he could protect his baby girl. He ducked into the tack room, and grabbed a sharp knife from the worktable in the center of the room. Stowing it in his belt, he returned to the aisle.

He turned into the first stall, closing and locking the door behind him. Nervous from the noise, the chestnut broodmare inside shied away. Christopher soothed the animal with a calm voice. He crossed the straw-covered floor and rose onto his toes to look out a small window high on the wall. From here he could see part of the house's rear yard. Bodies were strewn across the lush grass. More than one floated in the bright-blue pool water.

Everyone. The whole family. Dead. Mowed down in the middle of a barbecue.

Men dressed in black made their way across the grass, nudging bodies with the toes of their boots. Christopher watched a man roll Uncle Paolo onto his back and fire a shot into the old man's chest. Tears ran down his face into Luciana's hair.

"You must be quiet," he said into his daughter's ear. "Can you do that for Papa?"

Nodding, she hiccupped, her brown eyes opening wide in solemn promise. Did she understand? She was only a toddler, yet she seemed to sense his desperation—his terror.

He glanced at the horse pawing at the bedding. The mare had quick hooves. Nervous sweat gleamed on her side, but he'd delivered her last foal. She trusted him. And Christopher had few options. With a gentle pat to the horse's neck, he carried Luciana into the shadows. A bulging net full of hay blocked the view from the door.

"Close your eyes, do not move, and be as quiet as you have ever been," he whispered.

Her teary nod sliced his heart into pieces. A burst of gunshots reported. Luciana recoiled and turned her face into his shoulder.

Christopher stopped his imagination from conjuring images. He could not afford to grieve with his daughter in danger. He hugged her closer as footsteps pounded on the packed dirt of the barnyard. She lifted her head, and he put his finger to his lips. Luciana's mouth trembled. Her tiny arms circled his neck and held tight. And they waited.

Footsteps rushed into the barn.

"Check every stall. Quickly," a voice called out in Portuguese.

Hinges squeaked. Horses snorted and whinnied. Hooves shuffled in straw. Doors slammed.

Sweat soaked through the cotton of Christopher's shirt. Luciana's eyes were squeezed tightly closed. If she made a noise, they were dead. The thought of a bullet finding his child gripped him with enough fear to stop his heart. The stall door opened. A man's shadow fell across the straw. The chestnut mare spun around, putting her head in the corner and presenting her hindquarters to the intruder. A hoof rang out on wood as the animal kicked. With a curse, the man retreated and the door closed.

Christopher waited until the barn went silent of human sounds. Hours seemed to pass, but likely it was less than thirty minutes. Engines started, tires grated on dirt, and the rumbling of vehicles faded, and still he waited. He needed to be sure. Finally, he moved away from the wall.

Leaning over the half door, he peered around the wall. No men in black. What should he do?

He ran toward the house. He had to make sure there was no one who could be helped. Covering his daughter's eyes, he walked through the carnage. She was limp in his arms, her head lolling on his shoulder.

She sobbed softly, *"Bebé."* She'd dropped her toy. Somewhere. All Christopher could see were the people he'd loved, the only family he had. Everyone in the yard was dead. Women, children, old men. None had been spared.

He felt the numbness wash over him. The horror was simply too much for his mind to process, more grief than one man could bear. Christopher clutched his child close and wished he could shield his own eyes. The scene before him was instantly etched into his mind. There would be no erasing it, ever. Instead, he walled off his heart. Later. He would grieve later.

He went inside. His shoes rang on the tile floor as he made his way to the doorway of the main dining room. He didn't need to go into the room to know all the family members inside were dead as well. This part of the house was covered with rubble. The explosion had brought the roof down. Broken tiles and beams piled high. Dust drifted in the soot-scented air. Christopher could envision the scene too clearly. The ceiling caving in. Men bursting through the door. People ducking for cover. Machine-gun fire spraying the Vargas clan. Blood and grunts and screams and death.

He spotted a few bodies in the debris. One of the uncles was the closest to the door, the lower half of his body lying under a thick collapsed chunk of wood, his torso riddled with bullets. The heavy chair behind him rested on its back, as if he'd jumped up and knocked it over. Christopher's gaze darted to Franco's position at the rear of the room. Franco always sat with his back to the wall and a clear view of the doorway. Eva would have been at her father's side. Christopher moved deeper into the room, his eyes roaming the destruction. His heart lifted with the small possibility that maybe, just maybe, she wasn't here. Even as he thought it, he knew it was impossible.

He saw Franco on the floor ten feet away. He'd dived away from the explosion, toward his daughter. Under Franco, Eva lay on her side. Her father had tried to shield her with his own body. Beyond Franco's head, Eva's long, dark hair fanned across the tile. She faced away from the door. Blood darkened the back of the bright-red dress she'd been wearing this morning when he last saw her—when they'd fought. Christopher's breath locked in his chest for two heartbeats.

Before he got close enough to touch her, he knew.

Luciana sobbed into his shoulder, "Papa," breaking his trance.

Eva was dead. His body moved toward his wife, instinct propelling him across the floor. His feet stopped at her side. She was riddled with bullets from head to waist. Averting his eyes from her ruined face, he reached out and placed two fingers on her neck. The blood on her skin was still warm, but her heart did not beat. He rested his palm on her back for two seconds. Just above his hand, a few skinny rays of the Sun of May tattoo that adorned her back peeked out from the torn sleeve of her dress. The smiling face on the symbol of Argentine independence broke his heart.

I love you.

He tucked Luciana deeper into his shoulder. He couldn't bear for his precious daughter to see every member of her extended family massacred. She should never witness such a horror. This nightmare had already permanently stained Christopher's mind. As long as he lived, he would be able to picture every detail of this scene. Such a fate he could not bestow on his child. Yet leaving his wife felt wrong.

The decision was taken from him by a noise outside. Was someone coming? Friend or foe?

He had to get Luciana to safety.

He turned his back on the room—on the carnage, on his wife. If he were dead and Eva had survived, he would want her to do only one thing: save their child.

The men had spoken Portuguese with a distinct Brazilian accent. That meant the attack was likely orchestrated by the Vargas family's main enemy and business competition: Aline Barba. Was Christopher on the Brazilian's radar? She had enough reason to hate him. Eva had killed her son. Would he and Luciana be targets? Except for Eva's younger sister, Maria, who was away at school, they were the only members of the Vargas family still alive. Christopher hadn't been active in the business for the last eighteen months. Perhaps no one would miss him. But in case someone did, he needed to get Luciana as far from this place as possible.

Christopher carried his daughter into Franco's study. He set her in her grandfather's big leather chair and pushed it back against the wall. "Don't move, princess."

The child was still and silent as a doll, her eyes just as glassy.

Keeping one eye on his little girl, he rolled up the faded wool rug and pried up a large terra-cotta tile. Under the tile, a section of subfloor had been cut away and a wooden box suspended. The nylon bag inside was heavy. Christopher hauled it into the room.

He replaced the tile, rug, and desk. Then, picking up Luciana in one arm and the bag in the other, he ran for the car. The sound of engines and the swirl of dust on the horizon changed his mind. He raced for the garage. He should have learned how to fly the helicopter on the other side of the property instead of studying economics. Eva had been right. Pursuing a college education had been foolish.

Just inside the door, he grabbed a set of keys from the wall rack. He tossed the nylon bag inside the four-wheel-drive pickup truck. He strapped Luciana in the passenger seat and started the engine. He drove away from the buildings, hoping, praying, that whoever was in those vehicles approaching the ranch did not see their escape. The *whump whump* of a helicopter spurred him to drive faster. Was someone chasing them? He turned to scan the sky, but the sun obliterated his vision. All he could see was the glint of sunlight on the chopper. It disappeared into the distance.

They hadn't seen him. He exhaled. They had a chance. It was slim, but there wasn't anything he wouldn't do to keep his child safe.

Next to him, his daughter didn't make a sound.

CHAPTER TWO

Twelve years later, Westbury, Pennsylvania

She enjoyed revenge any way it was served. Hot. Warm. Cold. Or, in the case of Christopher Navarro, frozen solid would suffice.

Blending in to a group of parents, she tugged her scarf higher on her face and walked toward the school. Though the day was overcast, sunglasses shielded her face as she kept a sharp eye out for Christopher in the crowd. She'd tagged his Mercedes weeks ago as it sat in the parking lot at the winter festival. She knew where he was at all times. Although a glance at the GPS app on her smartphone told her he was nearby, she didn't see his car. It seemed odd that he wouldn't attend the school function since Luciana was in the competition. The event had been publicized in the local newspaper.

What would she do if he was here? Would he recognize her? The puffy circular scarf had been a strategic rather than a fashion choice. She tugged it higher to cover the line of her jaw. She would just have to spot him first.

She strode through the main entrance and followed the throng of adults down the wide hallway. No one checked identification. No one paid her much attention. With students from several schools competing, the staff wouldn't expect to recognize every parent. In a single, pathetic attempt to provide security, a teacher stood at the end of the hall to prevent visiting adults from straying beyond the main hall. She held back a snort of disgust.

If *she* had desired admittance, the rail-thin man on guard would not have stood in her way, at least not for long.

Parents packed the large room. Voices echoed off tile and wood. Pretending to wave at a few people, she sat down on a folding, metal chair near the front of the room as if she belonged there. She spoke to no one. She'd dressed like the other mothers, slim jeans, sweater, flat boots, nothing fancy, nothing to make her stand out.

Satisfaction swelled in her chest. It had been so long since she'd experienced it, she almost didn't recognize the pleasant sensation. Coming here today felt bold and invigorating. After years of careful research and months of planning details, her dream was finally coming to fruition.

A man crossed the stage and stopped in front of a microphone. Behind him, a few dozen plastic chairs were arranged in rows. He tapped the microphone, and the din of conversation faded to quiet as parents settled. The principal introduced himself and gave a quick speech about the hard work and dedication of the teachers and students involved in the spelling bee. She paid him little attention, her gaze riveted on the side of the stage where the heavy curtain shifted. No doubt the competitors waited in the wings. The principal introduced the twelve finalists one by one, in alphabetical order.

Lucia Rojas was the ninth child in line. Some of the children appeared shy and uncomfortable. Their shoulders curled, and they fidgeted in their chairs. But not her. Tall and slim, with a long mane of dark hair, Lucia took her seat with a straight spine and folded her hands in her lap with determination.

As she watched the teen, her breath locked in her throat. She'd seen the girl a few weeks before at a local horse show, but it had been from a distance, and she hadn't been sure. Up close, there was no question. She lifted her phone and opened the video application.

The girl was Luciana.

Her features were those of a Vargas, as was her composure. Despite her young age, she carried herself with regality when it was her turn to approach the microphone. She spoke with confidence, as if she fully expected to win. The girl was a Vargas, through and through. Over the course of the next forty minutes, the competitors were pared down until only one remained. The victor. Luciana.

Now everything could begin.

She slipped out with a group of other hurried parents and crossed the cement walkway, salt crystals and ice crunching under her boots. Glancing at the street, she froze. Not fifteen meters ahead, a Mercedes turned into the parking lot. The vehicle was silver, sleek, and powerful. She could not see the driver, but she assumed it was Christopher. The car was his, and he would not trust his daughter to anyone else easily. Men like Christopher knew better than to rely on anyone for important tasks. The world they'd come from, the world she still lived in, was a hard place where the trusting ended up dead.

Lifting the scarf higher on her face, she veered away. People surrounded her, but she felt alone and apart. Fury burned hot in her veins, and she welcomed the frigid wind. Her vengeance was close enough for her to taste its bitterness in the back of her throat. *Patience.*

Christopher had sneaked out of Argentina and hidden like a coward. She'd waited a long time for her opportunity to catch him. Patience was the only virtue that remained in her shriveled heart. And she'd been rewarded for her persistence and restraint. She'd found them.

But as satisfaction filled her, betrayal cleaved her heart in two. For years, she'd tracked Christopher across the United States. He'd always been a clever man. He didn't use personal credit. Assets, such as houses and cars, were purchased behind one of his numerous corporate shields, with many properties scattered throughout the country. He limited his personal connections to the bare necessities and, until recently, he'd moved frequently. This was the first time he'd stayed in one place long enough for her to catch up with him—to see them both with her own eyes—to confirm that Cristan and Lucia Rojas were Christopher and Luciana Navarro.

And now it was time for her to put her plan into motion.

She left the school yard and walked several blocks. Next to a small cemetery, a gray minivan waited at the curb. It was an ugly, ungainly vehicle, but one that went unnoticed, a sort of suburban-America camouflage. As she approached, the engine came to life. Her lieutenant stepped out of the driver's side and opened the passenger door for her. She climbed in without a word and settled onto the seat. Beneath her, the cold leather chilled her legs through her jeans.

He slid behind the wheel. "Where are we going?"

"We'll go back to the house and wait there." She'd chosen to rent a vacation home twenty minutes away, near a small but busy ski resort, where she and her driver would not be so noticeable among the vacationers. She'd come into town on a few occasions, each time limiting her exposure to events with enough of a crowd to blend, and each time, she and her driver had walked close together to feign the intimacy of a vacationing couple. There had also been a few midnight drives past Christopher's home. She had to admit, he'd established an easily defensible base, but his comfort in his surroundings had left her an opening at the winter festival.

"Was it her?" Her lieutenant turned onto another side road. Small houses with neatly shoveled sidewalks lined both sides of the street.

"Yes." She swallowed the burning in her throat. This slice of middle-class America was an odd place for him to hide. The town was quaint and comfortable. They passed a group of older children walking home from school. A boy scooped up a handful of snow, shoved it down the neck of his companion's jacket, and ran, grinning. His laughing companion gave chase. How could Christopher live in such a boring place? How much had he changed? Had he lost his edge?

"You are positive?" he asked.

"I am one hundred percent certain."

He glanced in the side and rearview mirrors. "Then we go on with the plan?"

"Yes." She pulled off her gloves and dropped them in her lap.

"I know you've worked hard to prepare for this, but we don't need to be creative. I could put a bullet between his eyes. He'd never know what hit him." He glanced sideways at her. He had never been a pretty man. His skin was rough and dark, and his once black hair was threaded thickly with gray. But she'd learned the hard way that loyalty was more valuable than looks.

"No," she said. Normally, she took his opinions very seriously. But she'd been waiting for this moment for a long time, and she intended to have her proper revenge.

"Are you sure? If we kill Christopher cleanly," he continued, "then you could take Luciana at your leisure. Without Christopher, she'll be an easy target."

"I didn't chase that bastard for more than a decade to kill him quickly." She unbuttoned her coat. "Don't worry. He'll die. But before he goes to his special hell, I want him to know I took Luciana. I want to look him in the eyes when he realizes that I took away the one thing he values most in this world and that all his scheming and running and hiding were a waste. We'll follow through with our original plan."

He frowned. He was a good man. He'd never had a taste for torture. It was a good thing that she didn't have that problem. Step two of the plan would be all hers. She couldn't wait to force Christopher to his knees, to make him pay for what he'd done.

"It's your decision," he said.

"He brought this on himself." Rage and excitement heated her skin. She lowered the window an inch. Cool, damp air rushed into the vehicle. "Do you think he's gone soft?"

Her sightings of him had been from a distance. One couldn't be too careful when tracking a killer.

"I suppose we're going to find out." He turned onto a rural highway and drove away from town.

She breathed more easily when they were removed from the intimate setting and all its quaintness. The wholesome little town that Christopher had chosen grated on her nerve endings. How dare he carve out such a pleasant life for himself.

Her driver dialed a number on his cell phone and gave the order. He lowered the phone and looked at her. "And now we wait."

They wouldn't have to wonder about Christopher's prowess for long. She was certain of only one thing: Christopher—or Cristan, as he now called himself—would die. But before his end, he would suffer. In order to understand what he'd done, he had to lose everything. And she had to be the one to extract retribution. The anniversary of the Vargas massacre approached. One week from today, Cristan would suffer the appropriate consequences.

CHAPTER THREE

How could such a good life be built on a foundation of lies?

A lone snowflake drifted onto the windshield as Cristan steered his sedan toward his daughter's school. Another afternoon. Another pickup. Never once did he fail to appreciate the quiet, ordinary life he and Lucia were blessed to lead. After twelve long years, his beautiful life still felt stolen.

He slowed his sedan. Cars crowded the entrance, and the parking lot overflowed. Minivans and SUVs lined the side street as well. There were way too many vehicles for a normal afternoon dismissal.

Had he missed something?

He skirted an illegally parked SUV and drove to the pickup zone. Angling the Mercedes to the curb, he scanned the sidewalk for his daughter. The school yard also seemed more crowded than usual. Parents teemed on the sidewalk. Had he forgotten some sort of event? He reached into his pocket and withdrew his phone. There were no school activities on his calendar.

Children emerged from the building. Despite the cold, they milled on the salt-dusted concrete and snow-patched grass. Their high-pitched chatter penetrated the closed windows of his car. Some headed for the line of yellow buses on the adjacent curb. Younger children met parents on the sidewalk. Older kids searched the line of arriving cars for their rides or started walking home.

Though the second week of March had arrived, winter wasn't quite finished with the northeastern mountains of Pennsylvania. Likewise, the darkness still had a grip on Cristan. He had to get through the next few weeks before the tension and sorrow would release him. He kept expecting this anniversary to get easier, but each year, he spent the final days of winter mired in the dark memories of his past.

Next to his car, two women, a blond and a brunette, stood on the pavement and talked as they waited for their children. The blond woman was the mother of Jenna Pratt, a coltish blond girl in Lucia's class who'd been to the house a few times recently. Jenna seemed prone to giggling.

Cristan looked away too late. Jenna's mother caught his gaze. With a short wave, she stepped closer to the car. Brushing a hand over her hair, she bent at the waist to look inside his vehicle. The brunette hovered just behind her.

With a reluctant sigh, Cristan lowered the passenger window and leaned over the console just enough to make eye contact. The brunette shot him a polite smile, but the predatory gleam in the blond's eyes gave him pause. When he'd picked this rural community for their new home, he hadn't anticipated the popularity of his widower status among the single-mother population. More mothers approached his car, gathering next to his Mercedes like hungry lionesses circling a safari Jeep filled with juicy tourists.

Cristan struggled to remember the blond woman's given name. Failing, he defaulted to formality, which was likely the best option in any case. Lucia had made friends in town, but he needed to keep his distance. "Good afternoon, Mrs. Pratt."

From the instant grimace on the brunette's face, Cristan sensed his choice was a serious *faux pas*.

Irritation flickered like frost in the blond's eyes. "It's Harper. After my divorce, I went back to my maiden name, but please, call me Vivienne."

"My apologies." Cristan scanned the crowd for his daughter. He had no interest in becoming better acquainted with Ms. Harper. Two years ago, he thought this small town would be a good place to stay. Perhaps he'd been wrong. The close-knit community demanded a level of intimacy he hadn't expected.

Ms. Harper wasn't put off that easily. She stepped closer to the car, her posture aggressive. She placed a hand on the vehicle door as if staking her claim. "Congratulations. You must be so proud of Lucia."

What did she mean? Confused, Cristan opened his mouth to ask when he spotted his daughter exiting the building with a thin blond girl at her side. He recognized Jenna. As if sensing his presence, Lucia swiveled her head toward him and tossed her long, dark hair over her shoulder. He caught his breath. So like Eva. One week from today would mark twelve years since his wife and her family had been executed. In all that time, he hadn't allowed himself any attachments, except to Lucia. But his aloofness was getting harder to maintain the longer he stayed in this community. Instead of his loneliness abating, the emptiness ate at him.

"Don't ruin the surprise," the brunette admonished.

Ms. Harper's smile went cold. "You're right. I'm sure Lucia wants to tell you herself."

Cristan's fingers tightened on the steering wheel. He didn't like surprises.

Lucia turned to her friend, her gestures animated, her body language excited. Laughter and voices drifted through the open car window. Thirteen-year-old girls were always excited, it seemed. Lucia left Jenna and bounded toward him, her dark eyes sparkling. In slim jeans, short sheepskin boots, and a bright, puffy jacket, she looked like every other child leaving the school. She was one of them, he realized with a small shock. Why hadn't he seen it this clearly before?

She opened the passenger door, dropped her backpack, and slid into the seat. The cold wind had reddened her nose, but her eyes and smile were bright.

"Don't forget I'm going to Sarah's house to babysit." She opened the front pouch on her backpack, pulled her cell phone from a zippered compartment, and turned it on. Technically, she wasn't supposed to have a phone in school, but Cristan's safety concerns trumped any school policy. In case of emergency, he needed to know Lucia could reach him at any time, and he refused to relinquish his ability to locate her via the GPS in her phone.

"I remember." Cristan wouldn't forget a chance to see Sarah Mitchell. Before he met her, he hadn't minded being alone. "She needs you Thursday as well, correct?"

"Uh-huh."

He waited for the click of her seat belt before pulling away from the curb. "How was your day?"

"Promise not to freak out?"

"I do not *freak out*." Indignation suppressed his apprehension. She rolled her eyes. "You do so."

Turning out of the parking lot, Cristan peeled his cramped fingers off the wheel and flexed his knuckles. "Tell me what happened."

"Today was the spelling bee." Radiating excitement, she bounced on the leather seat. "I won. Not just my school. Today's competition was regional and included kids from four surrounding schools who made the final round."

"That's wonderful." Perhaps. Pride mixed with unease. The competition explained why so many parents were gathered at the school. Why hadn't she invited him? "Is that why you've been spending so much time on your homework?"

"Yes. Last month, I advanced to the final round, and I've been studying hard since."

Cristan suppressed his surprise, along with a surge of hurt and concern. She'd been keeping this from him for a month. How? Why? Was she concealing anything else? "How did I not know about this?"

She picked at her cuticle. "I might have intercepted the letter and forged your name on the permission slip."

Shock silenced him. His daughter had gone beyond not telling him about this event. She'd passed lying and embraced outright deception. "Why didn't you want me to know about this spelling bee?"

Lucia leaned away from him, her attention shifting to the window. Through the glass, snow-covered athletic fields rolled by. "I know you don't like me to stand out."

He struggled with a response. She wasn't wrong, but the truth wasn't an option. "Why do you say that?"

"Because when I won that award in sixth grade in Miami, you packed up and moved us here a week later. I don't want to move again. This is the longest we've ever lived in one place." She turned her hand and examined her ragged, obviously chewed fingernails.

Cristan waved off her very accurate deduction. "We moved to take advantage of a business opportunity."

Her body stilled, and her attention shifted back to him. Her focus intensified. Her posture and tone challenged his statement. "You manage your real estate investments all over the country from your home office every day. I don't think we needed to move a thousand miles to buy a property."

"The house has a great view," he said, but his argument sounded weak. "And there were other opportunities. It turned out for the best, didn't it? You seem happy here."

"I guess." Her shoulder gave a quick lift. Her eyes were wary, as if she didn't want to admit, even to herself, how much she liked living in Westbury. "I like having a horse. I like living in the country. Having friends is nice."

"See? It all worked out." The move to Florida had been a mistake. Every time he heard Spanish spoken, it reminded him of Argentina—of his past—of events he wanted to forget, and put him on edge. He heard the language here occasionally, but not as frequently as in Miami.

Lucia picked at the peeling glitter polish on her thumbnail. "So if it was just a business decision, then this time we won't have to move, right?"

And now Cristan was paying the full price of keeping secrets from his daughter. "Not right at this moment. Unfortunately, my business requires frequent relocation."

"Why?"

"It's complicated." Lies generally were.

"I'm not stupid." Behind her impudent tone, Lucia's voice rang with heartache. "There's this really convenient thing out there called the Internet. You know all about it. It's the place where you do ninety-five percent of your work. You don't go to meetings. Why does it matter where we live?"

He didn't reprimand her for her disrespect. She was sad and hurt, and he bore the blame. Perhaps he should have been more honest with her, but he'd wanted her to have as normal a life as possible, which he now realized hadn't been very normal at all. Good intentions could indeed lead one in the wrong direction.

"I know that you are very intelligent." He just hadn't realized she was also perceptive and mature, or that she was just as good at keeping secrets as he was. "I am very proud of you."

"I've been invited to compete in the state competition next month. The winner goes to the national competition in Washington, D.C. in May." Lucia crossed her arms over her chest. "If you don't have an issue with attention, then I can go, right?"

What should he do? Could they stay in Westbury, at least until Lucia finished high school? In twelve years, no one had come looking for them. Was that because he'd moved them frequently, kept a low profile, and maintained his vigilance, or because Aline Barba had no interest in them? Cristan wasn't conducting any business that would compete with hers or draw her attention. Eva was dead. But the feud between the two families was long and ingrained. One violent killing spawning another. The back-and-forth acts of retribution had continued for decades, each side seemingly intent on wiping the other from existence. The last conflict, the one he believed had initiated the Vargas massacre, had cost Aline her son. Did she know Cristan wasn't responsible, even though he'd been there that day? Or would she find him guilty by association regardless? It had been Eva who'd pulled the trigger. These were the unanswered questions that had kept him in hiding for more than a decade.

He'd changed their names. Lucia would hardly be recognizable. She'd been an infant when they'd left Argentina. The years of worry had left their mark on his face. He no longer resembled the shaggy-haired young man he'd been at that time.

If his paranoia was unfounded, they could live a more normal life—or at least as normal as possible for two people living under false identities, something Lucia did not know.

Still, answering her question nearly choked him. Once he agreed, there would be no going back. But hadn't they already crossed that barrier by staying here for two years? He had to change the way he treated his daughter. She was no longer a small child. The days when she could make new best friends in a single afternoon on the playground were over. Uprooting her now without a concrete threat would be cruel. "I don't see why not."

"Really?" Lucia's voice rose with excitement. "We aren't leaving?"

He chose his words with care. "I have no immediate plans to move."

"Omigod." The stunned look on her face told him she'd been prepared for an argument. "I can't believe it. You mean it?"

"Yes." When his daughter was desperate enough to hide important events from him, when she lacked the very childhood he strove to protect, then it was time to reevaluate his decisions. "But you have to promise not to keep secrets from me. I would have liked to have seen you win this afternoon."

Her head bobbed. "I'm sorry. Next time I promise to tell you. But *you* have to promise me the same thing."

"And there will be consequences for signing my name on that document. Except for babysitting and taking care of Snowman, you are grounded for a month."

"OK." She didn't seem upset by her punishment. Her happy chatter filled the car—and his heart—during the short drive to Sarah's house. This was the reason he hadn't moved. Lucia was flourishing here. The only thing tainting the beauty of the afternoon was the knowledge that he could never be totally honest with his daughter.

Secrets could be deadly, but he knew how easily the truth could also kill.

CHAPTER FOUR

The stuffed kangaroo on the foyer floor nearly brought Sarah to tears. One marble, brown eye stared up at her, forlorn. Threadbare patches and a lumpy body attested to her three-year-old's attachment. Em dragged that animal everywhere, but she'd refused to take it with her today.

Hoppy might be scared.

Were Em and her five-year-old sister, Alex, as nervous as Sarah? Work had been a welcome distraction. Her job as a sous chef for the Main Street Inn kept her busy, but now that she was home again, she could think of nothing else. Today was her ex-husband's first court-ordered unsupervised visitation with their two small daughters. They should be home safe any minute. But every Tuesday and Thursday, plus entire alternate weekends, this was her new reality.

Looping the convenience store bag handles over her wrist, she stepped over the threshold and dropped her keys on the hall table. Her little black-and-tan spaniel mix, Bandit, hopped on his back legs, greeting her like a wagging, furry pogo stick. He put his front feet on her thigh and let her stroke his head. When his paws dropped to the floor, she bent and picked up the kangaroo. She held it toward the dog. "Did you bring this down from Em's room?"

At the sound of Emma's name, Bandit ran to the storm door and looked out the glass. He glanced back at Sarah and barked.

"Sorry, buddy. The girls aren't with me." Pulling off her gloves, Sarah went to the kitchen and stowed the milk in the refrigerator. Out of habit, she plucked the receipt from the bottom of the plastic bag and smoothed it between her fingers. She stopped midmotion. She no longer had to submit receipts to justify every penny she spent. With a deliberate curl of her fist, she crumpled the slip of paper and dropped it into the garbage can. If the house had a fireplace, she would have burned it in a more symbolic gesture.

She stood in the center of the kitchen, lost. The girls should be here, washing up, helping her make a simple dinner. The kitchen was too small for a table, but Em should be kneeling on her stool at the counter, hugging Hoppy and decompressing from daycare while Alex gave Sarah a detailed rundown of her entire day from drop-off to pickup. The house was too quiet without her oldest's constant chatter.

The dog cocked his head in question. She scratched behind his ears. "I'm not used to silence, and I'm sure you need to go out. Let's wait for the girls outside." Anything was better than sitting inside alone, waiting and worrying. She went back to the door, lifted the leash off the wall hook, and snapped it onto his collar.

Her phone vibrated in her coat pocket. She fished it out and read the display. Troy.

Her heart rattled. Something had happened to the girls. Terrible possibilities reeled through her mind. Fear clamped around her lungs. She pushed the Answer button with a shaky finger. "What's wrong?"

"Where are you?" Anger radiated through the connection.

She froze, startled by the hostility in his tone. "Is something wrong with the girls, Troy?"

"I want to know where you've been."

Sarah paused, her thoughts racing. Her location wasn't any of Troy's business. Their divorce was final, and he'd lost all rights to ask about her whereabouts the night he tossed her down a flight of stairs five months before. But she couldn't make him angry while he was alone with three-year-old Emma and five-year-old Alex.

She let out a frustrated, frightened breath. Before the judge had ruled in his favor last week, Sarah had refused to answer his calls. But the moment her two little girls had climbed into his truck that morning, she'd unblocked his number. He had control again, and he knew it.

Her words tasted like defeat. "I was at work. Now I'm home."

"I don't believe you."

Bandit growled up at her, as if he could sense the animosity in Troy's tone.

"You can hear the dog, Troy," she said in a tired voice.

"You were supposed to be home from work twenty minutes ago." His voice rose.

Conditioned to make peace, Sarah almost replied. Placating him had become a habit, and she wasn't hiding anything. She'd stopped for milk. But she couldn't let him drag her back into his control games. "Are the girls all right?"

"Why wouldn't they be?"

"You aren't supposed to call me unless it's about the girls, and you're ten minutes late."

"Maybe they just wanted to know where their mother is." He had an answer for everything. He'd gotten clever when he'd sobered up. "Or maybe I wanted to make sure you were home before I drop them off."

In the silent moment that followed, she heard the faint voices of her daughters in the background. Her lungs expelled the breath she'd been holding. The girls were all right. "I have to take the dog out, Troy. I'll see you soon."

Gathering her courage, Sarah pressed End. The phone wasn't even in her pocket when it buzzed again. She glanced at the display to make sure it was Troy and let the call go to voicemail. Her gaze drifted over the interior of the small house. The 1980s oak and country-blue furnishings were dated, but she didn't mind. She hadn't wanted anything from the house she'd shared with Troy. Her sister's fiancé, the local police chief, let her and the girls live in this little house rent-free. He'd insisted on installing an alarm, but she'd refused to allow him to renovate. He'd done more than enough. Her entire life had changed since she'd moved to this house. She had a job and her independence. Until today, her girls had been happy and safe. This was her haven, her sanctuary. It had taken Troy months of legal finagling to violate it. She'd gotten her swift divorce, but there was no way to sever her ties with him, not when they shared two children.

Easing onto the boot bench by the door, she scooped the dog into her lap. He leaned into her, and she wrapped an arm around his sturdy little body. "What are we going to do?"

She allowed herself two minutes of canine therapy before she set the dog on the floor and stood. "Come on. I'll take you out to do your business before I call my lawyer."

She would not—could not—let Troy take control. Her lawyer wasn't as useful as she'd hoped. Troy knew how to phrase his words so that without hearing his tone, his message could be interpreted innocently. But there was nothing innocent about anything Troy did.

Back in the house, she took off her coat, unleashed the dog, and changed into jeans and a sweater. Then there was nothing to do but wait until Troy's truck pulled to the curb fifteen minutes later. Standing on the back of the sofa, Bandit went ballistic. She'd wanted a little time with the girls before she had to leave for her self-defense class. No chance of that now. Her babysitter would be here any minute. By the time she settled the girls with Lucia, she'd have to leave. But she refused to show her irritation. A response of any kind would only encourage Troy.

He sat in the truck for a few seconds, glaring at her through the passenger window. Draping his wrists over the steering wheel, he twisted his heavy school ring, the same ring that had made solid contact with her head five months before. Sarah touched the scar on her temple, her fingers tracing the small indentation. Troy's gaze caught hers, and a smug half smile turned up the corner of his mouth. Sarah tensed as he got out of the pickup.

The girls popped out of the backseat like toast and raced toward her. Pushing the irate dog firmly back into the house, Sarah went out onto the stoop to greet Alex and Em. The girls ran up the driveway, and she crouched to hug them both. Holding their little bodies close, she breathed in the scents of sweat and No More Tangles. *They were OK.* Relief swept through her. "Go on inside. Don't let the dog out."

They went into the house. Alex pulled the storm door closed just as Bandit's feet hit the glass, muffling the dog's angry barks.

"Did everything go all right?" She'd be pleasant to him if it killed her.

"Fine." Troy took a step toward her. "But you have to stop spoiling them."

Sarah didn't respond, but feigning confidence, she widened her stance and stretched her head toward the sky. *Do not back down.*

"I'm serious, Sarah. Alex is defiant, and Emma cries all the freaking time." Troy stopped. Irritation and indecision flickered in his eyes.

Sarah clamped her molars together. What was she going to say? She doubted he'd be receptive to the truth. *Your children are afraid of you.* "What time will you pick them up on Thursday?"

"Same as today." Troy scowled, but he turned toward his truck.

"See you then." Sarah backed toward the house, praying he left before her babysitter—and her hot father—arrived. But she was destined to have the worst luck in the universe. At that very same moment, Cristan Rojas turned down her street and parked behind Troy's truck.

One more minute and Troy would have been gone.

Lucia leaped from the car and loped across the grass on long legs. "Hi, Sarah."

"Hi, Lucia," Sarah said. "You can go on in."

Cristan climbed out of his Mercedes and leaned on the closed door, his phone pressed to his ear, his eyes following Troy as he got into his pickup. Tension between the men was palpable in the chilly air, which was ridiculous because Sarah wasn't involved with either of them.

Troy pulled away from the curb. The moment the pickup disappeared around the corner, Cristan started toward Sarah. His athletic body was encased in jeans and a black wool coat that pegged him as foreign in a town where everyone else wore down and flannel. She tamped down the pleasure that sparked inside her as he walked up the driveway.

"Hello, Sarah." His smile softened otherwise hard features. He was dark and Latin, and the only thing sexier than his lean, chiseled face was his faint, slightly formal, accent. And Sarah realized she was staring. Again. Why did that always happen with him? She blinked and cleared her throat.

"Hello," she said. "Thanks for waiting. I don't know what he'd do if he saw you come into the house." Jealousy, no matter how unfounded, would make Troy even angrier.

"I know you wish to avoid provoking him." But the flash of anger in Cristan's eyes said he would welcome a confrontation with Troy. Fortunately, Cristan possessed the self-control of a monk. His voice never rose above a carefully modulated pitch, and he gave both his actions and words careful consideration. But under that steely control, his posture always suggested that he could explode in an instant.

"I just want what's best for the girls. Their needs have to come first."

"Of course." His expression relaxed with understanding and compassion. He was a widower and single father, and she had to admit that the bond between Cristan and his daughter was just as attractive as his dark eyes and broad shoulders.

"Thank you for understanding."

He acknowledged her comment with a slight incline of his head, but his eyes didn't break contact with hers. His focus intensified. "But I am at your disposal if you should change your mind. You deserve better. Much better."

Sarah's skin flushed. Cristan often appeared aloof and cool, but at that moment he radiated pure heat. The wind shifted, the damp chill reminding her that her life was complicated. Troy was already hostile. If he thought Sarah was flirting with another man, no amount of court-ordered anger management counseling would help.

It frustrated and depressed her that her ex-husband still controlled her life. Troy would eventually have to move on, and then maybe she could explore the feelings that bounced between her and Cristan. But for the girls' sake, for now she would have to make decisions with her head, not her heart.

She blinked, turned away from him, and led the way into the house. Lucia was hugging Alex and Em. The little girls' voices climbed to a high, excited pitch that soothed Sarah's doubts. They were worth anything she had to endure.

Sarah picked up a wrapped package on her bookshelf. "I have something for you, Lucia."

"It's not my birthday," Lucia said in a puzzled voice.

Sarah grinned. "I know. This is a just-because present."

"Just because?" Lucia asked.

"Just because I wanted to give it to you," Sarah said.

Lucia ripped off the brown paper. "Omigod." She squealed. "Look, Dad. It's Snowman and me at the show."

She turned the gift toward her father. Lucia had ridden her new horse, Snowman, in the indoor horse show at the winter festival. She'd been very excited to win a blue ribbon. When Sarah had seen their picture in the town newspaper, she'd had to frame it for the child. The photographer had captured a perfect image of the pair in midair over a low jump in the indoor arena.

"Thank you." Lucia grabbed Sarah in a fierce hug.

"You're welcome. I thought you should commemorate your first win," Sarah said.

Lucia turned the gift toward her father. Cristan's face tightened as he leaned closer and read the caption. "Lucia Rojas and Snowman win first place in the novice hunter division."

"I didn't know my picture was in the paper." Lucia beamed and enveloped Sarah in another one-armed hug. "I'm going to hang it in my room."

"You're welcome." Sarah warmed as she watched Lucia nearly skip back to the girls.

"It is a lovely gift." Cristan's voice was rigid. He'd shut down. "You didn't need to do that."

"It gives me great joy to make her happy."

"Thank you," he said. "What time should I pick up Lucia?"

"Is seven o'clock all right?" Confused, Sarah searched his face. Over the past few months, Cristan's formal demeanor had slowly shifted to friendly, maybe even more than friendly. But it seemed Mr. Uncomfortable had returned today. Why?

"Yes. I'll be back at seven." His deep brown eyes shuttered as he backed away.

He seemed to shake off his mood as he turned to the children. As always, his posture and smile relaxed the second he addressed the kids. He was more comfortable with them than her. Other than telling her his wife had died when Lucia was an infant, he was guarded when speaking about his past. Did he still grieve his wife?

But even if he did, why would her giving his daughter a gift put him on edge?

CHAPTER FIVE

Cristan backed out of the kitchen. How could he have let this happen? Lucia's picture was in the newspaper and surely on the Internet as well. Panic scratched at the edges of his control. He tried to reason with it. No one could possibly know her true identity. The local paper didn't circulate beyond the town's borders, and it had a very small readership within the community. He'd purchased only one issue, when the trash pickup schedule had been altered. He was being ridiculous. At this point in their new lives, being overly paranoid would attract more attention than a single article.

He went to his daughter, who was sitting cross-legged on the floor helping Alex line her stuffed animals up in a neat row in front of the television. Clutching her lopsided kangaroo, Emma climbed into Lucia's lap.

He crouched next to the children. "What do we have here?"

As usual, Alex answered. "We're going to watch a movie. Mommy said it was OK." She gave a small brown bear a seat in the front row.

"That sounds like fun." Cristan surveyed the pretend theater. "I see you've made sure everyone has a good view."

Alex positioned a small beanbag pig next to the bear. "The little ones get to sit up front."

Cristan turned to Emma. "Is Hoppy going to watch?"

Emma nodded and turned her bashful face into Lucia's shoulder, but the toddler's face turned back to him in a second, her eyes laughing.

Cristan leaned down to the kangaroo's level. "What's that, Hoppy? You would like to pick the movie?" He looked at Emma. "Hoppy says it's his turn to choose."

Shaking her head vigorously, Emma's eyes sparkled as she grinned back at him. "No."

"That's what he said." He turned up his palms and shrugged.

"No!" She burst into a fit of giggles. At the sound of her innocent laughter, Cristan's tension eased, and he wondered for the thousandth time what would have become of him if Lucia had not been born. Considering the path he'd been on, he'd likely be dead by now. Lucia had saved him.

"We already picked the movie." Alex showed him a colorful box with an animated princess on the front.

"That is a good movie." He and Lucia had watched it many times. Rising, he set a hand on his daughter's shoulder. "I have some errands to run. Call me if you need me. I love you."

"Love you too," she said.

Love for his child swelled his heart. Giving his daughter the opportunity to live with innocence had been worth all the sacrifices he'd made. But it was the least he could do after all she'd given him.

He stood. Sarah leaned in the doorway to the kitchen, watching him. Worn jeans and a simple sweater hugged her slim body. She wore no makeup. Wholesome and natural, she was nothing like the women he usually found attractive. Yet when he was with her, he often found himself staring, unable to look away. Her beauty was quiet and unassuming, and the longer he watched her, the more compelling she became.

Her brow creased. "Is everything all right?"

"Fine." As much as he tried to resist, those rich brown eyes always drew him in. He wished he could explain what must seem like erratic behavior, but it would be easier to put some distance between them. What did he have to offer a woman? He couldn't even give her his real name.

Time to go. Being with Sarah highlighted his loneliness.

He left the house, got back into his car, and pulled away from the curb. He would not think about his wife's death or his hopeless infatuation with a woman he couldn't have. Tonight he would make an effort to celebrate his many blessings. Lucia had made friends. People said hello to them in the grocery store. His daughter got straight As and babysat. Did the other residents of this little town appreciate the beautiful and uneventful nature of their lives? To him, ordinary life should be cherished, especially this week, when violent dreams vied for his attention.

He stopped at King's Tack Shop to order several new pairs of riding breeches for Lucia, then stopped at the Quickie-Mart. Cristan pushed through the glass door. The scent of coffee wafted, summoning him. He passed two customers standing in line, crossed the tile, and headed for the coffee station. He filled a cardboard cup with the darkest roast, then plucked a loaf of bread from a shelf.

A young woman with a quart of milk in one arm and a toddler in the other followed him back to the register. The woman looked familiar. Cristan skirted a display of automobile ice scrapers and took his place in line behind an elderly man buying lottery tickets.

"Hi," she smiled. "You're Lucia's father, right?"

"Yes," he said, trying to place her. She was in her mid to late twenties, pretty, with short dark hair. The little girl in her arms was all dark hair and eyes, like Lucia had been at the same age.

"I'm Kenzie Newell. This is Delaney." The toddler smiled at him. Kenzie continued, "I also have a daughter in kindergarten. We met at the school Christmas bake sale. You probably don't remember."

"Yes. I remember that day." Cristan had a clear remembrance of a gymnasium full of children and young mothers. A few fathers had been scattered in the crowd. Lucia had signed him up for the event. His daughter thought he spent too much time alone.

"I'm looking for a babysitter. Mine went away to college this year. You have no idea how hard it is to find a good sitter. Sarah Mitchell is my neighbor. She says Lucia is terrific."

"She is," he agreed with a smile.

Kenzie juggled her daughter and the milk to dig a business card from her coat pocket. "Here's my card. I'd love it if Lucia called me, if it's all right with you, of course. My husband and I haven't been out together since school started last September."

"Yes, I remember those days." Cristan stopped himself. He had almost shared a memory of his life with Eva. He was letting his guard down. Discomfort crawled over him. Standing apart, maintaining his vigilance, those were the factors that had kept Lucia safe, and he would do well to keep that in mind. Only one of them could live a normal life, and Lucia deserved the privilege. He hadn't done nearly enough penance for his multitude of sins.

The elderly man took his stack of lottery tickets and left the store. Another customer joined the line, a man in a dark-blue hooded sweatshirt. He was turned away, his hand over his face as he coughed. Cristan set the coffee and bread on the counter at the same moment the new customer stepped clear of the line and pulled a handgun from his pocket.

Adrenaline jolted Cristan's heart and shot through his veins. The shock sharpened his focus and reminded him how he no longer expected violence to be part of his life—and how much work it had taken him to find peace. Peace that this young thug had just destroyed.

Thank God Lucia was not with him.

Kenzie gasped. The oblivious child repeated a rhyme in a singsong voice, the innocent voice stirring Cristan's anger.

The young man held the 9mm with a steady hand. Staring through the gap between his hood and a bandana tied around the lower half of his face, the eyes that focused over the barrel were pale blue and cold and empty.

Cristan knew that look well. He used to see it in the mirror every morning.

Those were the eyes of a killer.

"Put your hands where I can see them." The robber gestured with the gun. A thin pair of black leather gloves covered his hands.

Moving slowly and avoiding the challenge of direct eye contact, Cristan raised both hands in front of his chest, palms facing outward. A feminine sob sounded behind him. He shifted his weight slightly to better shield Kenzie and her child.

The gunman moved behind the register. "Open the register and put the cash in a bag."

The skinny young clerk complied, his breath coming in short wheezes that would no doubt lead to hyperventilation in a few moments. The robber scanned the tops of the aisles, clearly looking for someone.

Who else was in the store? Cristan listened for voices or footsteps. A shoe scraped on tile behind him. He glanced at the round security mirror mounted in the corner. Two figures marched toward them. A second robber, dressed in a dark-red sweatshirt and jeans, dragged a bald, aproned man by the crook of his elbow.

Red Shirt pressed a gun to the bald man's temple. A gold pin affixed to the green Quickie-Mart apron read Manager.

"OK, Mr. Manager. Open that other register drawer." Red Shirt shoved the manager toward a register on the opposite counter. The manager stumbled and went down, landing in an awkward sprawl like a newborn colt.

"Get it done in ten seconds or I splatter junior's brains all over the floor." Behind the counter, Blue Eyes slapped the clerk on the side of the head. This man wasn't burdened by a conscience. If he was looking for a simple job and some quick cash, the only thing keeping him from pulling his trigger was the dislike of complication.

The manager scrambled to his knees, then pushed to his feet. Red Shirt followed him behind the counter.

Cristan sized up the clerk and manager. Both were familiar from his previous visits to the store. Neither seemed like the sort who would try anything foolish. The best possible outcome was for the robbers to take the money and run without injuring anyone. These two thugs were small time. No intelligent criminal would risk prison for the few hundred dollars in a couple of register drawers. The majority of the cash would be kept in a drop safe.

The manager flipped through keys with shaking fingers. It took three stabs at the lock before he managed to open the register drawer. By the time he got it, his face and scalp shone with perspiration. Red Shirt shoved him aside and emptied the drawer into a brown paper bag. "Next open the safe."

"I-I can't," the manager said.

"Bullshit," said Red Shirt. Then he directed his attention to Cristan.

"You." He flicked the muzzle of the gun. "Empty your pockets."

Cristan carefully slid two fingers into the chest pocket of his wool coat. There was nothing in his wallet that could not be replaced. Nothing that warranted risking his life to keep. He wanted no trouble. If anything happened to him, Lucia would be alone in this world. She had no family. She didn't even know her real name.

He withdrew his wallet. Red Shirt extended the paper bag, and Cristan dropped his leather billfold into it.

"Gimme your purse, lady." Red Shirt flexed his fingers twice.

Still holding the toddler on her hip, Kenzie dropped her quart of milk and shrugged the strap of the handbag off her shoulder. Cristan took the bag from her and handed it to the robber so she wouldn't have to get any closer.

"Thanks for doing business." Red Shirt turned toward the exit. Behind the counter, Blue Eyes paused to grab a handful of Power Bars from a display. He shoved them into his bag.

One more minute and it would be over. Cristan breathed.

Then Red Shirt stopped. His expression narrowed as he focused on Kenzie. "You. Come here."

A fresh wave of anger slid into Cristan's throat.

"Please. Don't," Kenzie begged.

The man moved closer. He pointed the gun at the child. "I said come here."

Kenzie took a faltering step toward him, twisting her body to turn the child away from the danger. "Just leave my baby alone. I'll do whatever you want."

He lowered the gun. "Then put the kid down. You're coming with me."

Kenzie tried to lower the little girl to the floor. Holding on to her mother's neck with a desperate grip, the child shrieked. Tears poured down her face, bright pink with terror.

"Shut her up!" Red Shirt demanded, aiming at the child again.

Kenzie shushed and soothed the child, while angling to cover the toddler with her own body.

"Why don't you take the money and go?" Cristan reasoned. "If you are quick, you might get away before the authorities arrive."

The gunman spun, took two steps, and pointed the gun directly in Cristan's face. "What the fuck did you say?"

Cristan stared down the barrel, his relief that the weapon was no longer aimed at the child short lived. His interference could orphan his daughter. But what else could he do? A man simply did not allow women or children to be harmed. He attempted to deflate the robber's anger. The best outcome for all was still a nonviolent one. "A woman will slow you down."

"Forget the girl, moron. He's the one we need." Behind the counter, Blue Eyes glanced at Cristan.

Why would they want him? They wouldn't. Blue Eyes must have meant they still needed the manager to open the safe.

"Get out of my way." Blue Eyes struck the clerk across the face with the butt of his gun. "I'm getting some Twinkies." He came out from behind the counter and sauntered down an aisle.

The clerk's legs collapsed. Blood welled from a cut on his cheek. The manager caught him and eased him to the floor.

So much for nonviolence.

In the corner of his eye, Cristan saw Kenzie gathering her child and slowly backing away. Smart girl, taking advantage of Cristan's diversion. He wanted the child out of the line of fire in case someone started shooting.

"One more fucking word out of you and I will blow your fucking face off," Red Shirt screamed, taking another step toward Cristan, but not close enough to put the gun within reach. His eyes were overly bright, and drugs would explain the sheer stupidity of this robbery. Who would risk an armed robbery in broad daylight for a few hundred dollars? "If I want the woman, I'll take the woman. Do you understand me?"

"I do." Cristan could see the desire to kill on the young man's face. Red Shirt wanted to pull the trigger, but something was holding him back, possibly the fear of having the event recorded on a surveillance camera.

"I think we'll take you both," Red Shirt said. "Hey, get back here, bitch," he yelled to Kenzie.

Cristan needed a weapon. Years of training and muscle memory took over. In one smooth and lightning-fast motion, he grabbed an ice scraper from the cardboard display next to him and arced it upward as if he were drawing a sword from a scabbard. The hard plastic handle caught Red Shirt in the forearm, a fraction of a second later the same motion carried the sharp plastic blade to his face. The gun flew out of his hands and slid across the tile. Blood spurted from his nose. The robber covered his gushing face with both hands. Cristan reversed the scraper in a circular motion. A downward strike brought the butt end of the hard plastic tool across Red Shirt's temple. He fell to his knees. A kick to his ribs sent him into a face-plant on the tile.

Cristan looked for the gun. Its momentum had carried it across the small store.

"What the fuck is going on?" Blue Eyes emerged from behind a display, his arms laden with white Hostess boxes. His gaze darted around the store and landed on his unconscious partner. "Fuck." He dropped the boxes and pulled his gun from his pocket.

But Cristan was already moving toward him, closing the critical distance. He was on the robber before the gun was leveled. He grabbed the weapon with his left hand, wrapping his fingers over the slide and redirecting the muzzle toward the floor. A solid right cross struck the robber's jaw. His head snapped back, and Cristan twisted the weapon out of his hands.

Blue Eyes cradled his hand. "You broke my wrist."

Adjusting his grip on the gun, Cristan aimed at the center of Blue Eyes's chest. "Get on your knees and put your hands on top of your head."

Blue Eyes complied. Cristan backed up and positioned his body to cover both robbers with the weapon. But Red Shirt was on his knees, a second gun in his hand. He pointed it at the manager.

"We're leaving or I shoot him." He yelled to his partner, "Come on!"

Blue Eyes ran out. Red Shirt backed out of the door, still aiming at the store manager. Cristan tracked him with the gun until both robbers ran around the side of the building, where they presumably had a vehicle.

The store clerk and manager stared, both white faced and open mouthed.

"Have you called the police?" Cristan asked without taking his eyes off the plate glass window, though he doubted the robbers would be back.

The manager's Adam's apple bobbed as he swallowed. "I hit the panic alarm. The police should be here any second."

Cristan lowered the gun. The men were long gone. "Kenzie, are you all right?"

She emerged from behind a low refrigerated case, where she'd been crouching. Pale faced and shaking, she clutched the sobbing toddler to her chest and babbled, "Thank you. Yes. Thank you."

Cristan surveyed his clothes. Blood from the robber's nose spotted his jeans, sweater, and wool coat.

He should run, before the police arrived. He could swing by the house, change his clothes, and grab the go-bags. He could pick up Lucia and disappear. Their flight plan was well planned and well funded. He didn't need to take the risk of being exposed.

So, why was he still here?

Sirens approached. A moment later, police cars pulled up and lights pulsed in the store, and Cristan's chance to flee had passed.

He set the gun on the ground at his feet and lifted his hands to shoulder height as police officers rushed into the store, guns drawn. The manager explained the situation. Cops swept the store and called for an ambulance.

Cristan went outside and dropped to sit on the curb. The enormity of the day's events washed over him. What was he going to do?

"Are you injured?" A policeman stepped off the concrete apron and scanned Cristan's body.

"No. It isn't my blood." He shook his head. His head and stomach reeled with the flux of adrenaline. He breathed through it. He might be out of practice, but this was hardly the first time he had committed an act of violence. But today, the aftermath felt different, as if it was no longer a purely physical reaction. Relief—and fear—swirled in his chest. How would he keep a low profile after this?

"What happened?" the cop asked.

Cristan kept his story simple.

"I'll need you to come to the station." The cop studied Cristan's face, as if deciding if he was being truthful. "We'll need a more detailed statement."

"Of course," Cristan said. But as he stared down at his blood-spattered clothes, one question consumed his mind. What now? The quiet life he'd built had come to an end, but that was the risk with basing one's existence on an elaborate deception. The robbery would draw attention from the police and media, and he needed to avoid scrutiny.

How would he handle Lucia? She'd be upset by today's incident. How would his daughter react if she knew the truth? That her mother hadn't died in an automobile accident. The thought of Lucia discovering her true heritage gave him nightmares. He could never tell her. The knowledge would put her at risk—and inspire her anger. He would rather die than lose her love, even if it had been gained in fraud.

No. Lucia would never forgive him if he told her that one week from today marked the twelfth anniversary of her mother's execution.

CHAPTER SIX

The forearm around her throat was gentle, but Sarah couldn't breathe.

He's barely touching you.

"Relax, Sarah," Brooke Davenport, her self-defense instructor, said in a calm voice. "You know Luke. He won't hurt you."

Luke Holloway, Brooke's man-friend and Internet security consultant, had played the role of attacker in the three previous classes. Sarah knew Luke. Her sister's neighbor, Mrs. Holloway, was his grandmother. Sarah had no reason to be afraid of him. She even knew exactly what he was going to do, yet every time he touched her, she froze. His body was huge behind her. Well over six feet tall, he towered over her. The padded training suit he wore for protection added bulk to his lean frame.

She had no difficulty practicing when she was paired up with another female student, but that wasn't very helpful. Women rarely attacked other women.

"You know what to do." Brooke stood in front of her, her kind brown eyes serious. "Come on, Sarah. I know you can do this."

Blood rushed in her ears, and Brooke's face spun. Despite the chilly air in the community center, sweat dripped down her back and soaked her T-shirt. "I can't."

"Yes, you can," Luke said in her ear. "Take a deep breath."

"Visualize the movement," Brooke said. "Just give me one elbow strike. One. You can do it."

Sarah breathed through the staccato beat of her heart. This was her fourth class, and she was the only student who couldn't perform a single self-defense technique on Luke. Her brain reeled with images of Troy's angry face, and today's hostile phone call.

"You can do this," Luke said. He lowered his voice so that only Sarah could hear him. "Don't let him win."

Frustration swelled into anger. She was tired of being powerless. Every time she made strides in her new life, Troy erected a new barrier in her path. It had to stop. Now.

Gathering every ounce of strength, Sarah moved her arm and popped an elbow into the padded vest. There were a few additional moves to the technique, but she didn't get any further. All her brain could process was the fact that she'd done *something*. She broken through her wall of fear.

Luke released her, and she spun around to see his grin. Next to the rectangular mat, a dozen women applauded.

A college-age brunette in yoga pants hooted, "Go, Sarah!"

Sarah stared at Luke. "I can't believe it. I did it."

"Attagirl." He raised his hand for a high five. Light-headed, Sarah lifted a weak arm and they slapped palms. Giddiness flooded her floppy limbs. She needed to start working out. A twenty-minute walk on her lunch break wasn't enough. "I really did it."

Brooke smiled wide. "You did."

Sarah had been afraid she'd never be able to shake the panic-induced paralysis, that she'd be stuck in a permanent state of frozen uselessness. But tonight, she'd taken another step forward.

"Now do it again." Brooke signaled to Luke.

He moved around her slowly and wrapped his arm around her neck again. This time, Sarah reacted almost instantly. Her elbow connected with his vest. He moved back a few inches and loosened his hold, mimicking the natural reaction to a blow to the solar plexus. Sarah looked over her shoulder, then retracted her arm and jutted her elbow into the palm he held in front of his face. Pivoting, she brought her hands in front of her face and backed away.

Luke grinned. "Yes!"

Joy flooded Sarah. The exercise was staged, but the accomplishment filled her with pride—and hope. Troy wouldn't give up easily. She knew that, but she would fight for her independence one little step at a time. She had a goal, and she'd reach it if she had to crawl. Troy's antics were no more than obstacles to be overcome, bumps in her road.

"One more time!" Brooke said.

Before the class finished ten minutes later, Sarah managed to break Luke's light hold on her wrist twice. She knew he was more aggressive with the other women and very gentle with her, but she didn't care. She'd get there. Baby steps. If she could do this, everything else would come with time.

"That's all for tonight," Brooke said. "Remember, all these techniques are your last resort. Your goal is not to get into a situation to need them. Be safe."

Brooke folded her floor mats. Luke stripped off his pads. Sweat soaked his T-shirt. The women gathered around Sarah. Their congratulatory back-pats and hugs filled her with warmth.

Sarah retrieved her jacket and purse. Zipping up, she followed the other women out of the brick building into the cold. A damp wind chilled her cheeks and salt crunched under her athletic shoes as she hurried across the lot and got into her van. Sarah locked her vehicle doors and started the engine of her minivan. Keeping all Brooke's safety tips in mind, she'd parked under a streetlamp.

Luke carried the mats and pads to Brooke's SUV and loaded the equipment in the back.

Waiting for her van to warm up, Sarah plugged her phone into the charging cord on the console. Before she could set the phone down, it vibrated with an incoming call. Sarah didn't recognize the number. She hesitated, but when she was away from the girls, she hated to ignore a call. She lifted the phone and pressed Answer.

"You fucking slut. Who was that man at the house?"

Her heart bumped her ribcage. "Troy?"

"Answer me."

"Did you change your phone number?" she asked.

"Maybe I borrowed a phone from a friend. Don't change the subject. Who is he, Sarah? Is that why you divorced me? I'll bet you've been fucking this guy for years," Troy yelled.

Recoiling, Sarah took the phone from her ear. She sent Lucia a quick text, on my way.

She hadn't met Cristan until after she'd left Troy, and the accusation that she'd been unfaithful stung. She took a deep breath. No more games. She couldn't allow Troy to manipulate her. If she did, it would never end. He would never understand that she was beyond his reach. And since when did he borrow a phone? Two possibilities occurred to her immediately. Either he thought she might not answer, or he didn't want a record of the call to exist.

Troy yelled, "I want to know who he is, Sarah."

Her phone vibrated as Lucia responded with OK. Knowing the girls were safe, Sarah set the phone on the console and stared at it.

"Sarah, God damn it. Answer me," Troy's bellow sounded small and tinny emanating from the speaker on her cell, but in her mind, she heard it at full volume.

Sarah held her finger an inch over the screen. She shouldn't have to tolerate this abuse. Because that's what it was. Troy might not be in her car. He might not be able to reach her with a fist, but the cursing and threats and yelling were all blows to her ego—and all designed for intimidation, something he'd perfected in their years together.

Be firm, her therapist had said, *but do not engage.*

"Sarah, are you still there—"

She sucked in some air and interrupted him. "Troy, if you continue to yell, I will hang up."

He exploded. "What the fuck—"

She touched the red End button, cutting Troy off midrant, and pulled her finger away as if the phone screen had burned her skin. Her heart thudded over the sound of the van's engine. To a normal woman, hanging up on her ex-husband might not seem like a big deal, but to Sarah, this was another first. Exhilaration and terror swept over her in waves.

A knock on her window nearly sent her into the passenger seat. She pressed a hand against her sternum, where her heart knocked. Brooke stood next to her car, her hands shoved into the pockets of her coat. Sarah lowered her window.

"Is everything all right?" Brooke's perceptive glance swept over Sarah's face.

"Yes. Fine." Sarah willed her face to relax, but smiling wasn't possible.

On the console, her phone buzzed.

"Are you going to answer that?" Brooke asked.

"No." Sarah met her gaze.

"Sarah, if you need help, please ask for it." Brooke knew her story.

Most of the town knew about her and Troy. His family owned one of the largest businesses in town, and her father-in-law had been on the town council before he'd gone to jail on corruption charges. The Mitchells hadn't exactly kept a low profile in Westbury.

The phone buzzed again. Sarah reached over and deliberately turned it off. "Thanks for asking, Brooke, but I'll be fine."

"Good night then. You made some real progress tonight. You should be proud of yourself."

"I am. Good night." Sarah raised the window and watched Brooke walk back to her SUV, then Sarah drove out of the lot.

When she'd first left Troy, the humiliation had been hard to get past. Her face had been battered, her arm broken, and her spirit shattered. There were days when she wanted to run as far away from her hometown as possible and start fresh in another town, where everyone didn't know about her failures. Gossip was part of living in a close-knit community, but so was support. As much as Sarah wanted to stand on her own, knowing that her friends and family were there for the girls kept her sane.

The drive home was short, and Sarah soon pulled into her driveway. She picked up her phone and turned it back on. Troy had called her three times and left a message. But Cristan had also called.

Taking her keys from the ignition, she tapped Cristan's name on her screen.

"Sarah," he answered. "I'm going to be late picking up Lucia. Is that all right?"

His tone was strained. In the background, she heard voices, phones, and movement.

"Of course," she said. "What's wrong?"

He sighed. "The Quickie-Mart was robbed tonight."

"While you were in it?" Concern tightened her grip on her keys.

Why else would he be detained? "I'm afraid so."

"Are you all right?"

"Yes. I'm at the police station. There's paperwork. I'm not sure when I'll be done."

"It's not a problem. Lucia can stay as long as necessary."

"Thank you."

"What do you want me to tell her?" Sarah asked.

"She should hear this from me. I'll call her now and tell her what happened."

"Keep me updated." Sarah ended the call. Pressing the voice-mail button, she held the phone to her ear while she got out of the car. Better to listen to Troy's message before she went into the house with the children.

"You shouldn't hang up on me." The false calm in Troy's voice lifted goose bumps on her arms. "I just want to talk. How will we manage our differences if you won't even have a conversation with me?"

The chill spread through Sarah's limbs. She had no record of his earlier, threatening call, and he was sure to keep his recorded message civil.

"We have children together, Sarah. The divorce won't change the fact that I'll be in your life forever."

CHAPTER SEVEN

A breaking news report played on the flat-screen television. She uncurled her legs and planted her feet flat on the floor as the newswoman stood in front of a convenience store. Police vehicles crowded the parking area.

"Two men who robbed a convenience store today were surprised when a customer fought back." The newswoman went on to describe an event, which was nothing like it should have been.

Disgust and fury tumbled through her. "Find out where they are."

"Of course." Her lieutenant whipped out his cell phone and pressed a button. He held the phone to his ear. "No answer."

"Cowards." She turned off the television and stood. "I don't like to be ignored. We need to find them." She lifted another remote from the coffee table and turned off the gas fireplace.

"Of course." He swiped a finger across his phone screen. "It appears they are headed to the warehouse where we had our first meeting."

"They'll try to run."

"Yes," he said.

"We have to get there before they leave. I don't want to have to chase them down." Her boots echoed on the glossy wood floor as she crossed the great room. The rental house was set up to accommodate families who enjoyed outdoor activities. A large utility room held coat hooks and cubbies. She'd used the convenient space to house some weapons, spare ammunition, and surveillance equipment. She grabbed her coat.

Outside, they climbed into the ugly minivan and drove fifteen minutes toward Westbury. Before they reached the actual town, he turned into the dark dirt lot of an abandoned warehouse. The sun was just dipping below the trees. A blue van was parked in the long shadows that stretched across the cold ground. The rear door of the vehicle was open. Two men stood behind the vehicle. Bags and boxes were piled around their feet.

The minivan came to a stop, and they got out. She rounded the front fender, hands loose and relaxed at her sides. "Rodney, you aren't answering your phone."

Rodney's nose was swollen. His shirt was stained dark red. "We're in a rush. We were going to call you back."

Sure they were. She gave their pile of belongings a pointed glance. "Going somewhere?"

Jerome clutched his arm to his chest. "We need to lay low for a few weeks."

"You didn't do the job for which you were paid," she said.

"You didn't mention we were supposed to kidnap fucking Jason Bourne." Rodney touched his nose and winced.

"It seems Christopher hasn't lost his edge," her lieutenant said without taking his eyes off Jerome and Rodney.

She took a step forward, the heels of her boots scraping the frozen ground. She walked closer to stand next to the man. "I gave you explicit instructions. You took the money and didn't hold up your end of the arrangement."

"Hey, we did what you said. You weren't straight with us." Jerome said, fear quivering in his voice.

"Did you attempt to use a woman or child to force him to comply?" she asked.

"Yeah." Rodney licked his lips. "That didn't pan out."

"What happened to the money we fronted you?" she asked.

"We deserve something." Jerome took a step back. "You lied to us."

No doubt they'd spent the money. They glanced at each other. From the wild-eyed expression that passed between them, she knew they suspected punishment was coming.

"Do not worry," she said. "You'll get what is coming to you."

She pulled a gun from her pocket and fired twice. Jerome flinched. The bullet struck him in the chest, the impact buckling his knees. He looked down, as if surprised to see a spreading patch of red on his jacket. He hadn't even had time to consider drawing the gun she could see bulging at his waistband.

"What the fuck?" Rodney said, looking down at the blood welling from his chest.

"Incompetent idiots." She felt nothing but annoyance as they crumpled to the dirt. These men were the dregs of society. No one would miss them. She walked closer and liberated their weapons: two handguns and a knife. She stared down at the bodies. One of the men groaned. His feet twitched. She aimed her gun and fired a second shot into each man's chest. The groaning man stilled. "You really need to start carrying a gun," she said to her lieutenant.

He raised a disdainful brow. "No skill is required."

"Killing isn't about ego. It's about getting the job done." She pocketed her weapon. "Put them in the van." The warehouse might be abandoned, but she preferred to leave scenes clean.

"I'm old-fashioned. A man should take pride in his work." With a grunt, he dragged the bodies, one by one, to the back of the van. Stooping, he hoisted a body into the vehicle. Sweat broke out on his forehead. He kept his body strong, but he was no longer a young man. He lifted the second robber into the cargo area and tossed a blanket over both bodies. "I will find a place to dump them tomorrow."

"Just park the van behind the house for now. It'll be out of sight. It's probably not a good idea to drive it around in case the police are looking for it." There was no reason for anyone to come to the rental house. She'd paid for the entire month. Her mind shifted to more important matters. Her thoughts had been spinning since she'd confirmed the child was Luciana Navarro. This initial plan had been a long shot, but she was just getting warmed up. An idea was forming in her head. One that could destroy Christopher, body *and* soul.

Her lieutenant closed the rear door of the vehicle. "It's a good thing we rented a property without close neighbors."

"That was not an accident." She liked to be prepared for all possibilities. The basement of the house would be the perfect place to hold an *interrogation* session.

He peeled the latex gloves from his hands, turned them inside out to contain the blood, and stuffed them into his pocket.

"You have blood on your coat." She pointed to his shoulder. "Dispose of it."

With a nod, he stripped it off. "Christopher will be a hard man to take."

"I'm sure he has lost some of his skills. Living here and raising a child must have softened him."

His head inclined toward the van. "Obviously, he hasn't gone too soft."

"Besting these two criminals wasn't all that difficult." She glanced into the rear window of the van at the still lumps under the blanket. Blood was seeping through the cloth in dark, wet patches. "Yes, I know you predicted these two would fail."

He lifted a shoulder. "No harm was done. The event appeared random, as was your plan."

"This is true," she agreed. "It should have been a simple job. How hard is it to threaten a woman or child? Christopher has weaknesses. One must use them as leverage. With a man like him, the mind is as formidable a weapon as the body." Christopher's chivalry was the chink in his armor.

"Why don't we just kill him?"

Because for years, her dream had been to mark the anniversary of the massacre by looking him in the eyes as he realized she'd won. He couldn't outrun her. There was no escape.

"I still have a week. I'm not ready to settle."

"Now who's being inefficient?"

"This is different." This was her life.

"What do we do now?" Her driver bent next to the robber's cargo van. He reached underneath the vehicle and pulled a black box loose. He tossed it to her, then opened the driver's door. His face creased with disgust as he surveyed the interior.

She caught the black GPS box in two hands. Technology had come so far in the last twelve years. "Fear not. My plan is evolving. First, you drive that," she pointed to the robbers' van, "to the house and park it out back. Then we'll decide what to do next."

She slid behind the wheel of the minivan and closed the door. Her mind strayed to Christopher. Soon, he would be as silent as the cargo in the back of the van. And he would stay that way. Forever.

CHAPTER EIGHT

Could this get any worse?

Cristan shifted his weight in the hard-backed chair in the Westbury Police Station. He twisted off the cap from a bottle of water and drank. The police had been apologetic, but the attention and legal scrutiny were still nightmarish for a man who wished to remain unknown.

"Can I get you some coffee? How about a sandwich? It's been hours. You have to be hungry." Officer Ethan Hale had typed Cristan's statement and questioned him. Ethan had also provided Cristan with the athletic pants and shirt he was currently wearing. The robbers had worn gloves, but the police were hoping to use DNA from the blood on Cristan's clothes to identify at least one of them.

"No, but thank you." Plans formed in Cristan's mind. He needed to get home. He needed to pick up Lucia at Sarah's house. His daughter had acted calm when he told her about the robbery, but he knew she would be upset. Events and repercussions had to be analyzed. Decisions had to be made.

The chief of police, Mike O'Connell, opened his office door. "Cristan, come on in."

Cristan crossed the room, water bottle in hand. He had known the police chief for five months. He and Lucia boarded their horses at a farm owned by Mike's fiancée, who was also Sarah's sister. Everyone in this small town was connected to everyone else.

In his early forties, the redheaded police chief was an inch or so shorter than him, but Mike's bulkier body carried a thirty-pound weight advantage, all of it muscle. He'd been a wrestler at one time and would make a formidable opponent. But the police chief was honest and honorable, two traits Cristan did not claim as his own. Being orphaned and living on the streets of Argentina had given him hard-scrabble survival instincts. Honor could be a handicap in a street fight.

He followed Mike into his office. Another man occupied the room. Cristan recognized the tall blond man perched on the credenza behind Mike's desk as the police chief's friend. He also recognized the lethal expression buried in the man's eyes. This man would not be burdened by scruples.

Mike waved him toward a leather guest chair, then rounded the desk, and sat behind it. "Do you remember Sean Wilson?"

Cristan nodded and reached over to shake hands. Sean acknowledged him with a nod that said they understood each other very well. Like all animals, predators knew their own kind. Cristan eased into the chair, exhaustion loosening his muscles. Adrenaline provided necessary quick energy for action, but the aftereffects drained him. And sleep had been an elusive adversary this past week.

"Sean is a security expert. He's helping me clean up the surveillance video from the Quickie-Mart." Mike spun his computer monitor so Cristan could see the screen. Mike pressed a button on his keyboard. The entire grainy clip took only moments to run. It had seemed much longer at the time.

The answer to Cristan's earlier question was yes. The situation was about to get much worse.

"You handled yourself pretty well in there," Mike prompted.

Sean leaned back. "I was impressed."

Cristan waited. Only fools volunteered information.

Sean scratched his chin. "Were you in the military in Argentina?"

"No," Cristan said, though Franco's men were trained as well as any legal army.

"How did you learn to fight?" Sean asked.

"I grew up in a very poor neighborhood. There were many gangs." Technically, this was true, but his vague answer felt hollow.

Mike's brow descended, and Sean folded his arms across his body. Clearly, they thought his answer thin as well. But deception was easier to pull off if one kept one's lies simple and as close to the truth as possible. Elaboration was the downfall of an amateur.

The police chief leaned back in his chair, the springs squeaking. Shrewd—and kind—blue eyes studied Cristan. Just because Mike was an honest man did not make him any less dangerous. "I have a few additional questions. Some I might have asked before. I apologize if this feels repetitive."

Again, Cristan waited.

Mike opened a file on his desk and donned a pair of reading glasses. "Are you married?"

"My wife died when Lucia was an infant." After all these years, that simple statement still stabbed him through the heart.

"How did she die?"

"She was in an auto accident."

"I'm sorry." Mike met his gaze with a brief look of sincere compassion before continuing. "You're the CEO of Rojas Corp. What exactly does Rojas Corporation do?"

"Primarily the conglomerate invests in commercial real estate and coffee," Cristan said. He understood that a small police force had few bodies to conduct an investigation, and following procedure would take time. Cristan had been patient and helpful, but his tolerance was wearing thin. He wanted to go home.

"Coffee?" Sean asked.

"The company owns an organic coffee plantation in Hawaii," Cristan clarified. "I've given a statement and answered all your questions. I'd really like to see my daughter."

"I understand." Mike paused. "But we'd really like to find those men before they hurt anyone else."

"That would be for the best." But Cristan was more concerned about Lucia. "But I don't see how interrogating me about my background will aid in your search for two local criminals. It was simply luck that put me at the scene. My skills are irrelevant."

"I'm just trying to get the whole picture," Mike said. "We're sending your clothes to the lab for a possible DNA match. We need more information to catch these guys."

"I understand, but I've already told you everything I know. And you have the video, which is much more accurate than my observations. Videos don't err."

"I'll probably need to ask you more questions," Mike added.

"You have my contact information."

Mike dropped his pen. "I appreciate what you did today. That little girl might be dead if you hadn't jumped in, but I really want to catch these guys. Is there anything you noticed about them, anything they said that might help us find them?"

"Jumping in, as you say it, was the last thing I wished to do." Cristan spoke carefully. "And I don't know how else I can be of assistance. You have my account of the incident and my description of the men. I've never seen either of them before. Surely, you have other avenues of investigation."

"I have a feeling your observation skills are as good as your hand-to-hand." Mike tilted his head. "Most civilians avoid confrontation. Yet you were able to disarm and overpower two men."

"They did not see it coming. Surprise is a formidable advantage." Cristan shrugged.

Sean's eyes called him a liar.

"True." Mike scratched his chin. He sighed, as if he was giving up. "The mayor called. He'd like to say thank you. Also, the woman with the little girl in the store wants to express her gratitude. Face it, you're a hero."

Cristan shifted his position. "I was hoping the incident could be kept low profile."

Mike sighed. "I doubt that's possible. Once that video gets out, the media will be looking for you."

"Is there any way to keep that from happening?" Cristan asked.

"Most people would be thrilled to get the attention." Mike dropped his glasses on his desk.

"I only wish for my daughter and me to live a quiet life," Cristan said. Was that too much to ask? Anger heated his blood. The fallout from today's robbery would threaten his daughter's happiness. Lucia would be devastated if he told her they had to move. But if the video went live . . .

Mike sighed. "I can try, but I suspect the state police will want to broadcast the video and set up a hotline in case these men are spotted by a citizen."

Mike's answer added to the argument for leaving town.

Cristan's muscles crawled with the need for movement. Frustration filled him with restless energy like an animal in a cage. "I should pick Lucia up. I'd like to shower and change before I do so, but I'm willing to answer more questions tomorrow."

"Fair enough," Mike said. The cell phone on his blotter buzzed.

He picked it up and read the text display. "Sarah wants to know if you're OK."

Cristan dropped his head into his hand.

Mike tapped on his phone screen. "I'll tell her you're fine, but you might want to call her. It sounds like she's worried about you."

"I'm sure she's wondering when I'll be picking up Lucia."

"I doubt that's the only reason she's asking." Mike set the phone on his desk.

What did he mean by that comment? Sarah did not so much as flirt with him. She was sweet and friendly and went out of her way to be kind to Lucia. His daughter adored her. But there was nothing between him and Sarah except a bit of longing on his part. As much as he enjoyed her company, he had nothing to offer her.

Mike straightened. "Thanks for cooperating, but I have to say, your hand-to-hand skills are impressive and a little shocking. Is there anything you want to tell me?"

Cristan lifted his head. Mike was a good man. He'd proved himself honorable and courageous several times over the past five months. But honesty could be a problem. He hadn't broken any laws today, but what Cristan had done in the past was illegal. Mike might feel obligated to turn him over to the proper authorities if he learned the truth. "I've taken Krav Maga for years. I suppose the training works."

Cristan stood. "I should be leaving. You'll let me know if you're able to identify the man from the blood on my clothes?"

Mike nodded. "No guarantees of getting your clothes back."

"Thank you, but I have no wish to have them back," Cristan said.

Mike stood and offered a hand. "I appreciate what you did today. You could have ducked and simply saved yourself. Instead, you risked your life to save a woman and a little girl."

Cristan accepted the handshake. In hindsight, his heroic actions had been foolish. Lucia didn't deserve to lose another parent. Plus, that video put their very existence at risk. Lucia would not be recognized as the infant he'd smuggled out of Argentina. He had changed as well, but there was no doubt in his mind that he could be recognized if the right people were watching.

———

He was hiding something.

Standing at the door to his office, Mike watched the Argentinean walk out of the police station. He closed his door. Sean was sitting in his chair behind the desk watching the video again. The former army ranger wasn't just a local security expert, he'd been Mike's best friend since grade school.

"Is the DNA really all you have?" Sean asked.

Mike slid his reading glasses onto his face to review his notes. "We have a witness who saw a blue van with a rusted rear bumper leaving the parking lot. She thinks the first letter on the license plate was *D*. Both men are injured. Looked to me like Rojas broke a nose and a wrist."

"Broken wrist will need to be set," Sean said.

"Right. We put out a BOLO on the van, and I have an officer calling hospitals." Mike leaned on the credenza. "What do you think of Rojas?"

"The ice scraper move was fucking brilliant," Sean said. "If I knew he was clean, I'd offer him a job."

"Why don't you think he's clean?"

"Remember when we had all that trouble in town last fall? I tried to find dirt on him and came up empty." Sean replayed the video. "Rojas has no record."

"Isn't that good?" Mike was torn. On one hand, Rojas's secretive nature put him on edge. On the other, his actions today were nothing short of heroic, and his skills damned impressive. Mike had watched the Argentinean interact with his teenage daughter. He seemed to be a caring if not occasionally frustrated single parent.

"I also found no record of his existence prior to ten years ago," Sean added.

"He wasn't in the States then."

"True." Sean gestured toward the computer monitor. "But his response is that of a well-trained fighter. He did not get lucky and take those guys by surprise. He reacted like a soldier or a cop. No amount of training in a gym produces that effective of a reaction. There was no hesitation. This was not the first time Rojas had a gun pointed in his face, that's for sure. The average Joe would have pissed his pants, but Rojas improvised with a handy weapon and disarmed two criminals like they were kindergarteners, and he walked away without a scratch."

Mike scrubbed a hand down his face. "I know."

"Let's analyze. Rojas kept his cool until the mom and kid were in danger. Then he kicked major-league ass." With a wife and two young daughters of his own, Sean took threats to women and children personally.

"But he seems to regret having to do it," Mike added.

"All in all, I like him. I would have done the same thing today," Sean said. "But, since Sarah is all hung up on him, the fact that he's a ghost that fights like a professional bugs me."

"I've been keeping an eye on that," Mike said. "Sarah's had enough trouble with Troy. I don't want to see her hurt again." Sarah and her two little girls deserved happiness and peace.

"I told you we should have killed Troy."

"Be serious." Mike rolled his eyes. But he suspected Sean's statement was only part jest.

Sean leaned forward, his interest peaked. "Has Rojas made any moves on her?"

"Not that I know of. Seems to keep his distance from her and everyone else except his daughter."

"What are you going to do about him?"

Mike shook his head. "I don't know. He hasn't done anything wrong."

"Not yet."

"I have no reason to think he will." Mike suspected Rojas was hiding something, but he knew the man had put his life on the line this afternoon to protect innocents. In Mike's world, that meant something. But his senses were telling him that Rojas was keeping secrets. Important secrets. To keep his town safe, Mike wanted to know if there was anything dangerous in the man's past. "He saved four lives today, and we're treating him like *he's* the criminal. That's just wrong, Sean."

Sean's vision of right and wrong was a blurred gray line. "So, you're just going to let the whole thing go?"

"Not exactly. I have a plan."

Sean tilted his head. "Tell me more."

CHAPTER NINE

Headlights swept across the living room as the Mercedes pulled into the driveway. Curled on the sofa next to Sarah, Bandit raised his head. A low growl rumbled from his throat.

"Shh." She set her novel on the coffee table and put a hand on his muzzle. "Don't wake the girls."

She carried the dog to the door and peered through the peephole. Cristan stood on the stoop. She opened the door and moved back to let him in. Bandit's tail swept in a frenzied arc. As cool as Cristan acted with adults, he'd neatly charmed her children and dog.

"I'm sorry it's so late." Cristan stepped across the threshold, one hand reaching out to stroke the dog's head.

"It's fine. Lucia fell asleep on Alex's trundle." Sarah lowered the dog to the floor. Her eyes swept over Cristan. His clothes were fresh and his hair damp, as if he'd just showered. But she saw no injuries. "I saw the robbery on the news. You disarmed two gunmen."

Cristan grimaced. "I surprised them."

"I'll bet." Sarah studied his face. The coolness he'd shown her earlier this evening seemed to have evaporated. She knew he was in his late thirties, but the fit cut of his body usually made him appear younger. Not tonight, though. Lines seemed to have cropped up on his face in a matter of hours. According to the news report, he'd saved several people in the robbery, including one of Sarah's neighbors and her little girl. He'd escaped physical injury, but his heroic act had obviously cost him.

"You look exhausted. Have you eaten?"

"No." He opened his mouth to decline any offer.

She didn't give him the chance. "Let me heat something up for you." She turned and walked toward the kitchen. He stood in the doorway for a few seconds, and she wondered if he was going to follow her or simply take his daughter and leave. But he closed and locked the front door and then followed her into the kitchen. He draped his coat over the short back of a stool, sat, and leaned his forearms on the counter.

Sarah went to the refrigerator. "I have some leftover pasta."

"Thank you. I'm suddenly very hungry."

"I imagine you are. It's after eleven." She heated the container in the microwave and then scooped the hot pasta and vegetables into a bowl. "I'm sorry there's no meat. The girls like simple food."

"I'm sure it'll be wonderful."

"Do you want to talk about it?" She shaved some fresh Parmesan onto the pasta and wiped the edges of the bowl before setting the dish in front of him.

"No."

Not a surprise.

He picked up his fork and froze. "Did the news show a video?"

"They did." Though she'd always sensed he was capable of violence, the speed and efficiency of his response had shocked her.

"How clear was the video?" he asked.

"It was pretty grainy. I could only tell it was you because I know you."

"The whole town will know it was me by morning."

"That would have happened with or without a video. It's hard to keep a secret in this town."

"This is true. My face was blurry?" At her nod, he dug his fork into the pasta.

Sarah filled a glass with water and set it at his elbow, then busied herself washing the container, giving Cristan time to eat in peace. He ate with efficiency then pushed the bowl away, and Sarah was pleased to see he didn't look quite as spent. She expected him to dine and dash, but he lingered.

"Can I make you some coffee?" she asked over her shoulder as she dried the container with a dishcloth.

"No." He got up and brought his bowl to the sink. Leaning over her shoulder, he set down the bowl and glass. His arm brushed hers, and his breath drifted over her cheek.

"Thank you, Sarah." His simple statement overflowed with emotion.

Goose bumps rose on her arms. Had they ever been alone? Usually, all three children were underfoot when he dropped Lucia off or when they saw each other at her sister's farm, where he kept horses. But now, with the house quiet and dark, her small kitchen made this meeting feel intimate. Though an inch of space separated them, she could feel sadness and tension radiating from his body.

She turned, slowly, and looked up into his dark eyes. Something lurked there. Something she knew well. Loneliness. He tried to act aloof, but she could see the truth in his eyes. The longing. Did he crave her or simple human contact? It didn't matter, she decided. Not tonight.

She wrapped her arms around his waist and hugged him. At first he stiffened, then a sigh eased out of his chest. His arms came around her shoulders, and he rested his cheek on the top of her head. She leaned her cheek against his shoulder. Whatever soap he'd used smelled like fir trees.

They stood, unmoving, for several minutes before he eased his head back. The shadows in his eyes had retreated.

"I would have frozen if someone pointed a gun at me," Sarah said. "But I suppose you weren't frightened if you were able to disarm two gunmen."

"I didn't have time to think in the moment, but afterward, there was plenty of fear." He exhaled. "Those men could have made Lucia an orphan. She doesn't deserve to lose another parent. That could have happened today."

Thinking about the possibility, Sarah tightened her hold around his waist. "Is Mike looking for the robbers?"

"The police are searching, but finding them is a remote possibility. Their faces were mostly covered, and they wore gloves. There is the possibility of identification through DNA analysis. Perhaps they are in a police database. I doubt this was their first crime."

"Mike will do his best."

"They could be many miles away from here by now."

"Let's hope."

His gaze dropped to her lips, and he brushed a knuckle across her cheek. "Thank you."

She nodded, not trusting her voice. For an instant, she'd thought he was going to kiss her. She'd wanted him to, even as she knew it was a bad idea. She'd only wanted to comfort him, but the intimate spark had gone both ways. Since she'd left Troy, she'd been focused on her girls and her job. Being alone had been a relief, and she hadn't been looking for male companionship. Physical intimacy hadn't been a consideration. But pressed against his hard body, breathing in the winter forest scent of him, she felt the first stirrings of need—and craved more.

A warning bell sounded in her mind. This craving had the potential to become addictive.

Her phone vibrated on the counter, and she instinctively stiffened. Only one person would call her this late at night. She moved farther away from Cristan and picked up the phone to read the display. This time Troy didn't bother to hide his identity.

Cristan tilted his head. "What's wrong?"

"Nothing."

"I don't believe you," he said. "But you've been an angel to me this evening, so I won't press you. If you need anything, day or night, I'm only a phone call away."

"I need to handle this on my own."

"And I applaud your determination, but the offer stands." Cristan reached out and cupped her jaw. His thumb brushed her cheek, and Sarah couldn't help but turn into his touch. "Don't take any risks to save your pride."

"I won't."

He dropped his hand. "I should go. Thank you for looking after my daughter tonight. I do not trust many people with her."

"You're welcome. Let me wake her." Sarah went into the girls' bedroom. Lucia was curled on her side on the trundle bed. She put a hand on the girl's shoulder, gave her a gentle shake, and whispered, "Your dad's here."

Lucia's eyes widened. Rising, she swung her legs off the bed and hurried from the room. Without speaking she walked into her father's arms. The sight of them embracing pulled at Sarah's heart. Lucia had acted bravely when she'd learned about the robbery, but the news had shaken her. If something did happen to Cristan, where would Lucia go? They must have family somewhere.

Cristan hugged his daughter tightly, then held her by the shoulders. "Let's go home."

He helped Lucia into her coat and herded her out the door.

Sarah locked up behind them and reset her alarm. That was

how a real father acted. Kind, caring, and selfless, Cristan was the opposite of Troy. He was the sort of man she should have married.

She walked through the house turning off lights. Grabbing her phone in the kitchen, she sighed. Troy had sent her a message. She pressed it with her thumb.

WHO IS HE?

How did Troy know Cristan was here? Sarah did a quick run through the house. She'd closed the blinds in the living room. But mature trees in the small backyard provided privacy from her rear neighbor, and she usually didn't bother to close the blinds. She twirled the lever and the slats swiveled shut. With no view, her tiny kitchen became claustrophobic.

Troy was winning. He'd made her a prisoner in her own house.

CHAPTER TEN

Cristan pulled into his driveway and drove up the hill toward his house. Built in the mid-1850s, the three-story colonial had been designed to withstand the elements. The solid stone construction would also perform well under the pressure of gunfire or fire. The house sat on the top of a hill with the slate patio in the rear overlooking a sloping, rocky yard and the Packman Creek. The waterway's name was misleading. Wide and deep enough for boating, the Packman was more of a river than a creek. Fueled by snowmelt, the normally placid water flowed swiftly between its ice-edged banks. Three acres of cleared meadow encircled the home, and woods flanked the open space. The view had been pricey, but the surrounding fields provided Cristan with a clear view of the possible avenues of approach, and he'd had the powerful outboard in the boathouse recently tuned up. Now that the ice had melted, the river was once again an extra avenue of escape.

The motion sensor lights illuminated as he parked in front of the house, flooding the front lawn with enough light to rival a stadium. In the passenger seat, Lucia huddled over her backpack. She'd been quiet during the entire drive home. Occasionally, he wished his daughter didn't speak nonstop for most of her waking hours, but tonight, the last ten minutes of silence had unnerved him.

He turned off the engine. "Are you all right with what happened today?"

Her fingers tightened around the straps of her pack. She nodded. "You could have been hurt."

"But I wasn't."

"What would happen to me if you were?" She lifted her gaze from her hands. Behind the gleam of unshed tears, fear lingered.

For a few seconds, Cristan didn't know how to respond. He'd made provisions for them both to run if necessary, but he trusted no one with his daughter—or the truth. In reality, Lucia had no one but him. His chest tightened when he thought of Lucia orphaned and all alone, like he had been. Would she fall prey to someone like Franco?

He swallowed. "The answer is, I don't know. You don't have any living family." The lie stuck in his throat, but he forced it out.

Maria Vargas lived. But his goal was to keep Lucia away from the Vargas family, even the last remaining member. Was that selfish? Should he tell his daughter that she had an aunt who looked so much like her mother, that when Cristan did his quarterly check on her whereabouts and activity, his chest hurt when he opened the digital photo files?

No. He could never tell her.

He held his daughter's gaze. "Nothing is going to happen to me. The incident today was a random occurrence. It won't happen again."

Lucia's eyes brightened with anger. "You can't make that promise. You could have a heart attack—" She choked on a sob. "You could be in a car accident like Mom."

The thought of her mother's death proved too much for her admirable control. Tears ran down her face. Cristan reached across the console and rubbed her arm. If they'd been in the house, he would have held her tight. But the console—and his lies—separated them. "I'm sorry I frightened you today."

"It wasn't your fault. You didn't do anything wrong. Those men who robbed the store did."

"I did the best I could under the circumstances. I always take care to be as safe as possible. I wouldn't do anything reckless."

"I know." She nodded. "But it was a serious question. What would happen to me if you died? I'd go to a foster home, wouldn't I?"

For once, Cristan had no choice but to answer with the truth. "Yes."

She was quiet. Her gaze drifted to the darkness beyond the light-flooded front yard. Cristan had picked the house because of its easily defended position and solid construction. Solitude was a benefit when you stored a cache of AK-47s in your basement. But seeing the property from his daughter's perspective made the house seem isolated and sad. They had a beautiful home. But they'd never once shared those views with others. Lucia occasionally had a friend to visit, but that was a relatively new occurrence, now that she had a few friends. Cristan had never hosted a dinner party or barbecue. For her birthday, they'd gone to dinner alone. She'd never even asked to have a party. Guilt weighed on him, but he hadn't had many choices. Living like this was far better than being dead.

"I don't want that." She sniffed. "I always knew we were alone. But tonight made me *feel* alone. Really alone. I was scared. I'm still scared."

"I'm sorry." Cristan rubbed at the hollow ache in the center of his chest.

"There's nothing you can do about it. You can't give me family." She wiped her cheeks with her hands. "Why didn't you ever get married again? It's been twelve years since Mom died. Don't you get lonely?"

"I have you." His entire world revolved around keeping her safe, but she didn't know that. Had he done everything wrong?

What would she do if he told her the truth now, after a lifetime of lies?

"You know what I mean." Irritation sharpened her tone. "Was it because you couldn't find anyone like Mom?"

"I will never be able to find anyone like your mother." That he could say with complete honesty. Eva had been one of a kind. She'd been everything he'd wanted in a woman. As sexy and lively as Eva had been, she'd had blade-sharp edges Cristan couldn't deny. Once, her callous nature hadn't bothered him. They'd been two of a kind, but after their child was born, he'd changed, and he'd been perplexed when Eva hadn't also wanted a new life. Now he wondered what would have become of their marriage if Eva had lived. He was no longer the same man. If he had talked her into running away, if he'd gotten her away from her family, would she have eventually gone through the same metamorphosis as he had? Or would her ruthlessness have divided them?

"You could try. I mean, you don't even date."

"I've never found anyone I wished to date."

"What about Sarah?"

"Sarah?"

"Yeah. Sarah." Lucia's voice held a note of *isn't it obvious?* "You like her, and she likes you. I can tell."

"You think she likes me?" Cristan asked. He'd assumed the comfort she'd offered him had been a friendly gesture on her part. Sarah was warm and nurturing by nature. Had he been wrong? Did she feel the same tug in her heart that he did?

"Oh, yeah." Lucia's nod became emphatic. "Her face gets brighter, and she smiles whenever she sees you."

The idea pleased him. "Sarah smiles at everyone."

"I know," Lucia said, her voice rising with interest. "You should take her out on a date."

"A date?" Cristan laughed. But it wasn't as if he hadn't thought about the possibility in the lonely, dark hours when exhaustion weakened his control. "Sarah has just gotten a divorce. I doubt she's ready to date."

"I wouldn't be so sure." The knowing tone of her comment made his thirteen-year-old daughter sound much older. "She was married to a creep. She doesn't miss him."

Cristan homed in on her statement. "How do you know?"

"Today, when he was staring at her, he made my skin crawl." Lucia gnawed on her thumbnail. "I think he's crazy."

"Why do you think that?" His daughter had good instincts, but he didn't want Sarah's ex-husband anywhere near his child. If he were back in his old life in Argentina, Cristan could have thought of many ways to ensure that Troy Mitchell never bothered Sarah again. But Cristan had sworn off violence. Since he'd left Argentina, he hadn't raised so much as his voice.

Until today.

"She changes when he's around or when he sends her a text or calls. Her body goes all tense. She gets jumpy. She tries to hide it, but she's afraid of him. The girls are too." Lucia dropped her hand to her lap. She cast him a sly glance. "If you married Sarah, she wouldn't have to worry about him anymore, and you wouldn't have to worry about me. It would be perfect."

"You have it all figured out." Cristan laughed. But his daughter was correct on one matter. If Sarah was his wife, she wouldn't ever have to worry about Troy again. "Mr. Mitchell isn't around when you babysit, right?"

Lucia shook her head. "No. Never."

"Good. If he ever shows up, you call me immediately." Cristan put his hand on the door handle. "Let's go inside. It's getting cold out here."

He did not like sitting still, spotlighted in the dark like targets. From the woods, a sniper would have a clear shot at them. He drove around the side of the house and pushed the button on the visor. The garage was under the house. The second half of the subterranean space was basement. The floor plan provided a quick exit, if necessary. The door rolled up, and he parked inside next to a Range Rover. Leaving a vehicle in the open invited tampering and incendiary devices.

"OK, but promise me you'll think about it." Lucia got out of the car. Her voice echoed in the cement-and-stone space.

Cristan followed her up the steps. He unlocked the door that led to the kitchen. "Think about what?"

"Dating Sarah," Lucia said, her voice heavy with exasperation.

"All right. I promise." Cristan would not forget that idea for a second.

They went through the kitchen into the foyer. He opened the hall closet and checked the security system panel. Lucia dropped her pack at her feet and waited at the foot of the steps for his all clear. When she visited friends, did she wonder why other families didn't go through the same obsessive safety checks? The rows of green lights assured him the house was secure.

Hanging up his coat, he leaned out of the closet. Lucia stood in the hallway. Cristan wasn't much of a decorator, and they hadn't stayed in a house long enough to get comfortable. But when they'd moved here, Lucia had been very disconnected and depressed. He'd hung a few pictures of her in the hallway to make her feel at home. Now she stood in front of a framed baby picture on the wall, a snapshot of Eva holding their daughter at her first birthday party. Cristan had grabbed it and a few other mementos when he'd returned to the Buenos Aires apartment to retrieve their passports. Lucia raised a hand and touched the glass over her mother's face. "I don't think she'd mind if you dated. If she loved you, she'd want you to be happy."

You didn't know your mother very well. Cristan didn't express his disagreement, but he doubted Eva would willingly relinquish him, even in death. For a Vargas, love, control, and possession were closely intertwined.

Lucia tossed her jacket over the newel post. "I'm tired. I'm going to bed." Lucia hefted her backpack onto one shoulder and headed upstairs.

Despite the green lights and his own assurances that tonight's incident was a random event, he walked the interior of his home. The damp rubber soles of his shoes squeaked on the wide, oak planks as he checked every window and door and searched each closet, nook, and cranny from the third floor to the basement. While he toured the interior, he also checked the locations of his hidden weapons.

Today's robbery had been an accident. He'd been in the wrong place at the wrong time. But as he slid his hand along the top of his medicine cabinet to feel for the knife taped there, he couldn't shake the nagging feeling that everything had changed.

He finished his weaponry tour, then he went back to the basement and pulled the go-bags from their hiding place behind a false wall of shelves. There were two backpacks containing the bare essentials, one each for him and Lucia. Another larger bag held additional supplies. What they would take would depend on the circumstances. Cristan updated the contents of the bags each season. There were smaller emergency kits in each of the cars as well.

He hefted the two backpacks to a scarred, wooden worktable and unzipped them. Then he began the painstaking itemizing process. He wouldn't be able to sleep anyway, and he'd feel more secure knowing that at any moment, they were ready to roll. He unfolded the master list and began checking supplies: AK-47, 9mm, ammunition . . .

As he reviewed his inventory, he thought about the years in which he used such weapons regularly, and how it all began.

CHAPTER ELEVEN

They say you always remember your first. First kiss. First love.

First murder.

But how many people can say they experienced those three things all in the same night?

Cristan remembered so clearly; the rush of images nearly stole his breath. Eva was the most beautiful girl he'd ever seen, though at thirteen and coming from a life on the street, he didn't have many comparisons. If he closed his eyes right now, he could see her just the way she'd looked that evening.

He'd been standing in the doorway of his small room in a building behind the house, the scent of warm, wet grass in his nose, the first strains of party music drifting across the lawn, a sharp spark of suspicion in his mind. Why was he here? Nothing was free. Franco Vargas wasn't a do-gooder prone to random acts of kindness. He was a gunrunner, not that Christopher had an issue with lawlessness. The only laws he respected were those of survival. A month before, in Buenos Aires, Franco had approached Christopher on the street and offered him money to deliver a message and bring back the response. Orphaned and homeless, Christopher had jumped at the opportunity. But when the task had been complete, Franco had offered him a job and brought him back to his *estancia*. Surely, a man like Franco would want something in exchange for this new life, payment of some sort.

Across twenty meters of grass and the lighted expanse of a swimming pool, she walked out of the house onto the patio. High cheekbones and an aquiline nose attested to her Spanish blood. Dark hair tumbled down her back in a sable wave. A white sundress showed off long, tan legs that ended in flat sandals. She looked cool and fresh in the Argentine summer night.

He'd washed after finishing his chores in the barn, but that night, heat hovered in a steamy layer over the pampas. A fresh trickle of sweat dripped between his shoulder blades. No matter. He could never be good enough for her. That must be Franco's oldest daughter, Eva. Franco might have opened his home, but no doubt his daughter would be off-limits.

The soft strums of guitar music floated from the house at her back. A patio door opened, and a voice called, "Eva."

She turned and went inside, and Christopher remembered how to breathe.

Christopher had learned several important lessons since his arrival. Franco was the indisputable head of the Vargas household. If he brought a stray teenage boy home from Buenos Aires, no one asked questions. Without so much as a shrug, the staff had prepared a room and scrounged up some clothing. Christopher adjusted his belt. The pants were still too large for his hollowed waist, but the cook pledged that condition would be temporary.

He'd spent the first week waiting for Franco to come to his senses and send him back. But that hadn't happened. Instead, he'd been fed, clothed, and given chores, as if he belonged. Learning to care for the sleek horses was more pleasure than work. He wasn't sure why, after years of backslapping him, fate had decided to play nice, but he knew how to live in the moment. This evening, instead of curling up on a cardboard pallet in an abandoned warehouse, he was preparing to attend a homecoming celebration for Franco's daughters, home on vacation from boarding school.

He had only faint recollections of family gatherings, from before his parents had become victims of Argentina's Dirty War. From a cupboard under the stairs, six-year-old Christopher had watched the soldiers drag his parents from the house in the middle of the night. Like thirty thousand other people suspected of being dissidents, they'd simply disappeared. With no family, Christopher had been on his own.

Shaking off the memory, he watched as guests arrived and people flowed onto the patio. He left his small room, his insecurities trampled by his need to see her again. The smell of grilling meat drifted over the lawn as he crossed to the main house. He spotted Franco's bulky frame standing by the pool. Surviving on the streets, Christopher had learned how to be invisible, an essential skill for a thief. He skirted the guests, his eyes sweeping the small groups of people for the only one he wanted to see.

Where was she?

A young girl, a smaller and childish version of Eva, waved at him. The sister. Her yellow dress bounced as she skipped over to him. She dipped her chin and gave him a shy smile. "I'm Maria. I'm nine."

"I'm Christopher."

"I know." Her grin showed a missing tooth. "Papa told us about you."

Heat seared Christopher's cheeks. He was the poor orphan boy.

She leaned close and whispered, "Don't be embarrassed. Papa says Argentina has too many orphans, and you're not the first he's brought home."

That explained the staff's ready response. Gratitude welled in Christopher's chest, and he vowed to earn his keep.

She smiled and looked up through her lashes at him. "Do you want some food? Cook makes the best empanadas."

Though Christopher was tempted to stuff his face once again, the habit of filling one's stomach at every opportunity ingrained, he resisted. The girl in white tugged at his attention. He wanted to find her.

"Where is your sister?" he asked.

Her smiled faded. "I saw her walking toward the barn."

"Thank you." Christopher turned away. The music quieted as he moved away from the house, and he could hear insects in the deep grass of the pasture. She wasn't in the barn. Walking through, he scanned the fence line and spied a slim figure on the other side of the barnyard, her white dress glowing ethereally in the moonlight. She leaned on the fence, watching the horses graze in the pasture beyond. At his approach, she turned and smiled at him, and his heart stumbled.

"I'm Christopher." He rested his forearms on the top rail.

"I know," she said without looking at him. "And I suspect you know who I am as well."

"Why aren't you at your party?" he asked.

She made a disgusted sound. "I have no time for such foolishness. I don't even want to go back to school. I want to stay here. But Papa insists. He promised Mama before she died."

Christopher studied her profile. He'd been told she was the same age as him, but the grave purpose in her eyes made her seem older. Perhaps, like him, she hadn't been a child in a long time.

His gaze swept the dark forms of horses grazing in the pasture. Above, stars glittered in an ink-blue sky. "I can't blame you for not wanting to leave here."

She glanced sideways. Consideration drew her brows together. "I suppose this is heaven for you."

"Yes." His feelings were a jumbled mess he couldn't explain with words. He looked away, but the darkness didn't supply any answers.

"Do you like to talk about the past, Christopher?"

"No," he said honestly.

"Good. Neither do I." She turned back to the horses. "That one is my favorite."

"The bay gelding?"

"Yes. He can follow the ball as well as most riders."

Christopher drank in the sound of her voice as she described each animal and its merits on the polo field. He wasn't sure how much time passed before she pushed away from the fence. "I had better make an appearance at my party. I don't want to offend Papa."

They turned to walk away when a soft scuffle caught his attention.

"No. Stop," a small voice cried from the barn.

In unison, they moved toward the dark building, their footsteps silent on the packed earth. In the shadow of the doorway, they paused. Christopher waited a moment for his eyes to adjust to the relative darkness. He saw a dark shadow and a brighter, smaller form.

Shoes scuffed. Fabric rustled.

"Please," a child's muffled voice pleaded.

Eva stiffened. She reached for a switch on the wall. Light brightened the aisle, revealing an older man and Maria. The man was at least twenty-five. His body pressed Maria against the wall. Her patent leather shoes kicked, seeking traction. His head swiveled, and he saw them.

Christopher lunged forward. Though smaller and lighter, he'd learned to fight to survive. He used surprise to his advantage, kicking the man in the back of the knee and punching the man in the kidney. The man dropped to his knees, and Christopher yanked Maria behind him. She sobbed quietly into the back of his shirt.

He turned to Eva. "You'd better get your father."

But she wasn't running for help. She raised a shovel over her head. Rage contorted her features. She swung. The shovel hit the man's skull with a dull, metallic *thunk*.

It wasn't the violence or the blood or the death that made the deepest impression on Christopher. He'd seen death before, and a man who preyed on children deserved the worst of fates. It was the gleam of angry satisfaction on Eva's face that branded itself into his heart. With her fierce eyes and white dress, she could have been an avenging angel. Her gaze met his, and he realized her beauty was the least important of her qualities. In a world filled with selfishness, deception, and greed, there was nothing more compelling than loyalty.

"We protect our own," she said.

"I understand." And he envied their bond.

"Good." She prodded the man's body with her toe. He lolled, dead and limp. With a nod, she tugged Maria out from behind Christopher's back and pointed at the dead man. "You never have to fear him again."

Maria's breath hitched over and over as she fought for control. "I-I-came to the barn to s-spy on you."

"This is *not* your fault." Eva smoothed the wrinkles from her sister's dress. "Go back to the party. Act as if nothing has happened." When Maria continued to cry, Eva dried her sister's eyes with gentle thumbs. "You must be strong. If Juan's boss finds out what happened, there will be retribution."

Maria's head snapped around. Her gaze locked with her older sister's. Understanding passed between them. With a final sniff,

Maria pulled her emotions in with a huge lungful of air. Her chin rose and she nodded. "I can do it."

"Good girl," Eva said. "If anyone asks why you are sad, just tell them you are missing Mama."

With a solemn nod, Maria left the barn.

"Help me hide him." Eva bent and took hold of the man's ankle.

Christopher took the other foot. "Who is he?"

"His name is Juan Menendez. He's a lieutenant in a local militia. His boss is one of our best clients."

Together they dragged the body down the aisle. They hid him behind a cabinet in the wash stall.

"Now what?" Christopher asked.

"We get Nicolas. He will know how to make the death look like an accident. It won't be difficult. Everyone knows how much Juan likes his tequila and cocaine." Brushing the dirt from her hands, she rose onto her toes to plant a kiss on his cheek. "Thank you."

Heat filled Christopher. At that moment, he would have done anything for her.

CHAPTER TWELVE

Sarah turned off the engine of the minivan and stared up at her childhood home. The old Cape Cod, with its peeling paint and torn window screen, looked depressed. A beat-up sedan sat in the cracked, stained driveway. Thursdays were slow at the inn, and she'd finished early. Troy wouldn't bring the girls home for a couple of hours. Now was a good time to check on her father, though her visits home were getting harder and harder.

She reached across the console and lifted the takeout container from the passenger seat, some lasagna left over from the inn's lunch menu. Her father didn't answer the doorbell, but then she hadn't expected a greeting. She used her key and went inside.

The smell hit her like a slap, a combination of rotten food and mustiness. Covering her nose and mouth with one hand, she walked through the dingy living room. The wide bay window couldn't let in enough light to offset the shroud of depression that smothered the house. She found the source of the odor in the kitchen: a sink full of dirty dishes and an almost empty quart of milk left to sour on the counter.

Worried, she deposited the takeout on the table and opened a window. "Dad?"

Apprehension raised goose bumps on her arms as she approached the den. Wooden blinds over the three windows blocked the daylight, and the light from the twenty-year-old console TV flickered over the room. Her father lay in his recliner. She walked closer, dread gathering in her belly, her eyes focused on his thin chest. At the first rise and fall of his ribcage, she exhaled in relief.

He wasn't dead, just drunk.

Ironically, the realization weakened her legs. Her father had been drinking himself to death since her mother died seven years ago. It was only a matter of time until he got his wish.

The darkness closed in on her, and her lungs constricted. She went to the windows and started opening blinds, letting the sunlight pour into the room. Dust floated from the wooden slats.

"What the hell are you doing?" Blinking, her father struggled to bring the recliner upright.

Ignoring him, Sarah opened the last blind, then fought with the window lock until it gave. She pushed up the sash. Cold, fresh air flooded the room, and Sarah inhaled. "I bought you some food."

He was on his feet and moving toward her on shaky legs. He pushed her out of the way. She stumbled sideways, grabbing for the arm of the sofa to steady her legs.

One rough hand slammed the window shut. An arthritic finger pointed at her nose. "Leave me alone." He closed every blind until the familiar gloom settled over the space.

"Fine." She backed away. Sadness tightened her throat. "You win. I can't keep doing this."

Returning to his chair, he lifted a glass from the end table to his lips. "You know where the door is."

"You have two grandchildren you've never met. If you decide you want to live, call me." Sarah glanced over her shoulder on her way out. "You have my number."

"It's a shame," he said in a slurred voice. "You were the good girl. Did too much time with your sister give you that smart mouth?"

He wasn't too drunk to try and manipulate her.

Sarah left without responding. There was no point, but guilt plagued her all the way home, where she decided she couldn't sit and wait. She changed her clothes, grabbed a plastic container from the fridge, and leashed her dog. "Let's go see Rachel."

Bandit rode shotgun. Fifteen minutes later, she parked her minivan in front of her sister's farmhouse and checked her messages. Her phone had beeped several times during the drive. Her phone showed three missed calls and messages, all from Troy. Though she suspected nothing was wrong, she pressed Listen with a nervous hand.

His voicemails accelerated from "You didn't answer my message" to "Are you fucking that guy?"

Instead of responding, Sarah phoned her attorney and dumped the situation in his lap. He'd mostly behaved while they were separated, but now that the divorce was final, he was ignoring the rules.

She got out of the van and collected her bowl. The dog jumped over the console and out of the car like a mountain goat, and Sarah slammed the door shut. Straining at the end of his leash, Bandit ran to the back door and barked. There was no need to ring the bell when she brought him along. She rubbed her aching arm. Though the sun shone from a clear sky, the March chill lodged in the knitted bone, a permanent reminder of Troy's temper.

"Hey." Rachel let them into the mudroom and used a towel to wipe Bandit's feet. "Where are the girls?"

"With Troy." Sarah stripped off her coat and carried her container through to the newly renovated kitchen. She set it on the island, and tossed her handbag on a counter stool. The little dog bolted past. His furry paws slid on the hardwood as he rounded a corner and ran out of the room.

"How did it go?" Rachel washed her hands at the white-aproned farmhouse sink.

"Troy picked them up at eight. Alex yelled, and Emma cried. By nine I had a call from my attorney that Troy is accusing me of spousal alienation, or turning his kids against him."

Rachel snorted. "Like he needs any help with that."

"It's been a long day." Sarah rubbed her forehead. "They'll be home in two hours. Then I can relax. I really don't want to talk about it right now."

"I'm sorry. He's a bastard. That's why you divorced him. Want some coffee?"

"Please." Sarah accepted a full mug and wrapped her cold fingers around it. Bandit trotted back into the kitchen, tail drooping.

"Sorry, buddy, Mike's not here." Sarah leaned over and stroked his head "I had to lock him up when Troy picked up the kids. He caught Troy's scent at the front door and went ballistic."

"Good dog." Rachel tossed him a piece of cheese. "He's a good judge of character."

"He hasn't forgotten what it's like to be on the angry end of Troy's boot." Sarah straightened. She hadn't forgotten what it was like to be on the wrong side of Troy's temper either. But she couldn't let her fear stunt the progress she was making. She'd made a lot of mistakes, but she was damned if she'd let them define her. She'd thought moving forward would be easier once the divorce was final and custody settled. But why was Troy so determined to control her? Every time he looked at her, she could feel hate emanating from his body, as toxic as a radiation leak. If she wasn't careful, it would bloom into something malignant.

Sarah peeled the plastic wrap from the bowl and opened Rachel's utensil drawer for a couple of spoons. "Taste this."

Rachel gave it a suspicious sniff. "What is it?"

"It's a lemon pepper dipping sauce. Just taste it." Sarah waved the spoon. "I promise. No vegetables."

Rachel tasted the sauce with the tip of her tongue like a child. "Oh, it's good."

"Why are you always so surprised?" Sarah asked.

Rachel licked the spoon clean. "I don't like fancy food."

Sarah said, "My three-year-old has a more sophisticated palate."

"True."

"What do you think about serving this with the chicken-skewer appetizers?" Sarah rooted through her handbag for the notebook she was using to plan the food for her sister's wedding reception. "After everything you and Mike have done for me, I want your wedding to be perfect."

"I wish you wouldn't worry about it so much." Rachel crossed the oak floor to the stainless steel fridge and opened it. She pulled a plastic container from a shelf. The fact that her sister had a container of actual food in her kitchen spoke volumes about how much her life had changed since she'd met the local police chief, Mike O'Connell. "We moved the wedding back. So there's tons of time." Both the barn reconstruction and kitchen remodel had taken longer than anticipated.

"What is that?" Sarah nodded toward the container her sister was opening.

"Chicken breast." Rachel removed the plastic lid and made a face. "Mike cooked it last night. No fat, no salt, no taste."

"Mike eats to fuel his body." Sarah laughed. Her sister's fiancé was a former athlete.

"He sure as hell doesn't eat for enjoyment." Rachel took two plates out of a drawer in the island. She forked some sliced chicken onto a plate and topped it with a spoonful of sauce. She ate a bite and offered one to Sarah. "The sauce helps. I bet it would be great with potato chips or hot wings."

"Good. I'll add it to the menu." Laughing, Sarah flipped through the notebook. Rachel retrieved a box of Pop-Tarts from the back of a cupboard and held it out.

"God, no." Sarah waved away the box.

"To each his own." Rachel opened a foil pouch and sniffed the pastry as if it were the cork of an aged bottle of merlot. "Now tell me what's up with Troy."

"He's been difficult lately."

"Why? Custody is settled. You didn't press for alimony or take anything except personal stuff from the house."

Troy had taken out a second mortgage to keep the sporting goods store out of bankruptcy. There hadn't been any marital assets to fight over.

"I don't know." Sarah took a long sip of steaming coffee. Troy was going to a lot of effort to harass her.

"I still can't believe any judge gave him unsupervised visitation." Rachel washed her pastry down with a glass of milk. "Troy shouldn't be allowed to raise livestock, let alone children."

"Troy can be charming when he wants to be." In high school, he'd been good-looking and athletic. He'd partied hard with the baseball team, but she'd thought he'd grow up eventually. Instead, he'd just grown bitter. "On the bright side, he's been clean and sober at every meeting, and he's required to attend AA and the anger management support group regularly. Maybe getting arrested really did change him. I'm hoping he really wants to connect with his children."

Rachel's expression disagreed.

"Please, Rachel." Sarah looked to the window. Flurries drifted across the glass. "I don't have any choice, so I might as well be optimistic. It would be best for the girls to have a relationship with their mother *and* father."

"You're right, but he hurt you. I can't forgive him for that," Rachel said.

And on the subject of family drama . . .

"I stopped to see Dad today." Sarah didn't meet Rachel's eyes. Her sister wanted nothing to do with their father. Sarah couldn't blame her.

But Rachel never judged her. She gave Sarah's shoulder a quick squeeze. "You're a much nicer person than I am."

Their own parents had been too consumed by their dysfunctional marriage and their mother's mental illness to tend to either of their children. And that was the real reason Sarah had married Troy: to escape. At the time, any attention, even the controlling kind, had felt like love. Her mother had just died, and her father had sunk deeper into depression. Troy's proposal had seemed like a lifeline. Their marriage had been all right at first. Sarah had been thrilled to start a family, though Troy's disappointment in having two girls had stung. Sarah thought he'd grow to love their children as much as she did.

He traveled during the baseball season, seemingly happy playing for a minor league baseball team, waiting for his big break. But no scout ever drafted him for the major leagues. Instead, he was cut from the team. With two babies to support, he'd gone to work in his father's store, something he'd sworn never to do. Bitterness drove him to drink, and drinking made him mean. When he'd pressured her to try for a boy, she'd refused. Another baby would only stress their troubled marriage further. And her defiance had proved to be Troy's tipping point.

"I only stopped by to make sure he was alive and take him some food," Sarah said. "But I told him this was my last visit. I can't do it anymore."

"You've done more than anyone else." Rachel wrapped an arm around her shoulders.

"He's getting worse. He's going to die alone in that house."

"That's his choice," Rachel said. "But it's time you moved forward. You should start your own catering business."

"I couldn't do that," Sarah protested.

"Why not? You're a fabulous cook. You're organized and motivated."

"There are lots of reasons." Sarah didn't know where to start. "I don't have the space or the money or the clients."

Rachel waved away Sarah's argument, but that was Rachel. Full steam ahead. "So start small. I'm not suggesting you take on formal dinners for five hundred, but you're handling a buffet for fifty."

"I don't know." But what was she waiting for? She needed more income than her job at the Main Street Inn provided. She wasn't optimistic about getting money from Troy. "Do you really think I could do it?"

"Why not?" Rachel gestured at her new appliances and acres of counter space. "You can use our kitchen. Mike's at work all day, and I'm outside. The place is empty."

Sarah pressed a knuckle to her lips. The idea of starting her own business was equally scary and exciting. "I'll think about it, but if I'm going to do it, I'll use the kitchen I have."

"Maybe we can upgrade it," Rachel said.

"No!" Sarah said firmly. "You and Mike already let us live there for free. I won't have you spending more money on me."

"We don't mind."

"But I do." Sarah softened her voice. "I appreciate everything you have done for me and the girls, but I have to be independent. It's important to me."

Rachel nodded. "Believe me. I understand that. But we're here if you get in a jam."

"Thank you. Knowing that helps me sleep at night." Her new job and independence were great, but knowing your kids had people they could depend on in an emergency was priceless.

The sound of car tires grating on gravel caught their attention. Rachel went to the window over the sink.

"It's Cristan and Lucia." Rachel headed for the mudroom. "I have to go out and check on Lady."

"No sign she's ready to foal?" Sarah asked. Her sister's favorite horse was two weeks overdue with her first foal.

"No." Rachel stepped into her boots. "What's up with you and Cristan?"

"Nothing's up. We're friendly. Lucia babysits my girls."

"Are you sure? The way he looks at you is more than friendly." Rachel's voice lowered.

Sarah's face heated. She played it cool, but when Cristan turned those dark eyes on her, the only word that came to mind was smoldering, and after the embrace they'd shared Tuesday night, she'd felt a shift in their relationship.

Through the glass, she watched him get out of his car. He was wearing a short, black wool coat and jeans. A shadow of dark stubble increased his mysterious aura. He wasn't exactly handsome. Except for when he looked at his daughter, his features were too hard, and his eyes held the shadows of a man who'd seen terrible things. After Troy, she didn't expect to be attracted to a man, at least not this soon. But there was something compelling about Cristan.

He went into the barn, and Sarah picked up her purse.

"You're looking at him like he's an ice cream cone and you want to—"

"Rachel!"

"What?" Her sister grinned. "The man is hot. There's nothing to be embarrassed about."

"It doesn't matter. I'm hardly in a position to take an interest in any man." Sarah followed her sister out into the cold and stopped in the barn to give Lady's nose a pat. "I have a new job and two kids, and thanks to you, I'm considering starting my own business. I have enough to juggle."

"If you say so." Rachel's grin faded to worry as she went into the stall and swept a hand over Lady's enormous belly.

"She'll be OK," Sarah said. "I was two weeks late with Alex. Babies come when they're ready, not a minute sooner."

"I know. The vet says there's nothing to worry about."

But Sarah knew her sister would worry until a healthy foal arrived—and probably for a long time after. Love created vulnerability.

Her phone vibrated in her pocket. She read the display. A message from Troy: CALL ME. NOW. Resigned, she dialed.

"I'm bringing them home in thirty minutes." Troy's voice sounded strained, not exactly angry. Frustrated? Whatever emotion he was projecting, the tension she felt over the connection lifted the hairs on the back of her neck.

"I'll be there," Sarah said. He was bringing the girls home more than an hour early, but she didn't protest. He couldn't bring her girls home fast enough.

"You'd better be," he said. "And you'd better start answering my fucking calls and messages, Sarah. You can't ignore me."

Not when he had the kids, she couldn't. But Sarah refused to be baited. "I have to get in the car now, so I'll be home in time. Good-bye."

"You—"

She ended the call. Shoving the phone in her pocket, she glanced back at the man on the horse. Cristan carried himself with the kind of quiet confidence that didn't need to be bolstered by hurting others. She turned away from Cristan. She'd see him later. Lucia was babysitting tonight so Sarah could attend her last self-defense class. But there was no point wanting things she couldn't have. Troy wasn't going to let her move on.

As long as he had her little girls, she was powerless.

CHAPTER THIRTEEN

"This is risky," her lieutenant said from the driver's seat of the minivan.

"It's a calculated risk." She watched the dot on the GPS settle on a patch of green in the middle of nowhere. The address listed was the stable where Christopher boarded two horses. She consulted the spreadsheet of his activities over the past few weeks. "They went riding. He shouldn't be back for at least an hour, and it isn't as if we don't know where he is at all times." She gestured with the GPS.

"Keep watch on that screen." He drove toward Christopher's house.

There was no point following Christopher. The stable sat on a flat, open expanse of ground that provided no cover for a clandestine observer. Plus, a member of local law enforcement appeared to live on the farm. Both times she'd driven past, an official vehicle was parked in front of the house. She did not wish to attract attention, and this afternoon created the perfect opportunity to survey Christopher's property in the daylight. Knowing he was occupied, they could get a closer inspection than they had on their previous drive-bys.

He slowed the car as they approached the house. "I don't see anywhere to conceal the van."

She pointed to the driveway. "I'm feeling bold."

"Foolish would be a better description." But he did as she requested, his reluctance evident in the stiff set of his shoulders and the thin line of his mouth.

She lifted a palm. "There's nowhere to park out of sight. We might as well keep the car close." There were times when one had to weigh the probabilities and make a decision. "You've been reluctant in every phase of this operation. Is there some reason you don't want Christopher to pay for his crime?"

"Of course not." He slowed at the driveway but didn't turn. "We'll park on the road and circle around through the woods. I'd rather cross some open ground on foot than be trapped. I do not wish to pay for revenge with my life." He stopped on the shoulder of the road a quarter mile past the house. "Or yours."

She caught the hesitation in his voice, as if the inclusion of her life in his statement was an afterthought. Neither did she appreciate his lack of obedience. She couldn't forget that he was the hired help, and that, for her, this vendetta was very personal.

"Everyone dies," she said simply. Her life had been filled with enough pain that death did not frighten her. "I'm tired of waiting. I want this finished."

"Then what?" he asked.

She didn't answer because she didn't know. She'd been consumed by hatred for so long, she couldn't imagine its absence in her life.

Putting the future out of her mind, she focused on the task at hand. She verified that Christopher's car had not moved, then slid the GPS into her pocket. She was bold, not stupid. Underestimated, Christopher could be deadly. Camera in hand, she got out of the car. They trekked through a short patch of woods and emerged in the side yard. Keeping her distance from the house, she aimed her telephoto lens at the front door. "First surveillance camera is on the front porch, under the eave." She snapped a picture.

"We won't be able to get any closer," he said.

"We don't have to."

They walked a wide perimeter around the house. Their trained eyes located several more cameras. She photographed them from different perspectives, zooming in close to note the direction of each camera's focus.

Folding his arms across his body, he frowned. "Door and windows will be alarmed, possibly booby-trapped."

"Yes," she agreed. "But there will be no police monitoring. Christopher would want to handle any transgressions personally."

After rechecking the GPS to make sure his car had not moved, she rounded the building and photographed the backyard. She estimated the distance between the house and the river and the woods that flanked the house. Then they walked back to the car, where she made a quick sketch of the property, noting the location of every camera they'd found. The dot moved on the GPS screen.

"We need to finish." She set aside her drawing. "He's on his way." She reached into the backseat and lifted the item she'd brought. "Stop at the mailbox."

At the base of the driveway, she slipped out of the car and tucked her gift into the mailbox.

Would he know what it meant? Would he remember?

She hoped so. She wanted him to completely understand why she had to destroy him.

She opened the video function on her phone and touched the thumbnail image of Luciana. The film she'd taken at Luciana's school filled the screen. She pressed Play. The young girl's voice sounded clear and confident through the phone's speakers. Anger burned deep inside her.

Today's venture was worth every ounce of risk. She must focus on her goal. By next week, Christopher would be dead.

"What time does Sarah need you?" Cristan shifted into drive and steered the sedan toward home.

Lucia looked up from her phone. "I don't have to be at her house until six. Her class is later tonight."

Cristan glanced at the dashboard clock. "It's after five already."

He'd lost track of time while they were riding. Sharing his favorite activity with his daughter had claimed all of his attention.

"Oh," Lucia said. "Maybe you should just drop me off now."

He gave her an exaggerated sniff. "No. You definitely need a shower. You smell like a horse."

She laughed. "I don't mind."

"I'm sure you can be quick."

Cristan turned into their driveway. As he pulled around to the side of the house where the garage doors opened, the hairs on the back of his neck quivered. His foot lifted from the gas pedal and the car rolled to a stop. He scanned the stone exterior but saw nothing out of the ordinary.

"What's wrong?" Lucia followed his gaze through the windshield.

He pushed a button on the visor. The overhead door rose, and he pulled into the garage. "Probably nothing." But he tucked Lucia behind him as they walked into the kitchen. The alarm panel displayed a healthy row of blinking green lights. There had been no disturbances. Cristan forced his muscles to loosen. The robbery had made him paranoid.

He was showered and dressed in a few minutes. Lucia wasn't the only one who'd smelled like horses. Leaving his bedroom, he heard the shower stop in her bathroom.

"I'll be in my office," he called to the closed door.

"Five minutes," she yelled in answer.

Downstairs, he booted up his computer and opened the security system software. He checked the feed for the surveillance cameras. All clear. Breathing easier, he shut his system down.

Lucia met him in the hallway, her still-wet hair spilling down onto the shoulders of her jacket. He grabbed a hat from a hook by the back door. Sighing, she tugged it onto her head as they returned to the car. Backing out, he waited until the overhead door hit the pavement before driving away. At the base of the driveway, the slightly open mailbox door caught his attention. He lowered his window and reached inside. On top of a folded stack of advertisements sat a stuffed brown rabbit.

"Ooo. What's that?" Lucia leaned across the seat.

Cristan turned the toy over in his hands. A ribbon around its neck bore a square gift envelope. New, it was definitely not the same toy she'd owned as a baby, but his gut cramped as he opened the card. "To Lucia, from a secret admirer."

"Really?" She lifted it out of his hands. Her voice rose to a squeal. "It's so cute. I wonder who sent it?" She whipped out her phone and snapped a picture of the toy.

"What are you doing?"

"Snapchatting Jenna." She looked up from her phone, her eyes lit with excitement.

"What?"

"Nothing." Smiling, she exchanged texts in rapid succession.

But Cristan knew it was definitely something that put that glow on her face. "What does Jenna think?"

Lucia set her phone down and turned to face him. When her brows lifted in challenge, the resemblance to her mother was striking. "Jenna thinks it was a new boy at school. She says he likes me."

"Boy? What boy? You haven't said anything about a boy."

"Because I knew you'd act all crazy-protective."

Cristan's jaws clamped together, stifling his retort. Lucia's assessment of his reaction was accurate. The thought of a boy showing interest in his daughter made his hands curl into tight fists. He drew a deep breath in through his nose and flexed his fingers. He needed to change his approach. He didn't expect a teenage girl to share *everything* with him, but he wanted her to feel like she could come to him with her problems. Clearly, she did not feel that way.

He smoothed his tone. "What is this boy's name?"

"Taylor."

"Tell me about him."

"He moved here from California," she said.

As Lucia rattled on about Taylor from California, Cristan frowned at the toy in her hands. Coincidence. It had to be. A stuffed rabbit was a common toy, especially with Easter approaching in a few weeks. No one could possibly know that she'd had a toy just like that one as a baby in Argentina.

But the sight of his daughter clutching the stuffed brown rabbit chilled his blood to ice.

CHAPTER FOURTEEN

Where were they?

Sarah fed the dog, started a load of laundry, and ran the dishwasher. The sound of a car engine pulled her to the front window. It wasn't Troy. Her next-door neighbor parked his sedan at the curb and went into his house. Apprehension rippled through Sarah. She checked her cell phone. They should have been home ten minutes before. She had no texts or missed calls. It was only ten minutes, and Troy had said he was ahead of schedule. And that was before she'd angered him by hanging up on him.

Relax.

But ten minutes turned into twenty. Sarah paced. Scenarios ran through her head. Her imagination covered the paranoid gamut from he lost them to he wasn't bringing them back. When the girls were another thirty minutes late, she started dialing Troy's number on her cell. The dog growled and ran toward the door. Troy's truck pulled into the driveway, and Sarah's heart sagged with relief. They were home.

Troy got out of the truck and opened the rear door. The girls jumped down and ran across the grass. Pushing the angry little dog back inside, Sarah stepped out onto the stoop and dropped to one knee for hugs.

"Mommy, I missed you." Alex threw her arms around Sarah's neck. Emma leaned her head on Sarah's shoulder.

"You've only been gone since this morning, silly goose," Sarah said, keeping the moment light. She didn't want the girls to feel any trace of the irrational fear that had gripped her just a few moments earlier, when her mind had been full of all the things that could have happened to them. Troy might hate Sarah, but surely, he loved his own children. Deep inside, he must.

Unmoving, Troy stood in the driveway. Just twenty feet separated them. Something about his posture was odd, almost apprehensive. Sliding out of Alex's arms, Sarah straightened. "Why don't you two run inside and wash up. I'll make macaroni and cheese."

"We had kids' meals." Alex opened the storm door and the two scampered inside.

"They were hungry." He hooked his thumbs in the front pockets of his jeans.

Determined to be reasonable and amenable and all the other things her attorney insisted she needed to demonstrate, Sarah said, "It's fine. We're new at this. We'll have to iron out those details. Next time just let me know if you're going to feed them."

He nodded. "I'll pick them up Tuesday morning then." He began to turn away, then stopped. "Sarah, I'm trying hard here."

"All right."

"I love you. I didn't want a divorce. I want you back."

No, he hadn't wanted to sign the papers, but with assault charges looming and his income tied up with his failing business, he hadn't had much of a choice. But love her? She saw nothing but hatred on his face every time he looked at her. Sarah reached behind her for the door handle. "Troy, that isn't going to happen."

His posture tensed. "You *have* to give me a chance."

"No, Troy. You hit me."

"You can't forgive me for one mistake."

"It wasn't one mistake, and we both know that."

His face and eyes narrowed. "You need to take some of the blame. You shouldn't have made me mad when I was drunk."

Sarah bit back her retort. *You were always drunk.* But she wasn't going to let him draw her into an argument. "I'm going inside now."

"Wait." His hand shot out to stop her. He curled it into a fist, then dropped it to his side, his forearm tense as if the restraint cost him. "I'm sorry. I miss you, baby."

Baby? He hadn't called her baby since before the kids were born.

"I'm sober. I haven't missed a single AA meeting. I've stayed away from you for five months. What else do you want from me?" he asked.

"Those are all great things, Troy. I'm glad to see you're getting your life back on track, but we aren't getting back together." There were some things that couldn't be forgiven. A broken arm and a concussion were two of them. That night hadn't been the first of Troy's temper tantrums. It had just been the most violent.

"Not even for them." He nodded toward the house.

"No." The girls had been so frightened that night that they'd hidden in their closet. "What happened between us wasn't good for them."

He leveled his gaze at her, and when she didn't break eye contact first, he looked away. Sarah exhaled. She could do this. *Be firm. Do not engage.*

"Good night, Troy." Sarah went inside and closed and locked the door. Had sobriety changed him? Had losing his family made him see the errors of his ways? It seemed hard to believe, after several years of control and abuse, and after what he'd done to her just five months before, that he was a new man.

But her opinion didn't matter. The judge had stressed that

children flourished best when they had active and healthy relationships with both parents. She and Troy had two children together. He would be a part of her life forever. She could not allow him to intimidate her—or talk her into attempting reconciliation. It had only been five months. He couldn't have changed that much, and even if he had, unlike skin and bone, their relationship was too damaged to heal.

She turned to the kitchen. Both girls were crowded onto the step stool in front of the sink. Alex reached forward to shut off the faucet. They scrambled down and dried their hands on a towel hanging from the refrigerator door handle.

Emma slipped into a kitchen chair. She rested her head on the table, her face turned to the side, her thumb in her mouth.

Sarah brushed a hair off her forehead. "Did you have a nap today?"

"She didn't." Alex dropped to her knees and opened the snack cabinet. "Can I have some cookies?"

"You may have one cookie," Sarah said. Should she ask them about their day? On one hand, she wanted to know how they felt about the time they'd spent with their father. But she didn't want them to think she would grill them every time they came home with Troy.

She went with a benign question. "Did you have a hamburger or chicken for dinner?"

"I had a hamburger." Alex pointed to Emma with a chocolate chip cookie. "And half of Em's nuggets."

"Weren't you hungry?" Sarah asked Emma.

"Uh-uh," the little girl said around her thumb. Sarah resisted the urge to stop her. The child was stressed enough. There'd be time to rebreak bad habits when they'd settled into their new routine, and she looked exhausted.

"Lucia is coming tonight." Sarah said. "Do you want to get a bath now or when I get home?"

"Later. Last time Lucia promised we'd play dress-up." Alex wiped her mouth with the back of her hand and skipped down the short hall that led to the bedrooms, calling, "I have to find my tiara and my rain boots."

Rain boots?

"How about you, Em?" Sarah turned to her youngest. "What do you want to do when Lucia comes?"

Em leaned over and vomited chicken nuggets and milk on the kitchen floor.

"Honey." Sarah rushed forward, avoiding the splatter, and carried the child to the bathroom. She put her down on a blue plastic step stool in front of the toilet. "Do you still feel sick?"

Emma nodded. Her eyes were huge and her face was as pale as the ivory ceramic tile around the bathtub. Sarah wet a cloth, wiped Em's face, and tucked some damp hair behind her ear. Em flinched. Sarah looked behind the child's ear. A bruise darkened the back of her head. She ran her fingertips gently over the area and felt a goose egg on the child's scalp.

"Ow." Em flinched.

"What happened, sweetie?" Sarah fought to keep anger and worry out of her voice. Had Troy hit her? No. She couldn't believe that. As awful as he'd been to Sarah, he'd never struck either of the kids. In truth, he'd never paid them much attention at all. During their marriage, Sarah had been the target of all his anger. But he was acting strangely.

Em's thumb had found its way back to her mouth. She looked up at Sarah with sad eyes.

"She fell," Alex said from the doorway. "Daddy told her not to climb on the 'splay, but she did it anyway."

"Fell from where?"

Alex put a hand over her mouth and mumbled, "I'm not supposed to tell you about it."

"Why not?" Sarah asked, suspicion creeping into her belly.

"Daddy said so. He said we can't tell you anything that happens when we're with him."

"OK. Just tell me how Em fell."

"She wanted the pretty balls, but they were up high and Daddy said she couldn't have them. When he went into his office, she climbed. I told her not to." Alex cast a worried look at her sister. "Is Em OK? Daddy said she was fine."

"I hafta frow up." Em's voice was teary and full of misery.

With an aching heart, Sarah lifted the lid on the toilet and held Em's hair while she lost the rest of her dinner.

Sarah mopped the little girl's face again, worry gathering beneath her sternum. Was the vomiting caused by the bump on the head, a virus, or the chicken nuggets? As much as she dreaded it, she'd have to call Troy to find out. "Would you please bring me the phone, Alex?"

The little girl ran down the hall to the kitchen and returned with Sarah's cell phone. Troy didn't answer her call. She left him a message, then dialed the pediatrician and left her number for an immediate callback.

The doorbell rang, and Bandit exploded into a barking frenzy. He raced for the foyer.

"If that's Lucia, you can let her in." Her phone rang. She answered the call as Alex bounced away. A few minutes later, she carried Emma out of the bathroom. Alex and Lucia were in the living room. Alex was modeling a plastic tiara. Sarah poked her head into the kitchen.

Cristan was putting a new bag in the garbage can. He returned a bottle of all-purpose cleaner to the top shelf in the pantry. The kitchen floor was clean, and the odor of vomit replaced by the lemon scent of disinfectant. He closed the window he'd obviously cracked to freshen the room.

"You didn't have to mop my kitchen floor, but you have no idea how much I appreciate that you did. Thank you."

"You're welcome." Cristan cast a raised brow at Bandit, sitting at the threshold, looking guilty. "Bandit offered to clean up. I thought it best if I took care of it."

The dog's tail thumped on the carpet, a canine version of *my bad*.

Cristan crossed the room and placed a palm on Emma's forehead, his dark eyes full of concern. "She's not feverish. Is she ill?"

"I don't know. She hit her head this afternoon. She's probably fine, but the doctor wants me to take her to the ER, just to be sure."

He frowned, his gaze meeting hers and understanding what she wasn't saying. "I'll drive you. Lucia will stay with Alex."

"You don't have to do that," she protested.

"No, I don't. You're perfectly capable of handling the situation. But please allow me to help. How will you attend to Emma if you are driving?" He made a valid point. From the driver's seat in the dark, she'd barely be able to see Emma in the back.

"All right. Thank you."

He ushered them to the foyer, where he picked up Emma's jacket from a chair and gently worked her arms into it. Then he helped Sarah with her coat before donning his own. Cristan drove the minivan. Sarah sat in the back next to Emma's car seat and held a plastic bowl in her lap, just in case.

Several hours later, Sarah sat next to the gurney, stroking Em's forehead while she slept. The cubicle was small, and Cristan had stayed out in the waiting room. Why couldn't she have met a man like him six years ago? A man who mopped up vomit and handled a gross little dog with humor instead of anger. Instead, she'd picked Troy, who'd left his *own* vomit on the floor and kicked the little dog. She reminded herself that Troy hadn't been an alcoholic when she'd married him.

"Where is she?" Troy's voice carried down the hallway. "Sarah?"

Sarah breathed, wishing she hadn't been required to call him. But the custody agreement was clear. The other parent must be notified in case of emergency. A trip to the ER was, by definition, urgent. Of course, he was also supposed to call her if one of the children was hurt or sick and he hadn't. But she was going to do the right thing, legally and morally.

Emma stirred. Making sure the bed rail was secure, Sarah slipped out of the chair and poked her head into the hall. Troy opened his mouth, but she put a finger to her lips as she stepped into the corridor. "She's sleeping."

"It was a bump on the head. She doesn't need a trip to the emergency room, Sarah," Troy whispered in a furious hiss. "What are you trying to pull here?"

CHAPTER FIFTEEN

"Pull?" she asked in a low voice. Shock straightened her spine as a chill formed in her belly at the accusation in his voice. "I called you. You didn't answer. She threw up twice, and I found a bruise and bump on her head. I didn't have much of a choice. You should have mentioned the fall when you dropped her off."

"She was fine. Kids fall all the time. You coddle them too much." He glared down at her, trying to crowd her with his body.

Though her knees were rubbery, Sarah held her ground. She'd have to deal with this man for the next fifteen years. If she let him intimidate her now, he'd never stop. "She's three, Troy. She can't articulate how badly she feels."

"If you think I'm going to let you get away with this, you're dumber than I thought." A vein on the side of Troy's neck throbbed. Sarah had learned to gauge his level of anger by the size of that vein, which was a sad fact all by itself.

But this time she was truly confused. "Get away with what?"

"You know what."

"Excuse me." Cristan walked up the hall. He held two Styrofoam cups. "How is Emma?" He offered a cup to Sarah, the extension of his arm forcing Troy to move back. Cristan's gaze swept over Troy from his Timberland boots to his baseball cap. The expression on Cristan's face was benign, but his dark eyes had gone intense. Sarah knew him well enough to sense a quiet threat behind his polite façade.

"Thank you." The smell of coffee drifted to her nose. She clung to the cup with both hands, hoping the warmth would seep into her fingers. "We're waiting on the MRI results."

As Sarah expected, Troy immediately put on his public face. When he was sober, he could switch his temper on and off with frightening speed. He held out a hand and introduced himself. Cristan accepted the handshake, but unmistakable coldness undercut his social niceties. He wasn't fooled.

She glanced back into the room. Emma was still asleep.

The ER physician, Dr. Wilson, walked down the hallway with a file in his hand. Sarah suppressed her humiliation. Dr. Quinn Wilson had been on duty the night Troy had broken her arm, and he was a close friend of Mike's. The doctor glanced in on Emma, then turned to Sarah. "The MRI shows no sign of bleeding in the brain."

"Of course there isn't," Troy interrupted. "She just bumped her head. Kids are tough."

"But she does have a concussion." The doctor leveled his blue eyes at Troy. "How far did she fall?" He pulled a pen from the chest pocket of his green scrub shirt and opened the file in his hands. With a click of his thumb, he poised the pen over the paper.

"Not far. A couple feet maybe." Troy backpedaled, his posture becoming defensive.

"What did she hit her head on?" Dr. Wilson asked.

"The floor." Troy moved toward Sarah. "I see what you're doing here. You're trying to blame me. This is a conspiracy."

Sarah froze. Her mouth refused to forms words, her body wouldn't respond to her commands. Cristan stepped in front of her.

Troy stopped short, his face reddening. "Who the hell are you, and why are you here?" His voice rose. Anger wiped away all traces of his company face. He stabbed a finger at Cristan. "Are you banging this guy, Sarah? Is that what this is really about? I'll bet you were cheating on me all along. All those weeks I was out of town when the team was on the road."

How dare he? She'd spent most of her marriage trying desperately to please him. She'd gone to his games, even hugely pregnant in the heat of summer, to support him. She'd kept his house and borne his children and put up with his outbursts to try and keep their family together. She knew now all that effort had been futile, but back then, with her parents' turmoil and her mother's death fresh, Sarah had only wanted to keep the peace. But appeasing Troy proved impossible. He'd made it his goal every day to point out some imagined fault. In hindsight, her utter stupidity filled her with humiliation.

She stepped around Cristan to confront her ex. As much as she appreciated Cristan's chivalry, she needed to stand up to Troy on her own. He would never respect her, and she would never respect herself, until she did. Her belly cramped and her leg muscles quivered, but she faced him. Keeping her response on target, she said, "Troy, this isn't about you or me. Tonight is about Emma. Aren't you worried about her at all? You didn't even go in and see her."

He blinked, as if just realizing his lapse. She watched the excuses spin in his eyes. His indifference to his daughters wounded Sarah all over again. How could he not love their two little girls as much as she did? And one question remained. Why did he pursue visitation and partial custody if he didn't actually want to spend time with them? Why did he claim to want to reconcile when his hate for her was palpable? What was he up to?

Troy glanced at Cristan as he answered. "This isn't about Emma. This is about you, Sarah. You've wanted to stick it to me since last fall. I made one mistake, and I'm going to pay for it for the rest of my life. If you think this stunt is going to get you alimony or high child support payments, think again." He pointed at Cristan. "Stay away from my wife."

"It's you who'd better keep his distance." Cristan's voice took on an icy tone that sent a warning shiver through Sarah. "I won't permit you to treat Sarah with disrespect."

Troy fell back, like a coyote confronted by a wolf. "You'll be hearing from my lawyer, Sarah." Troy turned and strode away. He'd backed down from Cristan, but that didn't mean he was giving in.

"I'm going to check on Emma," Dr. Wilson said. "You should call your case manager before Troy gets to her with his own spin on the incident."

The doctor went into the room.

Sarah watched Troy retreat. "He didn't even go into the room to see her. I want what's best for the girls. I had a tough relationship with my mother and father. I wanted more for them." Sarah sighed. Her head ached. She put a hand to her temple.

"It is not easy being both father and mother," Cristan said. "Not all people make good parents. If that were my child—" he nodded toward the doorway into Emma's cubicle, "—no one would have prevented me from seeing her with my own eyes."

Sarah couldn't imagine anyone trying to stand in his way. This was how a father should act, with a combination of ferocity and gentleness, to nurture and protect his children, not use them as pawns.

Was Troy using the kids to manipulate her? She wanted him to care about them. She wanted sobriety to have changed him, but obviously that was wishful thinking on her part.

Dr. Wilson proclaimed Emma fit to go home. A short time later, Sarah collected the hospital paperwork and tucked sleepy Emma into her coat before picking her up.

Cristan held his arms out. "May I carry you, little one, and give your mama a break?"

"She's not that heavy." Sarah hefted the child's weight higher for better leverage. Both of her girls were clingy when they were sick, especially Em.

But she nodded and lurched toward him. Cristan caught her and gently lifted her to his broad shoulder. She nestled her head against his chest.

Shocked, Sarah picked up her purse and the paperwork and followed him to the car. Usually, Em wasn't comfortable with any man other than Mike.

Cristan drove them home, carried Em into the house, and tucked her into bed.

"Do you need me to stay?" he asked while Lucia located her boots.

"No. We'll be fine. Thank you for your help tonight." She felt like all she did was thank other people for helping her. When she finally got her life back on track, she vowed to pay forward all the kindness in her life.

"I am glad I was here." He waited as Lucia put on her coat. His eyes were on Sarah. "I wish you didn't have to deal with . . . all this."

"Me too."

"I left my book in Alex's room." Lucia disappeared down the hall.

As soon as Lucia was out of earshot, he spoke in a low voice. "Sarah, I appreciate you want to handle your ex on your own, but I can't and won't allow him to threaten you."

"I know you mean well, but please don't interfere," Sarah said. "Troy is short-tempered. I won't let him bully me, but for the girls' sake, I also try not to make him angry. Please stay away from him."

Clearly unhappy with her request, he nodded and crossed his arms over his chest. "I won't provoke him."

It wasn't the promise she wanted, but she sensed it was the best she'd get.

His daughter returned, preventing Sarah from responding, even if she had the words.

"Goodnight. Call me if you need anything. I can be here in ten minutes." He gathered Lucia and left.

Sarah locked the dead bolt and leaned against the door for a few seconds. Was Cristan's response friendly concern, or was there more to his protective attitude? And why did the thought of him defending her fill her with warmth? She *should* want to stand on her own. It would be so much easier to let another man handle Troy, but she couldn't take the easy way out. That's how she'd ended up marrying Troy in the first place.

"Mommy," Alex called from the hall. "Can you tuck me in?"

"You're awake?"

"I heard you talking." Alex didn't like to miss any action.

Exhausted, she answered a thousand questions from Alex before getting her oldest child into her bed. Then she set her alarm for two hours so she could check on Emma. She made a quick round of the house, inspecting window and door locks, ensuring the blinds were tightly closed. The chore took only a few minutes in the tiny house. Testing the lock on the front window, she glanced outside. A large SUV sat across the street. It wasn't Troy's truck. In the darkness, she could see the outline of a driver sitting in the still vehicle, and she could feel him watching her.

Sarah shivered.

Troy could have borrowed a vehicle like he'd borrowed a cell phone. Or he could have asked a friend to watch her. Either way, she should probably call Mike. Troy's behavior had been too erratic. She reached for her phone. The truck's headlights turned on, and light flooded her driveway. The beams swept across her lawn as the vehicle pulled away from the curb and drove past the house very slowly before disappearing down the street.

She lowered the phone as the taillights faded into the darkness. Why would Troy be interested in her activities? She was home with two young children, one of whom had a concussion. What did he think she could possibly be doing? As Sarah called her sister's neighbor, Mrs. Holloway, to ask if she could babysit the next day—Em would need to be watched closely and Sarah didn't have any accumulated sick days yet—she almost wished she'd asked Cristan to stay.

Fuming, the woman leaned away from the eyepiece. Down the street, an SUV drove away from the house.

"Where to?" her lieutenant asked.

"I don't know," she snapped.

Christopher had a woman. He had a whole new life. He thought he'd left his tragedy behind in Argentina. Well, she was going to show him he was mistaken.

"The house." She twisted the cap off a bottle of water and drank. But the chilled liquid did little to cool her anger. That bastard! How dare he get on with his life when hers was ruined.

She lifted the digital camera from its dashboard-mounted tripod. The long, telephoto lens and night-vision attachment enabled her to see and photograph at a distance, even in low light. The images weren't perfect, but the subjects would be clear enough for identification. She didn't want to get any closer until she was sure she wouldn't be noticed.

She'd caught Christopher carrying a child and escorting the woman into the house. The porch light cast deep shadows on his face, and the way his body angled protectively around them fed her anger. Did he really think he could start over?

She put a finger on the LCD screen on the back of the camera. In the small, grainy image, the hard planes of his face were clear enough. He hadn't gone to fat. If anything, he was leaner, more dangerous and brutally handsome. "Do you think the child is his?"

Her lieutenant shook his head. "That child is at least three years old. Christopher has only lived in this place for approximately two years."

"Yes. Of course." She agreed. She wasn't thinking rationally. Of course that wasn't his child. But his body language toward the young mother indicated he was interested in her, and he was obviously still virile enough to obtain her if he wished. "He must be taught a lesson."

He nodded.

"Tomorrow, we will find out everything about that woman. I want to know where she works, where she shops, everything. I want her every movement tracked."

"It will be done."

She wrote down the woman's address and the license plate number for the minivan in the driveway. Drumming her fingers on the console, she watched as the windows went dark. Fifteen minutes later, she decided the neighborhood was quiet enough.

"Go around the block and meet me at the other end of the street." She opened the vehicle door. They'd disabled the interior dome light. She walked down the sidewalk at a leisurely pace. The street appeared empty. Working people went to bed early. She paused in front of the woman's house. The mailbox was empty, but she stooped to pick up a thin, tri-folded newspaper at the base of the driveway. Tucking it under her arm, she continued to saunter down the sidewalk. At the end of the street, she got back into the vehicle.

"Well?" he asked.

The newspaper was a local rag. She used her cell phone light to read the address label. "Her name is Sarah Mitchell."

A new plan formed in her mind. Perhaps Sarah Mitchell and her children could be used as leverage to control Christopher. He obviously cared about them, and that made him vulnerable.

CHAPTER SIXTEEN

Sarah parked in the rear of the Main Street Inn. Inside, she hung up her coat and stowed her purse in a cupboard in the back room. Nerves twisted in her belly. Even with the best babysitter in the world on duty, leaving Em today had broken her heart. Mrs. Holloway had known Sarah and Rachel since they were born, and Sarah had complete faith in the retired schoolteacher to care for Emma.

But that didn't make leaving her daughter the day after she'd spent the evening in the ER any easier. She checked her phone for messages. Nothing.

Jobs were hard to come by in her small hometown. She couldn't afford to lose this one. For a minute, she almost longed for the days when she didn't have to worry about working, when Troy's salary paid all the bills and she could concentrate on her house and her children. But that life had come with costs as well. It had put her in her current situation, tossing together a career like the chefs on *Chopped* scrambled to make an entrée in thirty minutes out of random ingredients.

She knew her new boss had given her this job as a favor to Mike. She was a good cook, but she had no formal training. While she couldn't let pride come between her and a steady paycheck, she was determined to do a damned good job.

Single parenthood came with issues she hadn't anticipated. Some days she loved her job. Being a person apart from a mother was refreshing and gave her a sense of individual accomplishment.

Other days, like today, she just plain hated it. There were even days when she felt guilty for enjoying her work at the inn.

But today, worrying about Em trumped all her other emotional issues.

In the hours before lunch, the kitchen was empty save for two dishwashers working at the dual commercial sinks. She removed a clipboard from its hook on the wall, where the head chef, Jacob, had left her notes on the lunch menu. After three months of watching Sarah's every move, Jacob had finally given her autonomy over the weekday lunch service.

"Sarah, what's wrong? You look exhausted." Herb Duncan, the owner of the Main Street Inn and former chef, poured coffee into a thick, black mug and handed it to her. In his gray slacks and dark-blue sweater, Herb looked every inch the successful country gentleman.

"Thank you." Sarah accepted it gratefully. The heat in the kitchen tended to melt makeup from her face. But this morning, she wished she'd given her dark circles a swipe of concealer. "Em hit her head yesterday. We spent the evening in the ER."

"Is she all right?"

"Yes. She was up and eating a waffle when I left."

Herb smiled. "Selfishly, I'm glad you're here. I could have called Jacob in early, but he gets ornery when his schedule is thrown off. I wish I could still be of use." Herb flexed his fingers. Arthritis kept him out of his apron.

"I know you do. I'd better get to work."

The next few hours passed quickly. Chopping, sautéing, plating, supervising a staff of four, her job as sous chef involved much more than cooking. By two thirty, the crowd had thinned enough for her to take her afternoon break. She stripped off her apron and grabbed her coat. She slipped her cell phone in her pocket. Leaving the inn through the back door, she ignored her minivan and walked toward Main Street. Sarah preferred to spend her thirty minutes of freedom outside.

She contemplated stopping home to see Em, but quickly dismissed that idea. Once she got home, her daughter would be attached to her body like a growth. Peeling her off to return to work would result in tears.

Crisp air swept over her face, refreshing her skin after an afternoon in the hot kitchen. She called home and checked in on Em. Mrs. Holloway assured her that the little girl was fine. They'd baked cookies, and Em was currently napping on the sofa. Sarah spoke to Alex and got a more detailed rundown of everything that had happened since she left at nine o'clock. Sarah hung up, feeling better about her decision to come to work. She turned her feet back toward Main Street.

Stopping at the red light in the center of town, she caught a movement out of the corner of her eye. She turned around. A block behind her, a man in a brown jacket stepped into the shadow of an awning. He stared in the store window, but Sarah could still feel his gaze on her, as if he were watching her in the reflection of the glass.

She continued to walk. In front of the consignment shop, she opened the door. The sun hit the glass and turned it into a mirror.

The man was still exactly one block away, this time inspecting the window of the butcher shop. Was he really watching her or was she paranoid?

She went into the consignment store and walked around the store once. Back outside, she glanced up and down the street, spotting the man in the brown jacket in the doorway of a gift shop. Confusion and apprehension eliminated her earlier feel-good moment. Downtown Westbury's meager tourist traffic was highest in summer. There were a number of antique shops nestled in the few blocks around Main Street, but strangers didn't typically wander the streets.

He was definitely following her, but why?

CHAPTER SEVENTEEN

She sat in the dining room of the Main Street Inn and sipped her tea. The newspaper lay unfolded on the table in front of her. Her driver had remained in the car. While she could fake a New York accent, one word out of his mouth would attract attention.

"Can I get you anything else?" the waiter asked.

She smiled. "Just the check."

The dining room was nearly empty. She paid her bill, left an appropriate tip, and gathered her belongings. Scanning the walls, she spotted a hallway and walked toward it. With a quick glance over her shoulder, she put a hand to the door of the ladies' toilet. Assured that she was alone in the hallway, she bypassed the bathroom. The short passage also led to the kitchen and some rooms beyond.

Christopher's woman worked here. Where was she? She peered around a doorframe into the kitchen. Three white-aproned men worked, but she didn't see Sarah Mitchell.

She stole across the rough-hewn floor and peered into a small office. Another larger room beyond held coats on hooks. She didn't see the coat Sarah had been wearing when she entered the inn that morning.

Pulling out her phone, she sent a text to her driver. He replied in a second. She left a few minutes ago. Didn't take her purse.

With one ear tuned to the hallway, she rooted through the cabinets until she found Sarah's purse. Then she slid the special device from her pocket into an exterior compartment of the handbag. It looked like a pen but was actually a voice-activated audio transmitter. She'd be able to hear everything that happened around Sarah's purse. At most, the battery would last four or five days, but that was plenty of time.

She couldn't make a decision about Christopher's woman until she knew more about her. She slipped from the back room into the inn's lobby without anyone seeing her and left through the front door.

A quick text summoned her driver. Soon she would know everything about Sarah Mitchell. Information was ammunition.

———

Cristan contemplated the knife pointed at his throat. In one swift movement, he twisted his shoulders, simultaneously grabbing his opponent's wrist to push the blade away from his neck and delivering a hard palm strike to the face. A knee in the belly doubled the man in half. The wristlock, takedown, and disarm followed a second later.

"Again," the instructor yelled.

His attacker, a police SWAT-team member, got to his feet. Cristan handed him the rubber practice knife. He repeated the technique a dozen times, and then they switched roles so his partner could practice. The weekly two-hour class ended with a knee-and-elbow strike drill that left him drenched in sweat. He shook his partner's hand and left the gym while his classmates were engaging in the post-class discussion. The advanced class was full of members of the military and law enforcement, and Cristan didn't want to get to know any of them too well. This was the same reason he drove nearly an hour to attend classes and an hour in the opposite direction to practice his marksmanship. There was both a gym and a gun range closer to Westbury, but he preferred to keep his private life private. The less his neighbors knew about his *hobbies*, the better.

A businessman with lethal combat skills was bound to attract attention, and if anyone knew about the cache of weapons, ammunitions, and other survival gear in his basement, interests would, indeed, be piqued. Not many real estate investors kept a go-kit containing everything from passports in multiple identities to three different types of currency.

He was still praying the video of the convenience store robbery didn't go viral. The fewer people who saw it the better. Regardless, if Mike found out about his treasure trove of unregistered weapons, he might view the store incident with different eyes.

He stopped in the locker room on his way out. Tugging a sweatshirt over his head, he grabbed his gym bag. Then he pushed through the metal door and walked into the parking lot.

The gym occupied a warehouse-type building in the center of an industrial complex. Cold air blew across his damp skin as he scanned the ice-crusted asphalt. A sedan parked at the opposite end of the rectangle caught his attention. The building on that end of the complex was marked with a For Lease sign. No other cars occupied that section of the lot, except for that lone sedan. Light reflected off the windshield, blocking any view of the vehicle's interior.

With a wary eye on the sedan, Cristan headed for his car. He dropped his duffel in the trunk and slid behind the wheel. Starting the engine, he slipped a hand under the seat of his car. His hand touched the handgun in the holster affixed to the underside of the seat. Next to it, a knife hilt protruded from a sheath. Satisfied his weapons were still in place, he checked his messages, taking an unobtrusive photo of the sedan and noting the license plate number.

A man couldn't be too careful, especially one with secrets to hide.

His identification had passed the police check he knew Mike had run months ago, when Rachel was being stalked. But there were other, unofficial channels through which a curious party could obtain information for the right price. Mike's friend Sean probably knew all about those less formal avenues. If he dug deep enough, could he find the truth?

The past could be altered, but it could not be erased.

Could this be the work of Aline Barba? After twelve long years, could she finally have found him now that he'd stayed in one place long enough?

He drove out of the lot. The sedan did not follow immediately, but he spotted it on the highway, maintaining a discreet distance that suggested a professional. Anger and apprehension sharpened his senses. His mind planned. Surveillance was the precursor to danger. Instead of driving toward Westbury, Cristan detoured.

He made three stops on the way. The sedan did not follow him into the parking lots of any of the stores, but every time he returned to the highway, it was five or six cars behind him. Whoever was behind the wheel wasn't an amateur. A person who wasn't always looking for danger wouldn't have spotted the vehicle.

He contemplated his options. He was not going to lead the driver to his home. His daughter's safety was not to be taken lightly. She had talent-show practice after school today, so he had some extra time. Cristan turned onto a country road that led to a state park where he and Lucia hiked when they desired a trail more difficult than the one that paralleled the river behind the house. The sedan dropped farther back, and he imagined the driver getting nervous as the road bisected a patch of forest. The scenery changed from open meadows and farms to rocky outcroppings and trees. A sheared-off rock wall flanked the left side of the road. The right shoulder dropped off into a rocky, tree-dotted slope. In the shadows of the forest, snow still covered the ground.

He turned onto a narrow lane that ended in a gravel parking area. There would be nowhere for the sedan to hide. If it followed him on this road, the driver would be trapped. There was only one way in and out. The sedan had not yet appeared in his rearview mirror.

Cristan parked at the end. He grabbed his coat, knife, and handgun, and sprinted for the woods. A fast-moving stream rushed next to the trail. Thin sheets of ice covered still pools. He ran up a trail to the first lookout area, a rocky ledge jutting out over the water—with an excellent view of the parking lot.

The appearance of the sedan erased any faint possibility of coincidence. On this trail, Cristan rarely ran into another human in the summer, let alone in the winter. The vehicle nosed into the lot, hesitating, as if the driver were nervous.

He should be.

Cristan glared at the vehicle making a three-point turn on the icy gravel below him. The man was planning for a quick exit. If he were smart, he would drive away and leave Cristan alone. But he wasn't. The sedan parked facing the road that led out of the parking area. Through the car window, Cristan watched the driver make a call. Getting instructions from his boss?

He should not have stayed in this town. He should have stuck to his original plan to stay on the move. He'd gotten sloppy. That needed to change.

He drew his knife from his pocket. The cold metal settled too comfortably in his grip, if not an old friend, at least an old ally. He might not trust people, but weapons and training had been faithful his entire life. Crouching, he watched the man complete his call and pocket his phone.

Cristan waited.

CHAPTER EIGHTEEN

Sarah crossed the street and sat down on a bench in front of the coffee shop. Pretending to look at her phone screen, she scanned the sidewalk over her sunglasses. The man had stopped in front of the small grocery store and was examining the specials listed on the blackboard out front. Enough foot traffic passed in and out of the café to give Sarah a sense of safety. Pulling out her phone, she yanked off a glove, dialed Mike, and described the man following her.

The police station was only a few blocks away. A few minutes later, Mike's dark SUV pulled to the curb next to the man. Mike got out, his burly body in full uniform. He spoke to the man, who pulled his wallet from his jacket pocket for Mike's scrutiny. Mike handed it back. Hand on his hips, he spoke to the man for a minute, then got back in his police vehicle and drove to the coffee shop. He parked at the curb and got out.

Sarah stood, her gaze drifting to the stranger heading in the opposite direction. "Who is he?"

"A private investigator. He wouldn't say who hired him, but he didn't deny it was Troy either." Mike said. "What's been going on with the divorce?"

"The divorce is final." Sarah told him about the scene at the hospital the night before. "But Troy says he wants me back."

"Em's all right?" he asked.

"Yes."

"There's no chance Troy hit her, right?"

Sarah shook her head. "No. The incident was recorded on the store surveillance camera. Troy submitted the tape this morning at the request of my attorney. She fell. In my opinion, he was negligent, but he claims she was never out of his sight. He just couldn't get to her quickly enough."

"Which could happen to anybody." Mike scratched his jaw, his ruddy complexion reddening in the cold. "It sounds to me like Troy is looking for some leverage."

"Leverage? For what?"

"Something to show you're not a fit mother or something to prove you were cheating on him would be my top guesses."

"But why? I don't understand. We're divorced. He has regular visitation."

"I can think of two reasons," Mike said. "The first is obvious. If he gets custody, he doesn't have to pay child support."

"I'm sure that's part of it."

"The second is because he wants you," Mike said. "He is using your love for the children to manipulate you." Mike's voice was deep and his blue eyes glittered with anger. "He said he wants you back, right?"

"Yes, but we all know he doesn't love me."

"Love isn't the issue." Mike shook his head. "He wants you in the same way he wants a shiny new truck. You were his possession and now you're not. You dumped him, and he isn't a good loser."

"No. He isn't." Sarah remembered Troy's fits of temper whenever he'd lost a baseball game or struck out at bat. "I thought he was just being spiteful."

"Think about it this way. When you were married, he had money. His family had a successful business and was respected in the community. After your clash last fall, you left him, and his life imploded."

"None of that was my fault."

"I know, but don't underestimate him, Sarah. He's not the sort of man who can lose with grace. He'll do anything to win. That type of man is dangerous when he has something to prove, and if he thinks he's in competition with Cristan Rojas, he's going to take that badly."

Sarah looked down the quiet street. Pretty shops. Not much traffic. Westbury was wholesome and quaint. She'd never wanted to live anywhere else, but now her hometown felt like a trap.

Mike sighed. "I can't stop that guy from observing you on a public street. He left because following you when you know he's there doesn't do him much good. Most PIs won't bother to follow you if you're forewarned. But watch yourself, Sarah. Ordinary things can look bad when taken out of context."

"But I don't *do* anything." Anger and frustration welled in Sarah's chest. "I go to work. I take care of the girls. I visit Rachel. That's about it."

"I know." But Mike looked worried. "Troy hired a private investigator. He's serious, and I wish I knew exactly what he was up to. Is there anything going on between you and Cristan Rojas?"

Sarah felt the blush in her cheeks. "No."

"I don't mean to pry, but how did he happen to be at your house last night to drive you to the hospital?"

"Lucia was supposed to babysit for me. Cristan was dropping her off when Em got sick." Sarah rubbed her head. "This is my fault. I should have driven myself, but I was worried about Emma."

"Sarah, this is not your fault. You haven't done anything wrong." Mike hesitated.

"But?" she prompted.

"But I wonder if that PI is also following Cristan. I don't know much about his personal life."

Neither did she. "I should call him and let him know."

"I'll do it," Mike said. "I want to find out more about him."

"I know you want to protect me, and that's very sweet of you. But Troy is my responsibility. I got myself into this situation, and I have to get myself out. I should be the one to tell Cristan."

"OK. I still might talk to Cristan." Mike held up a hand. "Your divorce is your responsibility, but this town is mine. I need to know about anything that might cause trouble."

"Thanks for coming, Mike."

"Call me anytime. I mean it. Be careful, Sarah." Mike got back into his SUV and drove away.

Sarah hurried back to the restaurant. A busboy carted dishes from the dining room to the sinks. Jacob was already in the kitchen, chopping carrots for soup—something Sarah was supposed to be doing. Typically, they spent fifteen minutes going over changes to the menu. She'd missed their daily meeting.

He pointed at her with his knife. His precision haircut and lean features sharpened his expression. "You're late."

Guilt flooded Sarah with heat. "I know. I'm sorry. I won't leave before I finish."

His blue eyes snapped to hers. "The kitchen doesn't run itself."

Offering an excuse sounded irresponsible. "It won't happen again."

She washed her hands and tied a clean apron around her waist. Grabbing a knife, she went to work on a pile of onions. Busy hands always helped calm her mind. But she couldn't stop wondering how long that investigator had been following her. Humiliation ebbed in her throat at the thought of a file filled with notes and photographs detailing her movements, scrutinizing her behavior, and documenting her whereabouts. Her eyes watered. The invasion of her privacy made her feel even more vulnerable.

The sound of blades hitting wood filled the kitchen. Jacob issued orders to the evening staff members as they arrived. Tables were set, dishes and utensils inspected, the special board updated.

Jacob scanned her face, his expression shifting from irritation to concern. "Is everything all right?"

She nodded and sniffed. "It's just the onions."

His scowl said he didn't believe her.

She finished chopping and consulted the clipboard. "Do you need me to do anything else before I go?"

"No." He stirred a pot of vegetables and stock. Steam wafted from the simmering mixture, and the kitchen filled with the scent of the inn's signature chicken chili. On the stainless counter behind him, one assistant diced tomatoes while another sliced strawberries for the goat cheese and balsamic salad on tonight's list of specials. Jacob switched gears, moving to the shelves of spices and mixing the rosemary rub for the pork tenderloin medallions.

Sarah stripped off her apron and gathered her purse and coat. She'd sent Mrs. Holloway a text earlier. Along with jeopardizing her job, Troy had the power to impact Sarah's coworkers and childcare providers.

Was that his goal? To simply make her life difficult? Was this payback, or was Mike right to suspect pure manipulation as Troy's motivation?

Her mind reeled with questions as she crossed the parking lot at the rear of the inn. She started her minivan. Blowing on her hands, she gave the engine a minute to warm up. She adjusted the heat vents and backed out of her parking space. The lot emptied into a narrow street that ran alongside the inn. Sarah shifted out of park and drove to the exit.

A horn blared and a fast-moving pickup truck nearly clipped the front end of the minivan. Sarah stomped on the brakes. The van lurched to a stop as the truck sped away.

Her stomach pitched as she recognized the Mitchell's Sporting Goods sticker on the pickup's rear window.

Troy.

Cristan crouched on the rocky ledge, peering from behind a tree trunk. His phone vibrated in his pocket. He pulled it free, along with his hat and gloves. Sarah.

Alarm rushed through him. Was Emma all right?

Keeping his eye on the lot below, he answered her call. Distance and the rush of water would cover the sound of his voice. Still, he kept his voice low. "Hello, Sarah."

The connection was weak and her voice broken with static, but he could make out her words.

"I'm sorry I have to tell you this," she began. "I'm being followed by a private investigator."

Shock jolted him. "Could you repeat that, Sarah?"

"Troy hired a private investigator to follow me."

Bastard.

"I don't know what he's trying to prove." Sarah's voice broke. "But I wanted to let you know. Considering what Troy said at the hospital last night, I wouldn't be surprised if you were caught up in this. I'm sorry."

"It's not your fault." All of the blame belonged on the poor excuse of a man she'd married, but Cristan was tempted to take his frustrations out on the PI in the sedan.

"I'm sorry anyway."

"Thank you for telling me," Cristan said.

"I'm so sorry. I'll get someone else to babysit the girls for a while. Please tell Lucia she didn't do anything wrong. You don't need to be involved in my problems."

"That won't be necessary. Do not worry about this, Sarah."

The man exited the sedan and walked a careful circle around the Mercedes.

"But thank you for the warning. I'll call you later." He ended the call and contemplated the man inspecting his car. Cristan didn't have to kill him. He didn't have to gather his daughter and leave town in the night. Aline Barba had not found him. Instead, he'd become embroiled in Sarah's divorce. How had he gotten involved in a domestic dispute? The answer was clear. He'd allowed himself to make personal connections in Westbury. Loneliness had taken its toll on him. He'd been weak. But Troy Mitchell did not have the right to dictate Sarah's actions, and Cristan would be damned if he let that bastard control him.

The man started up the trail. Dark haired and olive skinned, the man was in his midfifties and appeared reasonably fit. He wore a hat and gloves, but jeans grew heavy and cold when wet, and his street-type boots were not designed to navigate slippery rocks. He was dressed for urban surveillance, not a wilderness trek.

Cristan sprinted up the steep trail. His chilly muscles appreciated the movement. He would not kill the man, but he would teach him a lesson. He'd left clear footprints in the scattered patches of snow, and the man was following them. Cristan intentionally cracked a small twig. The noise reverberated through the trees. The man looked up, scanning the trail. He started up the slope. Cristan left a false trail heading up another, even steeper incline. Then he backtracked in his own footprints to a rocky patch and veered onto another path. He peered around a tree trunk. The man had progressed less than a hundred feet. He slid on a rock, his ascent hampered by his footwear.

Moving quietly, Cristan looped below his tail and doubled back to the parking lot. He used the hilt of the knife to smash the passenger window and access the glove compartment. The car was registered to A-Plus Private Investigations. Cristan took a picture of the vehicle registration with his cell phone. He'd run a check on the firm later. For now, stranding the investigator would have to suffice as payback. He slit all four tires on the sedan. Then he got into his own vehicle and drove away.

The PI had a phone. Cristan's stunt wouldn't kill him, but it would cost him.

Cristan sped down the highway. He still had some time before he needed to pick up Lucia from the talent-show practice. He headed into Westbury and cruised past Mitchell's Sporting Goods. He turned the car around and stopped at the curb in front of the store. Troy drove a pickup truck, but the vehicle wasn't parked in the lot alongside the store. Where was he?

As Cristan idled at the curb, anger simmered beneath his skin. He and Sarah had never gone anywhere together, except for that one trip to the hospital. Her ex-husband was trying to prove something that wasn't true. But then Cristan knew better than anyone that the truth didn't set anyone free.

What should he do? He wanted to goad Troy into attacking him. He didn't imagine it would be difficult. Sarah's ex had a quick temper and didn't seem prone to exercising self-control or thinking through decisions. If Troy was the aggressor, Cristan could legally defend himself—and teach Troy a valuable lesson.

Except that Cristan had given Sarah his word that he wouldn't provoke him, and breaking his promise to her felt wrong.

Movement in his rearview mirror distracted him. An SUV parked behind his sedan. Mike. The big cop got out of his car and walked up to the side of the Mercedes. Cristan lowered the window.

Mike pointed. "What are you doing?"

Cristan lifted a palm. "I wasn't aware that it was illegal to park on the side of the road."

Mike stared, clearly angry. "Diner. Now." It wasn't a request. "Sit with Sean. I'll be along in a minute."

The police chief walked away while Cristan debated ignoring his order. But curiosity, and his respect for Mike, won.

The Westbury diner was just a few blocks down the street. Cristan parked in the lot. The dinner hour hadn't begun, and only two tables in the dining room were occupied. One of the patrons was Sean, sitting in the corner booth with his back to the wall. Cristan slid into the other seat.

"Mike is pissed." Sean waved for a waitress.

She hurried over and poised her pen over her notepad. "What can I get you?"

Sean ignored the menu. "Coffee and a slice of cherry pie."

"Just coffee." Cristan had only been in the diner a handful of times. The restaurant was a local hangout, and the atmosphere felt intimate.

"Bring him a piece of pie, and the chief is coming." Sean leaned back, draping one arm over the top of the booth.

"I'll bring him the green tea he likes." The waitress hustled away.

"No pie for Mike?"

Sean rolled his eyes. "Mike doesn't eat food that has taste."

"My time is limited today," Cristan said as the waitress flipped and filled their cups. She brought them two slices of pie and utensils wrapped in napkins.

"Big plans?" Sean asked.

"I have to pick up my daughter at school."

"I have two girls. Five and seven." Sean dug into his pie.

Cristan ignored the slice of pie in front of him. "What is this?" He gestured between them.

Sean washed his pie down with a swallow of coffee. "Mike wants me to be your friend."

Of all the answers, that was the least expected. "What?"

"He wants to know more about you, and he figures the best way to do that is by being friendly." Sean dug his fork into his slice again. "Just so you know, I voted for asking a hacker friend to do an illegal background search. But Mike has all these moral dilemmas."

"Ethics can be a hindrance," Cristan said dryly.

"No shit," Sean laughed. "It's a good thing you and I aren't overly burdened."

A rush of cold air signaled Mike's arrival. He slid into the booth next to Sean and stared at Cristan over the table. "You can't park in front of Mitchell's. If Troy sees you, he'll flip."

Cristan drank his coffee. "His truck wasn't in the lot. Do you know where he is?"

"No, but I'm serious," Mike said. "I'm trying my best to defuse him, but that won't be possible if you're poking him with a lit match at the same time."

Cristan winced. Mike's description was uncomfortably accurate. If Troy had seen him, a confrontation would have been inevitable.

"You really think he can be defused?" Sean asked. "Cause I think he's gone bat-shit crazy."

"You're not helping," Mike glared at Sean, then turned to Cristan. "What were you going to do if Troy came outside?"

Cristan set his cup in its saucer. "I don't know, but I can't stand by and let him harass Sarah."

"Amen," Sean said. "I've been telling Mike for years that we should take out Troy."

Mike rubbed his forehead. "Please do not provoke Troy. Sarah is the one who will pay."

"You're right," Cristan said. "I won't provoke him."

Mike scrutinized him, as if not sure how to assess his statement. "You give me your word that you'll stay away from Troy."

"I said I wouldn't provoke him. But if he tries to hurt Sarah, I can't promise anything."

"Fair enough. I'll hold you to that promise." Mike tossed a few dollars on the table. "I have to go back to work."

Sean waited until Mike had left the diner. Then he ate the last bite of his pie. "If Troy hurts Sarah again, I'll help you dispose of the body." Though his grin and tone suggested humor, his eyes were serious.

"I suppose it's good to have friends."

"Damned straight."

But having an ally didn't mitigate Cristan's worries. Troy was unaccounted for. Who knew what he was planning?

CHAPTER NINETEEN

"Is it my imagination or is that dog barking nonstop tonight?" Sarah placed a card on the Candy Land board and moved her piece to the next purple square. Sitting cross-legged on the floor in front of the coffee table, she picked up her mug of lukewarm tea and sipped. Em crawled into her lap, and Sarah kissed the top of her head.

"Almost bedtime," she announced, more than ready to climb into her own bed.

Kneeling on the other side of the coffee table, Alex swiveled her head to the cable box. Her lips moved as she read the numbers. "It's not time yet." Now that she'd learned to read the digital clock, there was no more scooting her off to bed as much as a minute early.

Ruff ruff ruff. Bandit raced across the living room and leaped onto the back of the sofa, where he had a view of the street in front of the house.

She craned her head to look out the window. One of her neighbors and his elderly golden retriever shuffled down the sidewalk.

"Shh," Sarah said to the dog. "Goldie lives down the block. You've met her a hundred times."

His barks changed to whines.

"My turn." Alex flipped a card and counted the spaces on the colorful game board.

Sitting on Sarah's lap, Em took her turn in what felt like the longest board game in the history of the universe. Normally,

Sarah loved playing a game in the evening with her girls, but she couldn't wait to close her eyes tonight. Her lids felt as heavy as garage doors.

From his perch on the back of the sofa, Bandit growled, stiff-legged.

"I win!" Alex shouted, sliding her piece onto the Candy Castle space and raising both arms over her head in triumph.

The digital clock rolled to eight o'clock. Thank God.

"Bedtime," she said.

Alex gave the clock her full and intense scrutiny. "I have to put the game away." She began to collect the cards, carefully placing each one on top of the last and lining up the edges with an engineer's precision.

"I'll get it," Sarah said. Her eldest daughter was the queen of stalling. "You go pick out a book and brush your teeth."

"OK," Alex sighed. She got up and headed for their bedroom. "Come on, Em."

Emma picked up her bedraggled blanket from the floor, hugged it close, and followed her sister in a sleepy gait. As soon as the girls disappeared down the hall, Sarah cleaned up the game. She collected the empty cookie plate and cups, brought them to the kitchen, and loaded them in the dishwasher.

"Mom," Alex shouted. "Em frew up again."

Sarah ran for the bathroom. Alex waited outside the door.

Emma sat on the footstool. "I'm sorry, Mommy. I missed."

She certainly had. Sarah scanned Em's pink kitten pajamas. By some miracle, they appeared clean. Sarah handed Alex the fruit-flavored toothpaste. "It's OK, sweetie. Take your toothbrushes into my bathroom while I clean this up."

The doctor had said Em's nausea could continue for a few days. Sarah mopped the floor with paper towels and disinfectant.

Shoving the soiled mess into a plastic bag, she collected the kitchen trash and went through the laundry room into the garage. Avoiding the stacks of still-full moving boxes, she went out the side door. She kept the garbage can on the side of the house, hidden from street view by a piece of while trellis.

"Hello, Sarah."

Sarah jumped, her hand pressed to her chest. "Troy."

He slouched against a tree. Inside the house, Bandit barked. Sarah glanced back. Mature trees and shrubs lined the side and rear of the lot, providing privacy from the neighbors.

"What are you doing here?" Shivering, she clutched the edges of her sweater together. Her free hand slipped into the front pocket and closed over the fob for the alarm system.

He pushed off the tree and took two steps closer. "I wanted to see if Em was all right."

"You're supposed to call," she said.

"I didn't think you'd answer."

On that he was right. Her thumb found the oversized panic button on the alarm fob. How long would it take for the police to get here if she pushed it? Mike was at home. The only person in the station would be the dispatcher. Who knew where tonight's single patrol car was right now?

Troy walked closer. Sarah backtracked toward the door, trash bag dangling from her hand like a white shield. Could she get into the house before he caught her? What did he want?

"I need to put the girls to bed." Sarah moved sideways. "If you want to talk to Em, you can call her any night before eight."

"I don't want to ask permission to talk to my own kid. I don't want to talk to her on the phone either. I want to see them both every day. I want to see you every day. Why did you do this to us, Sarah?"

"You know why."

"You didn't need to break our family apart." His voice had that hollow, accusing tone that preceded anger.

"It wasn't my fault, Troy."

"Like hell it wasn't." He moved closer. Inside the house, the dog's barking rose to a shrill, furious pitch. "You made me sign those papers."

Sarah eased backward.

"I love you. I want you back," he said. "I did everything you wanted. I gave up drinking. I go to AA. I even took that anger management class. What more do you want from me?"

Cold wind blew through the knit of Sarah's sweater, chilling her. Clammy sweat broke out on her icy palms. "I'm going in now."

"That's not what I want to hear." He let out a *Why do you make me do this?* sigh. "If you don't come home, I'm going to take the kids away from you." Troy's voice sharpened. "The PI was just the beginning. You have a choice. Come back home where you belong and be the fucking good little wife I married, or you'll never see those kids again. Custody can be contested over and over. I'll never let it go."

Sarah's heart slammed against her breastbone. She shuffled backward another step. Her back bumped the door, and her hand closed over the doorknob. She dropped the garbage bag, slipped into the house, and shut and locked the door. The alarm reset with a click of the fob. She might have talked Mike out of renovating the house, but when he'd insisted on installing a security system, she hadn't argued.

Panting, she went into the house and searched for her cell phone. Spying it on the coffee table, she grabbed it. Her shaking fingers wouldn't cooperate with the touchpad numbers.

Damn it!

She stopped, lowered the phone, and took three deep breaths. She was inside. The doors were locked. The dog had stopped barking.

Troy was probably gone. He'd made his point and scared the hell out of her. There was no need for him to stick around any longer.

"Mommy?" Em called.

"I'll be right there." She called Mike, who said he'd be right over, then she went into the girls' room, an explosion of pink and white ruffles and stuffed animals. Sarah sat on a chair between the twin beds and read *If You Give a Moose a Muffin*. Em's eyes drooped, and she drifted off before Sarah finished, but Alex's eyes were wide open when Sarah turned off the light and left the room.

Sarah spied headlights just in time to scoop up Bandit and head off a barking frenzy. "Shh. It's just Mike."

She let Mike in and handed him the dog. Bandit's whole body wagged as Mike rubbed his head.

"Uncle Mike." Alex bolted from the doorway.

Mike set the dog down and caught Alex. "Aren't you supposed to be in bed?"

She grinned. "Uh-huh. Can you read me a story, pwease?" Alex faked a lisp and batted her brown eyes at him.

Laughing, he hugged her and set her down. "Maybe if you're real quiet and stay in your room while I talk to your mommy."

"I will." Alex nodded. "I'm not tired. I'll be awake." She ran back to her bedroom.

Sarah led the way into the kitchen. "Coffee?"

Mike shook his head. "No. Tell me what happened."

Sarah turned on the countertop TV and lowered her voice as she told him about the two encounters with Troy.

"You need a restraining order." Mike frowned. "You'll have to come to the station tomorrow and sign a complaint. Then you'll have to go before the judge on Monday."

"Who turned me down last time."

"Last time Troy hadn't done anything like this, but now he's stepped over the line. This is harassment," Mike said. "Did you call your attorney?"

"I called him on the way back to the inn this afternoon to tell him about the investigator." Sarah rubbed her temple. "I guess I'll be calling him again tomorrow morning. I'm supposed to work tomorrow."

"I thought you were off on Saturdays?"

"Not this week." Sarah had traded days with the weekend sous chef for a court appointment the previous Monday.

"You can come to the station anytime, but I don't have any control over the judge's schedule."

So Monday would be a problem as well. Jacob would not be pleased. Any proceeding at the courthouse involved several hours of waiting. She had to keep her job to keep her kids. But she might lose her job protecting her kids.

"Thanks, Mike. I don't know what I'd do without you," Sarah said.

"I wish I could do more." Mike stood. "Keep the alarm on. Call me if anything spooks you." His gaze went to the dog sitting on his foot. "Or him. Do the kids know?"

Sarah shook her head. "I didn't want to scare them. They have to go with Troy again on Tuesday."

Though the thought terrified her, legally, there was nothing she could do.

"Who's watching them tomorrow?"

"Mrs. Holloway has someone coming to her house tomorrow, so the kids are going there, but it'll be hard on Alex to be cooped up another day." Em needed rest, but Alex had the energy of a squirrel on Red Bull.

"Before Monday, you should let the daycare center know what's going on. You'll need to tell Mrs. Holloway too."

Everyone in town would soon know the dirty details of the Mitchell divorce.

"You know you and the girls can always come and stay with us."

"I know. Thank you. We'll see what happens tomorrow." She'd struggled hard all winter to establish her independence, and she didn't want to backtrack. But if she thought the girls were in danger, she could be packed in minutes.

Mike headed for the hallway and whispered for Alex. The dull thud of bare feet on carpet confirmed Sarah's prediction about her oldest's ability to stay awake. She heard Mike's deep voice in the living room reading to Alex. Her mind conjured an image of Cristan reading to Lucia as a baby. Men could be wonderful fathers. Sarah just hadn't picked the right one.

Ten minutes later, Mike sent Alex off to bed. He leaned down to kiss Sarah on the cheek. "Ethan's on patrol tonight. I'll have him drive by a few times just in case Troy decides to come back."

"Are you going to talk to Troy?"

"Yes," Mike said. "Stay safe."

"Wait." Sarah pulled out her phone. "He sent me some texts. You should read them."

Mike took her phone and scrolled through the messages. "Don't erase these. In fact, save them as screenshots and print them out. Make a copy for your attorney and one for me."

"OK." She nodded, then locked up behind him. She scanned her house. It felt smaller with the blinds adjusted to block prying eyes. A sense of claustrophobia closed down on her. She might have left Troy, but he'd still managed to make her feel vulnerable.

CHAPTER TWENTY

Mike turned into a tidy suburban neighborhood. Minivans and SUVs lined the curving street. Snow coated the lawns. He cruised past Troy's house. When Sarah lived there, the place always projected a cheery, homey image. But now that she'd moved out, the house looked abandoned.

The porch fixture was dark. A light glowed in the living room window, but the drawn blinds blocked Mike's view inside. Troy's truck sat in the dark driveway. Even in the scant moonlight, Mike could see damage to the front end of the truck and corresponding dents in the garage door, as if the pickup had rammed into the house. Several times.

So much for anger management classes.

Mike had handled Troy's temper in the past, but the smashed truck and garage door made the hair on his neck dance. Knocking on the door without backup wouldn't be a smart move.

He steered around a street hockey net and parked his vehicle at the curb a few house away. He picked up his cell phone and called dispatch. "Where's Ethan?"

There were only five officers on Mike's tiny force. Ethan Hale was on night shift.

"Out at the high school investigating a vandalism complaint. Do you need something?" the dispatcher asked.

"No." Mike didn't want to wait for Ethan. Who knew what Troy was up to? The texts he'd sent Sarah disturbed Mike, and it sounded as if the phone calls had been worse.

He ended the call and stared at the house for a few seconds. The thick scar on his thigh ached, and he massaged it through his jeans. He dialed Sean. "Busy?"

"Just finished putting the girls to bed. What's up?" Sean asked.

"I'm at Troy Mitchell's house. He's been harassing Sarah. I have a weird feeling. Want to come sit at the curb in case Troy does something stupid?"

"In case? This is Troy Mitchell we're talking about."

Mike sighed. "Can you help me out or not?"

"Leaving now. Be there in ten." Fabric rustled over the line. Keys jingled. "Wait for me."

"I will." Mike waited.

Sean was a little protective since Mike had been stabbed and nearly died back in October. Ten minutes later, Sean parked his SUV behind Mike's vehicle. They both stepped out and met in the street.

"What's the plan?" Sean asked.

"I'm going up to the door. You stand here and look threatening."

Sean scowled. "We should have killed Troy ages ago."

"So you've said." Mike was almost certain Sean was kidding. But just in case, he said, "You wait here."

Sean leaned against the truck, his arms crossed over his chest, his scowl directed at Troy's front door.

Mike stopped on the stoop and listened. He could hear the television through the front window. Angling his body to one side, he knocked on the door. No one answered. He knocked again. "Troy, I know you're in there."

Footsteps approached, and the door opened. Troy stepped out onto the stoop, leaving the door open. Over his shoulder, Mike could see through the living room and beyond into the kitchen. Broken bits of dishes and glasses covered the floor. The curtain over the sink hung in sliced tatters, and it appeared Troy had taken a sledgehammer to the cabinets.

"What do you want?" Troy folded his arms and glared. His eyes were clear and mean. Maybe sobriety wasn't his best option.

"I heard you visited Sarah tonight."

Troy cocked his head. "Where did you hear that?"

"From Sarah."

"Oh, from Sarah." Troy's tone turned condescending.

"Troy, you can't go there."

"I've been here all night."

"Sarah says differently."

Troy's words were clipped and cool. "Then I guess it's her word against mine. Frankly, I think the word of a cheating slut shouldn't weigh much."

Anger simmered in Mike's chest. "I'm not getting involved in your marital problems."

"Considering you're marrying her sister, that's the funniest thing I've heard all day." Troy laughed without smiling. He leaned closer. His lip curled and fury narrowed his eyes. "Be careful, Chief. Those Parker women are lying little whores."

Mike clamped his molars together. Listening to Troy always sent his teeth into grinding overtime. "I'm just trying to prevent a problem."

"No problems here."

"Anyone see you here tonight?"

Troy waved to the house behind him. "Do you see anyone else here?"

Mike's gaze strayed to the demolished kitchen. "Can I come in?"

"Do you have a warrant?"

"No."

"Then no." Turning his head Troy followed Mike's gaze to the demolished kitchen. "I'm doing some renovating." His lips parted in a creepy smile that would make Jack Nicholson proud. Was Troy losing it?

Mike got to the point. "You can't go to Sarah's house and frighten her. It's harassment."

Troy's eyes glittered. "She's easy to scare."

"So you were there tonight?" Mike prompted.

"I didn't say that. But a man should be able to see his kids whenever he wants."

"That's not how it works, Troy, and you know it," Mike said. "You have court-ordered visitation. If you want to see your kids more, alterations to that schedule have to be mandated by the judge."

"I guess I'll have to get my lawyer on that then." Troy leaned back and folded his arms across his chest, his expression shuttered.

"Where are your buddies tonight?"

"I've given up my friends as part of my AA commitment. They jeopardized my recovery and enabled my addiction." Troy sounded like he was reading from a script.

Mike sized him up. He'd thought a drunken Troy was bad enough, violent and prone to impulsive outbursts of temper. But intoxicated, Troy was easy to predict. Sober, he seemed much more dangerous, capable of thinking, planning . . . "How was that anger management course?"

"I'm practicing finding constructive outlets."

"Good, as long as one of those outlets isn't Sarah."

"You own the house Sarah is living in, right, *Chief*?" Troy asked.

"Yes."

"And after you get married, Sarah will be your sister-in-law." Troy's brows knitted. "Sure seems like your role is a conflict of interest."

"That's no excuse to break the law." Mike tamped down his frustration. "Stay away from Sarah, Troy. I know you were there tonight."

"It's a shame you can't prove it."

"I saw the texts you sent to her."

The cords at the base of Troy's neck tightened. He knew he'd made a mistake. "Private communication between a man and his wife should be kept private."

"Unless one of them is breaking the law," Mike pointed out. "She's no longer your wife, and that house is private property. My private property. Setting one foot on the lawn is trespassing. Don't do it again."

Troy backed into the house and shut the door. The deadbolt slid home with a deliberate click. Rubbing his thigh, Mike went back to his official SUV.

"You all right?" Sean asked, his eyes tracking Mike's hand.

"Fine." But every time he faced a threat, his thigh ached.

"How did that asshole ever talk Sarah into marrying him?"

"Sarah needed somewhere to go." Unfortunately, she'd traded a drunken, abusive father for a drunken, abusive husband. Mike told him about the trashed house.

Sean frowned. "Sounds like Troy is on a downward spiral. His wife left him. His father went to prison. His business is struggling."

"He can't drink or hang with his friends," Mike added. "He has no outlet for his frustration."

"And he can't handle it," Sean finished. "What are you going to do about it?"

Mike opened his vehicle door. "The only thing I can prove is that he sent her a couple of nasty texts. Unfortunately, there isn't much I can do until I can catch him in the act."

"Cameras," Sean suggested.

"You read my mind."

"I'll pick up some cameras tomorrow. I can put them in at the end of the day." Sean got into his truck. "We'll catch that little bastard."

"I hope so, Sean. I have a bad feeling. Troy is unraveling."

———————

At the top of an aluminum ladder on his front porch, Cristan tightened the final screw in the mounting bracket. He eyed the angle of the new surveillance camera and made an adjustment. The camera had a wide-angle lens with a seventy-five degree viewing arc and could capture images at night up to a hundred feet away. No more surprise visitors to his mailbox or driveway. He'd be able to see every car that drove past his house. He climbed down and carried the ladder back to the garage. Inside, he set the alarm before settling in his office.

He added the new camera feed to his existing software. The wide-angle was perfect, giving him a clear view of the entire front yard.

He should go to bed. Lucia had retired hours ago, but he knew attempting to sleep was pointless. With the massacre anniversary approaching, events that would normally be considered flukes, had put him on edge. Lucia was keeping secrets. He'd walked into a convenience store robbery. A private investigator had followed him. He'd been dragged into a domestic dispute. And someone had given Lucia a gift that looked remarkably like the one she'd cherished and lost as a baby.

Too many coincidences.

He'd start with the easiest of the incidents to cross off his list. The PI firm was supposedly hired by Sarah's ex. Cristan's virtual private network provided him online anonymity by hiding the IP address of his computer. Even if his inquiries were detected, no one would be able to locate him. Basic research on A-Plus Private Investigations yielded interesting results. The firm specialized in cheating and infidelity cases and appeared to be legitimate, although their reputation seemed somewhat sleazy. An investigator for A-Plus had recently been charged with impersonating a police officer. The firm had faced previous charges of trespassing and harassment. Most private investigators did not continue to follow their subjects once their presence was discovered. In all likelihood, the firm would cease surveillance. If not, then Cristan would deal with them. For now, it was enough to know that he hadn't been followed by one of Aline's men.

He moved on to the robbery. There wasn't much he could do without forensic evidence or access to law enforcement databases. As hard as it was, he was going to have to trust Mike to do his job.

He had only one avenue left to investigate. His past.

His inquiries yielded few results. He knew from previous reports that Maria didn't often leave her Mendoza vineyard. Her location would have to be verified by a local. Aline, though, was elusive. Tonight was no different. Relocating to the US had distanced Cristan from Aline's threat, but the move also put him at a disadvantage in obtaining information. But money helped to close that gap.

With an anonymous and untraceable e-mail account, he sent a message to the individual he paid to conduct quarterly investigations on Aline Barba and Maria Vargas. Payment for services rendered would be conducted through one of Rojas Corporation's offshore accounts. Cristan knew his contact broke laws getting information and thought it ironic that the person who provided the data that made him feel safe couldn't be trusted.

Unsatisfied, he logged off his computer.

He had no concrete reason to think his location had been compromised. But instinct didn't listen to reason, and every cell in Cristan's body was telling him to pack up his daughter and flee.

CHAPTER TWENTY-ONE

Sarah stared down at the flat tire on the minivan. Troy or accident? She didn't have time for this. She set Em down on the cold ground. At the end of his leash, Bandit sniffed his way to a bush and lifted his leg.

"I'm sorry, kids. Mommy has to change the tire."

Alex dropped her backpack. "Can I help?"

"The best way for you to help is to keep Bandit away from the car so he doesn't get hurt."

Alex choked up on his leash. "I've got him."

Sarah knew how to change a tire, but she'd never changed one on this vehicle. The spare wasn't under the cargo mat, and she spent ten minutes reading the manual to figure out how to lower the tire from the car's undercarriage.

Could they make this any more complicated?

When the spare was on the ground, she followed the instructions to use the retrieval tool and pulled the tire out from under the van. Once she had the actual spare in hand, changing the tire was simple, though not easy. She stifled a curse as she leaned on the tire iron with all her weight to loosen the lug nuts. She really needed to work an occasional push-up into her calendar.

With effort, she hefted the flattened wheel into the cargo area, and added *drop tire at auto service center* to her to-do list.

"We're all ready." She used baby wipes to clean her hands and then strapped the kids into their child seats. Using the hands-free setting on her phone, she called her boss and explained that she'd be late.

"I'll get things started," he said.

"Thank you." Sarah ended the call.

The flat tire was the last thing she'd needed this morning. Herb was kind and patient, but the restaurant needed to function. How long could he afford to employ her?

She dropped the kids and dog at Mrs. Holloway's house, turned around, and drove back to town. At the inn, she stowed her coat and purse and thoroughly washed her hands before entering the kitchen a solid thirty minutes late.

Herb stepped away from a chopping block and untied his apron. He tossed it into a hamper and rubbed his hands as if they were painful and stiff.

"I'm so sorry, Herb."

He nodded. "Is everything all right?"

"Just a flat tire."

"You've had a tough week." His blue eyes said he knew more about her situation than she'd admitted. But then, everyone knew everyone else's business in Westbury. One meal at the diner was more informative than the local news coverage, and Troy was hardly discreet.

Sarah smiled, but behind her happy face, nerves churned. How long could she keep faking it? Troy was dismantling her life.

She hustled to catch up on prep. At two thirty, she raced to the police station to sign her statement, then dropped the tire at the auto center. She stayed at work thirty minutes late to square away her paperwork and discuss the following week's menu with Jacob.

"I'll see you on Monday," Jacob said as he sautéed shallots and bacon.

"No." Hating what she needed to say next, Sarah tossed her soiled apron in the hamper with more force than she needed. "I need to switch shifts with someone on Monday."

Jacob stopped. His wooden spoon hovered over the pan. "Again?"

"I have to go to court. There isn't anything I can do about it." Helplessness paralyzed her for a few seconds. Getting control over her life was proving impossible. Tension constricted her lungs, making her next breath rasp. *Not here.* She reeled in her emotions and exhaled hard.

He frowned. "I'll cover your shift."

"I'm sorry," Sarah said. Frustration curled her hands into fists tight enough to feel the bite of her fingernails in her palms. Damn Troy. If his interference continued, she'd lose her job. It didn't matter how hard she worked if she wasn't reliable. She needed that restraining order. Not to keep Troy away. No piece of paper could do that. But the order would allow the police to arrest him for violations. He wouldn't be able to stand outside her house or leave nasty text messages without experiencing consequences, and the cameras Sean was installing would give her evidence if he showed up at the house again.

With a shiver, she remembered the tone of his last message. He didn't seem to be overly concerned with repercussions.

Resigned, Sarah drove to the auto center. The manager rang up her charges while a mechanic swapped her spare for the repaired tire.

"What caused the flat tire?" she asked as she swiped her credit card.

"Nail," he said. "Happens all the time."

Her tire could have picked up a nail at any time. Troy could be innocent. Though the doubt in the bottom of Sarah's gut didn't let her believe it. She vowed to clean the garage over the weekend so she could park her van inside.

She and the girls were having dinner with Mike and Rachel, so she went home for a quick shower and fresh clothes. Since Mrs. Holloway's house was just down the road from the farm, there was no point driving out there twice. She pulled into her driveway. A blue van sat at the curb at the edge of her property line. It was a commercial-type vehicle, with no windows on the sides. Rust laced the back fender and bumper. Had it been there this morning? Sarah got out of her minivan and scanned her neighbors' homes. Was someone getting work done on their house? On a Saturday? Sarah's next-door neighbor on that side was on a fixed income. Sarah's friend, Kenzie Newell, lived in the house kitty-corner. She hadn't mentioned anything when Sarah spoke to her the day before.

Kenzie waved from her mailbox, then started across the street. She gave the van a suspicious look. "Do you know who owns that van?"

Sarah shook her head. "No."

"Me either. It's been parked there all day." Kenzie wrapped her thick, knee-length cardigan tighter around her body.

"Has it? This morning was such a blur, I didn't notice." Sarah walked closer. "Maybe someone on the street has company."

"Maybe Mrs. Hill?" Kenzie nodded toward the house across the street from Sarah, Kenzie's next-door neighbor.

"Mrs. Hill's male friends drive nicer cars." Sarah laughed. Their mature neighbor had a reputation as a man-killer. "She could be getting something done in her house, but it doesn't look like she's home."

Something about the van set her nerves on edge.

Clutching her mail in one fist, Kenzie hugged her waist. Dark circles underscored her eyes.

"Are you all right?" Sarah asked.

"Delaney is sick. I'm tired and a little jumpy," Kenzie admitted. "I wish Tim wasn't away."

"You've been alone since the robbery?" Guilt swamped Sarah. She knew Kenzie's husband traveled. She should have checked on her neighbor.

"Yes."

"You're welcome to stay with us tonight. I'm running out to my sister's house for dinner, but I'll be back in a couple of hours."

"Thanks, but I'll be OK." Kenzie turned back to the van. "What is that on the door?"

A dark, red-brown substance was crusted on the driver's door, around the door handle. Sarah stepped back.

"Rust?" But as she answered, she knew she was wrong. Fear gathered beneath her sternum, pressuring her lungs. Her breathing grew tight. Colored lights danced in her vision.

"No." The color drained from Kenzie's face. "It's blood."

"It can't be." Sarah walked to the back of the van. More brown-red smeared the handle on the rear door. Without touching the vehicle, she shielded her eyes and peered through the back window.

No! She squeezed her eyelids shut and reopened them. *Oh, dear God.*

"What is it?" Kenzie stepped up next to Sarah.

"Don't look." Sarah tried to block her. Kenzie didn't need to see what was inside the van.

But she was too late. Kenzie's eyes rolled back in her head. She pitched forward as she uttered two breathless words. "They're dead."

CHAPTER TWENTY-TWO

Mike parked in front of his house in town, angling his SUV between Ethan's cruiser and the medical examiner's van. Crime scene tape cordoned off a rectangle at the curb, where a blue utility van was parked. The bumper was rusted, and the first letter on the license plate was a D. The rear doors hung open. A few yards in front of the van, Ethan wrote on a clipboard.

Mike got out of the car and walked over to Ethan. "Where's Sarah?"

Ethan pointed toward a white house kitty-corner to Sarah's. "They went to Kenzie Newell's house. Mrs. Newell's children were there. She was pretty upset."

"Did you run the van's plates?" Mike asked.

"I did. The van is registered to a Jerome Black," Ethan said. "Twenty-five years old. The address on the vehicle registration is an apartment in Scranton." Scranton was twenty minutes away.

Mike approached the van. The faint odor of decay wafted from the vehicle. "How the hell did two bodies sit in a van all day without anyone noticing?"

"Neighbors thought it was a contractor," Ethan said. "Nobody looked inside, and before I opened the back, you couldn't smell anything."

"Hi, Mike," the medical examiner, Gregory Caldwell, called over his shoulder. In his coveralls and gloves, Greg was leaning into the open rear door. His "tool kit" sat on the ground next to his feet. An assistant was snapping photos of the inside of the van.

"Greg." Mike nodded. "What's the status of the county forensics team?"

"On the way," Ethan said. "I called Pete too. Thought we might need some help."

The ME's assistant stepped back. Greg snapped fitted booties over his shoes and carefully climbed into the van. Crouching, he picked his way to the bodies with deliberate steps. The bodies appeared to have been tossed without care. Greg stopped even with the victims' hips and squatted. "I see two gunshot wounds in each chest. Mike, put aside your phobia of all things medical and come over here."

Mike sighed. One panic attack in the ER years ago, and he would never live it down. Though Greg was right. Mike had no desire to get closer to the bodies or the medical examiner, but he steeled himself and walked closer. The men were lying on their backs, arms and legs askew. Despite the beginning-to-bloat facial features, Mike could see the corpse on the left had facial damage. A sweet, metallic odor wafted from the van, like hamburger meat left in the fridge a few days too long.

Mike scanned the van's interior. The bodies lay on a bed of empty food containers, drug paraphernalia, blankets, pillows, and dirty clothing. "Looks like they spent a lot of time in the van. Maybe lived in it." He leaned out of the van. "Ethan, call the landlord at the apartment complex. See if Jerome was still living there."

"OK, Chief." Ethan went to his car.

Mike turned back to the ME. "Any idea how long they've been dead?"

"Not yet. I just got here. This is *CSI*, not *Medium*." Greg grasped the closest arm and moved it slightly, then glanced at the notes on his clipboard. "Rigor has come and gone." Rigor mortis, the port-mortem stiffening of muscles, usually passed in about thirty-six hours at room temperature. "If the van's been outside, cool temperatures over the past few days would have slowed decay considerably."

"This appears to be the van driven away from the convenience store robbery. The victim on the left has some facial damage. Can you check for a broken right wrist on the second body?"

Greg lifted the second corpse's hand and examined the wrist. "I'll need X-rays to confirm, but I'd say yes."

"Then for now, I'm proceeding on the hypothesis that these are the robbers. We know they were alive Tuesday evening," Mike said. "And their clothing appears to be the same as in the store's surveillance video. The van matches the witness's description. Could they have been dead since then?"

"Four days?" Greg considered. "It's possible. They've been dead at least two days, probably longer."

Greg took a scalpel from his kit. Positioning himself next to the closest victim's torso, he made a cut in the shirt. Checking the skin beneath, he made a small incision in the upper abdomen. Mike looked away, but he knew the ME was sliding his thermometer into the corpse to take the body's temperature directly from the liver. Greg read the thermometer, then made a note on his clipboard.

"When will you do the autopsies?" Mike asked.

"I suppose Monday isn't fast enough for you."

"Sooner would be better. I'd really like to know what's going on around here."

"OK. If I can get an autopsy assistant in tomorrow, I'll do it then. No promises, though. Tomorrow is Sunday. I might have to bribe someone."

"I appreciate it." Mike turned to Ethan as he returned from his patrol car. "Were the van's doors locked?"

"No, and the keys were in the ignition," Ethan said. "No answer at the apartment complex. I left a message."

Mike scanned the street. His gaze stopped on his house. Too bad Sean hadn't installed the cameras on Sarah's house yet.

A crime scene van rolled onto the scene. Mike and Ethan backed away as two navy-jumpsuited techs carried their kits to the van. Leaving Greg and the forensic crew to collect evidence, Mike went in search of Sarah. Who had killed the two robbers? And why had their bodies been left outside her house? Sarah had found the bodies. Sarah had a relationship with Cristan Rojas, who'd had a violent encounter with the two dead men. Or was this meant for Kenzie Newell? Had Cristan or someone else killed the men and left them as a sick gift for Kenzie?

After he talked to Sarah and Kenzie, Mike was going to pay Cristan a visit and find out where he'd been the night before. Kenzie had to be the reason the bodies had been left here. Mike couldn't fathom a connection between Sarah and the dead men.

Except for Cristan, who seemed to be the hub in this particular crime wheel.

Lieutenant Pete Winters, Mike's second-in-command, rolled up in his cruiser.

"Sorry about canceling your day off," Mike said.

Pete climbed out of the vehicle. His bulldog face creased. "My wife is hosting her book club tonight. I'd rather question witnesses or babysit dead bodies. Where do you want me to begin?"

Mike pointed to the crowd that had gathered in a driveway. "Start taking statements. This is a small, nosy neighborhood. Someone saw something. I was here at nine o'clock last night. The van wasn't there, so it must have been left after that."

"Got it." Pete headed for the gawkers.

Leaving Ethan with the van, Mike turned to study the street. The afternoon was cold, but the sun warmed the top of his head. Mike recognized everyone. He'd spent part of his childhood in the house, and his mother had left it to him when she died. He'd lived there alone for the last decade. He knew most of the residents who lived on the surrounding blocks, except for Kenzie Newell. She and her husband hadn't lived on the street long before he'd moved in with Rachel and turned his house over to Sarah.

A white sedan approached with obvious caution and pulled into the driveway of the small blue house directly across the street. Mike started toward the woman getting out of her car. Mrs. Hill had the best view of the van and Sarah's house. The trunk of the sedan popped open, and Mrs. Hill rounded her car to remove a canvas grocery bag.

A divorced sixty-year-old, Mrs. Hill had retired from selling real estate several years ago but still dressed every day as if heading off to work. Today's slim black slacks, white blouse, and wool trench coat showed off a trim figure that belied her age.

"Hello, Mrs. Hill." Mike stopped next to her car. "Can I carry these in for you?"

"Thank you. I'd appreciate that."

Mike hefted a canvas tote full of canned cat food and a twenty-pound plastic container of litter.

Unlocking her door, she led him into the foyer. "How are you?" Her gaze swept his body from bottom to top. "You look great. Rachel Parker must agree with you."

He flushed at her close appraisal. "Thank you, ma'am."

She tilted her head. Beneath a short cap of blond hair, her clear brown eyes flickered to the street over his shoulder, then returned to study his face. "But you're not here for a social call, are you?"

"No, ma'am."

Her gaze flickered to the medical examiner's vehicle. "Let's talk in the kitchen."

He shut the door behind him and followed her into a bright kitchen decorated in shades of gray.

"You can leave those by the pantry." She set her grocery bag on the black granite counter.

Mike set the bags down.

"Tea?" She lit the burner under a kettle on the stove.

"No, thank you." Mike took a seat at the kitchen island.

"Can you tell me what happened?"

"There are two dead bodies inside that van."

She paused, her hand on an upper cabinet. "Well, that's unexpected."

"It was," he agreed. "Did you notice that van on the street?"

"Yes." She took a delicate white cup from a cabinet and tossed a tea bag into it. "I saw it when I left to run errands after lunch. I assumed it was a repairman of some sort."

"Were you home last night?"

Her eyes sparkled. "I had a date."

Must have been some date. From the years he'd lived across the street, he knew she had an active *social* life. Mike had watched many men leave her house in the early morning hours. "What time did you go out?"

She toyed with a long strand of black pearls around her neck. "Oh, I didn't leave. Howard came here for dinner around seven."

Mike had been at Sarah's house at nine o'clock. The van wasn't there then. "So you didn't see any vehicles that didn't belong on the street after nine?"

"Honey, by nine o'clock, we were too busy to look out the window." Mrs. Hill wasn't known for her discretion.

Mike felt the blush heat his face. "Do you know Sarah Mitchell?"

"Yes. She has the most adorable little girls. If my son doesn't grow up soon, I won't see grandchildren before I'm dead. Can you believe he's almost forty and doesn't even have a steady girl? He says he's afraid of commitment. What a crock. He's just lazy."

Mike steered her back on track. "What about earlier, say about eight o'clock? Did you see a pickup truck that didn't belong on the street?"

Mrs. Hill raised her eyebrows and grinned at him as if amused by his discomfort. Then she sobered. "A pickup truck? Like the one Sarah's asshole of an ex drives?"

"Yes, ma'am."

"I didn't see it last night, but that son of a bitch has been all over this block for the last couple of weeks."

"Do you remember any specific times?"

Propping one hand on her hip, she hummed. Her chin dropped, and her fingers twirled a pearl for a few seconds. "No, I'm sorry. I wasn't paying attention."

"If you think of anything, give me a call." Mike offered her a business card.

She waved it off. "Honey, I already have your number."

Kenzie Newell's house was next in line. Knowing she had small children, Mike knocked instead of ringing the bell. She opened the door, clutching a child's stuffed kitten in front of her body. "Chief O'Connell."

"Hi, Kenzie. Can we talk?" he asked.

Her head bobbed in a tight nod. "Come in."

She led him to a small, warm kitchen. Sarah sat at the round, oak table. In the high chair next to her, a flush faced toddler played with a bowl of Cheerios. Through a doorway, he could see a little girl of about five staring at a cartoon on the television.

"I'll need to talk to you separately," Mike said.

"OK." Sarah got up from the table. "I'll wait for you at my house. If you need anything, call me, Kenzie."

"Thanks," Kenzie said.

The front door opened and closed. The kitchen was small, but Kenzie stood as far away as she could from Mike while staying in the same room. "Are those the men from the robbery?" Her voice trembled. From the circles under her eyes, he thought she hadn't been sleeping. "I don't know anything for sure yet, but it's possible," Mike said. "When did you notice the van?"

Kenzie leaned against the countertop. Her fingers rubbed the kitten's ear. "I noticed it this morning. But I was busy all day. Delaney had a fever. I finally got her down for a late nap and went out for the mail. I desperately needed a breath of fresh air. I don't know why the van suddenly bothered me then. I thought I was just being paranoid. I've been a little nervous since the robbery."

"Have you talked to anyone about what happened in the convenience store?"

Shaking her head, she clutched the toy tighter.

"The robbery was a traumatic event. It's perfectly normal to have some residual effects. A counselor might help."

The toddler swept her bowl of Cheerios to the floor. Her body stiffened and she cried, "Kitty."

Kenzie handed her the toy, liberated her from the chair, and lifted the child to her hip. "I don't know if we can afford that. I didn't go back to work after Delaney was born. Daycare for two kids cost more than I made."

Delaney rested her head on her mother's shoulder.

"Are you alone here?"

"My husband works for the mine. He's been in Australia looking at some equipment." Her eyes dropped. "He should be home Monday."

Mike dug out another business card. "I want you to call me if you can't get help through your insurance."

She took the card and stacked it with her mail. "OK."

But he doubted she would, and he made a mental note to follow up with her. At the very least, his secretary would know of a community or church-based support group that might help.

Mike went on to subject number two. "Do you know Sarah's husband, Troy?"

"Yes." The baby squirmed. Kenzie bounced and swayed to soothe her.

"Have you seen him around lately?"

She brushed a hair off her forehead. "I saw him last night. He was parked in front of my house."

Yes!

Mike whipped out his notebook. "Do you remember what time you saw him?"

"The truck parked there around seven thirty. I was trying to get Delaney to bed, but she was fussy so we were walking around the house. I'm always a little paranoid when Tim's out of town, but this week . . ."

Mike wrote down the information. "If I need you to sign a statement that you saw him here last night, will you do it?"

She hesitated. "He scares me, and Tim's not home. Is it important?"

"It is." Mike said.

She looked away for a few seconds. "If he scares me, he must terrify Sarah. I'll do it."

"Thank you."

"Is that all? I need to start dinner."

"Yes. Thanks for your help." Mike went outside. He didn't learn much about the blue van, but the two statements on Troy would help Sarah get her restraining order. He turned back toward his house.

Gotcha now, Troy.

"Mike." Greg climbed out of the van and waved him closer.

"Did you find something?" Mike approached, the uncharacteristic furrow between the ME's brow putting him on edge.

"I have two wallets." Greg held two nylon billfolds in his blue-gloved hands. He opened the first. "Jerome Black." Then the second. "Rodney Lint."

The dead men's identities weren't startling discoveries, but the envelope under the bodies was extremely interesting.

"Mike, there's one more thing." Greg motioned him toward the back of the van, where two morgue attendants were lifting a black-bagged corpse onto a gurney.

Mike walked to the side of the gurney. Greg unzipped the bag to the corpse's waist. He separated the edges and opened the man's shirt. Above the bullet wounds, someone had carved a *V* into the man's chest.

━━━━━━━━━━

Decisions. They had the power to change the course of a man's life. Cristan hadn't always made good choices. There was one in particular that stood out in his mind, a night that he could still picture as clearly as a movie in high-definition. The night he'd made the choice from which there was no return.

He spent his early years working with the horses, growing

stronger, and training to be one of Franco's fighters. His duties had gradually increased in scope. He went from being a lookout to a soldier. By the time he turned twenty-one, Christopher was fully integrated into Franco's private army.

AK-47s were the milk and bread of the arms trade. Lightweight, reliable, and abundant, Kalashnikovs accounted for twenty percent of firearms worldwide. Franco had sold a few crates of AKs to a Buenos Aires gang. Unfortunately, the gang had undergone a recent change in command. The new leadership, short on money and overflowing with ego, had ordered the ambush of the delivery, shooting Franco's men and demanding a payment renegotiation.

The last thing Christopher had wanted to do that night was drive into Buenos Aires to shake down a drug lord. Eva had been due to return to school the following day. He didn't fully understand what had grown between them over the past nine years. Companionship, camaraderie. Passion. Whatever it was, they understood each other, and when she was gone, he felt empty. He'd wanted to spend their last night together on a midnight ride on the pampas, not chasing drug dealers through a sprawling urban slum.

But what could he say? He and Eva had kept their relationship hidden. Once Eva graduated from college in a few months, they planned to bring her father in on their secret.

The alley had smelled of paco, a toxic cocaine by-product that two boys had been smoking. Both of the teens would likely be dead within the year. Standing at the entrance, he was hit hard with guilt. Franco had saved him from a similar fate. How could Christopher begrudge his benefactor anything he asked?

Franco had two objectives when a deal went awry: recoup his merchandise and make a statement. He was a hands-on leader. His team of well-armed, well-trained men swept through the dealer's shantytown headquarters like fire through the pampas. Under Nicolas's direction, Christopher and Eva went down the alley and crept up the back stairs of a building, where they were instructed to wait for the signal to enter. He tucked his machine gun into his hip and listened for the signal. At the familiar soft whistle, Christopher reached for the doorknob, intending on a silent entry. But Eva swung around him and burst through the door.

Wood smacked wood. Muzzle flashes flared in the dark room as someone opened fire.

Eva!

Christopher dove on top of her, covering her body with his own and pinning her behind the inadequate protection of a half wall. Bullets zinged above their heads. Bits of wood and stucco rained down on his back.

He lifted his head and scanned the dark room. Bright flashes gave away his enemy's location. He pushed Eva's shoulders down and slid off of her body. "Stay down," he shouted in her ear over the gunfire.

Christopher belly-crawled to the edge of the wall. He drew his knife from the sheath on his calf, balanced it in his fingertips, and threw the weapon with a flick of his wrist. The point stuck the gunman in the throat. He emitted a strangled sound and dropped to the floor.

Nicolas was behind him, helping Eva to her feet.

Anger narrowed her eyes. "I could have taken him."

"You—" Nicolas pointed at her nose, "—would be dead if Christopher hadn't acted."

She crossed her arms and sulked, her insolent expression looking more fifteen than twenty-two. Relief nearly buckled Christopher's knees. Fear for his own life never affected him the same way as a threat to Eva's.

Men flooded the room. At Nicolas's direction, the gang members were bound and dragged down the stairs to the dirt-floored main room where Franco waited. One by one, he scrutinized the men who had dared defy him. Wild-eyed, they knelt before him. There was no interrogation. No question-and-answer session. Franco didn't want excuses. He wanted to set an example. He wanted revenge.

But he turned his attention to Christopher.

"Nicolas told me what happened. Eva is impulsive. She needs to temper her anger." Franco cupped the back of Christopher's neck. "It was fate that brought you to my family. Thank you, Christopher, for saving my daughter. You are as much a son to me as if you were my own blood." He waved toward the gang leader as if presenting Christopher with a gift. "Now, like a true Vargas, claim our retribution."

Christopher had killed before, but always in the heat of a fight. Pulling the trigger in a do-or-die situation was entirely different from firing a bullet into a bound man's forehead. His heart rammed into his ribcage. Adrenaline from the earlier firefight faded, leaving a trail of nausea in its wake. His mind detached from his body as he lifted his weapon and fired. Blood spattered the concrete.

A barrage of conflicting emotions swept through him like a wildfire. Shame. Elation. Horror. What had he done? Embarrassed that his hand was shaking, he lowered the gun.

"You are worthy." Franco nodded, his eyes shining with pride.

Even as his conscience—and stomach—recoiled at the sight of the body, Christopher's heart swelled at Franco's praise. For the first time, he felt like he belonged. He felt like family.

CHAPTER TWENTY-THREE

"Let me help you with that." Cristan went into his daughter's purple-and-white room. "I thought you were working on that English paper."

"I am." Balanced precariously on top of her rolling chair, Lucia held a hammer in one hand and a nail in the other. "But I want to hang the picture Sarah gave me over my bookshelf."

"All right." Cristan took his daughter by the elbow while she climbed down. "Next time use the stepladder in the garage. A chair with wheels isn't the best choice for a step stool."

She blushed. "I guess not."

He took the hammer from her hand. "Where do you want it?"

"There." She pointed.

Cristan tapped the nail into the wall. He held out his hand for the picture, and Lucia handed it over. He felt for the metal hanger on the top of the frame and positioned it over the nail.

Lucia tilted her head and folded her arms over her waist as she studied the picture. "It's not straight."

Leaning back, he raised the right side a fraction of an inch. "Better?"

"Perfect." Lucia smiled, her eyes on the photo. "It was really nice of Sarah to do this for me."

"Yes, it was."

"She's really great." Lucia's voice turned wistful. "I wish I had a mother like her."

"That would be very lucky indeed." Cristan was not following her into another discussion about him and Sarah. It was too soon, for both of them.

Cristan examined the picture. His eyes were drawn away from the main image to the crowd leaning on the half wall that encircled the arena. Behind a large, bald man, a dark-haired woman stood. Cristan's muscles went lax as he stared at her. She was turned away from the camera, her face in profile. He took in her posture, the way she held her head, the angle of her jaw.

Eva.

He shook his head. Impossible. His wife was dead. All Lucia's talk about him dating must be triggering memories. He squeezed his eyelids closed briefly, then looked back at the picture. The camera had focused on Lucia and Snowman. The background was blurred.

He went downstairs to his office, took a magnifying glass from the desk drawer, and returned.

"What's wrong?" Lucia asked.

Cristan held the glass over the woman's face. The image was larger, but still fuzzy. "Nothing." But he couldn't shake the icy ball in the pit of his stomach.

He descended the stairs to the first floor, went to his office, and closed the door.

Sinking into his leather chair, he propped his elbows on the mahogany desk. Who was that woman in the picture? It couldn't be Eva.

He wanted to leave, to pile their packs into the Range Rover and drive until dawn. A few hundred miles of distance between Lucia and Westbury would make him feel more secure. He'd promised Lucia they could stay here. But if she was in danger, he'd have no choice but to break her heart.

Cristan paced. Frustration burned in his gut. He should have been honest with his daughter. His goal was to protect her from the truth and truly give her a fresh start. But he was beginning to see that his "fresh" start was nothing of the sort. Their lives were still controlled by what had happened in Argentina.

The doorbell rang, and Cristan startled. He glanced at the clock. Seven o'clock. He'd thought it was later. Not that it mattered. No one came to their house. They had no close neighbors, and they had never been bothered by solicitors. He left his office.

Lucia stood at the foot of the stairs. "Who's at the door?"

"You didn't invite a friend over?"

She shook her head.

Cristan peered through the tiny hole in the door at the police chief standing on the doorstep. "It's Chief O'Connell. Probably just follow-up paperwork."

He ducked into the closet and turned off the alarm system, then opened the door. "Mike."

"Cristan." The police chief stepped into the house. He held a yellow clasp envelope in his hand. "Hi, Lucia."

"Hi," she said.

Sensing bad news from the police chief, Cristan turned to his daughter and prompted, "Don't you have a paper to finish?"

She rolled her eyes. "I guess. Bye." She jogged up the stairs.

Cristan waited for Lucia to disappear down the upstairs hallway. "I assume this isn't a social call?" he asked Mike.

"No."

Cristan led the way back to his office. He shut the door. The cop's face was even more serious than usual. "What happened?"

Mike didn't waste words. "We found the robbers."

The tension in Cristan's chest eased. Not bad news. "Did you arrest them?"

"They're dead."

"Dead?" Imagining a shoot-out between the robbers and the police, Cristan rounded his desk and sat. "Did they resist arrest?"

Mike took a chair facing him. "No. Their bodies were found in the back of their van. They've been dead several days."

"Someone else killed the robbers?" Cristan asked, perplexed. If the police hadn't killed those men . . . "Who?"

"I wish I knew."

"Maybe they argued with other criminals," Cristan suggested. "They were obviously not law-abiding citizens. I imagine they associated with others of their sort."

"That's one possibility." Mike cocked his head. Suspicion narrowed his eyes. "The van was parked near Sarah's house. Kenzie Newell also lives on that street."

Cristan didn't know how to respond. Of all the news the police chief could have brought, this was the least expected. "I don't know what to say."

"You'll never guess what we found in the van."

Cristan waited, feigning calm. He couldn't even speculate. Mike tossed the yellow envelope onto the desk. Cristan opened the clasp and slid a stack of papers onto the blotter. He thumbed through at least twenty photographs of him. There was a picture of him and Lucia in the car outside the school and another of him coming out of the Quickie-Mart. He paused on an image of him carrying Emma into Sarah's house. The photo had been taken at night. From the grainy, greenish tint to the picture, he could tell that the photographer had used some sort of night vision module and a telephoto lens. The action captured was innocent, but his body language was protective male, not platonic friend. Clearly, he didn't conceal his feelings for her as well as he thought. Did he always appear this way around her? Maybe this was why her exhusband had reacted with jealously.

Cristan sat back, his mind reeling. "This appears to have been taken Thursday night. I drove Sarah and Emma home from the emergency room. This isn't a secret. Why would anyone care about this?" And who had been outside taking pictures? Someone had been watching him, and Cristan hadn't noticed. That alone was enough to *freak him out*, as Lucia would say. He'd lost his focus when he came to Westbury. He should have continued to move from city to city. Crowds protected their anonymity. Finding a lovely home for his daughter had been a mistake. He had made too many bad choices early in his life, and the price of his transgressions was a lifetime of running. For him, there would be no escape from the violence of his past.

Cristan moved to the last picture. His heartbeat stammered as he stared at a photo from at least twelve years ago: he and Eva in her favorite Buenos Aires restaurant. He slid it into the pile without commenting. There was no need to bring the old image undue attention, but his thoughts whirled. The picture, taken on Eva's birthday, had occupied a frame on their wall in their apartment in Buenos Aires. Who could have taken it?

Maria. As the sole remaining family member, she would have been given their personal possessions. He supposed the picture could have been stolen by Aline, but Maria would have had easy access.

"I'm just as confused as you are," Mike said. "But it seems there's some relationship between you and those robbers."

"But what could it be?" Cristan responded honestly. "I had never seen either of them before Tuesday."

The woman in the picture in Lucia's room spun in his head. It had to be related. Too many coincidences. Too many unknowns. Lucia would be devastated, but they had to leave. Tonight. He couldn't wait to find out what was going on. He had to preempt any possible attack.

Maria was here.

He thumbed back to the image of him and Sarah. The thought of never seeing her again left a hollow ache in his chest. "The only person who had an issue with me that night was Sarah's ex-husband."

"No deep, dark secrets in your past?" Mike rested his elbows on his knees. His clasped hands fell between his knees.

Cristan's smile felt as if it would shatter the frozen muscles of his face. "I live a quiet, boring life, Mike."

The chief didn't blink. "Except for this week."

"Except for this week," Cristan admitted. But he was going to put the past week—and all the associated danger—behind them. Tomorrow, they would be far away from Westbury.

"Have you checked with Sarah's ex?" Cristan asked. There was no better way to get rid of a cop than to dangle another suspect in front of him. "He is the only person I can think of who has taken any interest in me. He seems irrational and jealous. I was only being a good friend and helping Sarah that night."

Mike's eyebrow twitched. "Nice of you." Clearly, the cop didn't believe him.

"Troy?" Cristan prompted.

"Troy is next on my list." Mike stood, leaned over the desk, and swept the pictures into the envelope. "I might need you to identify the robbers."

"I only saw one of their faces, and his nose was bleeding heavily at the time. His features were distorted."

"Anything you can tell us will help," Mike said.

Cristan ushered him out of his office and toward the foyer. "Of course. I'll do whatever you need. Call me."

"Don't worry. I will." Mike went out the front door. "Good night."

Cristan shut the door on the police chief and went up the stairs. Despite his dread of the coming conversation, urgency quickened his steps. He knocked on Lucia's door.

"Come in."

He opened the door. She was lying across her bed, her laptop open to a text document in front of her. Her eyes locked on his face, and she sat bolt upright. "What happened?"

Cristan hesitated. "The two men who robbed the convenience store have been found."

"That's good, right?" she asked.

He sat down on the corner of the bed and took her hands in his. "They're dead. Someone killed them and left them near Sarah's house."

Confusion tilted her head. "What? Why? That doesn't make any sense."

"No one knows yet."

"But Chief O'Connell's going to find out, right?" she asked. "That's his job."

"It is." Cristan searched for the words to soften the blow and found none. "But we have to leave."

"No." Lucia snatched her hands out of his and backed away from him. "You promised."

"I'm sorry. I truly wish this hadn't happened." The pain in her eyes lanced his heart.

"I don't understand." A tear escaped from her eye. She swiped it away with an angry hand. "Those men robbed the convenience store. What does that have to do with us?"

"It's too much of a coincidence that their bodies were left outside Sarah's house."

"Sarah's house. Not ours."

"There were pictures of me in the van," Cristan said, wishing he didn't have to give her the details, but knowing he couldn't just expect her to blindly obey. She deserved answers if he was going to rip her life up by the roots.

Trembling, Lucia stumbled off the bed. She backed to the wall and wrapped her arms around her waist. Her face paled. "I'm not leaving."

"We have to. It isn't safe here anymore."

Two spots of color brightened her cheeks. "Safe from what? What aren't you telling me?"

He couldn't lie to her anymore. She wasn't a child. She needed to know. When the time came for her to be on her own, she would have to be on guard. In order for her to be prepared to live without him someday, she needed to know the nature of the threat she faced. "Your mother wasn't killed in a car accident."

Lucia's mouth opened, then closed before she uttered a word.

Cristan continued, "She was murdered."

Tears ran down Lucia's cheeks, but she ignored them. Her gaze was completely focused on Cristan. "You lied."

"I didn't want you to grow up afraid."

"You've lied to me my whole life." Her words ended on a sob she tried to swallow.

"I did what I thought was best. You were very young. I couldn't take the chance that you would give something away."

"In case you haven't noticed, I haven't been very young for a long time." Her palms flattened against the Sheetrock behind her, as if she wanted to go through the wall. "When were you going to tell me the truth?"

He had no more excuses. "I should have told you before now."

"Who murdered my mother?"

"An enemy of her family." He took a step toward her.

She slid along the wall away from him. "And?"

How could he tell her that the person trying to kill him could be her aunt? If so, he couldn't imagine that Maria would want to kill her niece, but could she want to take Lucia? Why, after all these years? The anniversary of the massacre was in three days. Perhaps that was the trigger.

He phrased his words carefully. "I am afraid the people who killed your mother will come for you." That was the truth. He had spent the last twelve years terrified that Aline would find them.

"This is why we've been running for my whole life? That's what we've been doing, right? All those moves had nothing to do with your job."

"Yes."

"I don't care. I'm not leaving. I have friends here. I have a life. What good is being alive if I'm miserable?"

"You can make new friends."

"No." She wiped her face with both hands. "I won't do it."

"I'm not giving you the choice." Cristan sharpened his tone, hating every word. "You have two hours to pack what you want to take. Everything has to fit in the back of the Range Rover."

"No."

"I'm sorry, Lucia. I wish it didn't have to be this way. But I love you more than life itself. I cannot allow any danger near you when I have the power to keep you safe." Cristan went to the door, his body heavy, his heart black. "Two hours."

"I'll hate you."

"I know, but at least you'll be alive." He walked down the hall and into his own room. He rubbed the center of his chest. Breaking his daughter's heart was fracturing his. But what could he do? Nothing. There would be no end to the price Lucia would pay for his sins.

He packed what he needed in ten minutes, then went to the basement to double-check their go-bags and load everything into the SUV. He never drove the Range Rover. It wasn't even a registered vehicle. He kept three different license plates that could be changed as he moved across the country. As he loaded the SUV, his mind drifted to the one subject he'd suppressed all evening: Sarah.

If those men had been placed intentionally near Sarah's house by someone from Cristan's past as a message to him, then he'd brought her into his nightmare. He reached into the bottom of the duffel bag and withdrew a small, locked box. The numbers spun easily as he set the combination. Opening the box, he pulled out passports and driver's licenses. Who should he be next? Each of his escape plans was complete with bank accounts and credit cards. Provisions had been made to dissolve Rojas Corp and funnel the assets into an offshore account.

But he'd led a killer to Sarah's door.

He stared at the passports in his hand. He couldn't do it. He couldn't leave and abandon Sarah and her children. They were targets now, and that was his fault.

But what was he going to do? His daughter had to come first. Maybe he could help Sarah after he got Lucia safely hidden. At the very least, he would warn Mike.

Heading for the steps, he went in search of his daughter. He had much more to tell her. It was time he was entirely—or at least mostly—honest with her. There were some things about the day her mother was killed that Cristan would never want her to know.

"Lucia?" he called as he approached her room.

No answer. The door was almost closed. He pushed against the wood. Her room was empty. The picture Sarah had given her was on the bed, the back of the frame pried open, the article removed. He checked the closet. No backpack. He ran through the upstairs calling her name. She couldn't have left. She couldn't be out there, alone. Cristan's mind ran to the woman in the newspaper photo, the one who reminded him of Eva, and to the two dead men with pictures of Cristan in their van. Something dangerous was out there, waiting, planning. He could feel malicious intent in the air. The thought of his little girl, alone and vulnerable while an unknown threat lurked, sent panic spiraling through him like a drill.

"Lucia!" He ran down the stairs and swept through the rooms on the first floor. In the hall, the wall frame that had contained the photo of Eva and Lucia was empty. A last check of the basement confirmed his worst fear.

Lucia was gone.

CHAPTER TWENTY-FOUR

The small boat rocked in the current. In the shadow of an overhanging tree, she trained her night vision binoculars on the back of Christopher's house. He'd chosen well. The house sat on a hill. Open ground on all four sides gave a possible intruder nowhere to hide. Likewise, there was no way for a car to linger in the road without being seen. Her lieutenant was sitting down the road. The best he could do was watch the end of Christopher's driveway.

And the only vantage point to view the rear of the house was the river. She'd borrowed a small boat and paddled downstream to a huge tree. Exposed roots clutched the bank like talons. She'd tied her boat to a root in the shadows. From here she was invisible.

She checked her phone. No messages. Christopher hadn't left by car. A light in the basement went on. What was he doing? When would he run?

At this point, he had to know someone from his past was after him. Carving the *V* into the bodies was a message she hoped he'd received. If not, the pictures in the van would speak loudly enough. He'd be prepping to flee now, and getting him out of that fortress he'd built was her first step. A light on the top floor went out. They were still in the house.

If she knew Christopher, it wouldn't take him long to put his gear together. He'd be ready.

The back door opened and a figure slipped out into the dark. She followed the movement across the meadow. The body was too small to be Christopher. Luciana!

The child raced across the field directly toward her.

Stunned, she lowered the binoculars. This was an unexpected, but welcome, event. If she took Luciana, she could make Christopher do anything. The child was his weakness.

The sound of steady footfalls and regular breathing approached. She stilled. Water lapped on the sides of her boat. There was no way she could get to the bank in time to intercept the girl. Better to wait and follow her into the woods, where there was no chance of Christopher hearing the encounter.

She held her breath as the girl passed within thirty feet of her, ran along the edge of the water, and disappeared into the forest. Once the footsteps had faded, she pulled the boat to the edge of the bank and climbed out. Her foot slipped in the half-frozen mud, and icy water invaded her boot. Ignoring it, she clambered onto the giant root ball.

Her gaze went to the house. She raised her binoculars. There was no sign of Christopher. Did he know Luciana was gone? Would he follow? Just in case, she checked her weapons. Handgun, spare clip, knife. She had a flashlight but preferred not to use it. Being in the dark for hours, her eyes had adjusted.

She headed into the woods on the trail Luciana had used. There was no sign of the girl, but the child had covered the meadow rapidly. She was obviously in good condition. Catching her would not be easy.

Especially for one in less-than-prime shape.

The cold bit into her lungs. Once the darkness closed around her, she slowed her pace, accessed the GPS on her phone, and viewed a map of the area. On the other side of this patch of woods was a local highway. If Luciana followed the river, that's where she would end up. She estimated the distance and time it would take to traverse the trail in the dark, then sent her driver a message.

When Luciana emerged from the woods, he would be waiting.

After the emergency vehicles had left her street, Sarah sat alone in her kitchen. Since their bedtime had come and gone, Mrs. Holloway had offered to keep Alex, Em, and Bandit overnight. The house was too quiet, and Sarah's nerves hummed. Every time she closed her eyes, she saw the bodies in the van. Mike was right. She shouldn't stay here alone tonight. She'd pack a bag and drive out to Mike and Rachel's place.

She dialed her sister's number.

"Hello?" Rachel answered, her voice sounding uncharacteristically weak.

"Is everything all right?" Sarah asked.

Rachel groaned. "I think I ate something bad."

"Do you want me to come over?"

"No," Rachel answered. "You'd better keep your distance in case this is a virus instead of food poisoning. I'd hate to give this to the girls. I'm going to crawl into bed and stay there."

"OK. But call me if you need anything." Sarah ended the call. Maybe she could sleep on Mrs. Holloway's couch.

Her phone buzzed in her hand. She tensed, expecting the caller to be Troy.

Cristan.

She answered. "Hello."

"Sarah, Lucia is gone."

"What do you mean, gone?"

His voice was low, angry, and desperate. "We had an argument. She ran away."

"OK. Calm down. How long has she been gone?"

"Maybe two hours. Maybe a bit less."

"Then she couldn't have gotten too far." Sarah could picture him pacing. "Call Mike. I'll come and help you look for her."

To her surprise, he didn't argue. She left the house, locked up behind her, and headed for Cristan's house. She knew where he lived. She'd dropped Lucia off once, but she'd never been in his house.

The big stone house sat on a hill at the end of a long driveway. Sarah parked and went up to the front door. Cristan answered before she knocked. He must have been watching for her.

"Did you call Mike?" she asked.

"Yes. He's notifying the state police and county sheriff's department. He's also calling in some firemen to help look for her."

"Good." Sarah stepped into the foyer. With the heavy stone exterior, she'd expected a closed-in house full of antiques, but Cristan's furnishings were sleek and minimalistic. He'd only bothered with the bare essentials. The sole attempt to make the space more personal was a row of photographs in the hall. She paused. One of the frames hung empty and crooked. Other than the framed pictures, the walls were mostly bare. She peered through the doorway into the living room. No knickknacks adorned the furniture. They lived here, but the sparse decor suggested a reluctance to make this place a home.

He paced the oak floorboards, one hand clutching the back of his head.

"I assume you searched outside."

"Yes." He pivoted and took three strides down the hall. "I drove several miles in each direction as well."

"How did she get out?" Sarah asked.

"I'm not sure. The security system was off. She must have turned off the alarm and walked out the door." He swept a hand through his thick black hair.

"Where were you?" Sarah asked.

"In the basement."

"Did you try to trace her phone?"

He pulled a cell phone from his pocket. "She left it in her room." *Smart kid.*

"I called her best friend. She's in New York City with her mother and hasn't heard from Lucia."

Sarah walked closer. His pain and fear were palpable. She reached out and touched his arm. "We'll find her."

He stopped, the tendons on each side of his neck as tight as electrical lines. "Thank you. But she was very upset with me."

"Want to tell me what you fought about?"

"Not right now, but she has every reason to be angry." Misery etched his face. "I haven't been the best father."

Sarah squeezed his forearm. "Parenting is hard. No one is perfect. All we can do is our best. Trust me. I know all about making mistakes."

He nodded. "I have to go out and look for her."

"What did Mike say?"

"He wants me to stay here in case she comes home, but I can't sit still while she is out there." His hand swept toward the door. The scope of his gesture suggested the motion stood for bigger fears than he could express. "Alone."

Sarah tightened her hold on his arm. The muscles under her palm were rigid. "Mike will find her. You need to trust him."

A painful sigh left his chest, and his face was twisted with misery. "I don't know if I'm capable."

She wrapped her arms around his waist, the muscles of his back hard and taut under her fingers. "I hate to ask this, but what do you think Lucia would do if she saw you? Would she come to you or would she hide?"

"I don't know." The weight of his chin settled on the top of her head.

"Can you tell me what you fought about?" Sarah's heart ached for him.

"No." His body shifted. His hands gripped her arms, and he pushed her away. His dark eyes closed off again. "I lied to her, and I don't know if she will ever forgive me."

"She loves you."

"Love isn't always enough. Tonight, Lucia feels as if I betrayed her, and I can't blame her. I deserve all of her hostility." He dropped his hands from her arms and took a step backward. "There are many things you don't know about me, Sarah. If I told you the truth, you wouldn't want to be anywhere near me either."

"Why don't you just tell me and let me decide for myself?" Apprehension swept through Sarah. He'd never volunteered much information about his past, and she'd always sensed he was holding back something important. But she'd never been afraid of him. Never once had she feared that he would hurt her. If anything, she'd felt safer in his presence, her instincts were certain that he would protect her from danger. But the storm rolling through his dark eyes put her on edge. Whatever he was holding back was big.

"Now is not the time. I need to find Lucia." He shook his head. "She is in grave danger."

CHAPTER TWENTY-FIVE

Sadness tasted like salt. Lucia sniffed. Her eyes watered as the freezing wind swept down the trail. She tugged her hat over her ears. When she'd been riding outside that afternoon, she'd been fine, but it felt much colder at night. And dark. Very dark. A thin cover of clouds obscured the moon.

She tripped, fell to her knees, and landed on something hard. The blow sang through her cold bones like the tuning fork her music teacher used in class. Tears slid from her eyes, the moisture running down her face in icy tracks. She swiped her cheek with a gloved hand. A sob trembled in her chest. She sucked it back.

Sitting on the ground and crying wouldn't accomplish anything.

She checked her watch. Knowing her father could track the GPS in her phone, she'd left it at home, hidden in a drawer on silent. Eventually, he'd figure out that she hadn't taken her cell with her, but every minute she could gain was more space between her and him.

He'd betrayed her.

She never wanted to see him again, but he was the only person she had in the world, and thinking about never seeing him again sent more tears spilling down her cheeks. She packed her sorrow deep inside. If she let it out now, she'd be paralyzed. She'd curl into a ball and die there on the trail.

Maybe that would be for the best. Right now she didn't feel like she had a reason to live.

Stumbling to her feet, she reached into her backpack for her flashlight. She switched it on. The narrow beam of light in front of her somehow made the woods seem even darker. She'd been afraid to use it when she'd been close to the house. But she was far enough from home now, and she hadn't heard any sounds to indicate he was following her. He'd been in the basement loading the car when she'd slipped out the door. Hopefully, he wouldn't notice she was gone before she'd put some more distance between them. When she'd left the house, she'd known better than to walk alongside the road. It was only a matter of time until her father came after her. Instead, she'd run across the meadow and followed the river toward the forest path. The ground was hard and cold and she'd made sure her hiking boots didn't leave prints. She'd covered the open ground as quickly as possible and sought the darkness of the woods. She breathed easier when she entered the cover of the trees.

To her right, the sound of the river gave her direction. She and Dad had hiked this trail often last fall, but they hadn't been out since winter hit. Dad didn't like the cold.

Shivering, she trudged forward. Inside her boots, her toes stung with cold, and her knee ached where she'd landed on the tree root. She pictured her father. He'd be terrified once he noticed she was missing. Part of her wanted him so suffer, but she also felt guilty, which was stupid. *Hello? He'd lied to her.*

Her mother had been murdered and he hadn't bothered to tell her. Grief raged in her chest, as fresh as if she'd just learned of her mother's death. How could Dad have done this to her? Her entire life was a lie. Anger fueled her steps and drove her forward.

She continued through the dark forest for a long time, until her feet felt like blocks of ice and the trail ended in a road. Lucia turned right and walked along the shoulder. She was visible on the open road, and a sense of vulnerability fell over her.

Her father's words rang in her mind. *I am afraid the people who killed your mother will come for you.* That is not the kind of information you keep from a person, she thought.

The forest ran alongside the road, but there wasn't a trail. She walked across the bridge, stopping in the center to watch the dark water rush underneath. She trained her flashlight on the river and watched a branch get caught up in the current and swept under the bridge. Her past felt like that branch, whisked out from under her feet faster than she could process. She didn't know how to react. She didn't even know where she was going, other than the barn. Wherever she went, she had to say good-bye to Snowman first.

She wished she could take him with her. If they had lived out West, it might have been possible for her to ride away and hide in the wilderness. But northeastern Pennsylvania was too crowded. There was no disappearing in the woods. She'd have to go to a city, where it would be easier to blend. She had the protein bars she'd taken from her go-bag, but only two bottles of water. Any more made her pack too heavy to carry. She'd also taken three hundred dollars, but she didn't know how far that would get her. Probably not very far. Where was the nearest bus station? If she still had her phone, she could call Jenna and see if she could help. Jenna and her mom were in New York City for the weekend, but she'd be back tomorrow. Maybe she could hide in their basement for a few days, just until she made a plan.

She left the bridge and continued walking along the shoulder of the road. The eight-mile trip to the barn felt much shorter when they drove, but she had to be getting close. She checked her watch. She'd been walking for almost three hours. Maybe her detour through the trees had added some distance to her journey.

An engine sounded behind her. She turned. Headlights approached.

Had he found her? Not already. She couldn't bear to see him. Lucia ran toward the woods. Hiding behind a tree, she realized she'd left her flashlight on. *How could she be so stupid?* Hoping the driver of the car hadn't seen the light, she switched it off. Darkness fell around her. Something moved in the branch above her head.

The vehicle slowed and stopped alongside the road. The driver must have seen her. Lucia peered around the tree trunk. A figure got out of the vehicle. Her heart rapped against her rib cage. Fear slid along her skin like cold water when she realized the headlights were too high for the vehicle to be a car—and the driver wasn't her father.

Cristan paced his kitchen. Trusting someone else to find his daughter was ripping a hole of frustration inside him. How could he be here, safe in his kitchen, when his little girl was out in the dark facing unknown dangers?

"Drink this." Sarah pushed a cup of coffee across the island toward him.

"I'm giving Mike thirty more minutes. If he hasn't found her by ten thirty, I'm going after her." Waiting was killing him.

"How long has she been gone now?" Sarah asked.

He glanced at the clock. "Three hours." The longest three hours of his life.

"How far could she get in three hours?"

"It's dark and cold, but she took provisions with her." He'd made it easy for her by keeping her go-bag in his bedroom closet. He'd always wanted them to be able to get out of the house quickly in an emergency. There was a fire ladder in his bedroom for a second-story exit, which she thankfully hadn't attempted to use by herself. But she had turned his paranoia against him. Her pack was loaded with a flashlight, power bars, and clothing. But how far could a thirteen-year-old get alone? "In better weather, we hike regularly. With a full pack, Lucia can manage three miles of flat ground in an hour. Allowing for the darkness, I would guess six miles."

Sarah took his hand. "So she hasn't gotten too far."

"Six miles is far. It's cold and dark . . ."

"I know." She squeezed his hand, and the comfort she offered tempted him. "I won't claim to know what you're feeling, but every time my girls are with Troy I have this ball of fear under my heart. Sometimes it feels like I can't breathe."

That was exactly how he felt, as if a deep breath would crack his ribs.

She wrapped both hands tightly around his. "Mike is one of the best men I know, and this town knows how to pull together. They'll find her. I know you want to be out there, but if she's as mad as you think, she'd probably run from you."

"She was very angry." Guilt rested on Cristan's shoulders. He wished he could go back twelve years in time and not lie to his daughter. But at the time, honesty hadn't been practical, and he knew if he had to do it all over again, he'd probably make the same choices. He'd hidden the truth from Lucia for multiple reasons. Yes, he'd wanted her to feel normal, but he'd also feared that a young child would not be able to keep such a large secret. There was no way he would have been able to allow her to attend school, and he couldn't imagine the stress knowing their true situation would have placed on her. As she got older, telling her the truth had felt more and more impossible.

"She's a teenager. They're volatile. She'll get over it."

"I doubt it." He simply had to find her. "I can't sit here any longer. I have to look for her. Would you come with me?"

"Of course."

"Thank you." He slipped into his coat and pulled the keys from his jacket pocket. His phone beeped. "It's Mike."

Cristan answered.

"I've got her." Mike wasted no words.

Relief nearly crippled Cristan. He covered the speaker and mouthed, "He found her."

"Thank God." Sarah exhaled.

Cristan listened to Mike for a few seconds. "I'll be right there."

He ended the call and turned to Sarah. "He spotted her walking on the shoulder of the road. She was headed toward the farm. I'm going there now." He hesitated. "I hate to impose, but would you still come with me? Lucia likes you, and at the moment, Mike says she doesn't want to speak to me. I think she could use a woman to talk to."

"Of course I'll come." Sarah donned her coat. "Lucia might be angry with you, but she loves you."

"I'm not sure she can forgive me that quickly." As he led Sarah out into the darkness, he wondered if his daughter would ever be able to forgive him.

———

Sarah followed Cristan out to Rachel's house. He turned into the entrance to the farm and parked in the gravel lot. Sarah pulled her minivan in next to his Mercedes. As Cristan got out of the car, Mike strode out of the barn. He jerked his thumb over his shoulder. "She's with Snowman." He put a hand on Cristan's chest, stopping him. "If I were you, I'd let Sarah talk to her first."

Fresh anguish passed over Cristan's face. With a resigned nod, he went to the house with Mike.

Sarah went into the barn. The dirt aisle was hard and cold under her shoes, and she zipped her jacket to her chin against the chilly night. Horses snorted and feet shuffled in straw. She stopped at a half door with a brass plaque that read *Snowman*.

The white gelding stood in the middle of his stall. Next to him, Lucia hugged his neck. The horse's head was bent around the child's body, as if he were hugging her back.

"I don't want to talk to you," Lucia said without moving.

Sarah rested her forearms on the door. "Lucia?"

The girl lifted her head and turned. Tears streaked her blotchy face. Seeing Sarah, she wiped her face on her sleeve. Behind the redness, her skin was pale. "Sorry. I thought you were my dad."

"Are you cold?"

Lucia shook her head. "I'm OK."

"I know you're angry with your dad, but you scared him tonight."

Lucia's face hardened. "He lied to me. About everything." Snowman shifted, bumping her shoulder with his nose. Lucia wrapped an arm under his neck.

"Do you want to talk about it?"

Lucia rested her temple against the horse's head. "No." Her face was as full of misery as Cristan's.

"I don't know what he did, but I do know that he loves you."

"He shouldn't have lied to me." Lucia stroked the horse's nose with a gloved hand.

"That's what he said."

Lucia straightened. "Really?"

"I think he regrets not being more honest with you. People make mistakes." Sarah had made plenty of her own. "No one is perfect. But I know better than anyone that regrets don't make bad decisions go away."

"No. They don't." Lucia sighed, sadness trembling in her breath. "I don't know if I can forgive him."

The child's love for her father made his betrayal even more painful.

Sarah sighed, her own regrets swamping her. "I wonder if my girls will feel the same as you do when they get older. Marrying Troy was the biggest mistake I ever made, but I can't undo it. My only option is to move forward and minimize the damage."

"You don't lie to them."

Sarah shoved her cold hands into her pockets. "I've omitted plenty. Some things they're too young to hear. They wouldn't understand, and the information would likely just frighten them. That's the best decision I can make today, but someday I might regret my choice."

Lucia met Sarah's gaze. Anger and defiance glittered in the girl's eyes. "He always told me my mother was killed in a car accident."

Apprehension stirred in Sarah's belly. "That isn't true?"

"She was murdered." Fresh tears escaped Lucia's eyes. "That's not something you hide from a person."

Shocked, Sarah opened the stall door and went inside. "I'm so sorry."

Lucia sniffed. A sob trembled on her lips. "He wants to move again. He gave me two hours to pack."

"I don't understand."

Lucia sobbed. "I don't want to leave my friends. I don't want to leave Snowman behind. This is the first time I've ever been really happy."

Sarah's chest ached with empathy for the distraught child. She moved forward and wrapped her arms around her.

Lucia leaned against Sarah. Words tumbled from the child's mouth, as if she couldn't hold them back any longer. "We used to move every year. Some places we didn't even stay that long. This time he said it would be different. He promised."

"What happened tonight?" Sarah rubbed her back. The child's body shook as she cried harder. Poor Lucia. And poor Cristan. His wife had been murdered, but why would he keep her cause of death a secret? It didn't make sense.

"Chief O'Connell came to the house. Dad sent me upstairs. After the chief left, Dad came into my room and told me to pack." Lucia sniffed. "It was all a lie. I don't want to start over again." Lucia pulled back and swiped a glove under each eye. "I don't want to leave you and the girls either."

"What can I do?" Sarah asked. Mike had likely gone to talk to Cristan about the dead robbers being found. Why would that trigger a decision to run from Westbury? What was Cristan hiding about his past?

"Talk him out of leaving. Please, Sarah," Lucia begged.

"I'll try, but I don't know why he thinks you have to go."

"He's afraid the person who killed my mother might come after me."

CHAPTER TWENTY-SIX

Cristan followed Mike into the kitchen, his heart thudding in his chest like an empty drum. Lucia was safe, thanks to the police chief. What would have happened to her if Mike hadn't found her, if she hadn't trusted him enough to get into his vehicle?

If Lucia wouldn't talk to him, he both hoped and feared she'd talk to Sarah. At this moment, all he cared about was keeping his daughter safe. Repairing their relationship, if that was even possible, would have to wait. But keeping his secrets at this point looked like a slim possibility.

He stepped into the warm kitchen. Mike poured two cups of coffee and handed Cristan one.

"Thank you for finding my daughter."

Mike nodded. "She was cold and tired and glad for a ride."

If Lucia didn't know the big cop well, would she have hidden? Would she still be out in the dark, alone?

"Where was she?"

"About two miles from here," Mike said.

"She was coming here?" Damn. Cristan should have thought of that possibility. The most important things in Lucia's life were Sarah, her girls, and Snowman.

"Teenagers usually head for a bus station or a friend's house, but you said Jenna and her mom were away for the weekend. Without a ride, the bus station is too far away, so the barn was the next likely option. If there's anything I've learned since I met Rachel, it's that girls love their horses more than almost anything."

Cristan set the coffee down on the island and eased onto a stool. He was relieved that his child was safe, and exhaustion hit him hard.

"Now you want to tell me what the hell is going on?" Mike asked.

"We had an argument."

"She was pretty upset."

"Teenagers are volatile." Cristan used Sarah's words.

"Lucia has always seemed like a pretty steady kid." Mike wasn't buying the story. "Look, I don't know what your deal is, but I can't help you if you don't level with me."

Cristan clamped his teeth together. Telling Mike, or anyone else, about his past went against the basic premise of his life. "That isn't possible."

"Why not?"

Cristan spun. "I'm not who you think I am."

Mike sighed. "I figured that out months ago."

"And you've done nothing about it?" Now Cristan was confused.

"Look, you've lived here two years and haven't done anything wrong. You helped me when Rachel was in danger. You stood up for Sarah. You saved four people in that convenience store. That said, I can't make promises. I'm operating in a vacuum, Cristan. I can't protect you or the other residents of this town unless I know what I'm up against."

"Lucia would be safer if we leave. We can start over in a new city. I told her this tonight, and she reacted badly." Cristan nearly choked on the truth. "She likes it here."

Mike set his cup on the counter. "Why isn't she safe here?"

"Because I suspect the people who killed her mother have come looking for her."

"We'll get into the whos and whys in a minute." Mike digested the information with a frown. "But do you really think moving her to another place will keep her safe? Whoever you're running from found you here. Why do you think they won't track you down again?"

"I know how to disappear."

"I'm sure you do, but I think you'd better look at this from a different perspective." Mike leaned his palms on the counter. "If Lucia runs away in a new city, who will pick her up on the side of the road? Who will make sure she's safe? And God forbid, anything ever happens to you, wouldn't you feel better knowing there are people who will step up and take care of her?"

Cristan opened his mouth to argue, but Mike held up a hand. "What happens to Lucia if these people kill you? Do you have a provision for that?"

"I admit there's a gap in my escape plan."

"Does she know about any of this?" Mike asked.

"Not until tonight." Cristan shook his head. "I wanted her to have the most normal childhood possible." But now he realized he'd put her in danger. "It was a mistake. I should have told her." He should have done many things differently.

Mike nodded. "Here's another thing to consider. Lucia won't be eighteen for five years. What if you're killed tomorrow? She's a child. She'd end up in foster care. I hate to say it, but the foster system isn't always a safe place. And if these people track her down then, she'd be on her own. I want you to think hard about this. She walked almost five miles in the cold tonight. When you were in the police station the other night, she stayed with Sarah. She came out of the woods tonight and got into my car. If you start again in another city, how long will it be before she has anyone she trusts?"

The turmoil in Cristan's chest burned. Mike was right. If he hadn't found her on the side of the road . . . If Lucia hadn't been heading for his farm . . . If she hadn't felt she had a safe place to go, then who knew what would have happened to her?

"What made you decide to leave Westbury tonight?"

Cristan inhaled and exhaled a single, long breath. Once he started talking, there would be no way to take back the information. Mike would know everything Cristan had been hiding for twelve years. But what else was he going to do? The cop was right. Lucia needed other people in her life other than him. She needed a safety net rather than an escape plan.

Cristan spied Lucia's backpack on the floor next to the kitchen island. He opened it and rooted through the contents for the two images that Lucia had taken from the house: the picture of her and her mother and the photo in the newspaper. Cristan found the pictures in a manila envelope and pulled them out.

He lined the images up next to each other. "When you came to tell me about the bodies, I was hanging this picture in Lucia's room." He pointed to the photo of Lucia and Snowman and pointed to the dark-haired woman in the crowd. "This woman looks like my wife." He tapped the picture of Eva and infant Lucia.

Mike squinted at the images. "It's blurry, and with the hat and scarf, not much of her face is visible."

Cristan turned up his palms. "I could be wrong, but the image took my breath away. Do you have a magnifying glass?"

Mike rummaged through his top drawer and pulled out a handheld magnifier. He held it over the newspaper photo. "It could be the same woman, but I wouldn't bet on it, and I thought your wife was dead?"

"She is, but she had a younger sister, Maria. The resemblance was strong between them."

"OK. Say this is your wife's sister, Lucia's aunt. Why did she kill those men?"

Cristan paced the kitchen. He scrubbed a hand over the top of his head. "I'm not sure. My best guess is that she wants Lucia. Wait." The robbery jumped into Cristan's thoughts. "During the robbery, one of the men told the other to forget about Kenzie. He said, 'He's the one we need.' At the time, I thought he was referring to the store manager, and that they needed him to open the safe. But now I wonder if *I* was the target."

"Why would they want you?"

"I wonder if Maria hired them to make me collateral damage in that robbery."

"You think the robbery was staged?" Mike asked.

"I don't know. But it makes sense. Maria hires those men to kill me, but she wants it to look like a tragic accident. When I'm gone, she either steals Lucia from a foster home or swoops in and says she's a long-lost relative. A DNA test would validate her claim. She wouldn't have to deal with me."

"Then when the men were unsuccessful, she kills them because they can identify her." Mike rubbed his leg. "But why not just dump them where no one will find them? It doesn't seem to make much sense to attract attention to the murders."

Cristan slapped his palm on the stone counter. He swore as the answer clarified in his mind. "She was hoping I'd run."

"You want to explain that?"

"She couldn't find a way around my home security."

"You have an alarm system. I assume you have some weapons." Mike held up a hand. "That I don't want to know about. You've built a stronghold, and she wanted to flush you out of it."

"And I almost did exactly what she planned." Cristan resumed pacing. He cupped the back of his head, where an ache pulsed.

"I'd like to know why you're running from this woman. You want to tell me the whole story from the beginning?"

The kitchen door opened and Sarah walked in. Her cheeks were reddened from the cold. "I want to make some hot chocolate for Lucia."

"I don't suppose she's ready to talk to me?" Cristan asked.

Sarah shook her head. "Give me a little more time."

"When you go back to the barn, would you check in on Lady?" Mike asked. "Rachel thinks it won't be long now. With her a couple of weeks late, she wants the vet on hand in case the mare runs into trouble with a big foal."

"OK." Sarah stripped off her hat, gloves, and coat, and set them on a stool. She opened a cabinet and pulled down a thermal mug. Lighting the burner under the teakettle, she added an envelope of hot chocolate to the mug. Then she stopped and studied the men for a few seconds. "Am I interrupting something?"

Cristan shook his head. "No. You should hear this too. I'm not who you think I am, Sarah."

She turned and gripped the edge of the counter, as if bracing herself for bad news.

"My name is Christopher Navarro. Twelve years ago I was living in Buenos Aires with my wife and infant daughter. My wife's father was an arms dealer. Franco Vargas's main customers were gangs in Brazil and Argentina."

"Is that Vargas with a *V*?" Mike asked, his face grim.

"Yes." Cristan took a breath. Sarah had not moved and her face was expressionless.

He continued, "Franco owned several properties, but his favorite was the ranch outside Buenos Aires, where he bred polo ponies. After Lucia was born, I took a leave of absence from the business. I cannot explain what happened to me when my daughter was born. From the first moment I held her in my arms, I was a changed man. I no longer wanted to be a part of the violent world I'd lived in all my life, and I certainly didn't want that life for my child. I tried to talk Eva into running away. I bought new identities for the three of us, but she was afraid, both of her father's wrath and of one of Franco's long-time enemies, Aline Barba.

"A meeting was held at the ranch. Eva had gone ahead. Lucia and I were late. We argued about that." The last time he'd seen his wife, they'd fought. "We arrived in time to see the beginning of the attack. There was an explosion and gunfire. I took Lucia and hid. I ran while my wife and her family were slaughtered. Every last one of them. I'm not proud of what I did, but at the time, I was concerned with only my child's safety."

Sarah's face had gone white.

"During the massacre I heard the men speaking Portuguese. I assumed the attack was orchestrated by Franco's Brazilian business rival. Aline Barba had a personal vendetta against the Vargas family. Her organization and my father-in-law's conflicted over a sale to a gang in Bolivia years before. Aline's son was killed in the ensuing altercation."

"Do you think this Aline Barba is the one behind all this?"

"I don't know. Aline had sworn vengeance against the entire Vargas clan. Eva was the one who killed Aline's son, so I would think her revenge was complete after the massacre." Cristan stopped pacing. "The only two people who would have any interest in me and Lucia are Aline Barba and Maria Vargas."

Mike's gaze dropped to the picture. "You're sure your wife is dead." With a quick glance at Sarah, he cleared his throat. "You saw her?"

Cristan didn't blink. The sight of Eva's ruined face and body was clear in his mind as it was that day twelve years before. "Yes." He lifted his glass and swallowed cold coffee. The liquid hit his stomach like pure acid. "There is a death certificate. DNA tests were done."

"Where was your wife's sister during the explosion?" Mike asked.

"At school in California. In addition to the ranch and penthouse, Franco owned a vineyard near Mendoza. That is where Maria usually stayed when she returned to Argentina during school breaks. She was supposedly studying business and interning at a winery in California, but Eva often complained that Maria was having too much fun. My wife was a very serious woman. She didn't believe in leisure activities, aside from the occasional polo match."

The teakettle whistled. Sarah jolted. She went to the stove and poured hot water into the mug. Steam rose, obscuring her face. "How much of this does Lucia know?"

"Not much," Cristan said. "I was afraid the knowledge would be a burden for a child, but it seems I should have been more honest."

"We all make mistakes." Sarah stirred the cocoa, her eyes studying his.

Could *she* forgive him for his deception? Because he realized that it mattered very much to him that she could.

"I'm not sure that, under the circumstances, I would have done anything differently. I've kept many of the awful things Troy has done from my girls because they didn't need to know." Sarah added milk to the cocoa and screwed the cap on the thermos. "I'd better get back to Lucia."

"Thank you," Cristan said. He wasn't sure which he appreciated more, Sarah's kindness toward his daughter or her empathy toward him. But would she still be as supportive if she knew about the men he'd killed? That was a conversation they'd have in private. He liked Mike, but a cop wasn't the audience he wanted for a confession.

She shrugged into her coat, put on her gloves, and went back outside.

Once she was gone, Mike said, "There are a few other things I didn't tell you about the bodies."

Cristan waited.

"We've withheld this information from the media, but each man had the letter *V* carved into his chest."

A chill slid through Cristan's blood. "*V* for Vargas."

"Seems like," Mike agreed. "Have you ever seen that before?"

"No." Cristan scrambled to make sense of it all. "Does that mean the men were killed by a Vargas or was the killer simply sending me a message?"

Mike shrugged. "Who knows that you're still alive?"

Cristan shrugged. "Everyone. I was a person of interest at the time. Once the police sorted out the identities of all the victims, they knew I was missing. Luckily, I'd gotten Lucia out of the country before that happened."

"Did they think you were involved?"

"I was a suspect for a period of time, but charges were never filed. Franco had many enemies. Eventually, the police concluded that the scope of the massacre was too big for one man, and they focused their investigation on Franco's competitors."

"So you're not wanted for murder in Argentina?"

"No," Cristan said.

"Do you know where Maria Vargas is today?"

"The last time I conducted a discreet query, she was living on the vineyard in Mendoza. Maria never had any interest in the family business. To my knowledge, she hasn't resurrected the enterprise."

"But this Aline Barba, she is still active?"

"Yes. Very. Her organization absorbed many of Franco's clients."

"I'm going to need more information to investigate."

"I have a dossier on both Maria and Aline, but I only have photos of Maria. Possibly there are pictures of Aline in some government database, but nothing I could hack into without triggering alarms." Cristan paced. "If you start making legitimate inquiries, the dust trail your investigation kicks up will let everyone know exactly where we are."

"It seems they already know," Mike said.

"I can't take that chance."

"I'll make a copy of Maria's photo, I'll check the local motels. She must be staying somewhere." Mike tilted his head. "Also, I have a friend I've used for digital inquiries that require discretion. Would you have any objection to pulling him into this?"

"My daughter wishes to stay in this community," Cristan said. "But if my identity is compromised, I won't be able to stay here."

"I'll do my best," Mike said. "You're going to have to trust me. I'm not looking to ruin Lucia's life."

"Trusting people isn't one of my skills."

"Maybe you can learn from your daughter." Mike set his coffee in the sink. "I don't see where you have many options."

CHAPTER TWENTY-SEVEN

Sarah leaned on the door and watched the chestnut mare.

Cristan walked into the barn and stood next to her. "Some mares won't foal while someone is watching."

"Rachel's worried about her."

He went into the stall and walked a circle around the gentle mare as she chewed her hay. Smiling, he stroked a hand over the horse's rounded belly. "She seems fine."

"Where did you learn about horses?"

"My father-in-law bred polo ponies on his ranch."

"I thought he . . ." Sarah searched for neutral words to say *sold illegal guns.* Lucia was in Snowman's stall at the other end of the barn. She needed to hear the truth from her father's lips. She went into the stall and rubbed Lady's nose.

"Horses were his love. The other was his business," Cristan said. "Franco was a hard man, and he did some terrible things, but he wasn't all bad." He paused, looking away as if afraid to see her response. When he spoke, his voice was low, almost a whisper. "I killed men, Sarah. Granted, none of them were innocent. They were all violent men, but taking a life leaves a stain on a man's soul."

"Then why did you do it?" Sarah asked, still trying to wrap her mind around all he'd told her. Try as she might, she couldn't see the man she knew as cold-blooded. Killing for a very good reason, that she could imagine very clearly. He would fight for a cause or to defend loved ones. Cristan had a warrior's nature. But she didn't see him as a murderer.

"I was a boy when I went to live with Franco. What he gave me went beyond food and shelter. For the first time in many years, I belonged. At the time in my life, I would have done anything for that feeling, to not be alone."

"It sounds like he manipulated you."

"If Franco recruited mass numbers of orphans and turned them into his soldiers, I would agree with you. But he only took three of us, one at a time, over the years."

"What happened to the others?" Sarah asked.

"They died in firefights before I joined the family."

"That's horrible."

Cristan shrugged. "Back then, I would have willingly given my life for Franco. Before he took me in, I wasn't really living." He paused, his dark eyes meeting hers. "I don't want to say I didn't know any better back then because it sounds like an excuse. So I'll say that I hadn't yet learned to value life. I was young and very alone. Having people who cared about me felt like everything."

As different as she and Cristan were, they had that in common. The very human need to love and be loved.

Sarah rested her forehead on the mare's neck. "I felt the same way when I married Troy. My mother was mentally ill. My birth sent her over the edge. Dad loved her more than he ever loved us. My sister was five when I was born, and she practically raised me. When my mother died, dad turned to alcohol. He couldn't cope. No, he didn't *want* to cope with my mom's death. Rachel had left for the European show-jumping tour. So, it was me and Dad in that house." She splayed her fingers on the horse's neck, absorbing some of the mare's tranquility. "When Troy said he loved me, I jumped at the chance to marry him. I don't even think I knew what love was, but I wanted it so badly, I didn't think. I said yes."

"Is your father still living?"

"He is, but my mother's life—and death—destroyed him. He loved her with his whole heart, and she wasn't capable of loving him back. She took drugs. She cheated on him, and he let her. Over and over again." Sarah shivered. "I used to stop and check on him twice a week, but this week I told him I couldn't do it anymore. He can destroy himself, but I can't watch. I feel relieved I don't have to witness his daily decline and feel guilty for abandoning him. To make it worse, I feel guilty that I'm relieved."

"I'm sorry." He took her hand from the horse's neck and interlaced their fingers. "Guilt and love shouldn't go hand in hand, but they often seem to. Do you still love Troy?"

"No." Sarah lifted her head. Troy had destroyed any feelings she'd had for him, but Cristan's wife had died. She hadn't betrayed their love. "Do you still miss your wife?"

"That's not an easy answer. When Eva died, I was still very much in love with her, but I don't know if she could have changed her ways or if the man I am now could have lived with her." He lifted her chin with a finger. "Anyway, it's time to move forward."

"Lucia will want to hear all this."

"And I'll tell her most of the truth." He stepped closer, his hand settling on her arm. "How about you? How do you feel about my lies? About my past?"

"I haven't had much time to process what you said." She *should* mind, and the fact that she didn't gave her pause. One thing she did understand was regret. She wasn't proud of the decisions she'd made when she'd been younger. "And frankly, when I'm with you, I have trouble considering the negatives to whatever is developing between us."

"What *is* developing between us?"

"I don't know." But it was definitely *something*.

"Fair enough." He dropped his hand.

She closed the gap between them. His news had surprised her. Her rational mind told her to be cautious, but she couldn't hold his lie against him. "I've always sensed you were holding something back, but your revelation wasn't quite what I'd expected."

His dark eyes held hers. "I'm sorry."

She studied his face. "If my girls were in danger, I'd do whatever it took to keep them safe. I don't blame you for lying."

"You are too forgiving. Definitely too good for a man like me." Cristan touched her cheek.

"I'm hardly perfect."

"I think you're perfect." He stroked her cheek with his thumb. "I feel like I could taint you with my touch. I did some things I'm not proud of in my old life, but I don't think of myself as that man anymore."

"I understand," she said. "I feel like an entirely different woman from the girl who married Troy. But I have children to consider. So I'm not making any decisions or promises."

His gaze dropped to her mouth. When he leaned in to kiss her, the brush of his lips to hers was featherlight. Her hand settled on the center of his chest, his heartbeat thudding under her palm. Desire simmered inside her. She knew whatever might happen between them would have to go on the back burner. Too many things were happening too quickly. But she wanted this man.

He pressed his forehead to her temple for two seconds before pulling away. "I wish it could be different. But there's someone out there who doesn't care if I've changed. Until I've dealt with my past, I can't look forward to a future, and being with me could be dangerous. I won't allow you or your girls to be caught in the crossfire."

She nodded, dropping her hand. "The children come first."

"That we have in common," he said.

"It's not all your fault." She stepped back. "I have enough going on in my life too. I need to settle things with Troy before I can move on."

His mouth twisted in a feral, almost cruel smile. "I could take care of Troy for you."

"I want to be independent."

"And I respect that." With a nod, Cristan zipped up his jacket. He led the way out of Lady's stall. Frowning, he stared down the aisle. "Do you think she'll talk to me yet?"

"There's only one way to find out."

"It's going to be a long night." He took Sarah's hand in his. "I don't know what I would have done without you tonight. Thank you."

It was going to be a long night for her as well. Sarah checked her messages. Her in-box was empty. She'd been trying to get Troy to stop calling and messaging her for days, but now that he had, she was even more worried.

Maybe he'd stopped harassing her. No. Troy would never give up so easily. If he hadn't called her, there was a reason.

The woman removed the earpiece and tossed it on the table. Outside the long window of the rental home, moonlight brightened the river that ran behind the house. They'd missed the perfect opportunity to grab Luciana. The policeman had beaten her driver to the girl by a minute. Damn this small town and its tight-knit community.

As if missing Luciana wasn't enough, the audio transmitter she'd planted in Sarah Mitchell's purse had picked up a telling discussion between Christopher and the pretty brunette. Christopher had told her everything. He'd trusted her with his secrets. Listening to tonight's conversation, an icy ball of hate formed beneath her heart.

He thought he could put his past behind him and play house? He was in for a rude awakening. There was no way in hell she would allow Christopher to have a happily ever after. His future was painfully clear. She was going to squeeze an incredible amount of suffering into a short period of time.

Only three days remained until the anniversary. Closing her eyes, she let her predicament percolate, and an idea bubbled to the surface of her mind within minutes. She'd show Christopher that his past wasn't going away. It was headed straight at him like a battering ram.

CHAPTER TWENTY-EIGHT

Cristan stopped in front of Snowman's stall. Lucia was running a soft brush over the gelding's flank.

"We're not leaving. Not now, anyway," he said.

She froze for a couple of seconds. Then the brush resumed its long strokes.

"Do you want to talk?" he asked.

She gave her horse a final pat and turned toward him. Her chin was up but her eyes were hurt as she shook her head. "Not really."

"Fair enough." Cristan wished he didn't have to push the conversation. But it couldn't wait. The past was hunting them. Lucia needed to know the risk. But how much detail would he give her about Eva? He'd loved his wife, but did their daughter need to know about her late mother's dark side?

"But I guess we have to." Lucia leaned on Snowman's shoulder, her face distrustful. "So, tell me about my mother."

She deserved to know the whole truth, but would she forgive him when she learned how much he'd been concealing?

Cristan told her the same story he'd given Sarah and Mike, minus the gory details of the carved letter *V* in the corpses and the fact that Eva had killed Aline's son. Eva was gone. There was no point in tainting her memory further.

"Is there anything else I need to know?" Her question was blunt, but many more lingered in her eyes. Perhaps she couldn't absorb any more information.

"No," he said. "I'm sorry I lied to you. I honestly didn't know what else to do."

"I don't know how I feel about it." But the hand holding the brush was clenched tightly enough to blanch her knuckles, and moisture shone from her eyes. She was barely keeping her emotions in check.

Relief eased the tension in Cristan's chest. She might not have forgiven him, but she was talking to him. For now, that's all he could expect.

"Wait." Lucia straightened, as if she was still processing all the information he'd given her. "This means I have an aunt."

"Yes."

"Do I have any other family alive?"

"I suppose it's possible there might be a few cousins floating around who weren't at the ranch that day," Cristan said. "If so, they could very well also be in hiding."

"But the possibility means I might not be completely alone, right?" she asked.

"Right, but looking for them would give away our true identities. That would be a very dangerous proposition. The world you were born into wasn't like this community." He waved his hand at the stall door. "There was family love and loyalty, but also greed and violence. Even now, I don't know if the family was betrayed that day."

If he didn't have a child to protect, Cristan wouldn't be hiding from anyone. But he wouldn't do anything to risk her life.

"But someday, in the future, we might learn the truth. Then I could look for my family."

"Maybe," he admitted. "But first we have to deal with the current threat. No more leaving the house without me. No more disarming the security system. No more leaving your phone behind."

"OK." She nodded, then her gaze leveled on his. "But only if you promise there will be no more lies."

"No more lies." He put his hand atop hers. Her return squeeze sent a shiver of guilt through him. He reasoned that the details he'd just kept from her weren't truly lies, just gory details she didn't need to know. But his gut said he would someday regret his omissions. But then, he had plenty of experience with regret.

———

There were defining moments in a man's life. The last time Cristan saw his wife alive was one of them. Reliving his story over and over reminded him that he never had the chance to kiss her good-bye. Twelve years after her death, he still regretted that they'd fought and parted angry.

He'd been seated at the desk in the study of the Buenos Aires penthouse apartment that afternoon, working on an economics paper, when she'd resurrected their breakfast disagreement.

"Christopher, I'm serious. You need to be at the meeting this afternoon." Eva sashayed across the room, her body showcased in a red summer dress and matching heels. His gaze drifted down her lush body. Despite the recent distance between them, she tried to wield her curves against him. But the tension between them had been building for eighteen months, and they'd both learned that a physical release was temporary. Once the sex was over, so was their truce. "I have to leave now. Don't keep my father waiting long." Her voice tightened. "Please?"

Saying no to Franco wasn't an option.

"I'll be along as soon as I finish this paper. It's nearly complete." But he would drag it out as long as possible, and she knew it.

Eva stopped behind his chair. Her hands settled on his shoulders. "I can only make excuses for a short time."

"I know." He rubbed her hand. "I'm sorry I put you in a difficult position." He was truly sorry about many things. None of this was her fault. She was exactly the woman he'd married. He was the one who had changed.

"You don't need a degree to work for my father. You are like a son to him. Papa appreciates your intelligence and versatility."

Franco valued Christopher's skill with a weapon even more.

Eva leaned over him and wound her arms around his neck. Her breasts pressed against his back, and her lips grazed his cheek. Her breath tickled his ear as she lowered her voice to a sultry octave. "He has a new horse to show you."

"Now that is tempting," he lied and turned back to his work. If they could get a fresh start, then maybe they could mend the rift between them. But at this moment, lust was no cure. "I do this for you and for Luciana."

"Luciana doesn't care if her father is educated. She knows that he adores her. That is enough for her."

"I want her to be proud of her papa." Someday, when he'd managed to take his family away from this lifestyle, he'd need to be able to support them. He'd tried to explain this to his wife before. She didn't understand.

"You're a smart man, Christopher." Her breath fanned his jaw. "My father would not have brought you into his business if you weren't. You don't need a piece of paper to prove your worth."

It did not take intelligence to ferret men out of their homes and drag them before Franco for their executions.

With a hot burst of anger, Christopher slid out of his wife's arms, stood, and turned to face her. "What will I tell Luciana when she asks what her papa does for a living?"

"There is no shame in defending the family." Eva bristled, her spine snapping straight as a ruler. Her red lipstick, seductive just a few minutes before, accentuated the hard line of her mouth. She paced to the window and back, her movements uncharacteristically jerky. "Papa wants us to move back onto the ranch. I don't want to return to the country. I love living in the city."

Her willingness to let go of their argument surprised him.

"I don't want to go back to the ranch either." Though Christopher missed the horses, moving back onto the Vargas family compound would put him under his father-in-law's watchful eye and leave Christopher no more excuses—or opportunities. They would never escape.

A small worm of panic slithered through his belly. Eva's father was a powerful man. On the surface, he bred horses, but the Vargas family had been selling illegal guns for generations.

"You know it's important to me that *we* raise our daughter, not a nanny." Christopher could not understand how Eva had returned to the business just a few weeks after giving birth. Did she not feel the pressure build behind her ribs every time she looked upon her child? Did Luciana's trusting face not demand that Eva be a better person? Did she not desire a safe place to raise their child, far away from guns and violence and love weighted with the burden of familial obligation and oppression? Just because they both had been raised in unhealthy environments didn't mean they couldn't do better for their daughter.

"You can't let being an orphan cloud your judgment." Eva enunciated her words carefully, but bitterness tainted each one. "All members of the Vargas family must earn their keep."

Christopher glanced around the four-bedroom Buenos Aires penthouse apartment they occupied. Like everything else in their world, the flat was owned by the Vargas family. Every luxury from the leather furniture to the floor-to-ceiling windows was paid for with Franco's blood money. Years ago, as a starving youth, Christopher had been easily bought. An empty belly and a strong survival instinct were powerful motivators, and his moral compass had been formed by desperation. His daughter shouldn't have to pay the price.

He needed more time. Time to plan. Time to convince his wife they needed a new life.

His gaze strayed to a photo on the wall. Two dark-haired young women smiled on horseback. Eva's little sister, Maria, was a younger version of his wife. "He indulges your sister."

"Maria is still in school, and we'll see how long he continues that." Like Eva, her sister had been sent to the United States to attend college, at the wish of Franco's late wife, an American expat. But Maria was not as focused as Eva had been in school. The younger Vargas sister showed more interest in the wine and vineyards that surrounded her California college than the family business. "She should have finished her schooling last year. My father values education, but he does not appreciate the waste of his time or money. He tried to bring her home for today's meeting, but she convinced him to let her finish out the semester."

So Maria would soon be dragged back into the family web, and once mired, attempting to escape was hazardous.

"Don't you ever want a different life?" he asked. He thought of the illegal passports he'd purchased. He didn't dare tell Eva. In fact, he should burn them before their existence destroyed them both. If Franco found out Christopher had gone behind his back, no one would ever find his body. "I want Luciana to have freedom."

Her spine weakened and her hands fell to curl into deceptively delicate fists at her sides. She lowered her voice, as if her father could hear their discussion from his ranch seventy kilometers outside the city. "Even if Papa agreed, which he would not do, there are other threats to consider. Here, we have Papa's protection. On our own, we'd have to stay in hiding. It wouldn't be much of a life. Aline will never stop trying to kill me. Being with me would put you both in danger."

The bluntness of her statement knocked sense into Christopher. Aline Barba, the head of a rival Brazilian arms dealer, had sworn death to the whole Vargas family, but Eva bore the brunt of her hatred. Eva would never be safe outside the protection of the family compounds.

But still, Christopher wanted more for his child. Luciana deserved choices. She deserved gentleness and beauty. She deserved a life untouched by violence. The Vargas family used loyalty and control interchangeably. Franco would show Christopher's beautiful baby that a powerful empire required ruthless rule. The thought that Franco would teach her to disregard and even take human life made Christopher's chest burn until it felt as if his heart would burst into flames.

A baby's cry drifted from the hallway.

"We've woken her." Christopher walked out of the room. He stepped into the pink-and-white nursery. At the sight of his child, he left his frustration and fear at the door. Luciana stood in her crib, tiny fists clutching the rail, tears streaming down her red cheeks.

"I'm sorry we woke you, my princess."

"Papa." On chubby legs, she bounced on the mattress. She would need to move out of her crib soon. Sadness enveloped him as he realized her babyhood was nearly behind her. Tiny arms stretched in his direction. "Up."

"You are a smart girl." Lifting her into his arms, he soothed her ragged breaths and hiccups, pressing her to his shoulder and rubbing her back. Once she calmed, he changed her diaper and carried her into the living room.

Eva's posture softened, and she walked closer to stroke the baby's cheek. "I will tell my father you were delayed by Luciana. He might not understand your motivations, but he loves his granddaughter." She leaned in to kiss the baby on the head. "And *abuelo* knows how cranky you can be if you haven't had your nap, little one." She turned back to Christopher and gave him a hard nod. "No matter what happens, remember that I have our best interests at heart, and that I love you."

She turned her back on them and left the apartment. The door closed behind her. He tried to shut off the memory, but the reel continued into a haze of machine-gun fire, screams, and blood. In the center of the carnage, Eva lay on the terra-cotta tiles, her red sundress soaked with blood. He reached for her, his fingers splaying on the Sun of May tattoo in the center of her back, her flesh still warm under his palm.

CHAPTER TWENTY-NINE

On Monday morning, Cristan parked at the curb in front of the school. "Are you sure I can't talk you into staying home this week?"

"Dad, you have no idea if or when something could happen. I can't hide forever. I promise not to go outside at lunch, and I'll wait until I see you at the curb before I come out at the end of the day." She got out of the car. "I have a big algebra test today."

Still struggling with the truth, she was frustratingly reasonable and a little too distant for his liking. Eventually, her emotions had to come to the surface. In the meantime, there was only so much Cristan could do.

Mike had called the principal and asked her to keep security tight. He'd bent the truth a little and suggested that a possible child predator had been seen nearby.

Lucia leaned into the vehicle to haul out her backpack. "Don't worry. Now that you've been honest with me, and I know there's a risk, I can be extra careful."

"I love you."

Nodding, she closed the car door.

He waited until she disappeared behind the glass doors before pulling away. He stopped at a diner on the interstate and killed an hour with coffee and the news via his electronic tablet.

He wanted—needed to go on the offensive. The first step was to find Maria. She had to be staying somewhere nearby. Mike was checking local motels, but a motel wouldn't provide enough privacy or the luxury Maria had been raised to enjoy. The next best option would be a rental house. There were many in the area as the mountainous region was a popular vacation destination. At nine o'clock, with his photo of Maria in hand, he drove from agency to agency to see if any of them recognized Maria's picture. He had no picture of Aline, but given that Maria had been at the horse show at the winter festival, she was the more likely suspect.

The first five real estate agencies denied having seen her. Most of their bookings occurred online. Typically, they only saw a client twice for a few seconds each time when they picked up and dropped off the keys to a rental property. But Cristan thought a single meeting would be enough to remember Maria. As he well knew, an accent was hard to lose, and people picked up on his immediately.

The sixth office was in the neighboring community of Cooperstown. The smell of musty carpet greeted him as he went inside. A woman in her midfifties turned her platinum-blond head as he approached her desk. "Can I help you?"

"I hope so." He smiled. "I'm looking for a woman." He pulled a photo of Maria from his pocket and showed it to the secretary. "She likely rented a vacation home in this area."

The secretary's eyes flickered to the picture. She stared for a few seconds, considering. "I'm not sure." She lifted her gaze from the picture. "Who are you?"

Cristan went with a near-truth. "Her brother-in-law. My wife is very worried about her sister. She isn't well."

"You're not the police?"

"No." He shook his head.

"Then you're out of luck." She turned back to her computer. "We don't give out any information about our clients. Good-bye."

So it was Maria. He thought of the way she'd tagged along behind him and Eva, the schoolgirl crush he'd suspected she had on him, and that night in the barn when he and Eva had saved her from being raped. Why would she want him dead? Why didn't she simply contact him if she knew he was alive? In order to learn the answers, he had to locate her.

"Good day." He left the building and slid into his car. Hacking into the agency's computer system shouldn't be that difficult.

He checked his phone. No call from Sarah. She'd promised to let him know how she fared in court. He drove home, ready to snoop through the real estate agency's client database.

Maria was here, and he was going to find her before she got to Lucia.

In his office, he opened his virtual private network. Hacking into the real estate management firm's records was simple, but sorting through possibilities in the client management database would be a time-consuming task. He wrote a basic query and turned his attention to his e-mail while it ran. There were several messages in the open account he used for Lucia's school and other unsecure communications. He scanned the list. A message from a TORmail account caught his eye. The TOR service was used explicitly to encrypt messages and hide a sender's identity. He should know. He used TOR for communications he wished to keep private and anonymous. Unease stirred in his chest as he opened the message. It was an animation of the nighttime photo of him and Sarah in front of her house—it played on a loop, with the recurring appearance of a bloody hole in the center of Sarah's forehead.

"Hi, Brooke. Is Luke here?" Mike asked as she opened the door to her yellow farmhouse. Luke Holloway, his neighborhood hacker, had moved in with the self-defense instructor over the winter.

"He's in the office." She led the way through her kitchen to the office in the back of the house. Her old collie, Sunshine, scrambled to shaky legs and greeted Mike with a wet nose and a wag. Mike paused to give the old dog a gentle ear rub.

"Sorry to make him work on a Sunday."

"We weren't busy, and he's happy to help." Brooke waved to piles of papers on the kitchen table. "I'm grading unit algebra tests anyway."

Luke stuck his head out of a doorway. "Hey, Mike."

Mike joined him in an office with an impressive row of computer monitors and hardware. Luke rounded his desk and sat down. His fingers danced across a keyboard.

"How are things?" Mike took a chair in front of Luke's desk.

"Things are good." Luke blinked up from his monitor.

"You really get paid to hack into computer systems?"

"Unbelievable, isn't it?" Luke grinned. A former Internet security analyst, he'd returned home and hung out his shingle as a freelance ethical hacker after being injured in a bombing overseas.

"I appreciate your helping me out."

"It wasn't that hard." Luke turned back to his computer.

"You're sure no one knew you were looking?"

"Please, Mike. This is what I do. I was invisible." Luke hit Enter. "Twenty-seven members of the Vargas family were killed in the attack." He turned his chair and collected a stack of papers from the printer behind his desk.

"Where did you find all this?"

"I told you when I agreed to do this that I wouldn't be able to reveal my sources." Luke stopped.

"I'm sorry. You did." Mike held up a hand. Luke had likely broken the law to get the information. "And thank you."

"Some of the images are disturbing." Luke dealt the pages onto the desktop like playing cards.

Guilt ripped through Mike as he scanned the images. Luke had enough nightmares of his own. He didn't need to borrow any visuals. "I'm sorry. I didn't know."

"It's OK. I'm glad I could help." Luke pushed the pages toward Mike. "I verified the death certificate for Eva Vargas. The medical examiner confirmed her ID with DNA taken from the apartment she shared with her husband. Christopher and the baby disappeared after the massacre. The case remains open, and he's still wanted as a person of interest. But charges were never filed against Christopher. The police suspect the crime was committed by a rival gang headed by a woman named Aline Barba. There's some additional background information in the pile."

"What about Maria Vargas?" Mike asked. So far, everything Cristan had told him was true, which was a relief.

"She was targeted by the tabloids for a time after the attack, but she keeps a low profile. Eventually they got bored and moved on to another tragedy."

Mike gathered the papers. "Thanks, Luke. I owe you."

"One thing, Mike. This crime scene was a mess. This is the official record, but it isn't the most reliable information in the world."

———————————

Though the judge had granted Sarah her restraining order, she felt no sense of victory as she left the courthouse Monday morning.

If anything, the judge's agreement brought a wave of depression over her. Troy could have no contact with her. He was supposed to take the girls the next day, but after listening to the messages he'd left on Sarah's phone, the judge had nixed that as well. Until Troy could demonstrate he had his temper in check, visitations with the girls would be supervised by a social worker. What would Troy do when he learned the judge had ruled in her favor?

Underneath her sadness, discomfort lurked. Troy hadn't shown up for the hearing. This was the first court appearance he'd missed. What did that mean? Could he be giving up?

She zipped her jacket against the chill and crossed the parking lot to her minivan. Settling inside, she started the engine. Em had woken with a headache, so she and Bandit were with Mrs. Holloway. Alex was at daycare and had made it clear she did not want to be picked up early. Sarah could stop for her paycheck, then go home and change her dress slacks for jeans before driving out to Mrs. Holloway's house.

She stopped at the inn. Behind the registration desk, Herb waved with a bandaged hand.

Before she could ask him about it, Jacob called from the hallway, "Can I see you in my office for a minute, Sarah?"

A sense of foreboding fell over her as she went into the small room behind the kitchen.

"Close the door," he said.

Uh-oh.

Not trusting her knees, Sarah lowered her butt into a chair facing his desk.

"What happened?" she asked.

"Herb burned his hand this morning while he was trying to do your job." Jacob handed her a long envelope. "Here's your check. I'm sorry to say, it'll have to be your last one. I'm sorry, but

I need a sous chef who can keep regular hours. Herb is too old and shaky to work in the kitchen anymore, and it isn't fair to leave him shorthanded."

Sarah's heart dropped. He was firing her.

"You're great in the kitchen. Please don't think this is a reflection of your abilities."

"I understand. Thank you for giving me the chance." She exited the office and slipped out the back door. Her van was in the back of the lot. Sliding behind the wheel, she took a deep breath. Employment opportunities were slim in her rural hometown, and until Troy stopped messing with her daily schedule, getting one was going to be impossible. What was she going to do? Wiping a stray tear from under one eye, she straightened her spine. She had no time for self-pity. Her energy would be better spent on starting her own catering business. At least she'd have control over her schedule.

She was almost home when her phone buzzed. Apprehensive, she glanced down, but the call wasn't from Troy. Cristan's name displayed on her screen. He'd texted her several times the previous day to check on her, and he'd known she was due in court this morning. She answered the call hands-free.

"How did it go?" he asked over the hollow echo of the speakerphone connection.

"The judge granted the restraining order and revoked Troy's unsupervised visitation."

"That's good to hear." But there was something else in his voice.

"Yes. I'm relieved the girls won't be alone with him tomorrow." Though her single victory felt like only one step forward when she'd been forced backward a mile, her girls would be safe. For now. While Troy had little interest in the kids, she didn't doubt that he'd used them to get even.

"You'll have to be careful," Cristan said. "He won't take this well."

"Probably not." She turned onto her street, scanning the curb for Troy's truck out of habit, but she saw no sign of him. On one bright note, Tim Newell's car was parked in front of his house, so Kenzie was no longer alone.

"Are you home?" An accelerating engine sounded over the connection. Cristan must be in his car too.

"Yes. What are you doing?" she asked.

"I'm on my way to your house."

"Why?" As much as Sarah wanted to see him, she needed to focus, and letting a man take care of her is how she got into this mess. She parked in her driveway. Her fingers closed over the fob in her purse and she slipped it into her jacket pocket with her keys. Switching her phone off speaker, she gathered her purse, got out of the minivan, and pushed the heavy door closed with her hip.

"I'll tell you when I get there." He paused. "But I want you to go inside and lock your door."

She balanced the phone between her face and shoulder. "What's wrong?"

"Please, just do it. I'll be there in a couple of minutes and explain everything."

"All right." She shuffled her purse to her left hand to retrieve her keys when Troy stepped out from around the corner of the house, the gun in his hand pointed straight at her. "Hello, Sarah."

He'd given up his guns for visitation rights, but she knew it had been an empty gesture. The sporting goods store was stocked with weapons. An avid hunter, Troy had used rifles, bows, and handguns since his boyhood. If he fired that gun at her, he wouldn't miss.

His eyes were cool and calculated. He wasn't consumed in a

fit of anger. Troy had planned this ambush. Sarah had never seen him this unemotional. Her fear amplified.

"Troy." Her purse and phone fell to the grass. Terror gripped her voice.

Thank God the girls weren't with her.

Troy walked closer and shoved her toward the house. She tripped, her feet suddenly uncoordinated.

"Fucking move, bitch." Troy shoved the gun into his waistband. His hand slid around her bicep as he maneuvered her toward the house. On the front walk, he slipped an arm around her neck. His forearm pressed on her windpipe, and she gagged.

No! She had to resist. Being alone with him would be the worst-case scenario. But what could she do? He had a gun.

The techniques she'd learned in self-defense class came to her in a jumble. Brooke's voice sounded in her mind. *Protect your airway!* Sarah turned her chin toward the crook of Troy's elbow, alleviating the pressure on her windpipe. Then she tucked her chin to her chest to keep him from getting his arm under her jaw again. Her breathing eased. But that wasn't enough. She had to get away from him. She'd seen him angry on many occasions, but this time seemed different. This wasn't a drunken outburst of violence. Troy was thinking and planning. Fed by his damaged ego, the violence inside him had grown. He wanted to hurt her with a deep and nourished hatred.

He dragged her up the front steps.

She brought both hands up to grab his wrist and elbow, pinning his arm across her collarbone and giving her another millimeter of space to breathe. Cristan was on his way. How long would it take for him to reach her? No one had been outside when she'd parked, but in case a neighbor was within earshot, she drew in a deep breath and yelled, "Help!"

"Shut up!" Troy screamed in her ear as his hand fumbled in her pocket. He pulled out her keys and the alarm fob. Unlocking the door, he hauled her over the threshold. The security system panel emitted a steady stream of beeps. Troy pressed the button on the fob. The beeping ceased.

"That stunt you pulled this morning was a big mistake." Troy tossed her keys and fob on the table next to the door.

Sarah released his arm with one hand, made a fist, and jabbed Troy in the ribs with her elbow. He sucked wind and dropped her. With the sudden release, she fell forward. Her knees hit the floor, and pain jolted through her legs. She got her feet under her body and dove toward the door.

But Troy was faster. His hand closed over her ankle. He yanked her toward him, and she fell to her belly on the carpet. He adjusted his grip on her foot. One hand closed over her toes; the other cupped her heel. With a twist of his hands—and her ankle—he flipped her onto her back, then stepped over her. She tried to roll away, but his short jab connected with her jaw. Pain exploded in her face as his high school ring hit her jawbone. Her head snapped back, and she slumped to the floor. Adrenaline pumped through her, numbing everything.

Troy loomed over her. He was dressed for hunting, from his hiking boots to his camouflage pants and shirt, to the smears of brown and green paint on his face. The white of his eyes shone crazy-bright from under his brown cap.

With a feral smile, he dragged her by the foot into the small kitchen. Stopping in front of the stove, he turned on all four burners and snapped off the knobs. The hiss of gas sent a fresh burst of terror shooting through her veins.

"Troy, stop," she pleaded, knowing her words would have no effect. Sarah had seen him lose his temper many times, but this was different. Fear seeped cold into her belly. Troy had gone beyond anger. He didn't want to hurt her. He didn't want to get even or make her pay for what she'd done.

He wanted her dead, and he was willing to kill himself in the process.

She needed to get away from him—and the gas that was filling the house. She kicked off his grip and shuffled backward like a crab through the doorway into the living room. Troy was on her in an instant. He lifted a foot, and Sarah curled on her side, raising her arms to protect her head from the imminent boot. But instead of kicking her, he planted a boot on her hip to pin her in place. Then he pulled a gun from his pocket and pointed it at her face.

CHAPTER THIRTY

The scream sounded tinny and helpless over the Bluetooth speaker in the car.

"Sarah?" Cristan pressed the gas pedal to the floor, roaring down the middle of Main Street. Horns and shouts protested his sudden acceleration. Then he dialed Mike and explained what he'd heard.

"On the way," the police chief said.

Cristan ended the call. In two minutes, he screeched to a stop two houses away from hers. He'd heard Sarah say her ex-husband's name. The bastard must have been waiting for her. Troy mustn't know he was here. He took his gun from under the driver's seat and slipped from the car. He pocketed the weapon. To stay out of sight, he crossed the neighbor's front lawn.

Sarah's minivan sat empty in the driveway. The front door was closed, as were the blinds over the windows. His gaze fell on the cell phone and packages lying on the grass. A movement in the narrow sidelight caught his attention. He ran for the front of the house and crouched behind a shrub. In a tiny sliver of space between the blinds and the window frame, he saw Troy pointing a gun at Sarah.

There was no time to wait for the police.

His vow against committing violence evaporated. He wanted to kill Troy Mitchell with every fiber of his being. But he needed to get into the house without Troy seeing him. Cristan jogged around the building. He crouched next to the garage window. Hoping the alarm wasn't set, he slid his arm out of his jacket, wrapped the fabric around the butt of his gun, and punched it through the window. The glass broke with a muffled sound. He unlocked the window and climbed into the garage. He skirted stacks of boxes and eased the door to the house open. He'd lost one woman to violence because he wasn't there to protect her. He couldn't let that happen again.

"What did you think you were doing?" Troy yelled. A fleshy smacking sound sent rage boiling through Cristan's veins. If Troy hurt her . . .

He crept through the laundry room to the doorway that led to a combination living room and dining area. Peering around the doorframe, he saw Troy and Sarah in the doorway to the kitchen. Sarah was on the floor. One hand clutched her jaw. A thin line of blood trickled from her lip. Troy stood over her. The gun in his hand pointed directly at her face.

"This is the end of all our problems, Sarah," Troy said in a calm voice that set Cristan's instincts on alert. Instead of red and distorted with rage, Troy's face was eerily relaxed, almost devoid of expression.

A familiar coolness washed over Cristan, chilling his anger and steadying his hands. He pulled his gun from his pocket and aimed it at Troy's chest. Cristan's finger curled around the trigger. He wanted to shoot the bastard with a desire that nearly overwhelmed him. But a thick, rotten odor hit his nostrils, and he froze.

Gas.

If he fired his weapon, the house would explode.

The continued hiss of gas gave Sarah new strength. Would he shoot her? Was there enough gas in the room to ignite if Troy pulled the trigger? Didn't matter. She was dead if she stayed.

She kicked at his hand. Her foot struck his fingers and he let go, only to catch her foot again almost immediately. Dropping to the floor, he straddled her. The gun was inches from her nose, but instead of shooting her, he wrapped his fingers around her throat and squeezed.

Her vision blurred.

"Just give up, Sarah," he said. "Admit it. I've won. You belong to me."

He wanted them both to die, but he wanted to go out a winner.

Her lungs burned. She clutched at his hand, trying to grab one of his fingers to bend backward, but she couldn't get a grip.

"I supported you. I put a roof over your head and food on your table, and you repay me by screwing another man. How long have you been fucking him, Sarah? Is it the money? You're like every other bitch, for sale to the highest bidder. What do you have to say for yourself?" He loosened his fingers.

"No," Sarah wheezed.

"Don't lie to me. I saw you together. If you think you can trade me in for a rich older dude, you're wrong." He shifted his position, pressing his knee into her sternum and cutting off her air again. Sarah gasped, her lungs unable to inflate. Tiny dots swam before her eyes. Unable to speak or move, she floundered.

Troy eased the weight off his knee. "Say it, Sarah. Say it and it'll all be over. No more pain. You and me. We'll go together."

Sarah inhaled, oxygen hitting her lungs in a rush. "The kids. Think of the girls."

"Why? They ruined everything. The day you got pregnant was the beginning of the end. No more fun for us. You didn't want to go out anymore. You were always tired. 'The girls have to be in bed early,'" he mimicked her voice. "*They* became the most important things in your life, and *I* got kicked to the curb."

She couldn't respond. He'd been jealous of his own children?

"The gas, Troy. You're going to blow us both up." She'd never see her girls again. A tear slipped from her eye. "You don't want to die," she croaked.

"Don't tell me what I want." Hostility glittered briefly in his eyes before they went cold again. His fingers tightened on her throat. Tiny lights danced in front of Sarah's eyes. She grabbed his wrist with both hands in a desperate attempt to loosen his grip.

Please, no.

"I don't have anything to live for. You've seen to that. No wife, no family, my father is in jail, and the business is going bankrupt. You ruined everything. You ruined me. Now you think you can move on?" He leaned closer. "I won't let you."

Sarah's vision darkened. Her grip on his wrist weakened, and his fingers around her throat tightened, cutting off her air.

He pressed the gun against her cheek. "If I can't have you, no one can."

Sorrow slid over her. This was the end. She was going to die. Troy had won.

A body hit him hard, knocking him off Sarah.

She gasped. Coughing, she rolled to her side to see Cristan and Troy locked in a brawl. Cristan had come. Relief was nearly as shocking as the flood of oxygen into her lungs.

The smell of gas intensified, choking her.

They had to get out of the house.

Sarah looked toward the door. Could she make it? No. She couldn't leave Cristan inside with Troy. Unable to stand, Sarah crawled into the kitchen toward the stove. Heaving to her knees, she tried to shut off the burners, but Troy had broken off the knobs. She needed a pair of pliers. A coughing fit seized her lungs. Dizzy, she dropped to her hands and knees and crawled out of the kitchen.

A lamp crashed to the floor as the men rolled across the carpet and bumped into an end table. Landing on top, Cristan grabbed Troy's wrist and banged it onto the floor until he dropped the gun. Then he plowed a fist into Troy's face. Troy bucked and threw Cristan off. Troy scrambled to his feet, lurched past the oak table in the adjoining dining area, and went out the sliding glass door. Pausing, he pointed at Sarah then Cristan. "I'm going to kill you both." He closed the door behind him and ran for the side of the house.

Cristan launched his body toward the door and jerked it open. Fresh air poured into the house. He hesitated, clearly wanting to go after Troy. But Cristan returned to Sarah, scooped her off the floor, and carried her out the front door. She rested her face on his chest and gave in to the solid feel of his arms around her. Her brain and body felt disconnected, as if she was unable to process what had just happened. She watched in a detached daze as Mike's SUV parked at the curb.

He jumped out of the vehicle. "Where's Troy?"

"Troy ran out the back door." Cristan inclined his head toward the rear of the property. "I opened the back door, but the gas is on. I wouldn't want a spark anywhere near the house."

Panic jolted her. She stirred, but Cristan held tight. "The girls. I have to get the girls."

"Where are they?" Mike asked.

"Em is with Mrs. Holloway," Sarah said. "Alex is at daycare."

"Call daycare and Mrs. Holloway and tell them Sean will pick up the girls." Grim, Mike talked on his cell phone as he jogged around the back of the house.

She made the calls. Hearing that both of the girls were fine allowed Sarah to breathe. Even though she knew the children would be safer with Sean than with her, her panic wouldn't fade until she saw them with her own eyes.

"Are you all right?" Cristan asked, frowning as he scanned her face. He moved her hair aside to inspect her throat.

Sarah lifted her head from his chest. "Thanks to you, yes." Her voice was raspy.

His arms tightened for a second, and she expected him to put her down. Instead, he walked to the back of Mike's SUV and sat on the bumper, holding her on his lap.

Mike returned. "I turned off the gas supply to the house. The fire department and gas company are on the way. No sign of Troy." He focused on Sarah. "Are you hurt? Should I call an ambulance?"

Sarah stirred, testing her body. As her adrenaline rush ebbed, small aches and pains came to life. Her throat throbbed. "I'm all right. I need to see the girls."

"Sean is on his way." Mike nodded. "We're notifying state, county, and local law enforcement. Everyone will be looking for Troy."

"I didn't see his truck near the house. I would have noticed." Suddenly realizing she was still sitting on Cristan's lap, Sarah pushed away from his chest and slid off of him. She regretted the move immediately. The vehicle bumper was cold under her butt, and the muscles in her arms and legs quivered. Though she still wore her jacket, she was suddenly freezing.

A police cruiser parked next to Mike's SUV and a fire truck rolled down the street. A gas company truck followed. Men emerged from vehicles and swarmed the front lawn.

"Ethan," Mike called. "Take Cristan's statement."

Cristan moved away.

Crouching, Mike lifted Sarah's chin and studied her neck. "You're sure you're all right? Your throat could swell."

"Some cold water and an ice pack should be enough."

"Tell me what happened." Someone wrapped a blanket around her shoulders, but her body seemed to be generating cold from the inside out.

"I left the courthouse and stopped at the inn." Sarah's voice cracked as she summed up the morning. The events gained clarity as the words left her lips. She'd lost her job to obtain a restraining order, which was completely worthless. No piece of paper would keep Troy away.

"Come home with me," Mike said. "You and the girls can stay with us until Troy is caught."

"No." Her relationship with Cristan had put him in danger. She couldn't risk anyone else. "I won't put Rachel in danger. You won't even be home. You'll be out looking for Troy."

Mike's mouth thinned. "What about Sean's place?"

"No." Sarah shook her head. "I won't put his wife or children at risk either." She gulped air. "Troy is suicidal, Mike. You're not dealing with a rational man anymore. He was going to blow up the house to kill me, and he didn't care who else he hurt in the process."

"What about the girls?" Mike's voice rose.

Sarah's chest tightened. She wouldn't endanger another person for her own safety, but her girls were a different matter. She'd mentioned the kids to Troy several times. He hadn't reacted.

"Troy has no interest in them." She never thought she'd be happy about his inattentiveness, but now she was nothing short of grateful. The thought of being separated from her kids filled her with panic, but they would be safer without her. "Would Sean take them for a few days?"

"Of course he will." Mike rested a fist on his hip, frustration and determination stiffening his posture. He would not give up easily. "You'll come back to the station with me, and we'll discuss this again."

Cristan approached. "Sarah will come home with me."

"No!" Sarah objected. She couldn't let her mistakes put Cristan in any more danger. Lucia needed a father, and he'd already risked his life for her.

Cristan held up a hand. "Troy has already declared me a target. It makes no difference whether you're with me or not."

"Your house is secure?" Mike asked.

"I've taken precautions against much more formidable opponents than Troy Mitchell," Cristan said. "I'm on alert anyway." He produced his cell phone and showed Mike the e-mail with the animation.

"Do you think that was Troy?" Mike asked.

"I doubt it, but it's not impossible," Cristan said. "The animation is crude enough, but the sender went to some trouble to encrypt the message and hide their location. Troy Mitchell seemed less than rational today."

Mike paced. "I'd like to put you all in a safe place, but we don't have safe houses here in Westbury. How about a hotel?"

"My house is more secure," Cristan insisted. "Troy won't get past my defenses." But his face was dark. "But I fear I could endanger Sarah more. Whoever is after me might come calling."

"I'll put a man outside your house," Mike said. "It'll be easier to watch you both at once."

Sarah sipped some water, the cool liquid soothing her throat. She wanted to protest, but what were her options? Going off on her own would be foolish.

A fireman interrupted them. "Chief, the gas is off and the windows open. You might want to air the house out for a few more hours, but you can go inside."

"Thank you," Mike said.

The firemen climbed on their truck and pulled away. The gas company vehicle followed.

"Can I go inside and pack a few things?" she asked Mike.

"Yes."

Cristan herded Sarah across the street. "Pack enough for a few days."

How had her life come to this? To keep her girls safe, she had to send them away.

CHAPTER THIRTY-ONE

Settled in the soft leather of the Mercedes, Sarah rested her head against the back of the seat. Cristan hadn't spoken on the short drive to his house, but the quiet between them was comfortable. Whatever reservations she'd had about him were gone. He'd risked his life to save her.

She'd sent a bag of clothes with Mike to Sean's house for Alex and Em. When she'd talked to the girls on the phone, Alex had been excited for a "sleepover." Sean's daughters were five and seven. Em was hesitant, but Sean had assured Sarah that he and his wife would distract her with games and movies. The former army ranger would keep the girls safe, but Sarah's chest ached with missing them.

Cristan parked in the garage and led her inside. The faint beeping of an alarm panel sounded from the hallway.

"I'll be right back." Leaving her in the kitchen, he disappeared down the hall. The beeping ceased.

He reappeared in the doorway. "Do you want something to eat or do you want me to show you to your room?"

Sarah leaned on the island. The events of the morning whirled in her head. She was shaking inside. Soon, those shakes were going to work their way to the surface and she'd prefer that happen in private. "I'd really like to take a shower."

"The guest room is upstairs." He showed her into a utilitarian room. The sleek, dark queen-sized bed and dresser contrasted with white linens. Other than the lamps on the nightstand and dresser, the furniture was bare. He led her to the edge of the bed. "I'll be right back."

He brought her clean towels, a thick robe that looked brand new, and her bag. On his way out the door, he said, "I'll make some lunch. Take your time. Lucia doesn't need to be picked up from school for a few hours."

She listened to his feet descending the stairs. Alone, the enormity of her situation crashed over her, as if she were standing in the ocean, glancing back at the shoreline, while a huge wave broke unexpectedly over her head. The feeling swamped her until she could barely breathe.

The image of Troy's gun in her face was branded in her mind. Had he always been this terrible? She tried to reconcile the young man she'd married with the one who'd nearly killed her but couldn't. Troy had been wild in a boys-will-be-boys way, partying hard with his teammates, but nothing suggested seven years later he'd want to kill both of them. Heaving to her feet, she hobbled into the adjoining bathroom. She placed her palms on the vanity and stared in the mirror. She couldn't reconcile her reflection with the naive eighteen-year-old who'd married Troy either.

Her lip was swollen, and a ring of bruises circled her throat. How much did she have to take? When could she say *uncle*? Last October, Troy had broken her arm and given her a concussion. She'd rebuilt her life, and he'd knocked it down like a Jenga tower. She gripped the granite vanity. She could not give up. More than her life was at stake. If she surrendered, her children would pay the price. She would do whatever it took to get through the next few days. Troy would be caught. He'd be arrested and put away. There was no way he'd be able to worm his way out of assault and attempted murder charges, not after what he'd done. There was too much evidence this time to fall back on the he-said-she-said argument he'd used in the past. This time, Troy hadn't bothered to cover his tracks.

Because he wasn't expecting to live to be arrested.

She shuddered. She dropped her jacket on the floor, reached into the shower, and turned on the water. She found hotel-sized shampoo and soap in a drawer. Unfortunately, she knew just what to do after having the hell beaten out of her: wash off the blood, ice her injuries, and take a couple of ibuprofen. She felt better with a plan of action, even if it only covered the next thirty minutes.

The hot water coursed over her skin. Sarah scrubbed her hair and body over and over. Still, she could smell the gas, Troy's sweat, and the oily smell of his gun. She rinsed her mouth, but the taste of her own blood lingered. Pieces of her week played in her mind. The two dead robbers. Troy attacking her. The barrel of his gun large as a cannon in her face. She put her back to the cold tiles and slid down to the floor. She hugged her knees until the water running over her skin grew cold.

"Sarah? Are you all right?" Cristan opened the shower door. Concern overrode the apprehension on his face. "I've been banging on the door. You didn't answer."

She shivered. "I'm OK."

"The water's freezing." He reached in and turned off the faucet. Snagging the towel from the vanity, he wrapped her in it and lifted her from the shower floor. He carried her into the bedroom and put her on the bed. Then he grabbed another towel from the bathroom and rubbed her dry.

She should have been embarrassed, but it was her emotional transparency that she found most humiliating, not her nudity. The first time he'd seen her naked she was a basket case. Not the sexiest of moments. "I'm sorry."

"Why? For being human?"

"I'm a blubbering mess." Her teeth chattered.

"You're hardly blubbering." He tugged the duvet off the bed and wrapped it around her shoulders. "The past week has been stressful. I think you handled it admirably."

"I don't know what I'm going to do. My ex-husband tried to kill me. I had to send my children away to keep them safe. I lost my job." She took a deep breath. "I know that Troy will eventually be caught. The girls are safe with Sean. But what can I do? I hate letting my family and friends do everything for me."

"Doing everything alone isn't usually the best option."

"But how long can I allow other people to carry me?"

"You've come a long way in a short period of time." Temper and regret flashed in his eyes. "Do you think it would be better to have no one? I made that choice, and my daughter suffered."

"I'm grateful for my friends and family every day. They're the reason I've stayed in this town. I don't know how the girls would have gotten through this divorce without support, and my kids are more important than my pride." Sarah's sigh trembled in her chest. "If only I didn't feel so useless."

"You are hardly useless. You give yourself no credit for what you've accomplished. You've fought hard for your children. You've been a wonderful friend to my daughter, and I've seen you take care of your sister." Cristan gently blotted her hair with the towel. "Every time you're knocked down, you get up again. That's the true test of strength." Cristan frowned as he scanned her face and neck. "You deserve a man who treasures you."

Sarah had no words. *What would that be like?* She couldn't imagine. The desire that bloomed inside her was nothing like she'd ever experienced. This man would never raise a hand to a woman. This man would never toss away his own child.

He set the towel on the bed and brought his hand back to her face. A gentle finger traced the bruises on her throat. "I should get you some ice."

Cristan leaned away, and Sarah caught his wrist. "Don't go."

His eyes darkened, and the muscles in his forearm tensed. "You don't know what you're saying."

She fought for the words to express what stirred in her heart. The best she could do was, "I need you."

For the first time since she'd left Troy, she didn't want to be alone. She needed to be touched. She needed him.

His lips thinned, and his body went rigid. "I've done some terrible things in my past, Sarah. You're wholesome and innocent. You deserve better than me."

"I don't care what you were in the past. It's what you are now that matters. Isn't that what you just said to me?" But what if he didn't want her? She stiffened. "I'm sorry. I assumed you were interested, but how could you be? Look at me." She waved a hand over her bruised knees.

Cristan took her by the arms and turned her to face him. "You are the most beautiful woman I've ever seen." His hand fell to caress her knee. The touch of his fingers sparked heat deep inside her. Her leg shifted, inviting him to stroke higher. "These are the marks of courage. You fought back."

When she looked at her bruises, she saw weakness.

"If I hadn't been concerned about an explosion, I would have killed him for hurting you. I still want to, more than I should." He dipped his head and pressed a tender kiss to the uninjured side of her mouth. "Inside and out. There is a light within you. Kindness and compassion. Those are the qualities that make you shine. Those are the sources of your strength."

His fingers trailed down the side of her neck. He stroked her shoulder and continued down her arm to her back. Pressing his palm flat against her lower back, he held her still as he moved closer. The hard ridge of his erection pressed against her hip. "Never think that I don't want you, but I don't want to hurt you."

"You would never hurt me." But as she said the words, she knew they weren't entirely true. He would never raise a hand to her, but she'd let him into her heart and made herself vulnerable. She'd given him the power to hurt her as seriously as Troy's fists had. But it was too late to pull back. He wanted her, and that was enough to push her desire from a simmer to a boil.

He hesitated, the muscles of his neck tightening with the effort. "Sarah . . ."

Her name sounded half protest, half plea.

She slid her hands up his chest and curled her fingers in his sweater. "Please."

CHAPTER THIRTY-TWO

Her trust leveled him. How could a woman offer him her bruised and battered soul? He wasn't worthy. But the soft body pressed against his was more than he could resist.

She squirmed closer. A restless leg slid against his thigh. The towel slid off her body. And the sight of her was his undoing. His hand slid down her collarbone and chest to cup one full, creamy breast. Her head fell back, and the moan that escaped her lips sent blood rushing to his groin.

"Sarah." He brushed a thumb across her nipple, his touch featherlight.

Her hands were pulling at his sweater. He helped her, peeling it off and dropping it to the floor. Her hand splayed on his chest, her fingers pale and slim and feminine against his darker skin. She was the light to his darkness, the kindness to counter the cruelty of his past. Everything about her made him feel stronger and more masculine.

He eased her back onto the bed, his intention to take her slowly and with great care. His gaze raked over the slim length of her. The bruises mottled in stark contrast to her fair, soft skin made him want to show her what it was like to be cherished. Every inch of her.

"You're so beautiful." He touched his lips to her shoulder.

She flushed, pinkness warming her creamy skin. He brushed his lips across her collarbone and continued to the side of her breast. When his mouth closed over her nipple, her body surged off the bed. Her hands clutched his shoulders, then moved lower to tug at the waistband of his jeans.

"There's no rush," he said. He hadn't touched a woman in years. He had every intention of making this special, of enjoying every second of his reintroduction to intimacy.

But her fingers were working the snap of his pants. "More, please."

"I don't have any condoms. I'm sorry, but I'm happy to give you pleasure. More than happy." He trailed his fingertips up the inside of her thigh. Satisfaction swelled in his chest as her legs separated to give him more room.

"I have some."

Surprised, he pulled away.

A blush rose into her cheeks. "They're in my purse. My sister gave them to me. She said I should, um, 'get back on the horse.'" The wry smile that tilted her mouth pleased him.

He chuckled.

"In that case." He lifted his body from hers. In two seconds, his jeans hit the floor.

"What's that?"

He unstrapped the sheath on his calf and set it on the nightstand. "A knife. I like to have a backup plan."

Grabbing her purse, he tossed it onto the bed next to them. She dug a condom out of an interior pocket, handing it to him.

"There's still no rush. I want to enjoy every second with you."

She reached for him. "Don't make me wait too long. Internal combustion would be a terrible way to go."

"I'll see what I can do to take the edge off." Naked, he stretched out beside her, their bodies pressing together. Her softness cradling his hard limbs. Her skin was smooth and silky against his. But those delicate hands on his body were going to hurry things along too quickly.

He slid down on the bed, his mouth cruising over her flat belly and hip. He licked his way to her center. At the first touch of his tongue, her body arced off the bed and her hands delved into his hair. He'd meant to give her a release to ease her need, but the sweet taste of her fueled his desire. And the way she responded had his erection throbbing. It didn't matter what he did, he needed her. Now.

Grabbing for the condom, he covered himself and rolled on top of her. His chest, and other things, aching with the need to be inside her.

"I'm not hurting you?" he panted in her ear.

"Hell, no." She took hold of his hips with both hands and guided him to her core. "Just keep me from exploding."

Laughing, he buried his face in her damp hair and slid inside her. Her silky heat closed around him as if welcoming him home. She bowed beneath him, her legs coming off the bed to wrap around his waist.

"I hope you have another condom. Against my best intentions, this isn't going to last very long." Was the pleasure this intense because he was inside of Sarah or because it had been a very long time since he'd been with a woman?

"Yes," she breathed. "I have more. Please save the finesse for next time," she begged. "I need . . ." Her voice trailed off as a groan ripped from her throat.

He levered onto his elbows. If this was going to be quick, he was determined it would still be meaningful. She met his gaze, her eyes darkened, the lids heavy with desire. He withdrew and thrust into her again. It was her, he decided. All her.

Her hands clutched his shoulders. The nails digging into his back spurred him to move faster. Her body bowed.

"Cristan." Her breathless cry grabbed him by the balls and drove him over the edge.

Her muscles went taut, and she closed around him, holding him tight. He held his weight off of her with a hand on the mattress while his breathing recovered. He rested his forehead against her shoulder.

Sweat coated their bodies, and her skin bloomed a healthy pink.

Lifting his head, he scanned her face for any signs of regret. His chest lightened when he saw none. He kissed her cheek. "Thank you. I can't express what you've done for me."

She brushed her fingers across his temple. "Right back at you."

His heart swelled. He took her hand and kissed her knuckles. "You've given me a great gift."

"You said it's been a long time since you've been with a woman. How long?"

"Long enough that I don't remember." He rolled to his back. "I told myself I was keeping my distance from people to protect Lucia, but in truth, I was punishing myself. I blamed myself for my wife's death. If I had demanded we leave, maybe she wouldn't have been killed."

Sarah rested her head on his chest. "*What if* is a pointless game to play."

"It is." He brushed his fingertips across her shoulder. "The good news is that I'm not willing to live that way anymore. Not everyone has the privilege of living. It's a sin to waste a single moment on regret."

"So you're going to allow yourself to be happy?"

"I'm going to try."

The lazy tilt of her smile stirred his blood all over again. "How long do we have before you need to pick up Lucia?"

He glanced at the clock. "More than two hours."

She grinned. "In that case . . ."

Laughter rumbled from his chest. "I'm supportive of a gift that keeps on giving."

Making love to her was no hardship. He'd do anything to keep the desolate look from her eyes. When he'd found her in the shower, she'd looked beaten. But now she was straight and her eyes clear. An hour later, she was more relaxed, curled under the covers as she slept soundly.

He stepped into his pants. Downstairs, he stopped in his office. His initial query had finished, eliminating all repeat clients of the firm. He doubted Maria had rented a house last year. He quickly programmed a new search, narrowing the client list down further by eliminating condos and attached units. Maria wouldn't want to share walls. Next, he excluded the few properties close to Westbury. If Maria had spent a significant amount of time in the small town, she would have stood out. His accent still garnered attention from the locals.

A short time later, he was left with several dozen properties outside of Westbury but within a thirty-minute drive. He printed the list, accessed the online Multiple Listing Service, and reviewed each house one by one. Maria Vargas would not make do with rough lodging. She was accustomed to the finer things in life. She would also prefer seclusion, so close neighbors wouldn't be desirable. On pure instinct, Cristan sorted the rental listings down to a final six. Four mountain properties for skiers, a farmhouse, and one waterfront property with a boat and dock.

Now what? He couldn't leave Sarah alone, and they needed to pick up Lucia in a short while. He could send the list to Mike, but what would the cop do with illegally obtained information? Not much. But Mike's friend Sean wasn't bound by the same legal restrictions.

Cristan had to face it. He needed help. He couldn't do everything himself. Not this time. He called Sean and explained the situation.

"Give me those addresses," Sean said.

Cristan read the list. "Thank you."

"I'll let you know if I find anything." Sean disconnected the call.

Shoving his phone into his pocket, he returned to Sarah. The waiting would be the death of him.

Dressed in clean jeans and a sweatshirt, Sarah punched a ball of risen bread dough in Cristan's gourmet kitchen.

"I'm so happy you're here." Lucia sat at the island.

"It's only temporary." Sarah used a rolling pin to flatten the dough into a rectangle, then rolled it into a loaf and placed it seam side down in a greased pan. She covered the dough and set it aside to rise a second time. "I appreciate your dad letting me stay."

Lucia glanced up from her schoolwork. Her pencil hovered over a sheet of lined paper. "Well, you couldn't go home, not with your ex-husband on the loose."

Cristan had insisted that Lucia deserved to know the basic truth. He'd left out a few of the more intimate details, like what had happened between them that afternoon, but she needed to be on her guard, both against Troy and the person who was after Cristan.

"I'm sure the police will catch him soon." Sarah moved to the commercial stovetop set into the island and stirred a pot of chicken, black bean, and sweet potato stew.

"You can stay with us as long as you want." Lucia stared at Sarah's neck for a minute before returning to her math problem.

Repeated applications of ice had minimized the swelling, but nothing but time would erase the black-and-blue ring. Too bad she hadn't thought to pack a scarf.

"Do you miss the girls?" Lucia asked.

Sarah sighed. "I do."

Cristan emerged from the door that led down to the basement. After they'd made love again, he'd taken her on a tour of the house. In addition to giving her the basic layout and showing her how to use the alarm system, he showed her where weapons were hidden in his house. In each bathroom, there was a knife affixed to the top of the medicine cabinet. The top edge of a framed painting in the family room held a handgun. In the kitchen, another handgun occupied one of the slots in the wine rack. And the stash of weapons in the basement could arm a small police force. If she hadn't seen the dead bodies of those robbers, she'd think Cristan was paranoid. Considering what he was facing, he was merely prepared.

He went to the coffeepot and poured a cup. "Coffee?"

She shook her head. Her stomach was already roiling. Coffee would not help. His gaze caught hers and held it. Despite their afternoon of intimacy, they hadn't graduated to displays of affection in front of Lucia.

Lucia shut her notebook. The slap of paper echoed. Cristan bobbled his coffee. Hot liquid spilled over the rim onto his hand. He shook the drops from his hand, picked up a dishcloth from the counter, and wiped his mug.

"Do you want me to leave the room so you can kiss her?" Lucia asked. "I know something is going on between you. Honestly, I'm thrilled. So don't feel like you have to hide it."

Cristan cleared his throat. "We're not hiding anything."

Lucia rolled her eyes.

"Really," Sarah said. "We're just not quite ready to define our relationship. It's all new, and a lot has happened in a short period. Give us some time, OK?"

"OK." Lucia smiled. She gave her father a look. "See? That wasn't very complicated."

Sarah checked the dough and moved the pan into the oven. The smell of baking bread filled the kitchen. Lucia's willingness to communicate with Cristan, albeit with some attitude, was a good sign.

Cristan scanned the kitchen. "Can I help?"

Sarah shook her head. "No. I have dinner under control."

Light poured from a set of French doors and gleamed on the black granite counters. The view was stunning. A lawn sloped to the river and a small boathouse constructed of weathered gray wood. The sunset rippled orange and pink on the river. "And this kitchen is amazing."

"I can't take any credit for this house. It came exactly as is." He moved to the wooden chopping block and minced the cilantro she'd washed. "Surely, I can help with something."

"You can cook?" Sarah stirred the stew.

His knife chopped in practiced motions. "My early efforts weren't pretty, but I learned."

"Dad makes great empanadas," Lucia said.

He finished mincing and washed the knife. "But nothing that smells like this."

Sarah checked the bread. "I love to cook, and I need to keep busy."

"Well, then feel free to use my kitchen at any time." He took a stool at the counter next to his daughter and watched as Sarah served the meal. "As long as you leave us samples."

The scene appeared relaxed but the undercurrent of tension couldn't be denied. Lucia picked at her food. Cristan ate with robotic motions that suggested he was fueling his body more than enjoying his meal. Sarah ate the tender stew, but her throat was too sore to swallow bread. She took an ibuprofen. Then she and Cristan cleaned up the kitchen side by side.

Now what?

Lucia took her books upstairs and Cristan poured another cup of coffee. "Tell me about your plans for a catering business," he said as if he understood her restlessness.

"They're not really plans just yet." Sarah dried the clean stew pot and told him about her sister's wedding.

"You're going to make the reception shine."

"Thank you. I hope so." She put the pot in the cabinet.

"Why don't you try to get some rest," he said. "It's going to be a long night."

"Do we have a plan?"

"I'll stay on watch tonight. In the morning, we'll meet with Mike and see how the search for Troy went."

Sarah paced the spotless kitchen. "What about the other issue?"

He rubbed his unshaven jaw. "Mike has made inquiries with motels and real estate agencies that handle vacation properties with no luck. Unfortunately, rentals are often completed online. So I did some research of my own. I'm waiting on results."

"Waiting is frustrating."

"Yes, but tonight, my only focus is keeping you and Lucia safe." Cristan took his coffee and headed for his office. "Go lie down. You've had a hard day. Your body might surprise you and sleep."

Sarah doubted she would relax. Every base instinct in her body told her to be on alert.

CHAPTER THIRTY-THREE

Her mother had been murdered. Not just her mother, her whole family. How could that be true? Lucia couldn't grasp the concept. Though her dad had lied to her in the past, she knew this time he was telling the truth. She'd watched him struggle to get the words out, saw the regret in his eyes as he gave her a likely sanitized version of the murders. He'd responded to most of her questions, but others he'd simply refused to answer.

She wasn't sure if it was worse to have never had any family or to know that once, she'd had tons of relatives, but they were all dead.

She was trying to forgive her father for fabricating her entire life, but how could she? And how could she suddenly process the fact that everyone in her family had been a criminal. The idea was too Hollywood to feel real.

Lucia lay on her stomach on her bed. She smoothed the newspaper article out next to the old photo of her and her mother. A third picture was of her Aunt Maria. Dad had copied it from a South American tabloid shortly after the Vargas family had been murdered. Putting the pictures side by side, it was easy to see the family resemblance. Her father said that the woman watching her at the horse show could have been her Aunt Maria, and that she might want to take Lucia away. But she couldn't believe a member of her own family would want to hurt her.

If everyone else in the family was dead, then maybe her aunt was lonely too. Maybe she just wanted to see Lucia. The Quickie-Mart robbery could have been totally unrelated. Things like that happened all the time. Her dad might be paranoid.

The thought that she had a relative out in the world warmed Lucia's heart, but at the same time, the knowledge made her sad. Why couldn't she ever see her aunt? Dad said he hadn't even talked to Maria since he'd sneaked them out of Argentina.

She held the magnifying glass over the newspaper picture. The photographer had focused on her and Snowman, so the background was blurry. She couldn't see the woman's face, but she wanted to more than anything. She wanted to see the only living connection to her mother so much her stomach ached and her chest felt hollow.

All her friends had grandparents and aunts and uncles and cousins. Except for her dad, she was all alone, and it seemed selfish of him to keep her that way. In twelve years, he hadn't even tried to find a wife. She liked to think it was because he'd been so in love with her mother, he had never gotten over her death. But maybe that had all changed now. Sarah was downstairs cleaning up the kitchen. The three of them had eaten dinner together, almost like a real family. Whatever happened, she wasn't giving this up. He couldn't make her. If he tried, she'd run away again.

A tear slid down her face as she stared at her mother's picture. Lucia had her dark wavy hair and olive skin. But her eyes were different. Lucia's were a lighter, softer brown. Her mother's eyes were almost black, and her gaze was sharp as she stared into the camera, almost as if she were challenging the photographer. Her mother had been beautiful, and she'd known it.

Yet someone had killed her. Her father had said there was an explosion and gunfire, but he'd refused to give her any details. *I will carry that image to my grave. I will not condemn you to the same fate.* At least he'd been honest.

She lifted the photo by the edges, careful not to damage the paper. Tomorrow she would return it to the safety of the frame. Her phone vibrated on the bed. A text message had come in. Lucia didn't recognize the number. Her finger hovered over the screen, an inexplicable tangle of apprehension twisting in her belly. She displayed the text. Hello Lucia. Another message followed immediately. A photo. I am your mother.

Lucia's breath stalled in her lungs as she stared at the selfie.

Her mother? How?

The woman held a newspaper in front of her and pointed to the date at the top. Today.

Anger welled hot in Lucia's throat, and a wave of other emotions she couldn't identify. They rushed over her like a tsunami, leaving her flattened. This was not her Aunt Maria. This was her mother. She responded with disbelief. I thought you were dead.

Another text came in. Is that what he told you?

Lucia went cold. He'd lied. Again. How could she ever trust him again? Maybe everything he'd told her was a lie. Maybe he'd been keeping her from her mother her entire life.

But her mother—she'd come for her. Maybe she'd been searching for her all these years. The thought of a brokenhearted woman in a tireless search for her only child warmed the empty space inside of her. She wasn't alone. She had the one thing she'd wished for all her life—her mother.

She texted, Where are you?

Outside. By the river. You can see me from your window.

Lucia went to the window and stared out into the dark. The full moon brightened the landscape, reflecting off the river in silver shimmers. A figure stood on the bank. An arm waved. Resentment and excitement warred within Lucia until it felt as if her body would burst. Her fingers trembled as she shoved the pictures into the envelope and stuffed them into her backpack. She could never trust her father again. Not after this. She sent a final text, I'm coming.

She moved to drop the phone on her bed but couldn't bring herself to lose the contact with her mother. What if she couldn't find her outside? She slipped the phone into her pocket. She'd dump it after she connected with her mother.

There was no way she'd let her father track her. No way.

She tugged on an extra sweater. Boots in hand, she tiptoed down the stairs. Dad was in his office. She stared at the yellow light in the doorway with hatred. How could he have lied to her all over again? She went to the foyer and slipped into the closet. She'd have to be quick. Once she hit the button, she'd have sixty seconds to get out of the house before the security system armed itself again. Plenty of time. But her father would hear the beeping. He'd know immediately what she'd done. She'd use the front door and run around the house. If he assumed she'd gone to the road, it might buy her a minute or so to get to the river before he caught her.

She entered the code, went out the front door, and ran.

———

Mike parked three lots away from Troy's house. Behind his vehicle, Sean's giant SUV cruised to the curb. They climbed out of their vehicles and met on the sidewalk. Two more Westbury PD cars parked on the street. Two officers, Pete Winters and Ethan Hale, got out.

The windows of Troy's house were dark, as was the porch light.

Sean scrutinized the house. "How do you want to do this?"

"Have to knock first." Mike waved the arrest warrant in his hand.

"That's bullshit." Sean snorted.

"It's the law." Mike tucked the warrant in his pocket and drew his gun. "Pete and Ethan, cover the back."

Sean's Glock was already in his hand. "Is he armed?"

"To the teeth." Mike led the way down the sidewalk.

"I know we have to go through the motions, but there's nothing in that warrant that says we can't reconnoiter the property first." Sean paused at the edge of the Mitchell property.

Mike scanned the house. Looked quiet. "When I went to the store, Troy's assistant manager said he took home three handguns, a rifle, and multiple boxes of ammunition."

"Terrific."

They veered across the grass and made a quick circle of the house. But they saw no sign of Troy. Pete and Ethan covered the back door, while Mike and Sean went around front. Mike climbed the front stoop. Sean hung back, covering him from behind a fat tree on the front lawn. Mike was not shocked when no one answered his knock. Sean joined him on the step and fished something from his pocket.

"Look over there." Sean pointed to the damaged garage door.

Mike turned his head. "What?"

"I guess it was nothing." Sean slid something back into his pocket. "Oh, look. The door is unlocked."

Mike shot him a look. The door had been locked thirty seconds before. But Sean was already going inside. Weapon raised, he slipped into the dark house. Mike followed, switching on the light.

"Holy shit," Sean said, as they worked their way from room to room. "Troy is officially whacked."

The last time Mike had been here, the kitchen had been trashed, but now the entire house was in ruins. More than trashed. Beyond the kitchen, where cabinets were ripped from the walls and sawn into pieces, obscenities in red paint covered the Sheetrock in the living room and hallways. In the bathrooms, mirrors and tiles had been smashed with a sledgehammer.

Mike spoke into his radio, letting Pete and Ethan know the house was clear.

Sean holstered his weapon. "What now?"

Good question, thought Mike. "Now we have to find the son of a bitch."

CHAPTER THIRTY-FOUR

Wired, Sarah stared at the dark ceiling. As exhausted as she felt, sleep would not come. The bed in the guest room smelled faintly of Cristan, and every breath reminded her of the intimacy they'd shared that afternoon. Despite the danger they faced, the memory sent a little thrill through her belly. She hadn't expected to enjoy the sex that much, not the first time. Sex with Troy had become one more means of manipulation and control. But Cristan had brought something more to the bedroom. She'd never been treated with reverence, and they'd joined in ways that weren't physical. Their connection should intimidate her. She was barely out of a bad marriage in which she was used and abused. But her body—and her heart—weren't listening to reason.

She flipped onto her side and fluffed the pillow, but she couldn't settle. A slight squeak caught her attention. She held her breath and listened. The sound was so faint, it wasn't as much a noise as a feeling. Her instinct told her that all wasn't right in the house. Tossing back the covers, she tugged a hooded sweatshirt over her flannel pajama bottoms and T-shirt. Her feet hit the floor automatically, drawn to the hall by the same intuition that notified her if one of the girls spiked a fever in the middle of the night.

Using her cell phone as a flashlight, Sarah went out into the hall. After listening to the silent house for a few seconds, she turned on the light. Her heart thudded against her breastbone, and her stomach twisted in that familiar something-is-not-right feeling. Lucia's bedroom was at the end of the hall. Barefoot, Sarah tiptoed down the hall and eased the door open. Light from the hall spilled across the empty bed.

Relax. Lucia could be downstairs. Maybe the child hadn't been able to sleep either. Her whole life had been turned upside down. But reasoning aside, Sarah knew this wasn't what had happened.

She ran down the stairs. A faint beep sounded from the closet in the foyer. She opened the front door to see Lucia disappear around the corner of the house.

"Lucia!" Sarah chased her, the grass wet and freezing under her bare feet. As she turned the corner, she heard Cristan calling out from inside the house. "Outside," she yelled, afraid to slow down. With long legs, Lucia loped across the back lawn like a gazelle. Sarah's thighs burned as she tried to run faster, but she was losing ground. Lucia was close to the river. What was she doing? Winded, Sarah panted. A stitch in her side slowed her pace.

She cupped her mouth and yelled, "Lucia!"

At the riverbank, the teen stopped and turned. A figure stepped out of the woods and beckoned the girl. Alarm burst through Sarah. She broke into a jog again, the cramp forgotten. It was a woman, dressed in dark jeans and a black jacket. She pulled something from her pocket and extended her arm toward Sarah. Moonlight glimmered off metal. A gun.

"No!" Lucia screamed. "Don't hurt her."

Sarah stopped dead. Cold, clammy sweat gathered under her thick hoodie. "What's going on, Lucia?"

The girl hefted her backpack and adjusted her backpack straps. "This is my mother."

Eva Vargas was alive?

Stunned, Sarah stared. How could this be? Cristan had said

his wife was dead. Disbelief and terror rolled down her spine. How could she be alive and why did she have a gun pointed at Sarah?

The woman stepped closer and swept a knit cap from her head. Long, dark hair spilled down her back. Even in the scant moonlight, the resemblance between her and the teen was striking. She also looked very much like the picture of Maria Vargas that Cristan had showed Sarah.

"But how?" Sarah asked, doubtful. This woman could have lied to entice Lucia from the house.

"No time to chat right now." The woman extended her other hand toward Lucia and beckoned with her fingers. "Come with me." The gun remained pointed at Sarah's chest.

Lucia walked forward. The woman snatched the cell phone from the teen's hands and tossed it onto the grass. "You won't be needing that."

Lucia flinched at the abrupt and harsh treatment. "Lucia, don't go. Wait for your father."

Teary eyed, the teen sniffed. "Why? So he can tell me more lies?"

Sarah panicked. She didn't know what had happened, but this woman was dangerous. "He loves you."

Eva's body shifted forward. "*I* am her mother. She needs to be with me. Christopher has kept us apart long enough."

Lucia wavered, her body frozen, indecision flickering in her gaze.

Eva said, "Luciana, we have to go now."

Sarah took advantage of the brief shift of the woman's eyes. She tucked her cell phone into the kangaroo pocket of her sweatshirt.

"Sarah! Lucia!" Cristan's shouts floated over the lawn, but Sarah couldn't see him. He must be in front of the house looking for them.

"Hurry." Backing toward the water, the woman gestured to Lucia. "There is a boat tied to the tree. Undo the rope."

Lucia strode down the bank. Her boots splashed in the shallows.

Sarah squinted into the shadows. An outboard skiff bobbed on the river as Lucia untied the rope.

"You're coming too," the woman gestured with the gun toward the boat. "Get in."

"No," Lucia said. "Sarah doesn't have anything to do with this."

"Oh, she most certainly does. I might need her for leverage, and if your father thinks he can take another woman while he is still married to me, he is mistaken." The woman walked forward. She pressed the muzzle of the gun to Sarah's forehead. "Get in the boat. Now."

"Don't do that to Sarah," Lucia protested.

"You'll do as you're told," the woman said in a cold voice. "Your father has pampered you. That will have to change."

The woman's accent sounded similar to Cristan's. But the harsh tones of her voice lacked the rolling warmth in Cristan's. Eva was bitter and hostile and dangerous.

Sarah turned her head. Where was he? She saw his shadow at the rear of the house. Two minutes. That's all it would take for him to get here. The woman turned away. She grabbed Lucia by the ponytail and pointed the gun at her face.

Lucia cried out, clamping her hands around the base of her ponytail to relieve the pain. Tears ran down her face. "I'm sorry, Sarah, but you shouldn't have followed me. I had to come. She's my mother."

"It's not your fault, Lucia," Sarah said.

What kind of person pointed a gun at her own child? Used her own baby for leverage? The kind that Cristan had been protecting Lucia from for over a decade. He'd been smart to keep her hidden. This woman shouldn't have responsibility for a child any more than Troy should.

Eva turned her cold, dark eyes on Sarah. "Get. In. The. Boat."

Cristan had said his wife was dead. Had he lied or was that what he truly believed? Sarah decided it hardly mattered. *He* would never put a gun in a child's face, just as Sarah couldn't take a chance with a child's life. She would do whatever Eva wanted to keep Lucia safe.

Sarah walked forward. The frigid water closed over her ankles and soaked her pajama bottoms from the knee down as she splashed to the boat and climbed in. The boat rocked as the woman jumped aboard. Still pointing the gun at Lucia, the woman moved to the back of the boat. She lifted the throttle, started the motor, and turned out onto the river. The boat shifted under Sarah's feet. She grabbed Lucia and pushed her down to keep her from falling overboard. The river water in March was cold enough to kill.

CHAPTER THIRTY-FIVE

"Lucia! Sarah!" Cristan yelled. No one answered. There was no sign of his daughter or Sarah on the lawn, but he knew he'd heard Sarah outside calling for Lucia. Fear fueled his steps as he raced for the side of the house. Turning the corner, he saw three figures on the riverbank: Lucia, Sarah, and a third slim figure climbed into a boat that bobbed on the water.

"Stop!" Cristan raced toward the river as the boat sped away. The glow of the white hull faded into the dark. Lungs heaving, he stopped on the bank. The third person had forced Sarah into the boat, but it had appeared as if Lucia had gotten in on her own. Spying a cell phone on the grass, he picked it up, tucked it into his pocket, and raced toward the boathouse.

As he threw open the door, he dialed Mike on his own cell phone. "Sarah and Lucia were taken away by boat."

"What? How?"

"I don't know." Cristan leaped up the steps into the small building. "The house wasn't broken into. Lucia must have turned off the alarm and gone outside."

"Why would she do that?"

"I don't know." Cristan turned on the hydraulic lift. The boat lowered onto the water. The process only took a few minutes, but it felt much longer. Cristan needed to move. Tomorrow was the anniversary of the massacre, and his instincts screamed that the date was a countdown.

"I'll get the marine police and sheriff boats out looking for them," Mike said. "Can you describe the boat?"

"Outboard. Open hull. Approximately fifteen to twenty feet in length." Cristan hadn't seen many details in the darkness. "The exterior was light colored, probably fiberglass, and it appeared to be fairly new."

"Got it. Let me call the sheriff now."

"Thank you." Cristan climbed into his boat. He pressed the button to raise the door onto the river and primed the engine. Thanks to a recent pre-spring tune-up, the outboard revved to life. He'd lost valuable time. If the skiff kept straight on the river, his larger, faster boat should be able to catch up.

"Is that an engine? What are you doing?" Mike asked.

"I'm going after them on the water."

Mike paused. "I'll call you back."

"Thanks." Cristan piloted his boat out of the building. He pulled Lucia's cell phone out of his pocket. He punched in the passcode and opened her last messages. His lungs shut down as he viewed the photo. Even as he stared at the woman's face, his mind claimed the image was impossible. Eva.

It couldn't be.

He blinked hard and focused again. No question. It was Eva. His heart stuttered. How? He'd touched her dead body. He'd read the death certificate. The medical examiner had verified her identity with DNA tests. But the ultimate evidence was right in front of him.

His wife was alive. Relief and joy and fear raced through him in rapid succession.

The phone vibrated. Mike. "Does Sarah have her phone? I'll trace the GPS."

"I don't know," Cristan said. "But I know who has Lucia. My dead wife." And he knew where they were going. "Call Sean," he shouted over the sound of the engine. "Tell him it's the riverfront property."

He turned the boat onto the open water and eased the throttle forward. The bow lifted as the craft accelerated, then the nose dropped as the boat planed out. The rumble of the engine drowned out any possible response from Mike. But all that mattered now was catching up with Eva.

Cristan's mind reeled with questions that went far beyond wondering how his wife could possibly be alive when he'd seen her dead body. Where had she been for twelve years, and why was she here? And more importantly, why had she kidnapped Lucia and Sarah?

The boat flew across the whitecap-dotted river. The hull slapped on the chop, each return to the surface a bone-charring jolt. Cristan gripped the wheel and spread his feet for balance. He had to catch them. With no jacket, the wind should have been cold, but Cristan was numb. His dead wife was alive. His child had been taken.

He'd been worried about a confrontation with Maria, but now his concern had exploded exponentially. Eva was a different level of antagonist. She wouldn't intentionally hurt her own child, but Eva was impulsive, and she had no attachment to Sarah. He had no idea where she'd been all this time or what had happened to her. Too many questions and not enough answers.

He knew only one thing for certain. His wife was a killer. She hadn't contacted him to see Lucia. Eva had hired men to kill him. Both Lucia and Sarah were in grave danger. He rounded a bend in the river. Ahead, he could see the faint glow of a light hull. The boat arced to the right. He eased the throttle back to slow the boat. Had she seen him?

CHAPTER THIRTY-SIX

The sound of an engine floated across the water. Holding the wheel, Eva glanced over her shoulder. Moonlight danced on the V-shaped wake of her boat, but she couldn't see far enough to get a visual on the boat following them. Sound carried farther over the water than on land. Whoever it was had his running lights off. Like she did. It must be Christopher. How close was he?

She pushed the throttle forward. She wanted to reach the dock before Christopher saw where she stopped.

"Does he have a boat?" she shouted to her daughter, but the girl didn't answer. Instead, the child shivered on the bottom of the boat with that other woman. What had Christopher done to the child to make her so weak? Likely, he'd pampered and coddled her like he had when she was an infant. Eva reached behind her and grasped the girl's arm, hauling her closer. Christopher's young plaything, Sarah Mitchell, reached for Luciana, and Eva kicked her away. Her boot struck Sarah in the shoulder. She spun around and fell to the decking on her hands and knees, an appropriate position for an inferior.

Eva yelled into Luciana's ear. But the girl recoiled in fear and tried to push Eva away. Christopher must have poisoned the child against her own mother.

The bastard.

Why should that have surprised her? He'd betrayed her entire family. Twenty-seven members of the Vargas clan were dead because of Christopher's traitorous act all those years ago. She'd kindled her hatred for more than a decade, and it flared to life as Eva looked at the woman kneeling in the stern, the whore who was sleeping with her husband. The whore was used to being beaten. Eva had heard the altercation between Sarah and her ex-husband. Sarah knew to stay down when she'd been put there.

I'll get even with him—and her.

Soon. Very soon, Christopher would get what was coming to him.

Looking for the right dock, Eva slowed the boat. She spotted the swaying lantern her lieutenant was waving at the end of the pier.

The boat bobbled on a wave, and Luciana grabbed a handrail to stay on her feet. The wind whipped her dark hair around her face. Pride surged as Eva noted the Vargas cheekbones and long, lean body. Whatever failings Christopher had ingrained into the child could be corrected. She was still young, still malleable. A few years with Eva would teach her what it meant to be a Vargas.

"Where are we?" Luciana asked, looking behind them. Except for a silver ribbon of moonlight, the water stretched endless and black behind their boat. There was no sign of their pursuer, but the engine behind them sounded closer.

Straightening the wheel, Eva took her chin in her hand. "Don't worry. He won't take you from me again. I'll see to it."

"What are you going to do to him?" Luciana shouted.

Eva pulled back on the throttle. The boat slowed. The wet rumble of the engine lessened. "What he deserves."

"You can't hurt him," the child said.

"I will do what I must, and you will do what you are told." Eva steered the boat toward Nicolas.

"Promise me you won't hurt my dad." Luciana crossed her arm. "And Sarah too. I won't go with you if you don't promise."

The cold air chilled Eva's teeth as she smiled. "It is not up to you."

Luciana turned to the dock. Her eyes widened as she saw her lieutenant standing on the edge. The lantern lighted him from below, making him seem larger and more intimidating. The child lunged forward, turned the wheel sharply, and shoved the throttle. The boat accelerated in a tight half circle and ran up against its own wake. The world swayed sideways as the craft banked hard. Eva went to her knees, sliding on the tilted deck. Scrambling for the console, she grabbed the wheel with both hands and fought to keep the boat from capsizing. A swell hit the boat on its starboard side, nearly flipping it over. Water sloshed over the gunwale. Eva turned into the wave. The bow rose into the air, topped the crest, then dove for the river nose first. She pulled the throttle back, and the craft leveled.

Panic scrambled in her throat as she scanned the deck. "Luciana," she called, her voice breaking with fear.

Sarah clung to a handrail. Staggering and sliding to her feet on the wet fiberglass, she lurched to the side of the boat. Raising an arm, she pointed out over the water. "There!"

Eva grabbed a flashlight from the deck box and played the beam out over the river, but Luciana had disappeared.

The flashlight illuminated a trail of bubbles. Sarah didn't think. Taking two running steps, she grabbed a life vest from a net strung along the stern, put a foot on the side of the boat, and jumped overboard. The icy water closed over her head in a shocking wave of cold that threatened to stop her heart.

How long could she remain conscious?

She floundered with numb limbs toward the bubble trail. Ducking under the water, she felt hair and grabbed a handful.

Pulling hard, she brought Lucia's head above the surface. The light cast a white sheen onto the girl's face. Was she breathing? Her eyes opened and she coughed. Relief almost made Sarah giddy. Lightheaded, she rolled onto her back and hugged Lucia and the life vest. The shoreline was closer than the boat. She kicked toward the man standing on the dock. Getting Lucia out of the water trumped any fears for their safety. She prayed that Eva didn't want to harm her own child. Lucia clung to Sarah and gagged. Sarah rolled her onto her side. Water spewed from her mouth.

The man leaned down and hauled Lucia from the water onto the dock. Sarah hugged a piling, unable to climb the wooden rungs with half-frozen limbs. Tossing his coat over Lucia, the man reached down, grasped Sarah's hand, and plucked her from the water as if she were a drowning kitten. He dropped her on the dock and turned back to the child. Lucia's body was wracked with violent shivers.

Something smacked against the dock. Eva jumped from the boat and fastened lines to cleats on the bow and stern. She dropped to her knees on the other side of Lucia. A stream of rapid Spanish flowed from her lips. Sarah didn't understand the words, but the anger in them was clear. Sarah's body shook so violently, it seemed as if it didn't fully belong to her. Surely, her bones would rattle loose of her skeleton.

Eva issued a command in Spanish. The man got to his feet with Lucia in his arms and carried her toward a house. Eva grabbed Sarah by the elbow and pulled her to her feet. "Move."

Sarah stumbled behind them, tripping over hands and feet she couldn't feel. She was beyond feeling cold. Exhaustion slid over her like a blanket. She wanted to lie down on the ground, curl into a ball, and go to sleep.

"Hurry!" Eva commanded, half dragging Sarah.

The back of a large house loomed dark over the yard. Unable to walk another step, she fell onto her hands and knees on the damp grass. She curled onto her side and shivered. "Where is Lucia?" Her words shook so hard they were barely intelligible.

"Her name is Luciana," Eva whirled. "And she is mine. Not yours."

Sarah's teeth chattered too hard to form the words on the tip of her tongue. *Then why didn't you jump into the water to save her?*

Eva leaned closer. She grabbed Sarah's wet hair and yanked her face off the ground. "I know what you're thinking. You pulled Luciana out of the water. Therefore, I should owe you." She laughed. "That's not the way I think. Moral debts are for fools. I could kill you as easily as I might stomp on a spider. The only reason you're still alive is in case I need to use you for leverage. Unlike me, Christopher has always been weak, and I am willing to use his code of ethics against him." She said the word *ethics* with disgust.

CHAPTER THIRTY-SEVEN

Cristan's heartbeat froze as he watched Sarah tow Lucia to the dock. A burly man hauled them both out of the water. Cristan recognized him from across fifty feet of river in the dark: Nicolas.

Franco's right-hand man. How had he escaped the massacre? Cristan thought back to that afternoon. He hadn't seen Nicolas at the house. He'd *assumed* Franco's head of security had been present. Obviously, he'd been wrong. But Eva . . .

How could she be alive? He'd touched her lifeless body. Her injuries had been too severe for anyone to survive. There was no way he'd imagined that. Not even in a state of shock would he have conjured up an image of his wife's bullet-ridden body.

"Stop!" Lucia's voice carried over the water, bringing him out of his thoughts.

He cruised his boat to the dock. With a quick leap, he landed on the boards, abandoning the vessel. He raced across the grass, gun in hand. Sarah was on the ground, pale, soaking wet and shivering. Eva held her by the hair.

Cristan aimed his gun at his wife. "Eva!"

She released Sarah and stood tall. Disdain creased her face. "You can't shoot me."

Cristan stared at her. She was right. This close, the light on the back of the house illuminated the strong line of her jaw, and snug winter apparel highlighted the lush body he'd made love to a thousand times. He stared, unable to process the sight of her in front of him. "How? I touched you. I saw you. You were dead."

"Disappointed?" Eva asked.

"God. No. I don't understand." Confusion filled him.

She pulled a gun from her jacket and pointed it at Sarah. "You killed my family. I should take away someone that you care about. Drop the gun or I will shoot her right now." Her eyes went ice-cold in the space of a heartbeat. Her face and body weren't the only things that hadn't changed much about his wife. She was still very much a killer, and he had no doubt she would pull that trigger.

His eyes locked with Sarah's. He couldn't risk her life.

"I did nothing. The Vargases were like my own family." The weapon slipped from Cristan's grip and hit the grass. In the corner of his eye, he saw Nicolas turn to face him. Lucia was in his arms, wrapped in what appeared to be his coat.

"Liar," Eva spat.

"Me a liar? What about you? You let me believe you were dead for twelve years!" Fury and frustration curled Cristan's hands into fists. The truth suddenly dawned on him. If Eva was alive, then someone else had died, because Cristan had not imagined that scene in the ranch dining room. "Who is the woman who died in the explosion, Eva? How did she look exactly like you?"

And what else had Eva been hiding all those years ago?

Ahead of them, Nicolas turned. "The child is cold. Let's take this discussion inside." He went into the house.

Pressing the gun against Sarah's temple, Eva grabbed her elbow and hauled her upright. She nodded toward the door. Cristan led the way through a tile-floored mudroom into a two-story great room decorated in leather and hardwoods. Nicolas set Lucia on a couch perpendicular to the fireplace. With a remote control, he ignited the gas jets and covered the child in a heavy comforter. Cristan had to get his daughter away from Eva, but at the moment, his greatest fear was for Sarah. Lucia was the only person on Earth that Eva wouldn't harm.

Behind him, Eva dragged Sarah across the room and dropped her next to the couch. Sarah sagged. Sopping wet, her heavy sweatshirt weighed her down. The overhead lamp highlighted her cold-blue lips and fingertips.

"She needs to get out of those wet clothes," Cristan said.

"Don't worry about her." Eva gestured. "She's not going to need anything soon."

Eva and Nicolas were alive. They'd hidden for twelve years only to risk exposure to kill him. What had he done except save Lucia?

"Why do you think I killed your family? I loved them all. They were the only family I had. There were children there, Eva. I would never harm a child. You know that."

Doubt softened Eva's features for two seconds, then her mouth tightened again. "You wanted out of the business. You were conveniently late to the meeting. You stole money. You ran. That's enough evidence for me."

"I took the money to take our child to a safe place." He had to convince her. "It wasn't planned. I didn't know what else to do. If the situation had been reversed, I would have wanted you to save Lucia at all costs."

"I don't believe you." Eva moved the gun to point at the center of Sarah's chest.

"No!" Lucia launched her body from under the quilt, hitting Eva's arm and knocking the gun from her grip. Eva fell backward, her head struck the edge of the coffee table, and she went still.

Nicolas charged. He hit Cristan in the midsection, his heavy body taking them both to the floor. Cristan landed on the bottom, pinned. He trapped an ankle with his own foot and bridged over his shoulder, flipping Nicolas onto his back. The older man scrambled to his feet with surprising speed and agility. He drew a knife from a sheath on his belt.

Cristan reached under the cuff of his jeans and withdrew the blade strapped to his calf. Nicolas lunged, but age had slowed him. Cristan slashed his forearm, blocking the knife. Blood welled from Nicolas's arm. But he didn't give up. He circled, stabbing at Cristan's midsection.

"Don't make me kill you." Cristan leaped backward to avoid the strike.

Nicolas stabbed again. "I taught you everything you know, and you betrayed me."

"Never." Cristan slashed downward, cutting his arm.

"Liar!" Nicolas shot in, his blade lunging at Cristan's belly perilously close to his vital organs. Cristan jumped back, arcing his body away from the weapon. But he wasn't quick enough. The point nicked his side with a hot sting. Blood welled, trickling in a warm, wet trail down his torso. The pain faded as adrenaline numbed the wound.

Cristan circled, dodging another strike. But Nicolas wasn't as quick or as strong as he'd once been. Breathing heavily, he lunged again, the knife lashing out at Cristan's face.

Cristan blocked the strike with a counterattack. He slashed downward. The blade of his knife sliced the older man's forearm again. Cristan reversed his motion and stabbed the older man under the ribs. The blade sank into his abdominal muscles. Cristan yanked the blade free with a twisting motion. Nicolas dropped his weapon. Both hands went to the wound, but the blood couldn't be staunched. His knees buckled. He fell forward, face-planting on the hardwood floor in a growing red puddle.

Breaths heaving, Cristan leaned on his thighs. Eva stirred, pushing her body up off the floor. She glanced at her gun. But there was no way she could reach it before Cristan reached her. And she knew it. Defeat slumped her shoulders.

He risked a glance at Lucia. She'd crawled across the floor to Sarah. Holding his daughter in a tight embrace, Sarah turned Lucia's head away. "Don't look."

Cristan picked up the gun. He staggered to Nicolas's side. His mentor wheezed. Blood dripped from the corner of his mouth.

"It didn't have to be this way," Cristan said. Confusion, anger, and pain churned. "Why did you attack me?"

Nicolas's next breath was a gurgle. His mouth moved as his lips formed the word, "traitor."

The accusation was a fresh wound. Cristan would never have betrayed those he loved.

"No," Cristan said. But it was too late. Nicolas's body went lax. His head lolled, and his eyes glazed over. Cristan pointed the gun at Eva as he tossed a blanket from the sofa over the body.

"Sit," he ordered. He grabbed a lamp from a table, severed the electrical cord with his knife, and used it to tie Eva's hands behind her back. Keeping one eye on her, he dropped to his knees beside Lucia and Sarah and wrapped his arms around them both. Relief topped all the emotions roaring through his blood. They were alive. He kissed his daughter's head, then leaned his temple against Sarah's forehead, his love for both of them overwhelming in its intensity.

"We need to call the police," Sarah said.

The door burst open, and a blond woman walked in. Three men followed her into the room. All four were armed with AK-47s.

"Isn't this convenient? Everyone I want to kill in one room."

CHAPTER THIRTY-EIGHT

Sarah stared at the four armed people pointing guns at them. A bleached blond in her late forties stepped forward.

Were those machine guns? She'd never seen one up close. And who was this woman?

"Isn't this cozy?" the blond woman said in a thick accent. She grinned at them, then her gaze shifted to Eva, who had managed to bring her legs through her arms and stand. Her hands were still bound, but now they were tied in front of her body.

"Thank you, Eva. You've made my job so much easier," the blond said.

"Aline," Eva breathed. "How did *you* find him?"

Aline? The Brazilian arms dealer? She was here too?

"I wasn't looking for *him*." Aline nodded at Cristan. "I followed you. *You* found Christopher for me." She squinted at Lucia. "I know who you are." Her smile widened. "I can't believe how perfectly this day has turned out."

"But I was dead," Eva said.

Aline dipped her chin. "Oh, please. You'll do anything to survive, and you're too mean to die that easily. I was there that day. I wanted to see you die. You killed my son. I was going to spit on your dead body. I saw you leave in the helicopter. Though, you did a fine job of faking your death."

Inch by inch, Cristan shifted his position until his body blocked Sarah and Lucia.

"Christopher, stop moving," Aline said without moving her eyes. "Get the child," she ordered her men. One walked forward and grabbed Lucia's arm.

"No," Lucia cried. The girl sagged, resisting with her body weight. Sarah and Cristan both reached for her.

"Ah ah ah." Aline shifted her aim to Lucia. "No one else moves."

Sarah froze. Inside her still body, her heart raced as she scrambled for a plan.

Next to her, Cristan's body trembled with rage. The tendons in his neck bulged.

"Grab him," Aline ordered.

The remaining two men took Cristan's arms, heaved him to his feet, and dragged him backward to the other side of the room and held him between them by his biceps.

The third man shoved Lucia in front of Aline. The teen fell to her knees. Her face lifted. Tears streaked her cheeks, and terror widened her eyes until they were completely rimmed in white. Her breaths came in short pants.

"I knew if I followed you long enough, you'd lead me to your child. I can't think of a more appropriate punishment than to take your only child from you the same way you took mine."

"You killed my whole family. Isn't that enough?" Eva cried.

"No." Aline pursed her lips. "Tell me? How does it feel to be betrayed by the one who is supposed to have your back?"

From across the room, Eva's body trembled.

Aline pointed the gun at Lucia's chest. "Isn't this how you shot my son? Two bullets dead center in his chest. Isn't that your calling card, Eva?"

Fear accelerated Sarah's pulse. This woman was going to shoot Lucia. Her eyes glowed with the hungry desire to kill.

"I have waited a long time to avenge my son's death." She settled the weapon on her shoulder. Her finger curled around the trigger. "He was barely a man. He had his whole life ahead of him."

Raising her bound fists overhead like a club, Eva dove at Aline.

Sarah launched her body at Lucia, tackling the child to the floor as the gunshot rang in the room. She covered the teen's head with one arm. The other refused to move. A burning sensation exploded in her shoulder.

———————

"No!" Cristan simultaneously back-fisted each man in the groin. Bending forward in pain, they released his upper arms. He grabbed a machine gun and struck its owner in the head with the butt, then swung around to shoot the other man in the chest. Backing up, he fired a three-shot burst into the second man's chest, and continued his spin to kill the last man.

The door stood open. Eva and Aline were both gone.

Terror clutched Cristan's heart as he knelt next to Sarah and Lucia. Sarah was on top, her body shielding his daughter. A dark-red stain spread across her back and arm. He slid her off of Lucia. His daughter's eyes were glassy, her breathing quick and shallow.

He pressed a hand to her throat. Her pulse beat a rapid tattoo against his fingertips. He ran his hands over her body. "Are you shot?"

She shook her head and swallowed. "Sarah."

At the sound of her name, Sarah stirred. She rolled to her side. "Ow."

"It's OK." He searched Sarah's body for more wounds but found none. He snatched his knife from the floor and used it to slit her sweatshirt down the back. A single shot had struck her high on the shoulder. He tore her T-shirt, and she flinched. The bullet had grazed her deltoid muscle. He staunched the bleeding with a piece of the torn shirt.

Lucia knelt next to him. "How badly is she hurt?"

Sarah's eyes dimmed with pain.

"It's bleeding heavily, but the wound is shallow. She should be all right." Cristan leaned closer. "This is going to hurt."

Her eyes closed and her mouth tightened. Cristan applied pressure to the wound, and she groaned. Her wound didn't appear life threatening, but he would rather take a bullet in his own body than listen to her sounds of pain.

"We need to call for help," he said to Lucia. "My phone had no service. Can you see if the landline works?"

"No need. The calvary is here." Sean jogged through the open door.

"You're a little late," Cristan said, relief sweeping through him.

"The directions sucked." Sean checked each of the downed men then dropped to a knee beside Sarah. "Ambulance is on the way." He checked Lucia's eyes. "Are you all right?"

She nodded, leaning on Cristan's shoulder.

"Where's Mike?" Cristan asked.

Sean removed his jacket and wrapped it around Lucia's shoulders. "Outside. He caught some crazy-ass blond chick with a machine gun running toward the woods."

"You caught Aline," Cristan said.

"If that's her name. Mike's got the bitch outside." Sean glanced at Lucia. "Sorry."

"Was there another woman? One with long, dark hair?" Lucia asked.

Sean tilted his head. "No. Should there be?"

Eva had escaped.

───────────

It was morning before Cristan could bring Sarah and Lucia home from the ER. Sarah leaned on him as he half carried her to the guest bedroom of his house.

"I can only stay tonight," she said. "The girls will need me tomorrow."

"Mm." Cristan made a noncommittal noise. He would keep her here as long as he could. Her girls were welcome too. "Do you need a pill?"

"Yes." Sarah eased onto the bed. "Normally, I don't like pain medications. But I have no desire to be stoic right now."

"Nor should you be." He crouched and removed her socks.

A shiver ripped through her. Her feet were freezing. He rubbed them between his palms and wrapped his hand around her toes. Dry clothes and warm blankets in the ER clearly hadn't been enough. "Let's get you under the covers."

She curled on her side. Rachel had brought yoga pants and a sweater to the hospital. Sarah's shoulder had been stitched. She and Lucia had been treated for hypothermia and released. Cristan had even submitted to a dozen stitches in his side where Nicolas's knife had landed.

"Do you need anything, Sarah?" Lucia said from the doorway. She'd changed into pink, plaid flannel pajamas that made her seem younger than thirteen. His heart and stomach somersaulted. If it hadn't been for Sarah, he might have lost his child last night. He wanted to gather them both close and never let them go.

"Would you fetch her a glass of water?" Cristan asked. With a nod, Lucia left.

"I meant it when I said I was going home tomorrow." Sarah nestled into the pillow. Her face relaxed as he tucked her in.

"We'll talk about that tomorrow." Cristan planted a kiss on her forehead. "I almost lost you last night. I won't let that happen again. Eva is still out there. I won't take my eyes off you or Lucia again until she's caught."

"Do you really think she'll be back?"

"She doesn't like to leave business unfinished." He tugged the comforter up over her shoulder. "If she comes back, I'll be waiting for her." He couldn't imagine she'd still be in the area any more than he could picture the authorities finding her. Eva was a most resourceful woman. "But I doubt she'd come back with all the police presence." There was a patrol car parked in the driveway. Eva had waited twelve years. She was obviously very patient. If the police didn't catch her, and Cristan wasn't hopeful, he might have to reconsider the promise he'd made Mike earlier.

"You're not tempted to go after her?"

"I admit I thought about it." He grimaced. "Mike and Sean talked me out of it." The pair had something planned. He was sure of it. But there was a statewide manhunt in progress. The FBI had been called in, plus other agencies with equally impressive acronyms. Cristan couldn't add anything of value to that amount of manpower. And he might trust Mike not to betray him, but he didn't trust anyone to protect the ones he loved. If Eva did show up, Cristan would be here to deal with her.

"You don't sound happy about that."

"I believe Mike has something up his sleeve."

"You can trust Mike."

"I hope so." Cristan had placed all his bets with the cop,

something he couldn't have done a week ago. This week had been full of firsts. He smoothed a hair off Sarah's forehead.

The police had found a GPS device hidden in the fender of Cristan's Mercedes. The device had allowed Eva to track his movements without taking the risk of being seen.

He still couldn't believe that Eva thought he'd betrayed her. He would never have left her unless he thought she was dead, and the fact that she'd so easily been convinced he was a traitor was a fresh wound as painful as the row of stitches across his ribs.

Lucia returned with a glass of water. "It's room temperature. I didn't think you'd want it to be cold."

"Good thinking. Thank you." Sarah lifted her torso and swallowed two pain pills.

"Do you need anything else?" Lucia asked. Her eyes were haunted and her face pale. Despite the youth in her features, her eyes looked as if she'd become an adult in the course of one night.

"Would you mind sleeping in here with me?" Sarah asked. "I don't think I want to be alone."

She knew exactly how Lucia felt. Could he find a better woman? No. Not in this lifetime.

"Me either." Lucia smiled as she rounded the bed and got in on the other side.

"Don't worry." Cristan carried an upholstered chair into the room and set it by the nightstand. "I'm not leaving either one of you alone."

"Troy is out there too," Sarah mumbled in a sleepy voice.

Cristan knew exactly how he'd deal with her ex if he dared show up anywhere near Sarah.

Troy was still on the loose, and Eva had escaped. But they'd deal with that tomorrow. They were all alive, and that's all that mattered.

CHAPTER THIRTY-NINE

Late the next night, Cristan nursed a cup of coffee. Sarah and Lucia slept upstairs. He'd talked Sarah out of leaving just yet. Though he had taken her to see her girls at Sean's house. Hugging her kids and pretending to be fine had taken its toll. When they'd returned, she'd taken a pill and gone directly to bed. Lucia went with her. His daughter couldn't sleep unless she was with one of them.

He rubbed his aching eyelids. Not sleeping was taking its toll on him as well. He could only survive on coffee for a short period of time. Sean had come to the house that morning and kept watch so he could get a few hours of sleep. Mike was tied up trying to find Troy and Eva.

A sound out back roused him. He jumped to his feet and went to the window, peering around the frame. A figure stood ten feet from the patio door.

Eva.

She held her hands at shoulder height, palms facing him, in a traditional pose of surrender. Meeting his gaze through the glass, she slowly lowered her hands and removed her jacket. Tossing it over a patio chair, she lifted the hem of her fitted T-shirt and pivoted in a slow circle. Then she raised each pant leg of her jeans. No weapons.

Shocked, but also curious, Cristan pulled a Glock from the wine rack. Covering her, he opened the door. A quick visual sweep revealed an empty patio and yard. Below, the river flowed in a black ribbon. No moonlight tonight to brighten its surface.

He closed the door behind him. "What do you want?"

"To say good-bye."

"I could call the policeman sitting out front."

"You could," she said.

"You didn't kill him, did you?" Cristan searched his heart for any sign of the love he once felt for this woman but found none. She was a stranger.

"No."

"Good," Cristan said. "He's a good man. Now why are you here? And why shouldn't I kill you right now?"

She tilted her head, as if unable to make sense of his statement. "I wanted to set things right between us before I left. To tell you what happened that day."

"I'm listening."

———

With a leaden heart, Eva tucked her purse under her arm and left the apartment. Closing the door felt final. She leaned against the corridor wall for a moment. Though she'd be seeing Christopher and Luciana again shortly, it would be for their last meeting for an unforeseen length of time. If her plan came to fruition, she'd never return to the apartment. Christopher would think her dead, and she didn't know how long it would be before it would be safe for her to contact him.

Her plan had to work. She was losing him. He was slipping away from her. She felt his absence in the pit of her belly. Luciana's birth had changed everything. Eva knew with absolute certainty that he loved her, but there had always been an aloofness about him, a part of him she could never touch. The only time she'd seen him truly engaged was with his child. When Luciana had taken her first breath, Christopher had come to life. And he wanted to make a new one—far away from the danger that hovered over the Vargas family every moment of every day.

For him, the decision was simple. They should disappear. As an orphan, Christopher's only blood relative was the child.

But for Eva . . .

How could she turn her back on her family?

The thought of leaving everything behind and starting new was both exciting and terrifying. She couldn't simply ask to be released from her obligations. It wasn't possible for a Vargas to walk away. Her father would see her wish to exit the family as a betrayal. The Vargas business had provided for her since the moment of her birth. Franco had always been an attentive father, but losing her mother to violence had hardened him, made him even more determined to best their number one enemy, Aline Barba. Any softness her father had possessed had died with his wife's kidnapping and murder. Although he lacked proof, he was sure Aline had been behind the crime. The desire for revenge had darkened his soul.

Eva took the elevator to the parking garage.

Climbing into her Mercedes, she tossed her purse on the passenger seat. Before Luciana was born, she and Christopher always made the drive out to the ranch together. But no more. Now they did everything separately. Pulling out into the crush of Buenos Aires traffic, she turned her attention to her task. Driving in the city required aggressive maneuvering and complete focus. Stoplights and road signs were mere suggestions to most Buenos Aires drivers. Once she'd left the city behind, she relaxed. For the next thirty minutes, she could pretend her life wasn't about to change forever.

That she hadn't made a life-altering decision.

All that was left was prayer. Christopher, forgive me. *Would he understand? Sharing the plan with him wasn't an option. He'd never agree to the risk she was going to take. But there was only one way to escape the Vargas family: death.*

Everyone, including Christopher, must think hers was real.

The drive ended too soon. She turned onto the long driveway, her tires grating as she left pavement for dirt. She stopped the car just inside the gates. The guards checked her vehicle's interior. She opened the trunk and they looked inside.

The family had experienced many acts of violence. Since her mother's abduction and murder, care was taken to ensure the ranch was safe. Large family gatherings were arranged with little lead time to give enemies less opportunity to plan an attack.

Perspiration gathered beneath her dress. She parked in front of the estancia *and, ignoring the armed guard, went through the mahogany door.*

"Papa." She greeted her father with a kiss and embrace, trying not to think that this would be the last time she'd see him.

His face glowed. "Eva."

He was a big man with an imposing frame. Even at sixty, his black hair held little gray and his shoulders refused to stoop. Guilt weighted Eva's steps. After today, grief would once again crease his features. But that couldn't be helped. It was Papa's own fault. He held the reins on his daughter too tightly. He was making her choose between him and the man she loved. Christopher would be devastated too. But she could not share her scheme with him either. He must play the grieving widower. As soon as possible, she'd contact him. Franco would allow him space to grieve. There would be no pressure to rejoin the business for a while. Franco would not object if Christopher wanted to take her child away to heal, and then they could vanish.

"Am I the last to arrive?" she asked in Spanish.

"But you are the most important. The others can wait." He looked over her shoulder. Disappointment and irritation tightened his jaw. "Where is Christopher?"

Eva smiled. "He will be late. Luciana was napping."

Her father frowned. "Luciana should have a nanny."

"I'm working on it, Papa. Christopher is enamored with his child. Surely, you can understand?"

Franco sighed. "And if I say no, you take offense?"

"Exactly, Papa." She patted his arm. "Have no worry. Christopher will be here soon. I made sure to tell him your new horse was coming today."

"You were always a clever one. I want to finish up the business discussion so I can give the beast a try." The prospect of a new polo mount brightened his mood and put a bounce in his step. He wrapped an arm around her shoulders and steered her toward the dining room. She nodded to the burly man who stood guard at the entrance. Nicolas was her father's most trusted man. He'd been employed by the Vargas family since before Eva was born. He'd been her ally her entire life.

Now he was her only confidant.

As usual, Eva was the only female in the room, but that did not worry her. Denied sons, Franco had responded in a practical manner. Instead of allowing a male cousin to take over the Vargas enterprises, he'd groomed his daughters for the role. Eva took the chair at his right. The chair to Papa's left was empty, to remind all that the seat was not for them to fill. Her younger sister, Maria, would take that place when the time came.

Maria would sit at this table sooner than she expected—or wanted, thought Eva. Guilt flickered. Her sister wanted no part of the business.

Eva sat, the high-backed chair hard under her thighs. Resting her forearms on the rustic table, she waited for the meeting to begin. Franco sent Nicolas to the cellar to retrieve a sample of their latest ammunition delivery. The family discussed the details of several impending deals. Eva grew restless. Just a few more hours before her world turned upside down. Before she took a step from which there was no retreating.

The ceiling exploded. Debris rained onto the table. The double doors burst open. Four men steamed in. Machine guns barked over the screams of men and the scraping of chairs as they tried to flee. But there was no escape.

Shock rooted Eva in her seat. What was happening? This was not part of her plan.

Her father dove off his chair. His arm caught Eva around the middle, forcing her to the ground beneath his larger body. But he hadn't moved fast enough. A bullet cut across Eva's midsection. Another seared across her neck, spearing her with agony. She hit the floor. Her head smacked the tile. Blood filled her throat, choking her. Gunshots and screaming became muffled. Franco landed partially on top of her. The weight of his body knocked the air from her lungs. His eyes blinked in shock and pain. Blood spread across his crisp white shirt. She felt her own life draining out onto the cold tile. Their mingled blood soaked her dress.

"I'm sorry," Papa mouthed before he died.

Eva's vision dimmed. Her eyes fixed on the ceiling fan, spinning in a lazy circle above her. Her only regret was that she hadn't said good-bye to her child or husband. A life built on violence ends in a bloody death. Christopher was right. They should have run long ago. Her heart weakened. Her breaths faltered.

"It is done." A man spoke in Portuguese.

Aline Barba was behind this. Retribution, no doubt, for the death of her son. This was Eva's fault. She'd been too eager to pull the trigger that day. And now she would pay.

Eva could barely draw air to inflate her lungs. Shallow breathing dimmed her vision.

The men left the room. Eva scanned the room. Dead. All dead.

She wheezed. Minutes later, a shoe scraped in the hallway. Her father's body blocked her view and pinned her upper torso and arms to the floor. He was too heavy and she was too weak to push him off of her. Unable to move, she waited for death, her breath rattling in her chest. Blood pooled on the tile around her and soaked her dress.

"Eva," a man's voice called.

Christopher?

She opened her eyes. Disappointment welled. Not Christopher.

Nicolas pushed Franco off of her and scanned her from head to foot. She remembered that he'd been in the cellar. The knees of his slacks were dark with blood, as if he'd crawled through a puddle of it to reach her.

"Shh." He rolled her onto her side and gave her a cursory examination. "It's not as bad as it looks. One shot. Straight through the shoulder. The neck wound is a graze. You've lost blood, though."

He folded two cloth napkins and bound them to the front and back of her shoulder with his belt. He placed another on her neck, moving her own hand to hold it in place. Then he righted a chair, picked her up, and placed her in it. "Put pressure on this. I'll be right back." He stood and walked toward the door.

"Where are you going?"

"We might as well proceed with the plan. Aline wants you dead. Let's let her think you are. Did you plant the toothbrush and hairbrush in the apartment?"

She nodded.

Nicolas disappeared through the doorway. Ten minutes later, he returned carrying an unconscious woman. She wore the same red dress and shoes as Eva. Her long hair fell over Nicolas's arm in a dark wave. When he positioned her on the floor, Eva could see the Sun of May tattoo between her shoulder blades. Nicolas picked up a machine gun from the floor. Stepping back, he fired a burst of bullets from her waist to her face. The blood that sprayed from her body blended with the existing carnage. After testing for her pulse, he rolled Franco on top of the woman's body.

The body's DNA would match the DNA Eva had planted in her apartment. Eva Vargas would be pronounced dead.

Nicolas carried her to the helipad and placed her inside the copter.

"I saw Christopher," Nicolas yelled over the sound of the rotors.

Eva pressed her nose to the window. "Where?"

"Running away like a coward." His mouth tightened. "He did this."

"He wouldn't." She shook her head. No one was more loyal than Christopher, except he was unhappy lately.

Nicolas stabbed a button on the instrument panel. "He was here while they gunned down your family. I saw his car, and he stole all the money from your father's study."

"No!" Eva's head spun.

"Why else would he take the money and run? He's been acting strangely lately. Did you know he purchased false passports? How the fool thought he could do that without someone finding out is beyond me."

He hadn't told her about any passports. She thought back to their argument.

She hadn't acted fast enough. He'd decided to go without her. He might love Eva, but his child was his life. For Luciana, Christopher would do anything.

The helicopter lifted, spun, and shot out over the pampas. Sunlight blurred her vision.

She vowed to find him. She would take her daughter back from the man who had stolen her child and left her to die. Christopher would pay for her family's massacre.

—————————

Cristan reeled.

"I'm sorry I believed Nicolas instead of believing in you," Eva continued. "Nicolas took me to a medical facility. You stole the cash, but thankfully, my father had money in his bank accounts as well. Maria funneled money to us. I don't remember much of the first six months." Her hand went to the scarf around her throat, tugging it down to reveal a ropey scar across her neck. "What the bullet wounds didn't damage, grief for my family and anger toward you destroyed."

"I don't understand. There was a woman who looked like you in the compound? What was your plan?"

She walked to the other end of the patio and back, her expression unreadable in the dark. "I was leaving the family for you. I'd been planning for months. The only person I told was Nicolas. We both knew that death was the only way to exit the Vargas family. So I had to die."

"But how . . ." Cristan was beginning to connect the terrible dots.

"Nicolas found a woman who looked very much like me. She was from Cordoba. A poor woman who would not be missed. He had a tattoo put on her back to match mine. I bought duplicate outfits. The day of the massacre, he'd been holding her in his trunk. Our plan was to put a bullet in her head, put the body in my car, and send it off the bridge into the river. We already had everything in place to fake my kidnapping and set up Aline Barba as the culprit. My father would have believed it without a doubt. Aline had made threats in the past.

"You killed a woman to fake your death?"

"Nicolas killed her." Eva waved a hand.

"But you knew about it." Horror swept through him.

Eva stopped and stared at him. His wife had arranged the murder of an innocent simply because the poor woman looked like her. Cristan might have done some bad things in his life, but Eva had crossed a line. Not just crossed it, she'd leaped over it at full speed like an Olympic hurdler. Yes, Cristan had killed men for Franco, but those men were his own equivalents in other gangs. They knew the risks associated with their activities, and if given equal chance, they would have killed Cristan without blinking.

But Cristan had never murdered an innocent. Judging by Eva's confused stare, she didn't comprehend his revulsion.

Anger flushed her skin and whitened her scar. "I had planned to take our daughter and kill you. Nicolas convinced me you had set up the massacre. You took the money in my father's study. You were out of the country in days. You had purchased fake birth certificates and passports. You were ready to run after the explosion. It seemed as if you planned the whole thing."

"I bought travel documents for all three of us, Eva. I wasn't planning to leave without you. When I confirmed you were dead, I did what I thought you would have wanted. I took our daughter to safety." If faced with the exact same situation, Cristan would make the same choice.

"If it wasn't you, then who told Aline about the meeting?" Eva asked. "The dates were never announced outside the immediate family more than a few days in advance. Yet Aline knew in time to plan a well-timed attack."

Cristan said, "Immediate family and Nicolas." Suddenly, part of Eva's story replayed in his mind. Who was the one person on the ranch that hadn't been hurt in the attack? Nicolas. "Convenient that he was in the cellar when the attack occurred."

For once, Eva looked stunned. "But he was with my family for decades. He helped raise me."

"I have no other explanation. Maybe Nicolas was tired of the life. Everyone else had their own agenda."

"True." Nodding, she digested this with a furrow of her brow. "Perhaps this is the reason Nicolas didn't desire revenge the way I did. He wanted to put a quick bullet in your head, steal Luciana, and find somewhere quiet for the three of us to retire." Her lip curled, as if the idea of retirement was distasteful.

If Nicolas had his way, Cristan would be dead. He wouldn't have seen the bullet coming.

Eva sighed. "I am leaving. I wish I could say good-bye and apologize to Luciana. But that isn't possible."

"You frightened her."

"I know." Eva sighed. "I was never meant to be a parent. Your woman, Sarah, her first instinct was to protect Luciana. It should have been mine. But it wasn't. Perhaps I am merely wired wrong. You deserve each other." She pointed toward her jacket. "I'm going to get something out of my jacket."

Cristan nodded, but he kept the gun on her. She would never intentionally hurt Lucia. She loved her daughter in her own way. But Eva was and always would be a killer.

She pulled an envelope and a small box from her pocket. "This is a letter for Luciana. An apology and an e-mail address so you or she can contact me through Maria in case of an emergency."

"Do you see Maria?"

"Occasionally. She is content on her vineyard. She never wanted more."

"I'm glad to hear that."

She shook the box. "This is for Sarah. A thank-you gift to her for saving my child. Do not let her open this until tomorrow."

"Where will you go?" He took the envelope and box.

"I don't know what I'm going to do. Everything is different than I thought."

"I shouldn't let you go." He should call the police, but deep in the recesses of his heart, feelings for Eva still lingered. He was no longer in love with her, but they'd shared defining experiences that had shaped the people they'd become. They also had a child together. That was a bond that could never be broken. "Why should I trust you? You tried to kill me."

Eva shrugged, a careless gesture that summed up her impulsive nature. "That was when I thought you were the enemy. I should have known you would never have turned on me."

"So we won't see you again."

She backed away from him and turned toward the woods. Glancing over her shoulder, she called, "You have nothing to fear from me, Christopher." And disappeared into the woods.

Not exactly an answer.

CHAPTER FORTY

"I can't stay here forever." Sarah perched on a kitchen island stool and pushed back the plate of eggs. She wasn't hungry. "I miss my girls. Who knows how long it will take to find Troy? He knows the woods around here. He can hide for a long time."

"We'll see." Cristan collected her dirty dish and carried it to the sink. The circles under his eyes attested to yet another night without sleep, but something about his attitude was decidedly less tense this morning. "There's no rush. You can't even use a knife or dress yourself. The girls can come here. I'm sure they'd love to have a sleepover with Lucia."

Sarah flexed the fingers of her left hand. She had to keep her arm immobilized in a sling until the stitches came out in seven days. "I'm sure they would, but what about Eva?"

The threat that his murderous wife was lurking was one of the reasons Alex and Em were still staying with Sean. Sarah wouldn't put her girls in any additional danger.

He tossed a dishcloth over his shoulder. His snug T-shirt outlined his well-defined biceps and chest. Maybe it was the drugs making her woozy, but he looked hot, which was ridiculous because she had problems in her life—problems so huge she shouldn't be thinking about her boyfriend's muscles. Both of their exes were trying to kill them.

Boyfriend. She smiled. It seemed like a silly title for someone as masculine as Cristan, but what should she call him? Lover? A blush heated her cheeks. He was definitely that.

"I'm not so worried about that this morning," he said.

Suspicion poked through her painkillers. "Why?"

"Sarah? Dad?" Lucia walked into the kitchen. Her tousled hair and wrinkled pajamas made her look unbearably young and vulnerable.

"Pancakes?" Cristan suggested.

"I'm not hungry." Lucia slipped onto the stool on Sarah's right.

Cristan frowned. "How about some hot chocolate?"

"OK." Lucia shrugged.

Sarah's heart squeezed. She wrapped her arm around the girl's shoulders. "Are you all right?"

"Yeah." Lucia rested her head on her shoulder. "I wish you were my mom."

"Me too," Sarah said.

The doorbell broke the moment. Cristan went to the door. A few seconds later, Mike's voice carried from the hall. He walked into the kitchen, his baby-blue eyes scrutinizing Sarah and Lucia. "How are you two feeling this morning?"

"Better," Sarah said.

Mike jingled his keys in his hand. "Can I talk to Sarah alone for a few minutes?"

"Of course." Cristan herded Lucia out of the room.

Mike took the stool next to Sarah. He took her hand in his. "Troy's dead."

"What?" Shock numbed her. Had she heard Mike correctly?

"We found him in the woods behind his house. He died from a single gunshot wound to the head. The cause of death isn't official, but it's likely he killed himself."

Shock closed Sarah's throat. Her next breath was a loud wheeze. Troy had seemed so intent on hurting her; it seemed impossible that he'd taken his own life.

Mike opened kitchen cabinets until he found glasses and filled one with water. He handed it to her. "Take a drink."

She sipped.

"He destroyed the house and took guns and ammo from the store. His computer search history was full of articles on husband/wife murder suicides." Mike rubbed her arm.

She'd never expected Troy to give up. Ever.

"I don't know why I'm surprised." Sarah's voice broke as sadness nearly overwhelmed her. "He tried to kill us both."

"Are you all right here? Do you want to come home with me?"

"I won't put Rachel in danger." Sarah shook her head. "Cristan is taking good care of me."

"Good. You deserve it." With a final pat to her hand, Mike stood. "We've seen no sign of Eva Vargas, so don't let your guard down."

Sarah rose onto her toes and kissed him on the cheek. "Thanks, Mike."

He left the room and she heard voices. Sarah settled in the chair. Troy's death would take a while to sink in. The combination of relief and sadness swirled in her belly.

Could it really be over? Troy had turned into a monster, but he hadn't always been that way. And she had never wished him dead. How would she tell the girls?

Cristan returned. He and Mike exchanged a few words, and then Cristan came to her. Sarah stood and turned her face to his chest. He wrapped his arms around her body. She cried in long, ragged sobs until her tears soaked his shirt. Cristan's hand rubbed a circle in the center of her back.

When she could breathe, Sarah pushed away, reaching for a napkin and drying her face. "I'm sorry." She sniffed. "Where's Lucia?"

"She's upstairs."

"Alone?"

"Yes. She's reading something." He brushed a thumb under her eye. "It's going to be all right, Sarah."

"How can you say that? Troy can't hurt us anymore, but Eva is still out there. And how will I tell the girls their father tried to kill me and committed suicide?"

"You'll find a way. Don't keep the truth from them. It will only hurt them more if they hear it from someone else. They're stronger than you think."

Light-headed, Sarah fought for control of her breathing. "Even if they catch Eva, what will happen to you and Lucia?"

"I would hope that if anything happened to me, you would care for Lucia."

"Of course."

"Sean has arranged a meeting for me with friends of his at the ATF and FBI. They want to offer me a deal. Immunity for information. Apparently, Aline isn't talking, and her operation has been on their radar for a long time, and they want all the background they can get. I don't know how useful twelve-year-old information will be, but I'll tell them everything I know. The potential charges against me for falsifying documents are trivial compared to Aline's organization. I also suspect Mike and Sean lobbied hard for me. They both seem very well respected in the law enforcement community. I can *be* Cristan Rojas. They can arrange for Lucia and me to have official documentation."

"Like witness protection?"

"Just like that." He kissed her. "Lucia gets to stay in the place she loves. I can stay here with you, and that makes me very happy."

Sarah almost smiled, then she remembered his murderous wife. "But we don't know where Eva is."

He glanced away. "That isn't entirely true."

"What?"

"Eva stopped here last night. She won't be bothering us again." He went to the cabinet and took out a small box. "She gave me a letter for Lucia. An apology. Eva recognized that she isn't mother material." He handed her the box.

"I don't understand." Sarah couldn't believe that Eva was no longer a threat. Wrapped in plain, brown paper, the box fit in her palm. "Do you know what it is?"

"No. She said it was her way of thanking you for saving Lucia. She also said you were the kind of woman Lucia deserved. She seemed sincere."

"Do you trust her?"

"No," he said. "But I believe she was telling the truth."

Sarah unwrapped the box and opened it. Her hand went to the scar on her temple, and her breath caught.

Inside, nestled on plain white cotton, sat Troy's high school ring.

———

An hour later, Cristan showed Mike and Sean into his office.

Mike took one of the chairs that faced Cristan's desk. "I hope you don't mind. Sean was with me when you called."

"Not at all." Sitting behind his desk, Cristan reached into the top drawer and pulled out the box with Troy's ring in it. He handed it across the desk.

"What is this?" Mike asked.

"Sarah says it's Troy's high school ring."

Mike shifted. "And how did you get it?"

"Eva gave it to me." Cristan summed up her visit to the house.

Sean whistled. "I know she tried to kill you, but you have to admire her style. If she were a dude, she'd have brass balls the size of Texas."

Mike set the box on the desk. "And you didn't think to call me when she was here?"

"Eva is no longer a threat to us," Cristan said. "I know her. She might be a killer, but lying was never one of her faults."

Mike rubbed his forehead as if it hurt. "I'll need to take the ring as evidence, but frankly, I don't know what the hell I'm going to do with it."

"Troy's dead, and Aline is sitting in a prison cell. So Eva got away. The only person she wanted to kill is Cristan, and he seems fine with it. Two out of three isn't bad." Sean lifted both shoulders. "You can't have everything."

CHAPTER FORTY-ONE

"You still look awful, and this is from someone who was shot a week ago." Sarah sat at Rachel's kitchen island.

"I'm fine."

"You are not." Sarah shifted in her chair. The wound in her shoulder was healing, but it still hurt plenty.

"I'm taking her to see Quinn tomorrow." Mike lifted a turkey breast from the oven and set the roasting pan on the stove. The three girls were in the barn with Cristan, checking on Lady and giving Snowman carrots.

Rachel sulked, but she was pale and pasty-looking. "A little food poisoning isn't a big deal."

"You've hardly eaten all week," Mike said.

The back door opened. Alex raced in, breathless and excited. "Cristan says call the vet. Lady is going to have her baby soon."

They rushed to the barn. The mare was lying in the center of the foaling stall. Sweat coated her flanks, and her sides heaved with effort. Cristan was outside the stall, leaning on the half door.

Looking scared, Lucia stepped up next to Sarah. "She looks like she's in pain. Are you sure she's OK?"

Sarah smiled and put her arm around the girl's shoulders. "She knows what to do." But she wished Alex and Em weren't here. What if something went wrong? They'd dealt with enough trauma this week. She looked at her daughters. They were standing on a bale of straw looking through the bars that topped the wooden wall.

The mare heaved to her feet and pawed at the straw bedding.

"She is restless." Cristan watched the horse with critical eyes. "It should be any time now."

Empathizing with the horse's discomfort, Sarah sighed. "I remember those days. Poor thing."

Rachel swayed. Her face was pale as marble.

Worried, Sarah put a hand on her sister's forehead. "You don't have a fever, but you look awful."

"Thanks." Completely focused on getting to her horse, Rachel's retort held no heat.

Cristan leaned over the door and scanned the bedding. As they watched, Lady got to her feet, paced a circle around her stall, then lay down again. She rolled to her belly and back to her side.

"Oh, no." Rachel hurried to the tack room and came back with a box. Lifting the lid, she removed surgical gloves and a pair of scissors from a plastic bag with shaking hands.

"What are you doing?" Lucia asked. "What's wrong?"

Cristan stepped forward. "Let me. I've done this before, and you're hardly in any condition to pull a foal."

"You've done what before?" Lucia stared at her father.

"Are those sterile?" Stripping off his jacket and rolling up his sleeves, he nodded toward the scissors.

"Yes." Rachel hesitated, then handed him the gloves and scissors.

Lucia's lip trembled. "What's wrong?"

"The foal is in trouble," Rachel said in a shaky voice. "The placenta is coming first. That means the foal isn't getting any oxygen. If it isn't born very quickly, it won't live."

Mike wrapped his arm around her waist, and she leaned into him. Lucia sniffed back a tear, the girls started to cry, and Sarah hugged the three sets of shoulders. "Do you want to go to the house?" she asked.

"No." Alex answered for all of them.

In the stall, Cristan donned the gloves and crouched behind the horse. He carefully cut the membrane with the scissors. Two tiny hooves, encased in a white sack, emerged. Cristan handed the scissors over the door to Rachel, then returned to the horse. He gently broke the white sack with his hands, then grasped the foal's legs and pulled. Forelegs followed hooves, then a nose. As soon as the head emerged, Cristan removed the sack from the foal's head and cleared its nostrils. Then he grabbed hold of the forelegs, leaned back, and pulled harder. Shoulders slid onto the straw. A few seconds later, the rest of the foal slipped from the horse and flopped on the straw, its thin legs thrashing.

Everyone exhaled at once. Rachel nearly fell over. Sarah felt tears on her face and blotted them on her sleeve. The baby lifted its head. Crouching in front of it, Cristan removed the white sack from the rest of the body. He glanced over his shoulder. "Could I have a towel?"

Sarah fetched a clean towel from the box of foaling supplies and took it to him. He rubbed the baby down and smiled back at Rachel. "It's a colt."

He was dark red with a white star on the center of his forehead.

"He looks like his daddy." Rachel wiped her face. Now that the baby was safe, Sarah's concern shifted back to her sister.

Lady lifted her head, looked back at her baby, and nickered softly.

"Is the baby OK?" Lucia asked. Next to her, Alex and Em stared up, wide-eyed.

Cristan stood. "He's perfect." He exited the stall, tossing the damp towel over the door. Peeling off the surgical gloves, he threw them in a garbage pail in the aisle.

"You should get back to bed before you fall down," Sarah said to her sister.

Rachel shook her head. "I need to make sure he nurses."

"I'll stay," Cristan offered. "And your veterinarian should be here soon."

"I don't know how to thank you for your help," Rachel said, her voice breaking.

Cristan glanced at Mike. "No thanks are needed. Friends help friends, right?"

"Right," Mike answered, turning Rachel and steering her toward the door.

Sarah followed them. "She needs to see a doctor, Mike."

Opening the door, Mike glanced back at Sarah. "I'm going to call Quinn."

As they left, Sarah could hear her sister protesting, which was a good sign. A compliant Rachel would have worried her even more.

Lucia hung over the door, her face full of wonder. "Oh, look! He's trying to stand."

"He's so cute," squealed Alex.

With a dreamy smile, Em leaned on Sarah.

In the stall, Lady got to her feet and turned to lick her baby. The colt splayed his forelegs, his first attempt to rock to his feet sending him sprawling face-first into the straw.

Cristan stood next to his daughter. "Do you mind if we stay here for the rest of the night?"

"I want to stay." Without looking at him, she said, "I didn't know you could deliver a baby horse."

"There are many things you don't know about me. I'm sorry about that."

"Will you tell me now?" She turned her head and studied his face.

He smiled. "*Right* now, I need a clean shirt. But yes, I will tell you what you want to know."

She nodded and went back to watching the horses.

"All right then." He stepped away from the door. "Can you watch them for a few minutes? I need to wash up."

"OK." Lucia rested her chin on her crossed forearms.

Cristan went out to his car and grabbed a gym bag from his trunk. Sarah grabbed his jacket and followed him to the wash stall. He stripped off his bloodstained shirt and washed his hands and arms.

"It would be warmer to do that up at the house." Sarah reached for a clean towel from a shelf on the wall.

"I'll survive." He took the towel and rubbed his body dry.

Sarah tried not to stare at the lean muscles rippling in his chest and arms. There was no question the man was hot, but it was the gentleness he'd shown the mare that attracted her. Troy had been an athlete with a rocking body when she'd married him. Looks were nice, but they didn't mean much in the long run. Kindness was for keeps.

"Thank you for saving my sister's horse. You have no idea what that mare and baby mean to her."

He tugged a clean T-shirt over his head. "I think I do, and it was my pleasure."

"Lucia was impressed."

"I'm just happy she spoke to me. Perhaps someday she will even forgive me."

"I think she will. She just watched you save Lady's foal. That's bound to help."

Lucia was smiling when they returned. "He's trying to stand up again."

The little girls *oohed* and *ahhed* as the colt staggered to his feet and careened the few steps to Lady's side. Instinct drove him to nuzzle at her flank. A few seconds later, he was nursing. Sarah's eyes filled with tears again.

Mike poked his head into the barn. "I'm taking Rachel to the emergency room. She just fainted."

"Do you want me to come with you?" Sarah jogged to the door.

"No." Mike shook his head. "If you and Cristan could see to the horses, I'd appreciate it."

"Of course we will." Worry filled Sarah. "You'll call me when you know something or if she gets worse?"

Mike nodded. "Thanks, Sarah."

The vet pulled up just as Mike's SUV left the driveway.

An arm came around her shoulders. Lucia. "It'll be all right, Sarah."

Sarah hugged the girl back and rested her cheek on Lucia's head. "Thank you for your help."

"That's what friends are for," Lucia said. "Right Dad?"

"Yes." But as Cristan met her gaze, she saw her own worry reflected back at her.

Dr. White walked into the barn, his huge frame outfitted in the usual coveralls and heavy boots. Cristan showed him to the mare's stall.

"You missed the whole thing." Lucia gave the vet the details on the birth.

"You are worried about your sister?" Cristan took Sarah's hand.

"Yes." What would she do if something was really wrong with her sister?

Sarah took her phone from her pocket and turned up the ringer. She didn't want to miss a call from Mike. Not much kept her sister down, and she'd been waiting for this foal for many long months. If she let Mike talk her into a trip to the ER, she must be much sicker than she'd admitted.

Hours later, Cristan watched dawn break clear and bright over the field. Sarah had taken a half-asleep Lucia up to the house a few hours before. Alex and Em had been carted off to Mrs. Holloway's place down the road. Rachel's sole employee, a young man named Brandon, arrived to clean stalls. Cristan helped him feed the horses, then checked in on the mother and baby again. Lady nuzzled her baby as he suckled. After the dangerous and hurried birth, mare and foal had showed no signs of complications.

The sound of a car door pulled him to the barnyard. Mike and Rachel got out of the SUV. Mike gestured for Cristan and he walked to the house.

The scent of brewing coffee greeted him as he entered through the mudroom. In the adjoining kitchen, Sarah stirred a huge pan of scrambled eggs. Lucia put bread into the toaster, and the scent of bacon made Cristan's stomach growl. The sight of his daughter and Sarah working in the kitchen together warmed him. Twelve years ago, he would never have guessed this scene would appeal to him. But now, he couldn't imagine anything better.

Rachel stripped off her coat, dumped it on a stool, and attacked a piece of bacon on a plate at the island. Mike stood next to her, grinning like a fool.

Cristan helped himself to a cup of coffee. "All is well?"

"She was dehydrated," Mike put his hand on his wife's shoulder. "And pregnant."

Sarah dumped her pan of eggs in a large bowl and ran around the island to hug her sister. "Oh, my god. That's so exciting."

Smiling, Lucia brought a platter of toast to the island and filled a plate with food.

Rachel reached for another piece of bacon. "Wait. It gets better."

Mike looked as if he would burst. "Twins."

Cristan had never heard a grown woman squeal, but that's the only way he could describe the sound that burst from Sarah's lips.

Face beaming, she hugged her sister hard. "How do they know so soon?"

Rachel sighed. "They did an ultrasound. I'm already seven weeks."

"And you didn't notice?" Sarah asked, laughing.

"I guess I wasn't paying attention. I was preoccupied with Lady." Rachel crunched through another piece of bacon and reached for more.

"Your appetite seems to have improved." Sarah went back to the cooking side of the island. "How about eggs or toast?"

"Yes, please, and extra bacon." Rachel made a face. She narrowed her eyes at Mike's disapproving glance. "The doctor said I should eat whatever appeals to me."

He held up his hands in surrender. "You can have whatever you want."

Rachel turned up her nose at orange juice and went to the cabinet for a Pop-Tart. Mike opened his mouth, then closed it. She ate it cold with a contented sigh. "I'm going out to see my baby."

Lucia wolfed down a plate of eggs. "I'll come with you."

Mike filled a plate and sat at the island. His ruddy face was lined with exhaustion. No doubt Cristan looked the same.

He took a piece of toast from the plate. "Is everything all right?"

"Yes. As soon as they rehydrated her, she felt better." Mike scooped eggs with his fork. "But the doctor wants her to take it easy. That will be a challenge."

"She's going to be tired." Sarah stood on the other side of the island, holding a mug of coffee with both hands. "It might not be as hard as you think."

"Do you need any more help today?"

"If Brandon is here, all is good." Mike shrugged into his jacket. "Thank you for your help last night. That horse is very important to my wife."

"You are welcome, but I would have done it regardless," Cristan said. "Has there been any progress tracking Eva?"

Mike shook his head. "Her fingerprints weren't on the ring she gave to Sarah or on the gun we assume she used to kill Troy. Do you think she'll be back?"

Eva had been different when she'd appeared on his patio. For the first time ever, she'd been humbled. Her world had been completely upended.

"I hope not. I felt like she was telling me the truth." Eva had her own, skewed sense of morality and justice. "As I said before, Eva is a killer, but she isn't a liar."

"And that makes you feel better about the situation?" Mike asked.

Cristan laughed. "I know it's odd, but yes."

"Odd doesn't even come close."

======

316

Eva got out of the SUV. She looked up at her sister's house. The square stucco structure squatted in the middle of a plateau. Beyond the house, the vineyard stretched across the moon-brightened plateau. She wrapped her leather jacket around her shoulders against the night chill. The high altitude brought cold nights, but the slower ripening period gave Mendoza wine its distinctive, rich flavor.

Using her key, she went inside the *estancia*. After disarming the security system, she headed to the kitchen. Her sister lived simply. No servants. No armed guards. Just a basic alarm system.

Maria was in the study, a book in her lap and a glass of wine at her elbow. She looked up in surprise. "I didn't know you were coming. You should have called." She set aside her book and stood to give Eva an air kiss.

A small fire cracked in the hearth. The room was warm and cozy. Maria had built a safe haven here. She lived in quiet seclusion. The same tranquility that gave her sister peace made Eva restless.

She paced the study. "How do you live here? Nothing happens."

How could Maria be content watching grapes grow?

"You need to relax." Maria went to a side table and poured a second glass of red wine. She handed it to Eva. "The 2011 Cabernet is our best yet."

Eva held the glass up to the firelight. It glowed like a liquid ruby—or blood. A sniff brought hints of blackberry and clove to her nose. Looking at her sister was like looking into a mirror, minus a few years. Except Maria's face was relaxed, her posture content.

"You are happy, aren't you?"

Maria smiled. "I am."

"How long did it take to feel happy?"

"What do you mean?" Maria asked.

"After. How long after the family was killed did you grieve?"

Maria shrugged. "I don't know exactly. But it's been twelve years, Eva. Maybe you should let the past go."

Eva set her glass down. "I still have a hard time believing Nicolas betrayed us."

"There isn't anyone else," Maria said. "He was never blood, after all."

How does it feel to be betrayed by the one who is supposed to love you the most? Aline's words rang in Eva's head. At the time, she'd thought Aline was referring to Christopher, but the statement didn't make any sense when applied to Nicolas. He wasn't family.

"Isn't there?" The truth speared Eva like a sharp blade. How much was Maria willing to sacrifice for the life she wanted? "Why did you do it?"

"Do what?" Maria asked, but a secret lurked in her eyes.

Despite the heat of the fire, Eva's skin went cold. "You betrayed the family to Aline. You had them all killed."

"How can you even suggest such a thing?" But Maria's protest didn't reach her eyes.

And Eva knew the truth. "You did it. Why?"

Heat flared in Maria's face. "Why? *Why?* Our father was a monster. He was in the business of selling death. He murdered people. You and Christopher killed people. You all did. I was almost raped as a child because of the type of men our father welcomed into our home, and you wonder why I never wanted anything to do with the business. Why I wanted out of that life? Papa kept telling me I had to come home and take my place at his side. That was the last place I wanted to be." She spat.

"There were children there, Maria. *My* child could have been there." It was only by chance that Christopher had escaped with Luciana. "You had Papa killed. You tried to kill me."

Death was no stranger to them, but family loyalty was an unnatural bond to break.

Maria didn't respond. Hatred shone from her eyes.

Without a word, Eva turned and walked out of the house. If she stayed any longer, if her sister issued one more word from her lips, Eva would kill her.

And she didn't think she could live with that. Not now. Not after seeing Christopher and Luciana and the happy, domestic life they lived. There had been too much death. He'd been right all along. If only she'd listened to him sooner. If only she'd loved him more than her family. Maybe they could have gotten away and started a new life together.

She inhaled cool, dry air deep into her lungs. Who was she kidding? The thought of living in that little town, of spending her days running errands, of the endless boredom, made her skin itch. She would never be able to adapt to the unrelenting tedium. The pain rocketing through her soul right now was preferable. In the long run, it was probably best that Christopher raise Luciana on his own or with his new woman. Sarah Mitchell suited his new life far better than Eva.

Maria didn't follow her outside. Eva got into her car and drove away from the house into the dark. She had no idea where she would go, but she hadn't killed her sister, and for tonight, that was enough.

CHAPTER FORTY-TWO

Two months later

Sarah adjusted the bodice of her sister's wedding dress. Plain silk and strapless, it fell from a gray sash from the bodice straight to the floor. Simple, classic, and no-fuss, it suited her sister perfectly, except the sash restricted her almost four-months-pregnant belly. In a dove gray, Sarah's dress mimicked the style, but with a just-above-the-knee hem. Sarah wore a cropped silk jacket to cover the scar on the back of her shoulder.

"Aunt Rachel, you look boot-i-ful." Em stared up at Rachel.

"You're perfect." Eyes shining with excitement, Alex spun. The hem of her poofy white dress twirled around her legs. "I love weddings."

"They're right," Sarah said to her sister. "You're gorgeous."

"Thanks. Oh my God, this dress is tight." Rachel pulled at the waist. "I had it let out twice. According to the book, I'm not supposed to be this big yet."

Sarah wrapped an arm around Rachel's shoulders. "Honey, you are manufacturing two human beings. It's bound to take a toll."

Her sister patted her barely rounded stomach. "I guess I can't back out, considering I'm carrying his twins."

"Why on earth would you want to back out? You love Mike and he loves you."

"I do. So much." Her eyes went misty. "It's the pregnant part that's scary. What if I'm a horrible mother? Ours wasn't exactly Donna Reed."

"It's going to be all right. You're going to be a great mom." Sarah hugged her. "I might make plenty of mistakes, but I'm a good mother. Neither of us is Mom."

"You're the best. I guess if you can do it, so can I."

"Now stop blubbering. You'll ruin your makeup." Sarah plucked a tissue and blotted Rachel's eyes. "Are you ready?"

"I am."

They went downstairs. In the kitchen, the servers bustled. Sarah pointed at a chafing dish. "That Sterno needs to be lighted."

Rachel poked her. "I let you plan and prepare the food. But you're not supposed to be working today, remember?"

"I remember." Sarah herded the girls through the chaos before one of them ended up covered in something sticky. White dresses and preschoolers were a dangerous combination.

They went outside. Friends gathered under a tent in the backyard. In front of a lattice-and-flower pergola, Mike waited in a dark-blue suit and tie that made his shoulders seem impossibly broad. As best man, Sean stood next to him. He leaned over and whispered something in Mike's ear. From Mike's expression, the comment was typically funny but inappropriate. Grinning, he jabbed Sean with an elbow.

Sarah scanned the crowd. Everyone from the police department was there. Brooke and Luke were in the back row. Mike's friend, Jack, and his enormously pregnant wife, Beth, sat with her children. Sean's wife and his little girls occupied seats next to them. Sarah smiled at Lucia, but her gaze fell on Cristan—and stayed there. Incredibly handsome in a charcoal suit and silver tie, he held two seats in the front row for Alex and Em. But it was the smile on his face that transfixed her. He looked content and relaxed, two words she would never have used to describe him eight weeks ago.

Em tossed her flower petals with care and precision, while Alex skipped down the aisle and flung them over guests' heads. Sarah and Rachel walked between the chairs together, the way they'd gone through life, Rachel had said. Sarah hadn't heard from their father since she'd walked out of his house that last time. Nothing could be perfect, she supposed, but today was awfully close. The ceremony was short and sweet, and by the time the "I dos" were exchanged, Sarah had tears in her eyes.

Cristan was at her side the second the nuptials were over. His arm curled around her waist as he whispered in her ear. "You are the most beautiful woman here."

She blushed, happiness flooding her. A thin whinny punctuated Rachel's arrival at the aisle between folding chairs. The colt ran a circle around his grazing mother.

"Lucky!" Alex and Em raced for the fence. Their long-legged playmate trotted over to greet them. Officially named Lucky Feet, after his show jumping champion father, Fleet O' Feet, the colt acted more like a puppy than a horse with the children.

"I'm on them," Lucia called, jogging after them.

Alex and Em didn't know all the details of their father's death. Sarah didn't know when they'd be old enough. Maybe it'd be best if the truth came out in small pieces. She'd promised herself that if they asked questions, she would give them answers. She wouldn't offer details until she thought they were ready, but she wouldn't lie to them. For now, they were happy, and that's all she could want.

The colt stuck his head between the boards and wiped dirt on the front of Em's white dress.

"I hope you weren't planning on Emma wearing that dress again." Cristan smiled at the children. "They're both going to be filthy by the end of the day."

"But they're having fun." Sarah laughed. "I'm shocked those dresses stayed clean until the ceremony was over."

"Your food is very popular." He swept a hand toward the buffet table, where guests lined up. "You'll have plenty of new orders after today."

Sarah's business was building at a slow and steady rate. Her friends and family were spreading the word, and she'd garnered several local events already.

"I hope so. I'd love to be able to pay rent to Mike and Rachel."

He turned her to face him. "Or you could move in with me and Lucia."

"I'm not ready to get that serious just yet." But the fact that he'd asked pleased her.

He kissed her on the cheek. "And yet, you can continue to use me for my gourmet kitchen."

She flattened her hands against his chest and teased him. "It *is* a great kitchen."

"My kitchen," he smiled, his eyes darkening, "and anything else of mine you desire, is at your service. Then the more orders you have, the more I get to see you."

"You see me almost every day." Sometimes when all the kids were at school . . . Sarah flushed with the memories. Lover was definitely the correct term for him.

Cristan tucked a stray hair behind her ear. "Someday I intend to stand at an altar with you. I love you, but I'm a patient man. I'll wait until you're ready."

"Who knows how long your paperwork will take anyway."

"True." Though his official paperwork would declare Cristan Rojas a single man, a divorce was being arranged for his Argentinean alter ego. "None of that matters if we're together. I love you, Sarah. I want to spend the rest of my life with you, raising children, growing old, making love." He leaned closer, kissed her jaw, and whispered, "Especially making love. I could be with you every moment, and it wouldn't be enough."

"I love you." She rose onto her toes and wrapped her arms around his neck. Over the last few months, she'd decided she didn't have to be alone to be independent. Cristan respected her, and that made all the difference. The time they spent together felt right in a way she couldn't describe with words, but her heart understood. Cristan was trust and passion and friendship.

"*Tienes mi corazón*," he whispered in her ear.

"That's beautiful. What does it mean?"

"You have my heart." He pressed her hands against the center of his chest, where his heart thudded under her palms. "I don't commit easily, Sarah. But when I do, I don't hold back." He lifted her hands to his lips and kissed them. "You have given me your trust and restored my faith in love and life. You are my forever."

You have my heart. He'd summed up her feelings perfectly. Sarah rose on her toes to kiss him. "*Tienes mi corazón* right back at you."

ACKNOWLEDGMENTS

As always, credit goes to Super Agent Jill Marsal. She is the best.

I also need to thank the entire team at Montlake Romance, especially author herder and tech goddess Jessica Poore, who keeps everything in order, and editor Anh Schluep. Special thanks to developmental editor Charlotte Herscher for helping me pull this book together, and Mary Buckham, writing teacher extraordinaire, for helping me plan it.

ABOUT THE AUTHOR

Photo © 2014 Marti Corn Photography

Melinda Leigh abandoned her career in banking to raise her kids and never looked back. She started writing as a hobby and became addicted to creating characters and stories. Since then, she has won numerous writing awards for her paranormal romance and romantic-suspense fiction.

Her debut novel, *She Can Run*, was a number one bestseller in Kindle Romantic Suspense, a 2011 Best Book Finalist (*The Romance Reviews*), and a nominee for the 2012 International Thriller Award for Best First Book. Melinda is a three-time Daphne du Maurier Award finalist and the winner of the Golden Leaf Award. When she isn't writing, Melinda is an avid martial artist: she holds a second-degree black belt in Kenpo karate and teaches women's self-defense. She lives in a messy house with her husband, two teenagers, a couple of dogs, and two rescue cats.